Praise for
STARFIST I: FIRST TO FIGHT

"CAUTION! Any book written by Dan Cragg and David Sherman is bound to be addictive, and this is the first in what promises to be a great adventure series. *First to Fight* is rousing, rugged, and just plain fun. The authors have a deep firsthand knowledge of warfare, an enthralling vision of the future, and the skill of veteran writers. Fans of military fiction, science fiction, and suspense will all get their money's worth, and the novel is so well done it will appeal to general readers as well. It's fast, realistic, moral, and a general hoot. *First to Fight* is also vivid, convincing—and hard to put down. Sherman and Cragg are a great team! I can't wait for the next one!"

—RALPH PETERS
New York Times bestselling author of
Red Army

By David Sherman and Dan Cragg

Starfist
FIRST TO FIGHT
SCHOOL OF FIRE
STEEL GAUNTLET
BLOOD CONTACT
TECHNOKILL
HANGFIRE
KINGDOM'S SWORDS

By David Sherman

Fiction
The Night Fighters
KNIVES IN THE NIGHT
MAIN FORCE ASSAULT
OUT OF THE FIRE
A ROCK AND A HARD PLACE
A NGHU NIGHT FALLS
CHARLIE DON'T LIVE HERE ANYMORE

Nonfiction
THERE I WAS: THE WAR OF CORPORAL HENRY J.
    MORRIS, USMC
THE SQUAD

By Dan Cragg

Fiction
THE SOLDIER'S PRIZE

Nonfiction
A DICTIONARY OF SOLDIER TALK
GENERALS IN MUDDY BOOTS
INSIDE THE VC AND THE NVA (with Michael Lee Lanning)
TOP SERGEANT (with William G. Bainbridge)

KINGDOM'S SWORDS

Starfist
Book Seven

David Sherman
and
Dan Cragg

BALLANTINE BOOKS • NEW YORK

A Del Rey® Book
Published by The Ballantine Publishing Group
Copyright © 2002 by David Sherman and Dan Cragg

All rights reserved under International and Pan-American Copyright Conventions. Published in the United States by The Ballantine Publishing Group, a division of Random House, Inc., New York, and simultaneously in Canada by Random House of Canada, Limited, Toronto.

Del Rey is a registered trademark and the Del Rey colophon is a trademark of Random House, Inc.

www.delreydigital.com

ISBN 0-345-44371-3

Manufactured in the United States of America

First Edition: May 2002

OPM 10 9 8 7 6 5 4 3 2 1

Dedicated to:
O. A. Lock
Former Airman, Cold Warrior,
and Most Loyal Friend

PROLOGUE

Clouds made the night so dark a Soldier of the Lord would have had to step on a raider to know one was in the area, and the rain and thunder masked what little noise the raiders made as they crawled through the muck and ground cover toward the Army of the Lord outpost. Lack of visibility didn't bother the raiders; their plan was detailed, they knew their routes. Nor did the rain bother them. The receptors that lined their sides detected and located life-forms, could tell the difference between their own kind and others and were more effective in the rain than on a clear, dry night.

The Soldiers of the Lord were all gathered in their barracks or in the duty office. None of them manned the observation posts; on a night like this, they knew, there would be no one about to guard against. Most of the eighteen soldiers in the duty office ignored the displays from the remote sensors; the effectiveness of the sensors was seriously reduced in severe weather, and they were unlikely to detect the approach of any mass smaller than a mob or an army, though no mob or army would be on the move on such a night. The Soldiers of the Lord had grown to like dark and stormy nights, for it gave them a break from the toils of guard duty at that remote outpost.

Which was why the raiders selected a dark, stormy night.

A Master led the night's raid, though with only fifty Fighters slithering and crawling toward the barracks and duty office, it needed no more than a Leader in command. This raid was the first direct strike in several months against the Army

1

of the Lord, and the Over Master in command of operations in that sector of Kingdom greatly desired certainty of success.

Sword Worshipful, the duty noncommissioned officer, briefly glowered at the displays. He took security duty in the farming lands more seriously than most; he thought most of the soldiers in the outpost risked their immortal souls with their laxness. But glowering at the displays did nothing to improve their efficiency.

"I am going to make the rounds," Sword Worshipful announced.

The other soldiers looked at him curiously as he donned his slicker. What posts would he check? Everyone who should be manning a post was huddled in the duty office, reading sacred tracts, talking, or sinfully playing cards. There were no manned posts for him to make the rounds of.

"Soldier Truth, Soldier Hellsbane, come with me."

Soldiers Truth and Hellsbane grumbled at having to leave the dryness and warmth of the duty office, but they didn't grumble loudly or long; Sword Worshipful was an easy taskmaster, but a harsh disciplinarian. They shrugged into slickers and picked up their weapons, then stood next to the exit while Sword Worshipful gave instructions to the assistant duty noncom.

Outside, rain battered the three men as they headed toward Post One. It drummed on their heads and shoulders, cascaded down their slickers, and gusts of wind blew it up under their raingear. Except when bolts of lightning allowed brief glances of the surrounding farmland, they could see no farther than a rod through the driving rain. Yet, with the ease born of constant repetition, they found their way unerringly to the post.

Sword Worshipful stepped down into the unmanned watch post. Under the woven-reed overhead the rain dripped rather than pelted, but water flowed steadily into the pit, and muddy water sloshed over the tops of his boots. Soldiers Truth and Hellsbane huddled together on the post's leeward side.

Careful not to allow water to drip onto the infrared scanner Sword Worshipful raised its waterproof shell and leaned his eyes into the viewing port. He scanned the area assigned to Post One, saw nothing but wind- and rainswept grain as far as the treeline windbreak. Carefully, he secured the scanner, then called in an "all-secure" report.

They repeated the process at Post Two and Post Three. Soldiers Truth and Hellsbane looked forward to returning to the warmth and dryness of the duty office.

The five Fighters were close to each other, and had a Leader seen them, they would have been ordered to maintain the proper interval. But neither Leader was close enough to detect their bunching up. Suddenly, a Fighter hissed at the others—something—*three* somethings—was approaching from the left. They needed a Leader to tell them what to do.

One of the five had a genetic defect—his intelligence was far higher than Fighters were bred for, and he quietly harbored the ambition to become a Leader. He growled an order to his four companions to get on line facing the oncoming trio. The four hesitated; obeying orders from another Fighter was as unheard of as a Fighter giving orders. But the one growled his orders more harshly, and the four recognized the command voice of a Leader even though they knew it came from another Fighter. They formed the line as ordered.

Three humans loomed out of the darkness, two slightly to the rear and flanks, one centered and leading. The Fighter with the genetic defect aimed the spout of his weapon at the centered Earthman, the obvious Leader, and shouted the command to fire.

Each Fighter fired at the closest Earthman. Fluid, vaguely greenish in the dark, shot from the muzzles of the Fighters' weapons and splashed on the Earthmen, eating through the waterproof fabric, through the soldiers' uniforms, and into their flesh. The screams of Soldiers Truth and Hellsbane were drowned out by a crack of thunder. Sword Worshipful didn't scream; the fluid had struck him square in the face, was sucked into his lungs, and he began burning from the inside.

The defective Fighter barked another order, and the other Fighters fired again at the Earthmen. He ordered them to cease fire and crawled to the downed Earthmen to make sure they were dead. One wasn't, but would be soon. The Fighter turned away, leaving the Earthman to die agonizingly in his own time, and ordered his companions to resume the crawl toward the duty office.

Some minutes later the assistant duty noncom noticed that Sword Worshipful was late reporting in from Post Four. As he wondered why, the door of the duty office burst open and ten shrieking, growling, barking, manlike hellspawn were in the office, spraying greenish fluid. The soldiers screamed as the viscous fluid began eating into their flesh. Five who weren't hit in the initial volley scrambled for their weapons, but two of them were doubled up in agony before they reached the rack. A third was hit before he could bring his weapon to bear. The fourth was hit by three streams, and his finger spasmed on the trigger of his fléchette rifle, spraying miniature darts into the ceiling of the duty office. One man got off a directed shot, and one of the demon creatures screamed as fléchettes shredded its chest. Half a dozen streams of fluid struck that soldier, and he died much faster, though with no less agony, than the others.

Simultaneously, twenty raiders burst into the barracks. The weapons of the off-duty soldiers were locked in racks. The slaughter was one-sided.

A Leader and three Fighters raced into the small side building that housed the First Acolyte and Lead Sword who commanded the outpost. They caught the First Acolyte in the bath and the Lead Sword at his prayers. Both died before they could begin to fight.

The Fighters who had been left outside as a blocking force saw no action. In less than a minute the fifty-six Soldiers of the Lord who manned the outpost were dead.

The Master commanding the raid ground his teeth when

told of the Fighter killed in the duty office. He ordered the body to be bagged and all interior surfaces of the office to be sprayed with acid from the weapons, then had the building burned down. The few helix traces left should prove impossible to find.

CHAPTER
ONE

Big Barb's, the combination bar, bordello, and ship's chandlers that served as third platoon's headquarters when the men were on liberty in Bronnysund, was jumping.

To start the evening out, Gunnery Sergeant Charlie Bass, along with Joe Dean, Rock Claypoole, and some others, had shoved three tables together in what they called the banquet room and ordered beer. Hours had passed, during which the other members of third platoon had trooped in by ones and twos, each new arrival greeted by loud cheers and hardy backslapping. Eventually almost the entire platoon was crowded around the tables, drinking, eating, and singing, as Bass held court at one end. Sitting nearby was Lance Corporal Chan, the unofficial honoree of the evening. Chan would soon be the newest corporal in third platoon, and Bass and the other NCOs were flexing their arms and clenching their fists in anticipation of the pinning-on ceremony. Chan sipped his beer happily, eagerly anticipating the sore shoulders that would plague him for a week after Captain Conorado pinned on the new chevrons.

Owen the woo perched comfortably on Dean's shoulder, glowing the bright pink of wooish contentment, rocking gently back and forth, seemingly taking in everything with his enormous eyes. Top Myer had taken good care of the woo while Dean was away on Havanagas, but he confided to the lance corporal upon his return, "Dean, the little bastard never got beyond light gray the whole time you were away. He missed you, lad!" Owen extended an appendage and snatched up a ceramic fragment from a stein someone had broken earlier. The fragment disappeared down Owen's gullet and stayed down. It seemed to like ceramics. Several Marines applauded, and Claypoole, who was watching the woo carefully, was sure the little creature appreciated the attention. Claypoole had not forgotten the corpsman's story about the woo shouting a warning when the Skinks attacked his aid station on Waygone. Though Claypoole had never heard the woo make any sound that could be interpreted as words, he believed the story.

Barmaids flitted in and out of the room, trays loaded with one-liter steins of Reindeer Ale. The women slapped away eager, groping hands and enthusiastically traded verbal barbs with the Marines, to everyone's great enjoyment. To be a barmaid at Big Barb's, a girl had to know English well and be able to think and move quickly, because after a few beers many of the patrons forgot who was a barmaid and who was a whore. But Big Barb's other girls were there too, matching the Marines beer for beer, joining in with the singing and holding their own in the repartee. To be a whore at Big Barb's a girl had to know some English, work fast, and move men quickly to the upstairs rooms and give them what they bargained for—and if they were really good, more than they bargained for. That's what kept 'em coming back.

But that night was special, not particularly because Lance Corporal Chan was anticipating his forthcoming promotion, but because it was one of those nights fueled by the magical chemistry of alcohol, companionship, and shared experiences. It was just one of those magnificent nights for drinking with friends. They'd worry about their heads in the morning.

Occasionally a Marine would get up, his arm around one of the girls, and drift out into the bar, headed for the stairs. Everyone cheered and clapped and shouted ribald advice to the pair, and those behind loudly ordered more rounds of beer to celebrate a comrade's good fortune.

Out at the bar, sailors from the ships in port crowded three deep. Someone had brought an accordion and another man a fiddle, and they wheezed and scratched lively sea chanteys.

Men and women stomped onto the dance floor, shaking the boards with the pounding of their feet. The bonhomie was infectious: sailors wandered into the banquet hall and were made welcome at the tables with the Marines. And as Marines stumbled through the crowded bar to the rest rooms, they were swept into the arms of the dancers and whisked around the room, to the delighted cheers of the patrons.

But sometimes at Big Barb's it wasn't all just beer and skittles and a headlong rush to the private rooms upstairs . . .

A new girl was holding court, seated on the bar in the main room. Hilma was above average height, full-breasted and broad-hipped, with her hair a blond that would have given even Mother Nature pause to wonder whether that shade of yellow actually existed anywhere in the spectrum. Her laugh was full and nearly as brassy as her hair. A dense knot of Marines and fishermen surrounded her, eager to get acquainted. She laughed and sang and joked—and urged her throng of admirers to drink up and eat more. The men roared approval with each sound she emitted, every move she made. And her movements were many; exotic, graceful, and sexy all at the same time.

So nobody noticed particularly when the door opened and John Francis walked in. One of the many off-worlders who'd come to Thorsfinni's World to pursue the wild and free-wheeling life of the fisheries, Francis had the build of a tugboat and short-cropped black hair above a moon face. He walked with a limp occasioned by an encounter with a trawler that wanted to occupy the same space he and a dinghy happened to hold. Looking around just inside the entrance, Francis saw an open space at a table occupied by some acquaintances. He worked his way through the crowd and slowly, like a davit lowering a fragile cargo into a ship's hold, levered himself into the empty chair. The fishermen exchanged greetings. A harried serving girl popped up at his shoulder almost immediately to take his order for beer and brownies.

John Francis slowly shrugged off the satchel slung on his

left shoulder. Moving just as deliberately, he opened it and withdrew a portable trid viewer.

"Were any of you at Einaar's Fjord on First Day?" he asked. Without waiting for an answer, he continued, "Rumbart Tomison ran his sprint-hover." He turned on the viewer and popped a trid crystal into it. "I had my cam with me, got some beautiful pictures." While he talked he fiddled with the viewer's controls, then turned it toward the other fishermen. "Look at this. He hit 225 kph in the half-K run. He let me into his pits and I got to work on the engine."

The others exchanged glances before they turned toward the viewer. They weren't ready to talk about the races just yet, but they knew they had a choice: listen to John Francis talk about the hovercraft sprints and watch his trids, or get up and leave the table. There wasn't another open table, so moving wasn't much of an option.

John Francis talked and talked and showed his trids of the previous First Day's sprints. His tablemates felt twinges of jealousy that they hadn't been there. He drank his beer and ate his brownies. Every time the laugh of the new girl, Hilma, cut through the din, he cocked his eyes toward her, and each time he did, his eyes glowed more brightly. Francis wasn't known as a ladies' man, so the fishermen who watched his sprints trids paid his glances no attention.

At length one of the fishermen in her circle broke through Hilma's mesmerizing spell long enough to announce that he was taking her upstairs. The announcement was greeted by an uproar of protest from the others.

"Excuse me," John Francis said to his tablemates, "I have to take care of something. You know how to use this; you can look at more pictures." Then he ponderously levered himself to his feet and heavily limped toward the bar, where a good-natured argument was in progress about the selfishness of the one fisherman who wanted to take Hilma away from the rest. Hilma, for her part, laughed about it with raucous delight.

Limp or not, no crowd could divert John Francis's progress. He waded through like an icebreaker in pack ice until he stood with his belly against Hilma's knees. He looked seriously into her face. She looked back and a laugh dribbled away before reaching full throat. Her broad grin melted into a sweetly timorous smile.

"Hi, sailor," she said softly, but not coquettishly.

"I'm John Francis," he said. "You're Hilma."

She nodded shyly. He backed just far enough to turn around without pushing her knees, looked out at the surrounding men, and said in a voice that sounded like the foghorn on the tugboat he was built like, "This one's mine!" He turned back to Hilma and offered his hands. She slid off the bar into his grasp, and he gently lowered her to the floor.

A hush fell over the bar and a way parted for them to the stairs. They went up. They didn't come back down.

The next time anyone at Big Barb's saw Hilma, she was on John Francis's arm, flaunting a wedding band on her finger.

Sometimes at Big Barb's everything wasn't just beer and skittles and a headlong rush to the private rooms upstairs.

"I have a song!" Corporal Raoul Pasquin shouted, standing up and waving his arms. The Marines listened attentively. That he could stand and wave his arms so soon after what he'd been through on Havanagas was a bit of a miracle in itself, but he was not the kind of Marine who'd let a few missing body parts keep him down very long.

When Pasquin had joined 34th FIST from his old outfit, 25th FIST, he'd given every indication he was a problem child, and gotten off to a bad start at Camp Ellis. He and Dean had serious words just before they deployed to Society 437, but once there, and during the Avionian mission, Pasquin proved he could handle himself in combat and was accepted in third platoon as a trusted NCO. More important, on Havanagas, where the corporal had withstood vicious torture at the hands of the mobsters who'd been running the place, he'd proved to Dean and Claypoole that he was far more than a Marine corporal, more even than their fire team leader. He was a proven comrade, a man Marines could trust their lives to.

But the best proof that Corporal Raoul Pasquin was not

the ass he'd started out as was that Owen the woo had taken a liking to him. Everyone was sure Owen could tell good from bad, and the Marines trusted his judgment.

So when Raoul Pasquin stood up, he was given a measure of respect. Dean and Claypoole shouted for silence. Bass gestured him to continue.

"I learned this song in 25th FIST," Pasquin said. "It's called 'Erika.'" He nodded at Dean's companion, whose name just happened to be Erika. "No offense to the beautiful lady here." Erika, who'd been leaning her head on Dean's shoulder, smiled and blushed. "It's just coincidence, Erika, and the song's not dirty or insulting." Several men loudly groaned their disappointment. Pasquin gave them the finger. "It was the unofficial marching song of 25th FIST," he continued. "It's an old song that's come down from the twentieth century or earlier. It's in a good march tempo. Here, listen . . ." He hummed a few bars. "Get it? Here . . ." He sang the first verse: "In the meadow blooms a tiny flower." Boom-boom-boom-boom, he stamped the floor with his foot to get the cadence. "And we call her Erika! Get it?" He took a deep breath and sang:

"In the meadow blooms a tiny flower / And we call
     her Erika.
The bees cannot resist her power / Little Erika,
'Cause her heart is soft and sweet
Her petals trim and neat / Dainty little Erika!

In the village lives a tiny maid / And we call her
     Erika.
She's prim and sweet and oh, so staid / Little Erika!
Yet she lets us kiss her, but not too long
And when we're done we sing this song:
'In the meadow blooms a tiny flower / And we call her
     Erika . . .'"

Pasquin's singing voice was not the best, but the tune was catchy, and as Pasquin warmed to his singing, he got better.

Soon others began to join in, hesitantly at first and then with more confidence as they learned the words. Everyone at the table began to sing, and as they sang they stamped their feet at the appropriate place in the music—boom-boom-boom-boom!—like a bass drum beating out the cadence. When they got to the name Erika, they shouted it out at the top of their voices so it rang in the rafters far above them. The real Erika's face turned brick red with pleased embarrassment, and Owen the woo actually began to sway in time to the music.

It was a soldier's song, the kind men far from home have sung since the dawn of warfare to keep up morale. But even if hearing it for the first time—as the men of third platoon were—its subject was familiar and dear to all men who've ever worn a uniform. Each man had known an Erika back home, or in a foreign town somewhere, or hoped he would someday meet an Erika. Young men need young women as much to comfort their souls as to relieve their hormonal urges, and "Erika" emphasized the gentler side of sexual relations. It made Claypoole think of Katie, back on Havanagas; and despite the real Erika snug against his side, Dean was reminded of Hway back on Wanderjahr. Every man at the table cast his thoughts back to some Erika, not thinking about sex with her, just wanting to relive the experience for a few moments.

But they were young men, and young Marines at that, and ten seconds after the music was done they'd all be thinking about the women around them again.

Pasquin jumped up on the table and led them in chorus after chorus. Between the Marines' singing and stamping their feet in the banquet hall and the sailors' dancing in the bar, the whole building shook.

A crash echoed through the building as the door to Big Barb's private office suddenly slammed open and she sallied forth, her vast bulk bouncing startled men out of the way. But the music and dancing did not slow a beat. She headed straight to the banquet hall. Big though she was, none of the Marines noticed her rolling down on them. Pasquin squawked in mid-verse as she grabbed him, one hand on the seat of his pants, the other by his shirt collar. She picked him up bodily and dropped him heavily into an empty chair.

Huffing and puffing with the effort, she waggled a massive finger at Gunnery Sergeant Bass. "Charlie!" she gasped, "vat you doing? Ve haf der erdquake, mine whole place comin' crashin' down!"

Everyone went silent for a moment. Several patrons from the bar, expecting the fight of the century, stuck their heads cautiously through the door to watch. And then Bass began to laugh. Big Barb couldn't help herself. She smiled. She was soft on Gunny Bass. "Siddown with me, Barb, and have a goddamned beer," he said.

"Vell . . ." Big Barb frowned at the Marines. "Okay! Bud only one." She eagerly slid into a chair beside Bass, snatched a nearby stein and drank. She made a terrible noise, spit the beer out in a spray and threw the stein across the room. "Goddamn! Somebuddy, he puts oud his segar in dat one!" A barmaid quickly offered her mistress a fresh stein, and she drank thirstily. "Aaah." She wiped foam off her upper lip and belched. "Pasquin! Dat song, is gut one, ya! You sings gut too. Owen, he likes it too, dat liddle woo! But you gotta stop pounding wit der feets! You crazy Marines, you gonna wreck my place!" She laughed and drained the rest of the beer in one vast gulp. Someone thrust a full stein into her massive hand and she drank again, one arm draped affectionately across Bass's shoulders.

"Charlie, ven ve gettink married?" Barb roared, her chins jiggling with merriment. Although she was huge, Barb—whose real name was Freya Banak—carried her massive weight well. She was more a solid woman than a fat one.

"Tonight! Right goddamn now!" Bass shouted, pounding the table enthusiastically. The Marines roared approval. Bass winked clandestinely at Barb and her face turned a bit redder. She was reminded of that time Bass was alone with her in her office . . . that had been a sweet moment, but that was all it had been, just a moment. Big Barb and Charlie Bass were the kind of man and woman who could be good friends but never man and wife. Bass grinned fiercely at Barb over the rim of his stein as a thought struck him: on a cold night, what did a man need most, another blanket or an ample woman? And a girl, even a girl like Big Barb, could dream.

The onlookers at the door, realizing it would be just another night of drinking and bonhomie, returned to the dancers in the bar, and Big Barb's establishment settled down once again into the dull roar of drunken camaraderie.

Ten kilometers from Camp Ellis lay Mainside, the fleet naval base that was the hub of Confederation military operations for that quadrant of Human Space where Thorsfinni's World was located. Ten kilometers from Mainside was the dependent housing area where the men who were authorized to have their families with them lived. Marines in the grade of staff sergeant and up and equivalent naval ratings were allowed to marry, but only those men occupying "key" command and staff positions could have their families with them on hardship tours. And if a man was authorized to have his family with him, his tour was automatically extended. The Confederation Navy was not about to ship dependents to far-off worlds and then let their sponsors return to civilization on a normal two year rotation. Not that that meant much to the men of 34th FIST just then; they'd found out that somebody had secretly slapped them with involuntary extensions.

The dependent housing on Thorsfinni's World was known as Safe Harbor and consisted of two separate areas—one for the enlisted's families and one for the officers'. Everything the residents needed was provided for at Safe Harbor—a commissary, an exchange, medical facilities, a school for the children, recreational facilities. Regular transportation between Safe Harbor, Mainside, and Camp Ellis was also provided. For most of the family members a trip to Mainside was a regular outing; dependents were not normally allowed on Camp Ellis. But trips to New Oslo and other cities were a regular feature of the recreational programs available to them.

Senior field-grade officers—commanders, lieutenants

colonel, colonels, and navy captains—occupied single-family dwellings; all others lived in apartment-style buildings. The grade of the sponsor and the number of dependents in his family determined the size of individual quarters. All furnishings were provided by the navy and were passed from family to family until they wore out. The Confederation was not about to bear the expense of shipping anyone's furniture from one side of Human Space to another. Permanent personal possessions were generally limited to the family's personal transportation mass allowance, and when a family rotated out of Thorsfinni's World, the things it had acquired while there were either given away or sold to those who were staying, or to new families just coming in.

Life could be dull at Safe Harbor, but it was better than living years away from husbands and fathers.

Unmarried men called navy wives "camp followers" (or worse) and their children "navy brats" (and much, much, worse), and at Camp Ellis the enlisted Marines referred to Safe Harbor disparagingly as the "Bay of Pigs."

In general, the Confederation military policy was that if it wanted its men to have wives, they'd have been issued one.

Captain Lewis Conorado trudged wearily up the sidewalk into Tarawa Terrace, the apartment building housing the families of company-grade officers. The Conorados had not been living there long. Because of the shortage of family quarters when he was assigned to 34th FIST, his family had originally been placed in spare housing operated by the Confederation's embassy in New Oslo. Their apartment in Tarawa Terrace had only recently been vacated by a navy family.

In the lobby, the children of a naval lieutenant in the supply corps were screaming shrilly at their play. The shrieks reverberated painfully off the bare walls and floor. "Shaddup!" Conorado bellowed. The children went silent instantly; Conorado was known in the community as a man who tolerated no insubordination.

One of the children had urinated in the corner by the elevators, and the acrid odor was heavy in the still air of the lobby. Conorado wrinkled his nose. "Who did that?" he demanded, pointing a rigid finger at the large puddle. There were three of them, ranging in age from six to nine. None answered. Conorado addressed the eldest child: "Brian, you are in charge of your brother and sister. You let it happen, you clean it up. If it's still here when I come down, I'm coming after you." He pressed his palm into the entry pad and the elevator door hissed open. He turned and smiled fiercely at Brian as the doors closed.

The Conorados' one-bedroom apartment was on the top floor of the building. As the building's senior occupant, Captain Conorado could have squeezed a two-bedroom apartment out of the billeting officer, but he felt that he and his wife, Marta, should give up the larger quarters for some officer whose family was larger.

Two hours later, when the Conorados descended to the lobby on their way to the commissary, the noisy children were gone. But the puddle was still there.

CHAPTER
TWO

Colonel Israel Ramadan, deputy commander of 34th FIST, believed firmly that a Marine officer should at all times demonstrate austerity in his personal lifestyle and official conduct. He made it a point to eat in the enlisted messes several times each week, and when a unit went on a field problem he would often accompany it and share living conditions with the men. In this regard he was a carbon copy of Brigadier Sturgeon, the FIST commander. The two officers complemented each other perfectly.

Ramadan's bachelor living quarters were spartan, enlivened only by a wall of bookshelves containing volumes of military classics bound in the old-fashioned way. While almost everyone else was satisfied to get his reading material from vids and trids, Colonel Ramadan had spent a fortune collecting his books, and he had read them all many times. Books were his greatest indulgence.

But Colonel Ramadan had one other weakness, if you could call it that. He loved fine cigars. Oh, there were the Clintons and the Fidels and they satisfied most smokers. But for the real connoisseur, the Clintons left a lingering and slightly unpleasant aftertaste, and the Fidels, although an excellent smoke, were too big, too "long-winded"—at 400mm, they just seemed to go on and on. His favorites were Davidoffs, particularly the Anniversario No. 2 brand. The cigars were grown and produced on New Geneve according to the centuries-old traditions of the Davidoff family. Rumor had it they were rolled on the thighs of nubile native maidens just out of puberty. A box of twenty-five cost the colonel a month's pay. They were his only indulgence other than his books. He husbanded his supply carefully because it took months to get a reorder. He owned three state-of-the-art humidors, one for the cigars in his quarters, one for those he kept in his office, and the third a portable unit he kept filled when traveling.

That morning, as he sat at his desk reviewing the incoming message traffic from Fleet, he decided to have an Anniversario. He pressed a button on the office humidor and its lid hissed open, releasing the rich aromatic fragrance of the cigars stored inside. He picked one carefully and ran it under his nose. Ah, delicious! He noted there were only ten left. Hmm. Must bring some more from my quarters, he thought, and then: Better put in a reorder! It could take up to eight months for a new shipment to reach him. He calculated: 240 days, and he had about six boxes left. That'd be one cigar every other day with a few left over for special occasions. In a pinch he could get some Fidels from New Oslo. Perhaps the tobacconist he dealt with there might even have an Anniversario or two in his private stock. A man could never have enough ammo or enough good cigars!

Carefully, the colonel clipped the end off his cigar and struck an old-fashioned sulfur match. He drew slowly as he rolled the cigar over the flame, drawing in the rich, aromatic smoke and exhaling luxuriously. Sulfur matches were also an indulgence, but a real connoisseur never lighted a good cigar with one of those mechanical devices! Thank God the 'Finnis were traditionalists who appreciated their cigars. Sulfur matches were hard to get anywhere else.

Wreathed in cigar smoke, Colonel Ramadan briefly reviewed the incoming message traffic on his screen. He could have delegated the chore, but as Brigadier Sturgeon's deputy he felt it his responsibility to check everything personally to be absolutely certain the action and information assignments were correct. He was careful to forward to the brigadier a copy of every message he thought would interest him, but he directed routine traffic to the appropriate staff office, with terse comments where necessary. He and Brigadier Sturgeon had worked together for so long, Ramadan knew precisely what the FIST commander would want to see.

Suddenly the computer bleeped and a yellow warning flashed across the screen: SPECAT! EYES ONLY, CO 34TH FIST.

"Oh, shit!" Ramadan muttered. A deployment order. The colonel was both excited and disappointed. Excited because any Marine worth his salt wants action; disappointed because he knew he would not deploy; he was still on a light-duty profile after being severely injured in a Dragon accident.

He set the cigar in an ashtray and typed in his password. Only he, the F2, and F3—intelligence and operations officers—and Brigadier Sturgeon were authorized to read "special category" messages. And the F2 only got them if he and the brigadier agreed he should see them. The message flashed on his screen. It was very short but he had to read it twice. "Print!" he said to the system.

Then: "Delete!" The hardcopy would suffice to execute the order.

"Get me the brigadier!" he ordered the computer system. The screen went blank for an instant, and then Brigadier Ted Sturgeon's face appeared. "Sir, I've got to see you right away. Message from Fleet."

"Come," Sturgeon replied.

Colonel Ramadan limped from his office so quickly he left the Anniversario smoldering in the ashtray.

Stor Evdal, mayor of Bronnysund, sat contentedly in a comfortable chair at the coffee table in Brigadier Sturgeon's office. Mayor Evdal visited the brigadier regularly to coordinate and discuss events of mutual interest with the commander of 34th FIST, usually some terrific fight the night before between his townspeople and 34th FIST's Marines. But far from complaining about the incidents, Evdal enjoyed Monday-morning quarterbacking the fights. The citizens of Bronnys liked fighting second only to drinking, and often Evdal thought that without the fights, he might not be re-elected when his term of office was finally up.

In his eighties, Stor Evdal was still as rugged as the fjords that ringed the seacoast he had fished for most of his life. He was a big, hardy man with a deep voice, rugged, hamlike fists scarred by years of deckwork, and huge mustaches that drooped down the sides of his face. He was smoking a Fidel, courtesy of Brigadier Sturgeon's private supply. The purpose of his visit was to discuss the Marines' "Toys for Tots," the annual Christmas drive to collect toys for the children of Bronnysund. Privately, some enlisted men referred to the program as "Toys for Snots," but generally the Marines derived a lot of satisfaction from participation in the program.

"You know," Mayor Evdal said as he regarded his cigar appreciatively, "the worse times for us here is when da Marines is on deployment. Yah. Tings too quiet den for us in Bronnys!" They both laughed.

"Those are usually bad times for us too, Your Honor," Sturgeon replied.

"Huh? Oh," Evdal nodded, "yah, you lose some gud fellows on dose deployments. Gud fellows." He nodded seriously. "Well," he prepared to get up, "den we is set for der toys raising program dis year! By golly, Brigadier, I can't tell you how much we appreciated vat you does for us!"

Brigadier Sturgeon's computer bleeped. "Sir, I've got to see you right away. Message from Fleet," Colonel Ramadan said.

"Come," he told the machine. Then: "Well, Your Honor, business intrudes." He smiled apologetically and extended his hand as he rose. They shook.

"Anodder of dem goddamn 'deployments' maybe?" Evdal asked. He held up his hand. "I knows, business iss business but schnapps is schnapps, and we done talkin' about da schnapps. Tank you agin, Brigadier, and God bless." He turned to go.

"Your Honor, even if it is another deployment, the stay-behinds will take care of the toy program. My Marines have never left anyone in the lurch and we aren't going to start now, especially not your kids."

Evdal paused and drew deeply on his cigar. "Yah," he said

gravely, "we all knows dat too." He nodded amiably at Colonel Ramadan as he left.

"Look at this goddamned thing!" Ramadan raged.

Sturgeon glanced briefly at the paper. It ordered Captain Lewis Conorado to report to Headquarters Marine Corps in Fargo on Earth by the quickest possible method of transportation. Nothing else, just a fund citation to pay for his transportation. Sturgeon sighed. "I know what this is, Ram. Please sit down."

Colonel Ramadan did not know what had happened to Lima Company on Avionia. The only reason Brigadier Sturgeon knew was because General Cazombi, the army general in command of the operation, had stopped on Thorsfinni's World and filled him in on the details on his way back to Earth. Now Sturgeon told Ramadan. The colonel took it all in silently. "So I guess despite this army general's promise, this Hoxey woman really has filed charges against Lew for letting her guinea pigs go," Sturgeon concluded.

"This army general—Cazombi, you said his name was?"

"Yeah. Lew swears by the guy, so I guess he's okay, did his best to kill the damned incident, I'm sure. Goddamnit, Ram!"

Sturgeon slapped the order with his hand. "They're keeping us here on Thorsfinni's World like lepers, quarantined, because we have knowledge of alien sentiences the government wants to keep quiet. That's what I found out when I went back to HQMC. All right, I accept that. But this— this—" He slapped the paper again. "—this crap goes too damned far! They're taking away one of my best officers because some dried-up old . . ." He let the words trail off. Then: "Okay. Ram, get Van Winkle at Battalion, tell him to have Lew report to me personally, on the double. We keep this to ourselves. But you know, all this hush-hush stuff, I really don't give a damn anymore. My Marines are taking it on the chin because a bunch of goddamned government bureaucrats don't trust anybody but themselves with the truth.

I'm up to here with it! Let them sentence me to Darkside. All right, Ram, see to it."

Back in his office Ramadan discovered the Anniversario had gone out. He relit it. These were the only cigars he knew of you could do that with and lose none of the flavor. He got Commander Van Winkle on the system.

Captain Conorado finished reading the message and looked up at Brigadier Sturgeon. "I guess General Cazombi wasn't able to get Dr. Hoxey to withdraw the charges."

"Are you ready to go back to Fargo and face these charges then?"

"Yessir, I am," Conorado replied evenly.

"Nobody from 34th FIST is being subpoenaed except you, Lew. Plenty of the men in your company witnessed what went on at Avionia Station. Seems to me the court's being packed against you."

Conorado thought about that for a moment. "General Cazombi will be there. So will Mr. Nast from the Ministry of Justice. I think they're all I'll need to support me."

"Didn't you tell me that this Hoxey woman tried to get Dean to give up the woo for experimentation? And Charlie Bass was there with you when you released the Avionians. Can you think of anyone else in your company who witnessed what she was doing to the creatures? I'll have them deposed, and you can take the depositions back with you."

"But sir, this is all ultrasecret information, and the staff judge advocate isn't cleared—"

"Lew, how long have we known each other?" Sturgeon interrupted.

"Years and years. Since I was a corporal and you were an ensign." Conorado laughed. "Since Caesar was a road guard."

"Since Christ was a corporal," Sturgeon added. "Well, I'm not going to let you go down by yourself on this, Lew. You put your career on the line out there for something you believed in. I believe in you and the other Marines in this FIST, and by the cheeks of Mohammed's hairy ass, I don't give a damn for 'security' when it comes to this business. Good God, those pirates knew all about Avionia! By now every crook in the Confederation must know. So the Confederation wants to keep only the honest citizens in the dark? And we haven't even mentioned the Skinks! What the hell are things coming to with all this 'security'? We all know now that they're keeping us here because of this 'alien sentiences' crap! It's wearing mighty thin, Captain.

"Now, I want Bass and Dean deposed by the SJA. I've already talked to the judge. Have them report over there when you get back to the company."

"Yessir. And sir? Thanks."

"Don't mention it. We'll team up on Darkside and make a breakout.

"The F1 and the finance people have arranged for your transportation back to Earth. The next ship leaving for there takes off from New Oslo in two days. It's a civilian job, the SS *Cambria*. It stops somewhere en route, but even so, it'll get you back to Earth before any naval vessel we can scare up on such short notice. Turn Lima Company over to your XO." He stood and extended his hand. "Lew, we're going to miss you."

"Thank you, sir. I'll be back." They shook hands for a long moment.

"I know you will, Lew," Sturgeon replied, but he wasn't so sure.

CHAPTER THREE

It was a case of garbled communications, miscommunication, and bureaucratic arrogance right from the start. Not to mention ignorance brought about by secrets kept too tightly.

Ambassador Friendly Creadence, emissary of the Confederation of Human Worlds to the human planet formally known as the Kingdom of Yahweh and His Saints and Their Apostles, but more commonly called simply "Kingdom," wasn't certain who the invaders were, or even that they were invaders from off-world. So his dispatch to the Ministry of State didn't make that fully clear. Moreover, he was a career diplomat whose only military contact—not experience; he had no experience—was with military attachés who more often owed their appointments to political connection than to military acumen. Consequently, he had a dreadfully minimal understanding of the nature of military weaponry, which ignorance caused him to omit information about the invader's armament.

The dispatch Ambassador Creadence sent to the Ministry of State on Earth requesting Marines noted horrendous fighting, death, and destruction in the outlands, against a foe of unknown origin, armed with weapons evidently superior to those used by the armed forces of Kingdom.

Associate Vice Consul for Consular and Ambassadorial Affairs Moyamenssing, the mid-level Ministry of State bureaucrat who was charged with disposition of the dispatch, began by looking up Creadence in the *Blue Line of Ambassadors, Ministers, and Consuls*. The five paragraph entry outlined an undistinguished career. Creadence seemed to be a competent enough man with no great political connections but sufficient social ones to assist him in gaining advancement through the ranks slightly faster than routine. Kingdom was his third ambassadorial assignment. The earlier two— one as a consul, the other as an ambassador—were, like the present one, to unimportant worlds. Kingdom had to be unimportant; Associate Vice etcetera Moyamenssing had never heard of it.

He looked it up in the eighteenth edition of *The Atlas of the Populated and Explored Planets of Human Space.*

The governing body of the Kingdom of Yahweh and His Saints and Their Apostles was an ecumenical theocracy. Reading between the lines of the short entry, he concluded that the government must be repressive: over the past couple of centuries it had suffered more than ten major rebellions and numerous lesser revolts; on six occasions Confederation Marines had been dispatched to put down the revolts. The entry included an annotation that requests for military assistance were handled by the Office of the President of the Confederation of Human Worlds.

Then there was that passage in the dispatch: "Certain images of one of the possible invaders indicates that they might be of a nonhuman origin. "So where are the images?" Moyamenssing muttered. Well, the suggestion that the possible off-worlders might be an alien sentience was simply too absurd to even consider. Everybody knew that *h. sapiens* was the only sentience anywhere near Human Space.

Moyamenssing duly queued Ambassador Creadence's urgent dispatch via routine channel to the President's office, where two days later it reached the top of the queue of Second Associate Deputy Director for State Affairs Lumrhanda Ronstedt.

Ronstedt's hobby was the history of the lesser worlds of the Confederation. He recognized the world in question immediately and laughed with delight. *"Again?"* The follies of humanity never failed to amuse him. After a second reading of the dispatch—it was marked "urgent," but obviously State didn't think it was, since it had been queued to him via routine channel—he looked up Creadence's entry in the *Blue Line* . . . And laughed with yet more delight; the man had absolutely no experience that would allow him to make a considered judgment on whether military assistance was necessary. Further, his dispatch didn't note any immediate threat to either Interstellar City, the off-worlder enclave outside Kingdom's capital of Haven, or to Confederation citizens outside Interstellar City—the prerequisites for Confederation military intervention on Kingdom.

And the intimation that it might be an alien invasion? He laughed again. It was absurd. The comedic possibilities of ambassadorial level appointees who lacked experience outside diplomatic circles were just too rich!

In total, Ronstedt saw no justification for military intervention. Still . . .

If memory served—and he was confident it did—the Confederation hadn't used military force on Kingdom in more than twenty years, even though there had been two or three uprisings during that time.

He pondered. The simple fact the "rebels," if that's what they were, were allegedly using weapons superior to anything in the Kingdom arsenal at least *theoretically* implied a threat to the security of Interstellar City and Confederation citizens. And there was that silly *intimation* of aliens. Yes, he could find justification for Ambassador Creadence's call for Marines.

Ronstedt chuckled. If he was patient enough to wait for the Marines to get to Kingdom—which meant if he didn't forget about it during the many months it would take for orders to reach an appropriate unit, for the Marines to travel to Kingdom, and news of the mission to get back to Earth—it could provide him with months of amusement.

He marked the dispatch "Approved, Office of the President" with not even a twitch at exceeding his authority, and queued it via "fast"—he wasn't prepared to exceed his authority far enough to queue it "urgent"—channel for the offices of the Combined Chiefs of Staff.

The next day the dispatch reached the top of the message board for Colonel Alleghretti Adoni, Confederation Army, the Assistant Director of Civil Affairs of the Combined Chiefs.

Colonel Adoni checked the authenticity certificate of the "Approved, Office of the President" annotation, and then read the dispatch. Since the dispatch was marked "Approved . . ." he didn't bother to look up Ambassador Creadence. He did, however, look up Kingdom. When he interpreted the diplomatic language of the brief entry in military edition of *The Atlas of the Populated and Explored Planets of Human Space,* he sadly shook his head. Adoni had spent his entire career as a staff officer in higher command headquarters, but he was enough of a humanist to realize the necessity of decent treatment of people. His own subordinates almost invariably thought well of him and did exemplary work, which made him look good, and he rewarded it as well as he could. It was evident to him that Kingdom's governing body probably brought the repeated revolts on itself.

Even though he could request Headquarters Marine Corps to dispatch up to a FIST to quell a civil disturbance or put down a revolt—only the Combined Chiefs could actually order it—he decided that, given the history of Confederation military interventions on Kingdom, his boss should make the decision.

He queued the dispatch urgent to Major General Michael Khanzhak, his boss and the Director of Civil Affairs of the Combined Chiefs, checked that General Khanzhak was available, and walked down the hall to his office.

"Big Mike" Khanzhak, Major General, Confederation Army, rumbled, "Come on in, Al," when Colonel Adoni appeared in his office door. "Big Mike" certainly was, but the bigness of muscle he'd had when first given the name as an artillery officer had morphed into fat from too many years spent cocking a desk instead of a cannon. "What do you have for me?"

"Thank you, sir," Adoni said, taking the seat Khanzhak

waved him to. "What I have is a situation for which I want to see if you come up with the same solution I did. My authority is sufficient to deal with it, but my solution exceeds my authority."

Khanzhak cocked an eyebrow at his deputy and reached a hand to morph the console from his desktop.

"I queued it urgent," Adoni said, "and attached an entry from *The Atlas* . . ."

Khanzhak nodded and turned to his console. He diddled a control, then read Ambassador Creadence's dispatch and the attached entry on Kingdom from under lowered brows.

"You checked the authentication?" Khanzhak asked.

Adoni didn't answer; the question was pro forma.

Khanzhak leaned back in his chair and considered the situation. He came to a conclusion and sat up, facing his deputy.

"You're right, Al, you could handle this under your own authority. Most likely, all this peasant revolt will take is a company or two of Marine infantry. But I think it's time those theocrats saw a real sample of Confederation military power. What do you think?"

Colonel Adoni grinned. "I wonder if I should say 'like minds.' That was my thinking."

"That's why I keep you on as my deputy, Al. You come up with the same solutions I would."

"Thank you, sir."

"Draw up a request to HQMC to dispatch one FIST with another on standby. I'll sign it and kick it upstairs as soon as you get it to me."

Neither of them gave a thought to the nonsensical hint that Kingdom was dealing with an alien invasion rather than a peasant revolt. There weren't any sentient aliens, everybody knew that.

Lieutenant Colonel Rory Torn, Deputy Director for Civil Affairs, Marine Corps, snorted when he read the request from the Combined Chiefs. What are they spiking their caf with over there? he wondered. Don't they realize how many deployments the Marines already have? An entire FIST—with another on standby—to put down a peasant revolt on a rinky-dink little world like Kingdom? He didn't have to look Kingdom up, he'd been a corporal with the company 37th FIST sent to put down a peasant revolt that threatened Interstellar City more than twenty years earlier. *An entire FIST?* If the damn army could get its damn act together *it* could send a military police company to Kingdom, maybe reinforced by a special services platoon, on permanent garrison duty to keep the peace, and leave the Marines to perform more important missions.

But it was an official request from the Combined Chiefs, so he assumed the commandant must know about it and be in agreement.

Lieutenant Colonel Torn didn't think of an alien invasion at all; the request merely quoted selections from Ambassador Creadence's dispatch instead of containing its full text. He passed the request on to his boss, queued through "fast" channel and added an annotation that 34th FIST on Thorsfinni's World, currently not on deployment, was the closest unit to Kingdom.

Assistant Commandant of the Marine Corps Aguinaldo didn't find out about the deployment until after the orders were dispatched. If he had, he would have quashed them and assigned the duty to a different unit. But then, nobody had told the Marines there might be aliens involved. Aguinaldo was virtually the only Marine outside of 34th FIST who knew there really *were* sentient aliens, and that dealing with them was 34th FIST's primary, albeit secret, assignment.

CHAPTER
FOUR

Lieutenant Humphrey, Company L's executive officer; First Sergeant Myer; and the company's platoon commanders stood crowded in Captain Conorado's tiny office. He had called for this meeting as soon as he got back from his talk with the brigadier.

"Men, I'll be brief. I've been recalled to Earth, and Lieutenant Humphrey will take command of the company during my absence."

At first the men received this news in shocked silence, and then, "For how long, sir?" "Why?" "What the hell?" "Goddamn!" Of them all, Lieutenant Humphrey was the most shocked. He thought, Command of the company? Me? He was both frightened and elated. Frightened because nobody could follow Conorado's act as a Marine company commander; elated because if he did well, his own captaincy was assured. But if he screwed up . . . He was like any junior officer, self-confident and anxious to prove himself, but scared silly he'd make a mistake. Humphrey was in his mid-thirties and he'd been a corporal before commissioning, but still, company commander? The Old Man? Actually, as company executive officer and nominal second in command, he had proved himself a very capable and brave officer, and he was respected by the men of Lima Company. But being the happy-go-lucky number two was a lot different from being commander and dealing with all the responsibility that entailed.

He smiled.

Well, he thought, thank God this didn't happen during a

combat operation! At least he'd have time to work his way into the billet, since there were no deployments on the horizon. Lieutenant Humphrey was well-aware that command in combat is the ultimate test of an officer's ability.

Conorado raised a hand. "That's enough. I leave in the morning. Lieutenant Humphrey can make the formal announcement at formation then. I don't know how long I'll be gone—months, of course. Nobody say anything until Humphrey makes the announcement. I know you'll all give him your total support while he's in command. Otherwise, he'll just kick all your asses." He turned to his ashen XO. "Isn't that right, Phil?" Humphrey made a sickish grin in reply.

"That's all, men. Phil, Top, Charlie, would you stay behind for a moment?" They remained standing until the platoon commanders had filed out. "Take seats, gentlemen," Conorado ordered. He sat down himself. "I think you should know the score. It seems Hoxey has filed formal charges against me for what I did on Avionia and I have to return to Headquarters, Marine Corps, to face a court-martial inquiry."

Charlie Bass swore violently. "That is the biggest load of—"

"I know, Charlie," Conorado interrupted.

"Any of us would've done the same, Skipper!" Top Myer protested.

"And if we didn't, sir, you'd have kicked our asses!" Humphrey added, his trepidation about taking command of the company having vanished.

"Nevertheless, gentlemen, it's gone down and I have to go back and face the charges. Don't worry; General Cazombi and Special Agent Nast will be there with me, and I couldn't ask for two better witnesses. Speaking of which, Charlie, the brigadier has ordered that you and Lance Corporal Dean be deposed about what you know, especially how Hoxey tried to get ahold of Owen to experiment on him, and about the reaction of the Avionians when we let them loose. So after this meeting, get over to the SJA. They're expecting you. By the way, speaking of Owen, where is that little devil?"

"Over in my office, sir, dining on some rocks." Top Myer laughed.

"Top, Charlie, I'm coming back when this is over, so don't you let anybody write me off." He laughed too. "All right, you two are dismissed. Phil, stick around for a minute, will you?"

The two NCOs filed out, closing the door behind them.

"Phil, you can command this company as well as anybody. I know you. I've watched you in combat. There couldn't be a better replacement for me. The men and officers of this company will give you their total support and confidence. And you know the old maxim—rely on your noncommissioned officers and you'll never get a bum steer."

"I know, sir, and thank you. It's like the old joke, 'Sergeant, put up the flagpole!' "

Conorado laughed. The story went that a group of officer candidates had been given a practical exercise to erect a flagpole. They'd been given all the tools and equipment plus a sergeant and two enlisted men. They attacked the problem like trained engineers but each candidate had his own suggestion on how to get the job done. They argued and demonstrated, drew up detailed plans, but after fifteen minutes of talk they still had not started on the job. "Gentlemen," their tactical officer had said after the confusion had gone on long enough, "allow me to demonstrate how this is done." He turned to the sergeant and said, "Sergeant, have the men put up the flagpole." In five minutes it was done.

"Okay, Phil, I've got a lot of administrative trivia to get through before I go home and pack. Leave me alone for a while, would you?"

Conorado remained in his office most of the rest of that day, authenticating reports, writing instructions to his staff, reviewing dozens of personnel matters, generally trying to clean up as much detail as he could in order to leave Lieutenant Humphrey free to concentrate on taking over command. He knew that Humphrey would have plenty of time to get himself bogged down in the administrivia of running an infantry company, not that as XO he hadn't had enough of that already.

At 1500 hours Top Myer knocked on the captain's door. "Sir, Lance Corporals Dean and Claypoole have requested to see you." There was a quizzical look on the first sergeant's face.

"What about, Top? I've got a lot of stuff to get through here before I can leave."

"They wouldn't say, Skipper."

"All right, send them in," Conorado said, a tone of annoyance in his voice.

The two lance corporals marched in and stood at attention before Conorado's desk.

"What is it, Marines?"

Dean and Claypoole looked at one another. Claypoole nodded, evidently designating Dean as their spokesman. "Sir, we heard that you are leaving and—"

"Goddamnit!" Conorado shouted, slamming a fist onto his desk. The two lance corporals blanched and Top Myer stuck his head in the doorway. "It's okay, Top. Men, I apologize. You caught me by surprise. What do you have for me?" Conorado kicked himself mentally. He was letting the stress get to him. The worst was yet to come, when he went home and told his wife he was leaving. But with all his experience, he should have known that in the company news of his imminent departure couldn't be kept secret longer than five minutes. Nobody could keep a secret for very long in an infantry company.

"Well, sir, we heard you're going back to Earth and, uh, well, we wanted to give you something like a going-away gift. Sort of, that is," Dean said, fumbling for words.

"Something you'd appreciate, sir. Gunny Bass said it was okay," Claypoole added.

"Well, thank you, men." He stood up.

Dean handed him a small leather case. It was heavy.

Conorado hefted it and smiled. "Hope it's not a watch." He laughed. Dean and Claypoole laughed with him, but nervously.

"It's definitely not a watch, sir," Claypoole offered. Conorado heard something in his voice and glanced up at him. There were tears in his eyes.

"Well, well . . ." Conorado unzipped the case. Inside lay an old-fashioned projectile weapon, a pistol. He took it out and examined it. The instrument was jet-black and shiny. He pressed a stud on the handle and the magazine dropped out into his hand. It contained six old-fashioned gunpowder rounds in shiny brass casings.

"It's called a POS, sir. That means—"

"I know what it means, Dean. When I was your age that's what I called the first landcar I ever owned. It really was a POS."

"Sir, you put the magazine back into the handle and work it by pulling the slide back. That puts the first bullet into the chamber. Then you just sight it and squeeze the trigger. It's .25 caliber, six rounds, weighs only a little over four hundred grams. You kinda gotta hold it tight when you shoot it because it'll kick. But first round's what counts, they say. The cops, that is. They gave them to us."

"Is this the pistol you used, Claypoole, back on Wanderjahr?"

"Yessir!" Claypoole answered proudly.

"The police gave us each one, sir," Dean repeated, "as sort of a badge of honor. When we were working for Chief Long. When he was the FIST F2, you know, after Commander Peters got wounded?"

"Claypoole, you actually shot a man with this thing, didn't you?"

"He sure did, sir! Turned the tables on the sonofa—er, 'scuse me, sir."

"I killed him deader'n hell, sir," Claypoole said. "One round, right in the forehead, and he went down like a goddamned sack of—" Dean signed for Claypoole to be quiet. "Well, the sonofabitch roughed me up, sir," he continued in a quieter tone of voice, "and nobody handles a Marine like that and gets away with it," Claypoole added lamely.

"Sir, we figured, well, a man should always have something to fall back on. And you have a long trip, and who knows? And we don't have time to get you a proper gift. So we talked it over, sir, and decided to give it to you. Claypoole doesn't have any need for it. And Gunnery Sergeant Bass approved," he repeated hopefully.

"Well, thank you, Marines. Thank you very much," Conorado said, slipping the gun back into its case. It was highly irregular to accept a gift from enlisted men, but Conorado could hardly refuse it under the circumstances. "I'll take good care of it. Now I have work to do. Dismissed."

The two lance corporals did a smart about-face and marched out of the captain's office, huge smiles on their faces.

Conorado shook his head and smiled. He slipped the tiny pistol into his briefcase. When he got home he'd secure it in his private safe and forget about it.

His work done, Captain Lewis Conorado stood silently behind his desk. The walls of his office were bare, and where other officers might have framed trids of themselves or their various awards, Conorado had none. He didn't even keep trids of his family on his desk, just a few artifacts, mementos of things past: the butt of a ten pound mortar shell fired at him on Elneal; the fuse plug from an explosive shell fired from the main gun of a Diamundian tank; the set of ensign's bars issued to him when he was first commissioned; and the staff-sergeant chevrons, which he'd given up when he reported to officer candidate school. He stood looking down at them. Not much to commemorate a lifetime of service, he thought. Slowly, he packed them into a box, examining each one lovingly as he wrapped it and put it away.

As he turned to place the box into the cabinet behind his desk, a dull blue glow suffused the room. He turned and saw Owen the woo, standing in the doorway. "What's up, Marine?" He really liked Owen; all the men in Company L liked the woo. He was their mascot, but in the time since Dean had brought him back from Diamunde, the Marines had taken to treating him as one of their own, like another Marine. Some believed he was highly intelligent, and everyone talked to him as if he could understand human speech. Many thought he did.

Owen wobbled into the captain's office and jumped lightly up on his desk. He stood there swaying, his great saucerlike eyes staring plaintively up at the officer. Blue was a color of distress for a woo.

"Aw, what's the problem, you old grunt, you?" Conorado asked, genuine affection in his voice. "You sad I'm going away? Shake." He held out his finger, and one of Owen's many delicate appendages wrapped itself around it. It felt like the tendril of a tiny plant, and immediately Owen's color began to change from blue to pink, the sign of satisfaction and happiness. "I'll be back, Owen. While I'm gone, you help Lieutenant Humphrey run this company. I'm counting on you. You do a good job while I'm away and I'll promote you to honorary lance corporal when I get back."

The creature wobbled comfortably on the edge of the captain's desk, on their stalks his huge eyes were raised to the man's face, as if it were trying to tell him something. Captain Conorado smiled.

"Good luck, Skipper," Owen the woo said.

Bass sat comfortably in Sergeant Major Shiro's quarters, a liter of cold Reindeer ale on the table beside him. The FIST sergeant major often invited select senior NCOs to his quarters after duty hours, to unwind and discuss among themselves important matters affecting the enlisted men of 34th FIST. These sessions were an unofficial form of NCO Call, but they often accomplished more business than any formal meeting ever could.

First Sergeant Myer, Lima Company's top kick, occupied another chair in the sergeant major's tiny sitting room. Next to him Sergeant Major Parant of the FIST's infantry battalion stretched his long legs and sipped an ice cold beer. The room was hazy with cigar smoke, proving the old adage that in the Corps all you needed to find your way to an NCO meeting was to follow your nose.

The topic under discussion was Captain Conorado's imminent departure.

"Will there be any problems with this Humphrey?" Shiro asked Myer directly.

Myer glanced at Bass. "Not if Charlie and I can help it," he answered. "Besides, the kid's been around." To Top Myer, anybody under fifty was still a kid.

Parant laughed. "There isn't much you two old grunts can't handle. Hell, we've all been training junior officers since Christ was a corporal. That's what NCOs do, and the Corps knows it."

"There'll be no problems with Lieutenant Humphrey," Bass said quietly. "He's been shot at and missed and shit at and hit and he's come through just fine. Top and I'll keep an eye on him, though, in case he's forgotten anything since he was a corporal. Thankfully there're no deployments on the horizon. Humphrey probably won't want to give the company back when Lew returns." They all laughed. They knew Lieutenant Humphrey would be just fine as Company L's commander.

"What's with this recall anyway, Charlie?" Shiro asked. "Oh, I know the bare bones, but what happened out there that could get such a fine officer in so much trouble?"

Bass shrugged. "Fred, I've never seen an officer display so much guts as Lew did on Avionia Station." He explained briefly what had happened. "I gotta tell you, Lew has it all, he's brave in combat and he's morally courageous. That's what that army general said of him, and for once the army is right."

"Sounds like you're describing yourself there," Parant interjected. Bass's face turned red at the compliment. "I mean it, Charlie," Parant continued. "What the hell are you doing, sitting there as a gunnery sergeant, 'platoon commander' notwithstanding? There's not an officer in the Corps better fitted for command than you are. You're still young enough. Get a goddamned commission!"

They had discussed this many times before. Bass gave the same answer: "You know I could ask any one of you that same question. But Bern, I don't want to lose contact with my Marines. I'd take a commission as an ensign, maybe even a lieutenant, but I'm a platoon sergeant. I want to stay where I can work with Marine infantrymen. I'm good for them and they're good for me. I become an officer and next thing you know I'm off to some charm school or some rear-echelon assignment. You know how every officer is supposed to be a potential general, so the Corps shifts them around to get all the 'experience' they need to command a FIST or be the commandant. Besides," he added, "I become an officer, and you guys won't let me play poker with you anymore! I'll take Frank's job, though." He nudged First Sergeant Myer in the ribs.

"What? Give you my cushy job? Never happen said the cap'n!"

"We don't like to play with you anyway, you lucky bastard," Parant said.

"You guys," Shiro said, shaking his head. "Well, you're right about one thing, there are no deployments coming up so we can enjoy garrison life for a while. Now, we have successfully disposed of the matters affecting human life in the universe, so let's get down to real business. Deal the cards!"

Captain Conorado trudged wearily down the hallway to his apartment. Now came the hardest part. The door opened soundlessly in response to his voice pattern. He set his briefcase on a table in the tiny foyer and stepped into the living room module.

"Lew!" Marta exclaimed as she came out of the kitchen module, a dish towel over her shoulder. The Conorados couldn't afford the servomechs most civilian households used for housework, so Marta did it herself. The smile washed off her face. She realized from her husband's expression that bad news was coming. "*Another* goddamned deployment?" She pulled the dish towel from her shoulder and flicked it to emphasize her anger.

"Marta . . . No, not another deployment. I've been re-called to Earth." He pushed some pillows out of the way and sat on the sofa, letting out a deep sigh as he settled in.

"You mean, we're going back to Earth?" She brightened at the prospect.

"No, Martie, I mean I'm going back. You stay here." One of Conorado's failings was that he did not know how to sugarcoat bad news. He was not a diplomatic person.

"Well, why? Lew, why are they sending you back?"

"I can't tell you, honey, it's classified." He knew how that would go over and braced himself, but he didn't know how else to put it.

Marta stared at him silently for a long moment. "God-damnit to hell!" she shouted. She threw the dish towel into the kitchen. "Classified? What in the hell are you doing that's classified, Lew? What's not 'classified,' Lew, is how goddamned hard I've worked all these years to be a good Marine wife, to make a home for you and raise our kids! What's not 'classified' is how I get to live alone all the time because my husband is off on a deployment light-years away. What's not 'classified' is how I raised our children es-sentially by myself, Lew, because you were never there! What's not 'classified' is how the Corps jerks you around, sends you here, there, everywhere, to get yourself killed fighting some goddamned battle some goddamned fat-assed politician thinks is the 'cause of the moment' with his god-damned brain-dead constituents! I'll tell you again, Lewis Conorado, Captain, Confederation Marine Corps—not a single one of those bastard government creeps back in Fargo has a kid in the Fleet or a husband or a wife laying their asses on the line somewhere out there," she gestured toward the ceiling, "and now you come in here and blithely an-nounce this crap—" She began to cry.

The Conorados had had that kind of fight before, but

nothing quite as serious as this was turning out to be. Lew realized that Marta was venting deeply suppressed emotions. He also realized that once they got out they'd never go back where they came from. Lewis Conorado loved his wife as deeply as he loved the Corps. Neither had the market on his affection. He just loved them in different ways.

"Honey—"

"No. No, Lewis, sit still." She wiped her eyes on a sleeve. She was calm now. "Lewis, tell me what's up. Tell me everything."

So he told her everything. He told her what he knew from personal experience and what he suspected from what he'd learned over the months. He knew he was committing a felony by revealing classified information. But the worst that could happen is he'd be removed permanently from command—and his family. He knew Marta would never subject him to that. Alien sentiences? Conorado thought. What the hell did anyone back at Fargo know about "alien sentiences" anyway? Here, they'd had one living among them for months and nobody'd really figured out that not only was Owen the woo sentient, he'd learned to speak English! Conorado wasn't about to tell anyone either. The scientists and bureaucrats could all go straight to hell.

Marta seemed to wilt as Conorado talked. "My God," she whispered at last, thinking of the Skinks, "and they're not telling anyone? And they're going to court-martial you for doing what any decent man would've done in that awful birdman situation?"

"Well, not exactly a court-martial, Marta. Just an inquiry. I don't think it'll fly but I've got to be there. Look, I'd take you with me, honey, but you know we can't afford it. And look on the bright side—I won't be in any danger back there."

"Lewis, that was not funny. You have to resign, that's all there is to it. Resign. Tell them to stick their court-martial right up their—"

"Marta, be reasonable. I can't resign, not while this thing

is hanging over my head. All favorable personnel actions are suspended when a man gets into a situation like this. You know that."

Marta nodded. "Yes, Lew, I know it. I know you love those Marines in that company of yours too. I'd be jealous if I didn't love them too. Goddamnit, Lew, every time you go on deployment I worry as much about your Marines as I do about you!" Her face began to crumple but she got hold of herself. "I'll help you pack," she said at last, a tone of resignation in her voice.

The packing did not take long, and Marta said little as they went about it. Conorado stood in the living room, his bag hanging loosely from one arm. "You look splendid in your reds," Marta whispered. "Just as splendid as the day I first saw you when I was young."

"Marta . . ." Powerful emotions were welling up in Conorado's breast. He swallowed and suppressed them. The Conorados were not the kind of people who showed emotion readily; they never billed and cooed and whispered sweet nothings to each other. They were alike in that they both believed action spoke louder than words. They knew they loved each other, and that was all either needed to know about the other. They just didn't think it necessary to remind themselves of that.

"Martie, the shuttle to New Oslo leaves soon. I've got to go now."

"Good-bye, Lewis." She made no move to approach him.

Conorado hesitated for a moment, as if expecting more from his wife. Then: "Good-bye, Marta." He turned and walked toward the door.

"Lewis!" Conorado whirled around. "Lewis, don't count on me being here when you get back."

That statement hit Conorado like a plasma bolt in the chest. She meant what she'd just said. He knew that, knew there was nothing he could say to her about it, and also knew she'd been working up to saying it for a long time now. But now he got mad. "Well, we'll just have to cross that bridge when we get to it," he said as he turned about sharply, grabbed his briefcase, and went out the door without a backward look.

"Captain, may I have a word with you?" someone said as Conorado crossed the lobby of the apartment building.

"Huh?" He turned. It was that naval lieutenant, his neighbor—of sorts.

"Captain, my son tells me you threatened him the other day. I won't stand for that!"

"What? Who?"

"My son, Brian. He said you accosted him in the lobby here and said you would 'come after' him. You have no business threatening my children."

Yes, he remembered now. Brian. That was the kid's name. The kid or one of his siblings had pissed all over the floor, and he had told him to clean it up.

"Well, Lieutenant . . ." Conorado turned to face the man. He wore the insignia of the naval supply corps and two ribbons on his tunic, one for deep space service and the other some sort of navy commendation. "I apologize."

Thinking he'd made the Marine captain back down, the lieutenant preened himself, "Well, of course there must've been a misunderstanding, Captain. I—"

"No, no. No 'misunderstanding,' Lieutenant. I really should not have threatened Brian." Conorado stepped very close and put his face right up to him. "Tell you what. Next time one of your brats pisses all over the floor, or screws up generally in any other way, I won't say a word. They're only kids. They're learning. From their dad. Instead, I'll come and get you. I'll give *you* the spanking, Lieutenant. And if you don't like it, you pasty-faced little shit, I'll just right here and now reach down your fucking throat and pull your goddamned tongue out by the roots. Now shove off, Mr. Squid!"

CHAPTER
FIVE

The Confederation Marine Corps' Fleet Initial Strike Teams, known as FISTs, were expeditionary forces. They were designed to deploy on short notice to anyplace there was a problem that might require a military solution. Sometimes the mere arrival of a FIST in orbit around a problem planet—or a planet with a problem—was sufficient to calm matters enough that military intervention was no longer needed. Sometimes it was necessary for the Marines to make planetfall and simply look able to take on and defeat any opposition. Often they had to fight.

Infrequently, a FIST—or, rarely, more than one—went in to kick open a door so the Confederation Army could walk through.

From the hand-blasters carried by officers and senior non-commissioned officers all the way to the Raptors flown by fighter pilots, the Marines were more lethally armed than any force they were likely to come up against. Their communications devices were the best the Confederation could provide. Their normal combat uniform was chameleon, made of material that mimicked the color and pattern of whatever it was closest to—a combat-ready Marine was effectively invisible. When they weren't on deployments, the Marines of a FIST trained incessantly so they'd be ready for whatever they might face when they next mounted out.

Deployments for any FIST could come back-to-back or be a year apart. Orders to mount out could come at any time, and almost never had advance notice. Sometimes the need for Marines was urgent and an entire FIST would be aboard

Confederation Navy shipping and en route within two days. Other times the need was less urgent and there might be a week or so between the receipt of orders and the time the FIST boarded navy starships.

Nobody thought there was any particular need for urgency when the Confederation ambassador to Kingdom made his urgent request for military assistance. There was rarely any urgency to dealing with a peasant revolt, especially one on Kingdom.

Morning formation, an age-old military ritual. It was an easy means for a commander to make sure none of his men were missing and that all were fit for duty. It was also an easy means for commanders to pass the official word to their people and make other necessary announcements.

Company L formed up behind the barracks on a balmy spring morning at Camp Major Pete Ellis. "Balmy spring morning" at that northerly latitude of Thorsfinni's World meant the breeze was stiff but seldom howled or gusted to gale force, and the temperature was a bit above ten degrees Celsius. The air was damp with moisture from the snow evaporating from the mountains that lurked on the windward horizon—nobody but the new men noticed the constant, pervasive, smell of fish.

"Sir!" Gunnery Sergeant Thatcher barked, and brought his hand crisply up in salute as Lieutenant Humphrey marched up and halted two paces in front of him. "Company L, all present and accounted for."

Humphrey returned Thatcher's salute. "Company L, all present and accounted for," he echoed. "You are dismissed, Gunnery Sergeant."

Thatcher cut his salute, said, "Aye aye, sir," and executed a sharp about-face. He marched to the barracks and disappeared into it.

Everyone's attention was piqued; the lieutenant carried a clipboard. Captain Conorado never carried a clipboard to morning formation unless he had some important news to give them.

As Humphrey looked over the formation from one end to the other, each Marine before him was trying to guess what Humphrey would say. There could be an important visitor coming, or a FIST commander's inspection, or a deployment. The platoon commanders, standing at attention in a line behind him, also gave no hint. A deployment was most likely. Even though Company L had deployed by itself recently, and its third platoon not long before that, the entire FIST hadn't mounted out in a couple of years, an unusually long time.

A couple of years. The normal tour of duty for a Marine assigned to a hardship post such as 34th FIST was two years. Many of the Marines had been with 34th FIST for much longer than two years. Maybe Humphrey had word on when rotations would resume. Probably not. He'd dismissed Gunny Thatcher, so maybe it was an unexpected training exercise and the Gunny needed extra time to make plans for it.

Humphrey didn't let the suspense last overlong. "At ease," he said in a voice that carried clearly, and stood easy himself. "Thirty-fourth FIST has a deployment."

The announcement was met stoically by the men who had been with the FIST the longest and were most looking forward to transfer. It was received with nervous anticipation by the newest Marines who had never been on a deployment.

"Eight days from today," the acting company commander continued, "we will board the CNSS *Grandar Bay*, an Amphibious Landing Ship, Force, for transport to the Kingdom of Yahweh and His Saints and Their Apostles. I know a few of you have been to Kingdom in the past. It appears the peasants are revolting again. Thirty-fourth FIST's mission is to restore peace and order." Humphrey didn't sound happy about the deployment, and with good reason; he was one of the Marines in Company L who had been there before and had no love and less respect for the world's government.

"During the coming week you will have time to put your

affairs in order. Most of the time, though, we will undergo refresher training on civil strife response actions. There are no further announcements. When you are dismissed you will proceed to your quarters and commence preparations for deployment. You will be notified of the time and place of the first training evolution.

"COMP-ney, a-ten-HUT!" he barked, and snapped-to himself. There was a crisp *snap* as the Marines returned to the position of attention. Humphrey looked them over again, then said, "Platoon sergeants, take your platoons!" He stepped off and led the officers back into the barracks.

The sergeant of third platoon, Wang Hyakowa, pivoted to face his men. "At ease," he said, and held up a hand. "No questions. This is the first I've heard of this deployment. I don't know anything about the training we'll be having other than the civil strife response action training I've had in the past, and most of you have had that training as well. I've never been to Kingdom, so I can't tell you anything about it either."

That last statement wasn't totally true. Hyakowa had heard about it from other Marines who'd been there, and seen the trids and vids they'd made of conditions on that world. He knew it to be an agrarian world on which the overwhelming majority of the population lived and worked in the countryside; communication with the outside universe, including books and all other forms of entertainment, was forbidden to the general populace; literacy beyond what was needed for scripture study was almost nonexistent; life expectancy for all but the ruling theocracy was little more than half the 117 years in the Confederation at large.

The little Hyakowa knew about Kingdom made him wonder why the Confederation assisted its government in putting down the frequent peasant revolts instead of aiding the rebels. But that was something he couldn't say to his Marines.

What he did tell them was: "You heard Lieutenant Humphrey. Go to your quarters and start packing. Dismissed."

The platoon broke formation and the Marines headed for the back door of their wing of the barracks, talking among themselves. Hyakowa didn't try to listen to them as they went past, but he couldn't help but overhear comments, and so it was obvious to him that the more experienced Marines didn't like the deployment, and that it had nothing to do with resentment over their indefinitely delayed rotations to more civilized, more mainstream duty stations than Thorsfinni's World.

Few Marines who'd ever been on a mission to put down a peasant revolt had any stomach for another. Generally, peasants were poorly armed and trained, and more often than not their leadership had little or no knowledge of military tactics. Thirty-fourth FIST's deployment to Wanderjahr three years earlier had been an exception; the leaders of the rebels had excellent military training. Even so, when the Marines and rebels had met, it was a slaughter. It was one thing to meet a properly trained and equipped soldier in combat and kill him—he at least had a chance, no matter how small. It was altogether something else to kill an untrained, poorly armed farmer—especially one who might have a legitimate grievance.

But they were Marines, Hyakowa thought. They went where they were sent and did their job. Nobody said they had to agree with the mission, much less like it.

When the second fire team of third platoon's second squad reached its room on the second level of the barracks, Corporal Kerr, the fire team leader, went straight into the head they shared with the squad's third fire team and bolted both doors, though the head could accommodate all six men simultaneously. He needed a few minutes' privacy. It had been on a mission not too dissimilar, one that required heavy civic action, that he was savagely wounded and spent many hours in surgery while the doctors put the inside of his chest cavity back into a working arrangement. That was followed by months of recuperation, and even more months of physical therapy while he regained his full strength and agility.

Since his return to Company L after an absence of nearly two years, Kerr had been on two deployments: Third platoon went to the exploratory world nicknamed "Waygone," and then Company L went to the quarantined world of Avionia. On the first one, they encountered strange beings from elsewhere, the ones they called Skinks. On the second, they dealt with smugglers who were trading with a backward alien sentience. Contact with that sentience, the existence of which was a closely guarded state secret, was the reason for the cancellation of all transfers out of 34th FIST.

When he'd first returned, Corporal Kerr was uncertain whether he'd be able to function properly as a combat infantry noncommissioned officer. But after an initial fright on Waygone, he'd been the same cool, collected Marine corporal he'd always been. But neither of those missions had been a civil action. Neither had any relationship to the mission on which he'd been almost killed. This one did.

Quite unexpectedly, Corporal Kerr found himself terrified at the prospect of a civil strife response action. He knew he had to get hold of himself and overcome this fear. If he didn't, he not only risked his own life, but would unnecessarily place the lives of his men, and other Marines, in jeopardy.

Lance Corporal Schultz noted Corporal Kerr's disappearance and chose to ignore it. He knew Kerr was a solid Marine who would get over whatever was bothering him. He turned immediately to his own preparations. He had little in the way of personal possessions that he couldn't take along; his packing could wait until the last day or until he was ordered to pack. First, he wanted to learn about Kingdom.

This wasn't his usual first step in preparing; usually he made sure—for him an unneeded operation—that his weapons were ready. Next, he wanted to undergo any training that might be needed for the mission. Learning about the mission world was low priority because, he figured, people were people no matter where they were in Human Space. But Schultz had heard a few comments when morning formation broke up, and thought he detected an undertone to Lieutenant Humphrey's voice when he told them about the mission. This made him curious. He got out his reader, flipped it on, and checked the index. Yes, it still held the Confederation Intelligence Agency's *FactBook Overview*. He called it up and opened it to the entry on the Kingdom of Yahweh and His Saints and Their Apostles.

Three short paragraphs. Founded by an ecumenical group of religious fundamentalists, Kingdom had a closed, agrarian culture. It was well away from normal shipping routes and had little interstellar trade. The small off-worlder community was restricted to one settlement, Interstellar City. Congress between off-worlders and Kingdomites was limited to official contacts. The entry was followed by a short listing of references, none of which Schultz had in his library. He was linking into the Camp Ellis library to see which of those references it had when Corporal Doyle, the fire team's third man, interrupted him.

"L-Lance Corporal Sch-Schultz?" Doyle was afraid of Schultz. In fact, Schultz was the kind of man who inspired fear, but Doyle's fear ran much deeper—he was secretly afraid of all warriors.

"Speak." Schultz kept his attention on his data search.

"What's it like?"

"What?" Schultz found a reference and downloaded it for study. He kept searching.

"A civil strife response action? You've been on one." Doyle's most recent duty was as Company L's senior clerk. His entire Marine career had been as a clerk, so he was familiar with the careers of the Marines of the company. This was his first *assignment* as an infantryman.

"Chickenshit." Schultz found two more references and downloaded them.

"What?"

"Hmm." Schultz had found and downloaded a total of seven references, precious little for a Confederation member world.

"Wh-What do you m-mean, 'chickenshit'?"

Schultz glowered at Doyle. He wanted to read the material he'd downloaded. "Farmers acting up. We put them in their place. Almost like Elneal. Chickenshit." Schultz returned to his reader.

"Farmers acting up?" Doyle's mind flashed on an ancient vid he'd once seen that showed peasants in homespun, swinging scythes and hoes as they attacked a castle. Then he flashed on a Hieronymous Bosch painting of hell, with Marines as the devils and farmers as the damned souls. He shuddered. That wasn't anything like the action he'd taken part in on Elneal. Absently, he fingered the material of his shirt above the left pocket—where the Bronze Star medal he'd been awarded for that action hung on his dress reds.

Farmers acting up? A Boschian hell? What?

He shuddered again.

Schultz was immersed in his study. The "chickenshit" was about more than farmers acting up. He knew 34th FIST was secretly designated as the Confederation's official alien-contact military force. Why were they being sent to deal with a Mickey Mouse peasant revolt?

The company classroom could comfortably seat fifty. All 120 Marines of Company L crammed themselves into it. The platoon sergeants stood against the wall on both sides of the entrance. Lieutenant Humphrey stood outside, waiting to make his entrance. Top Myer, the company first sergeant, stood at one side of the small stage opposite the entrance, Gunnery Sergeant Thatcher at the other. They gave the men a moment or two to settle themselves, then mounted the stage.

"AT EASE!" Thatcher bellowed.

The susurration of voices stilled and all eyes turned toward the stage.

"We have a week before we mount out. We will spend that week in training for the coming mission."

Myer looked through the entry door and caught Humphrey's nod. "COMP-ney, a-ten-HUT!" he roared.

There was a cacophony of scraping chairs, shuffling and clicking boot heels as the Marines jumped to their feet and snapped to attention.

Lieutenant Humphrey strode into the classroom, followed by the platoon commanders, who peeled off and took station next to their platoon sergeants.

"As you were!" Humphrey called when he was halfway down the aisle between the chairs. The men relaxed from their stiff postures but remained standing under the glares from Top Myer and Gunny Thatcher.

Humphrey reached the stage and stood at the lectern, looking out at the Marines for a moment. It wasn't formally necessary for him to make the appearance, and he had nothing to say that Myer and Thatcher wouldn't, but almost none of the men had known a commander other than Captain Conorado during the time they'd been with Company L. He needed to get them accustomed to seeing him as the commander until Conorado returned or another captain replaced him.

"Sit," he ordered.

When the Marines were seated, he began. "You know we have a mission. You know it's a civil strife response action. All of you have had training in civil strife response actions, but Company L hasn't trained in it for quite some time. On Kingdom, Brigadier Sturgeon expects us to function in company-, platoon-, and squad-size actions. Therefore, during the short time we have before we mount out, we will train accordingly. The training will continue as conditions allow while we are in transit. By the time we make planetfall, I expect every man jack in this company to be so well versed in civil strife response actions, he'll be able to take a squad or larger unit of the Kingdom army and train it into proficiency."

Humphrey cracked a smile, knocked it off his face.

"Don't misunderstand, we won't integrate with the Kingdom army as we have with some other planetary armies. I don't think the ruling theocracy would allow such contamination of their true believers." This time he couldn't keep a wry smile off his face. A few of the Marines got the joke and chuckled. "We won't be training the Kingdom army, but I expect all of you to achieve that level of expertise. With good fortune, and a few Marines, this mission should be wrapped up in a matter of weeks. We should be back on Thorsfinni's World in time to undertake training with the flies and mosquitoes of high summer." That elicited groans from the Marines who had trained at Camp Ellis during the local summer.

"Now I'll turn you over to the good graces of First Sergeant Myer and Gunnery Sergeant Thatcher." He stepped away from the lectern and strode down the aisle to the exit.

"COMP-ney, a-ten-HUT!" Top Myer barked, and the men snapped to attention. He took station at the lectern and glowered at the men for a moment, then snarled, "Siddown and listen up. You heard the Skipper." He too would reinforce who was in command during Captain Conorado's absence. "You're going to learn, and you're going to learn well. You will train so hard you'll be able to do it all in your sleep. You'll need to be able to do it in your sleep, because even a whole FIST isn't big enough to deal with a planetwide uprising. Don't expect to get any sleep while we're on Kingdom. Everybody's going to have to do double and triple duty.

"Now, to get started on this. Gunny." He nodded to Gunny Thatcher and left the stage to join the platoon sergeants at the rear of the room.

"There's something I want to get out of the way immediately," Thatcher began, "because I don't want anybody worrying about it instead of paying attention. *No* nonlethal weapons. We don't know how the rebels are armed, so we go in with blasters and assault guns fully charged and at the ready."

He paused to let the murmurs run their course. On their

last mission, the men of Company L had been armed with nonlethal weapons. That had caused quite a bit of upset among the Marines, and might have led to a degree of laxity. Even though they hadn't suffered any fatalities as a result, there were a few casualties that might have been caused by overconfidence—if their opponent wasn't dangerous enough to require lethal force, the opponent couldn't be dangerous enough to harm them.

"The Rules of Engagement for this mission are still being developed," Thatcher said when the murmurs had gone on long enough, "but I can tell you what some of them are likely to be. Given the nature of Kingdom, one of the top rules will be no contact with the native population except under clearly prescribed conditions. Here's one way of interpreting that rule: any of you who believes in a girl in every port, tie a knot in it. You *don't* get a girl in this port." He went on for several more minutes. Most of the probable rules he discussed had to do with restraints on contact with the Kingdomites. Then he got into the training regimen.

"We're going to train in small unit ops, platoon and smaller, with heavy emphasis on squad and fire team actions." He cocked an eyebrow at the squad and fire team leaders, who grinned at the news; the junior NCOs relished the opportunities to act independently. Time to stabilize their excitement, he decided: "Many of you squad leaders and fire team leaders have been on operations before where you functioned as leaders of independent units. There's a difference in this one." He paused, satisfied to see the grins slipping. "A probable ROE that I didn't mention is—*no* firing until fired upon." That was met with muted exclamations of disgust. No firing until fired upon sometimes caused casualties. Thatcher smiled inside. "You have to challenge any armed people you come across. These are peasants, not soldiers; you have to give them a chance to surrender." All the grins were gone; the mission had suddenly become more difficult.

Thatcher talked a little longer about the training, then dismissed the Marines with, "All right. Make a head call. Even if you don't need to go, go anyway. It'll be several hours before you have another chance. Form up behind the barracks in fifteen minutes. Go!"

There was clattering, shuffling, and shouts as the Marines left the classroom.

CHAPTER
SIX

Thirty-fourth FIST began boarding the Amphibious Landing Ship, Force, CNSS *Grandar Bay* three days after it arrived in orbit around Thorsfinni's World.

The *Grandar Bay* was a Mandalay class ship, modern in all respects, including its berthing and the training spaces for the Marines it carried. Mandalay ships had the same troop-carrying capacity as the Crowe class Amphibious Battle Cruiser, but lacked the Crowe's planet-busting armament. The integral weaponry of the Mandalay class was purely defensive. Given the generally slight capability for space combat of most planets, and the fact that amphibious landing ships normally traveled in convoy with fighting ships, the class was effectively unarmed.

The first thing Lance Corporal Schultz did when his weapons and other gear were secured in second squad's compartment was hook into the *Grandar Bay* library. The little he'd learned about Kingdom from the resources available on Thorsfinni's World had only made him more curious about why 34th FIST was assigned to this mission. Neither could he find anything in the very extensive *Grandar Bay* library to explain why a FIST with a specialized and classified mission would be sent to put down a peasant rebellion. He would have scoffed had anybody suggested to him that routine bureaucratic machinations and ineptitude might be the reason.

Midway through the second day after the first elements of the FIST launched into orbit to board the *Grandar Bay*, the last of its supplies were secured in the ship's holds and the starship eased out of orbit and headed in a direction perpendicular to the planetary plane. Mandalay class ships were fast, and she reached jump point only three days after leaving orbit.

Klaxons blared throughout the ship. "All hands, now hear this," a melodious female voice intoned. "All hands, now hear this. All hands not at required duty stations, secure for jump. All hands not at required duty stations, secure for jump. Jump is in zero-five minutes."

None of the Marines had required duty stations. They'd already been restricted to their compartments in preparation for the jump into Beamspace. Fire team leaders made sure their men were properly strapped into their racks, then strapped themselves in. Squad leaders checked their fire team leaders, and platoon sergeants followed up on the squad leaders.

Everyone was ready before the computer's female voice announced, "Jump in one minute. All hands not in required duty stations, secure for jump."

Jump into Beamspace was routine for the Marines. Even the greenest Marine, fresh from Boot Camp, had jumped from Space-3 into Beamspace and back no fewer than half a dozen times. Navigation between stars wasn't a precise science, and on a typical voyage a ship would have to return to Space-3 two or three times to recalculate its course.

There was a moment of vertigo when the ship's gravity was turned off, then the female voice counted down the final seconds to jump. ". . . three, two, one, jump."

Abruptly, the entire universe turned gray or black or red or purple. It shattered into colors so fragmented they couldn't be identified. Weight vanished; it wasn't a floating sensation like null-g had been, but a total absence of weight, as though mass had been turned off. All the weight that ever was, was now, and ever would be, settled onto every individual on the ship. There was no sound, yet there was such a volume of sound it seemed the universe must be ending in the collapse of everything into a primordial speck that instantly exploded in a Big Bang.

Then the transition from Space-3 into Beamspace was complete. Colors returned to their proper places in the spectrum, sounds resumed normal audibility, and Newtonian mass reigned once more. The ship's gravity was turned back on.

"Aargh!" PFC MacIlargie cried out as he unstrapped himself from his rack. "Does anybody ever get used to that?" He lay supine in a top rack.

Corporal Linsman, his fire team leader, stood up from his middle rack and smacked MacIlargie on the top of his head. MacIlargie yelped indignantly.

"Nobody ever gets used to it so there's no point in complaining." Linsman checked the time. "Who's for chow?"

"How can you think of food after that?" MacIlargie said.

"The galley's open, that's how," Corporal Kerr said, standing up. "Let's go eat," he said to his men. "We've got time before we hit the classroom."

Corporal Doyle shakily hauled himself out of the bottom rack. He looked more than a bit green, but if his fire team leader said "Let's eat," he'd get something down and try to keep it there.

"Later," Schultz grunted. He had already plugged his reader back into the library jack.

Everyone but Schultz filed out of the compartment. A couple of them glanced oddly at him, wondering what it was that interested him so much, but none dared disturb the big man by asking.

One modern convenience of the *Grandar Bay* was its galley arrangement. The main galley was large enough to accommodate two infantry companies at a time. The FIST's elements rotated through it three times a day, and each had an hour for each meal—not that any unit had an open hour for dining in its training and study schedule. Two smaller galleys were open around the clock except during the half hour prior to a jump into or out of Beamspace. Those satellite galleys doubled as lounges for Marines who might find themselves with some unexpected leisure time. But once in a while they did.

"How are you holding up, Dorny?" Corporal Kerr asked when he and Corporal Dornhofer found themselves relaxing over mugs of real coffee.

"I'm doing fine," Dornhofer replied. "Why not?"

"You were almost killed on Avionia. For a little while after you got shot we thought you *were* dead."

Dornhofer laughed. "Yo, Kerr, I understand where you're coming from. But I wasn't almost killed the same way you were. I got drilled pretty bad, but it didn't tear up my insides like what happened to you."

"You sure?"

"Hey, I'm a Marine. Gotta expect to get dinged once in a while."

"That was one hell of a ding you got."

"Want to compare scars? I'll bet yours is a whole lot bigger than mine."

Kerr grunted. If Dornhofer had a scar, it was bigger than his own. After the doctors reconstructed the inside of his chest, they did just as good a job on the outside; he didn't have any scars from that wound. No visible scars anyway.

After four days the *Grandar Bay* returned to Space-3, got its bearings, and jumped back into Beamspace on a slightly different heading. The Marines continued their civil strife response action training.

During the downtime at the end of a training day of the second period in Beamspace, Schultz jacked out of the library and announced, "No peasants."

"What do you mean, 'no peasants,' " Kerr asked idly without taking his eyes from the novel he was reading.

"Kingdom. Not a peasant rebellion."

"Then what is it?" Kerr kept reading.

"Don't know."

Kerr grunted and hoped Schultz would drop it. He was just getting into a tricky section of the novel's plot and it demanded his attention.

When Schultz didn't reply immediately, Doyle nervously asked, "What is it, Hammer?"

Schultz just looked at Doyle. Doyle might have more rank than he did, but he had no experience. Well, not much experience. He knew that Doyle wouldn't understand if he told him. Schultz jacked back into the ship's library, not to do more research, but to wall himself off from the other men in the squad so he could spend time thinking.

Corporal Doyle, former company senior clerk now filling the billet of an infantry PFC, was headed into an unknown danger. He felt a lump of cold in his chest. The lump grew into a bar that fused to the ventral side of his spine and grew toward his sternum. He spent a paralyzed moment wondering whether he could move without shattering, then crawled fully dressed into his rack, pulled the blanket over his shoulders, and hugged himself tightly. He hoped his violent shivering wasn't visible to the other Marines.

Doyle's shivering was visible, but those few who noticed it misinterpreted the movement and thought he should have waited until lights out.

During the second jump, the Marines were introduced to a new piece of equipment they'd be using on Kingdom. The *Grandar Bay* didn't have a space large enough to gather the entire FIST, so each unit assembled in its normal classroom, where the men watched the introduction given by Brigadier Sturgeon and the equipment technician over the ship's trid system. At first Gunnery Sergeant Bass wondered why Top Myer was watching him instead of the trid projection. But when the presentation started, he forgot all about the first sergeant and concentrated on not erupting in a compartment-mangling fury.

"What the hell is with those people?" Bass roared when the company's officers and senior NCOs assembled in the company office after the all-hands briefing. "Who in Fargo is getting paid off?"

"Now now, Charlie," Lieutenant Humphrey said placatingly. He patted the air for Bass to lower his voice.

"Are they getting money, women, are they being black-mailed?" Bass continued in a hardly lower voice. "That's it! Terminal Dynamics has something on someone high up in procurement and is blackmailing him into buying this piece of shit!"

"Charlie," Top Myer said quietly, "calm down."

"No I will not calm down! That thing kills Marines!"

"Gunnery Sergeant!" Myer roared. *"You will belay that shit!"*

Bass's teeth clacked together as he shut his mouth and snapped to attention. His face was so deep a red it verged on purple, and his chest heaved with each deep, fast breath he took.

Bass's eruption was caused by the introduction of the Universal Positionator, Up-Downlink, Mark III. The first two UPUD Marks had been a combination radio, geographic position system, and motion detector—one piece of equipment designed to replace three. The Mark III also had the capability of data and detailed mapping reception.

It had been Bass's misfortune to field-test the first two versions of the UPUD under combat conditions. The first, on Fiesta de Santiago, had exposed a design flaw the manufacturer had glossed over. That flaw had gotten fifty Marines lost and out of communications. More than half of them died before they were able to reopen communications. Over his protests, Bass field-tested the Mark II on Elneal. It turned out to be too sensitive and burned itself out, again leaving Bass and his Marines isolated, with no communications or means of knowing exactly where they were.

Now, after Bass thought the demon was dead and buried, its latest incarnation was being given to 34th FIST to field-test on a live operation.

"I understand your feelings, Charlie," Myer said when he saw Bass had regained a measure of control. "This isn't Fiesta de Santiago, it isn't Elneal. It's a Mickey Mouse peasant revolt. The thing can die the first time you power it up and it won't hurt a thing."

Still at attention, eyes fixed on the bulkhead above and behind Humphrey, Bass said in a strained voice, "Elneal wasn't supposed to be Elneal either."

With two days remaining in the third and final jump, Company L assembled in a classroom compartment for its final briefing before making planetfall on Kingdom. Communications with a ship in interstellar transit could only be accomplished by physically intercepting it at a jump point. Such interceptions had to be planned well in advance and were used only in the event vital information had to be passed on. Nobody in the Confederation government thought there was any information regarding this deployment that 34th FIST didn't already have, so there was no attempt to intercept it. Lieutenant Humphrey merely reiterated what the Marines already knew; he had nothing new to impart to them. He could have given them a pep talk about the importance of the mission, but he had misgivings and couldn't come up with anything that justified it in his own mind. Besides, he knew First Sergeant Myer would do a much better job of, as Top put it, "Tuning up the troops," than he could. So when he finished repeating what everybody already knew, Humphrey handed the company over to the first sergeant for his unofficial briefing. Then he and the platoon commanders retired to the company office to listen in on the ship's intercom. Top Myer's unofficial briefings were supposed to be restricted to the enlisted men, but everybody knew the officers listened in.

Top Myer waited until Gunny Thatcher dogged the hatch behind the departing officers, then bowed his head, clasped his hands behind his back, and began pacing to and fro. He hadn't spoken a word to anyone about it, but he believed the Marines should not be sent in to put down a peasant revolt on Kingdom. He'd never been there himself, but he'd undertaken as deep a study of the world as possible since the FIST got its orders. What he learned fleshed out everything he'd heard during his long career from other Marines who had been deployed to Kingdom. Fleshed it out and underscored it. Personally, he believed the Confederation should simply stand back and let the peasants overthrow the government.

But they were Marines. They went where they were sent and did their jobs. Nobody said they had to like the mission, much less agree with it. His job just then was to tune up the Marines so they'd go in alert and ready for anything. The sharper they were, the less likely any of them were to get wounded or killed. No matter how much he disliked the mission, he liked having Marines wounded or killed even less.

He stopped pacing and faced the Marines of Company L.

"Peasant revolt," he began in a booming voice. "Most of you probably think this is going to be a cakewalk. You imagine we're going to face a bunch of poorly armed, ill-trained, badly led farmers.

"Maybe we will meet unprepared peasants. Probably not, though. You may not be aware of Confederation policy regarding peasant revolts. No military intervention until Confederation lives and property are threatened." He carefully neglected to say that policy applied only to Kingdom. "Confederation officials and Confederation property are at threat on Kingdom. That's why Earth saw a need to deploy Marines. Not only are Confederation lives and property being threatened, the revolt must be very widespread. Otherwise we wouldn't have an entire FIST deployed to deal with it. If it was the Mickey Mouse rebellion many of you may be thinking, the Confederation would send in a couple of companies from an army engineering outfit, or send in military police to deal with it. But they aren't sending the army, they're sending Marines. That means someone high up thinks this revolt is a very serious matter, and that the 'revolting peasants' present a clear and present danger.

"Now, just how dangerous can peasants be, you wonder? A millennium and a half ago, China was the most powerful nation on Earth. It had been united under one emperor for centuries, it was the most populous and geographically the largest nation-state on Earth. China secured its borders against potentially hostile nation-states by conquering and administering its immediate neighbors.

"One of those neighbors was a small country that occupied not much more than a river's valley and its delta. The country was called Nam Viet. Ah, I see some glimmers of recognition. Yes, the old United States Marines fought in Vietnam, but that was a much later version of the country after it had done its own expansion and was considerably bigger. But the Nam Viet I'm talking about was much smaller, and the Chinese thought it was weak.

"Two young women, the Tranh sisters, raised a peasant army and threw the Chinese out of Nam Viet.

"You heard me right. A peasant army, led by two young women, threw the most powerful nation on Earth out of their country. And they did it without outside assistance.

"In the fifteenth century England was clearly the most powerful nation in Europe. During the Hundred Years War, England conquered France, arguably the most powerful nation on the European continent. A peasant woman by the name of Joan raised an army and threw the English out of France.

"The American colonies' revolution against England in the eighteenth century qualifies as a peasant revolt, as does the French Revolution a few years later.

"The history of the first two-thirds of the twentieth century is the story of peasant army after peasant army in far-flung places rising up and throwing out colonial powers or overpowering despots: Kenya. Tanzania. Congo. The Dominican Republic. Cuba. Algeria. Vietnam. Iran.

"In the twenty-first century, United Central and Southern Africa was ruled by a despot who controlled one of Earth's largest and best equipped armies. Two hunters, N'Gamma Uhuru and Freedom Mbawali, raised an army of illiterate villagers—peasants—and defeated that army.

"Many of you were with 34th FIST when we went to Wanderjahr. The rebellion we dealt with there falls under the heading of 'peasant revolt.'

"Are you getting the idea that peasant rebellions aren't necessarily easy to put down? History is full of examples of peasant armies that rose up and defeated the professional armies of powerful nations. We cannot, we will not, join the ranks of professional armies that were defeated by a peasant army. Be aware, people! We are headed for something that could be far worse than anybody imagines."

He was through. It didn't matter that every one of the "peasant revolts" he'd just enumerated was righteous, just as he thought the one on Kingdom probably was. The right or wrong of the mission was irrelevant; the important thing was to save the lives of his Marines.

"That is all." Top Myer began to head for the exit, but a loud voice stopped him.

"It's not peasants!"

He turned to the speaker; Lance Corporal Schultz.

"What do you mean?" he asked in an ominously soft voice.

"Study it. No justification for a FIST."

Myer gestured for Schultz to continue.

"History, few interventions. No full FIST deployed to Kingdom in past eighty years. Peasant rebellions aren't strong enough for a FIST."

"So what makes you think this one isn't an exception?"

Schultz had to chew on his answer for a moment. He didn't like to use words, but he had to now. He had figured out something that nobody else had—they had been misinformed about what their mission really was. He had no idea why they were given a false reason, but he knew there was no peasant revolt waiting for 34th FIST to put down. How could he put that in words that would convince the others, especially Top Myer?

"Only one rebellion was big enough to need a FIST. It had a messiah. Took years to build up. There were many reports before it began. This time, no reports, no news. Everything was quiet until the orders came." He took a deep breath. The next thing he had to say was a mouthful for him.

"A spontaneous, widespread rebellion is a major nuisance, but not a major threat. If this is a widespread, spontaneous revolt, it needs time and local forces. Not a FIST. If it is small and aimed at Interstellar City, it will be over before we get there. Don't need a FIST for a peasant revolt."

He took another deep breath to calm himself after that speech, and looked at Myer for confirmation or argument about why he was wrong.

The first sergeant returned the look for a long moment. Schultz's reasoning was sound. There wasn't any military necessity he could see for deploying an entire FIST to put down a peasant rebellion on Kingdom. Kingdom's rebellions simply weren't that big.

"If it's not a peasant revolt, what do you think it is?"

Schultz swallowed and slowly blinked. In his entire life he'd only encountered one thing that frightened him, and he thought it was waiting for them on Kingdom.

Still, his voice was strong and clear when he said, "Skinks."

The reply startled Myer so much he didn't cut off the sudden cacophony of surprise from the Marines. He regained his composure quickly, though.

"As you were, people!" he bellowed.

The uproar cut off. Some of the Marines looked at Schultz, wondering how he came up with Skinks. Others looked at Myer, wondering how he would respond. A few, all in third platoon, closed their eyes and shook their heads.

"I read the dispatches, Hammer. There is no indication of Skinks or of any nonhuman sentience being present on Kingdom. You're wrong. It's peasants." He shook his head. "What I'm going to say now doesn't leave this room." He looked around for agreement and waited until it appeared that everyone agreed.

"I'll give you benefit of my vast experience in this man's Marine Corps. Sometimes the Confederation decides to make an example. There have been a lot of rebellions on Kingdom. What I suspect is, the Confederation decided to make an example, to hit the rebels so hard it'll be generations before they even think of another rebellion. So we're going in with a lot more force than we need to put down a simple peasant revolt. I think we're going in to cause enough damage to stop it from happening again for a long time to come."

He looked at the faces in the classroom as the Marines absorbed what he said. It was obvious that none of them liked the idea, but they were Marines, they'd do their job.

"One more thing, people. Just because I think we're going in with massive overkill doesn't mean we won't be facing a serious threat. We are professionals. Amateurs can hurt professionals very badly because sometimes they do things that no professional would ever think of. And remember all those times peasant armies have beaten professional armies."

He turned around and left the classroom. Behind him he heard a few men utter the word "Skinks."

In the company office the officers looked at each other uneasily. Gunnery Sergeant Charlie Bass was the only one who had encountered the Skinks. The others had secondhand knowledge. Skinks were a bad prospect, but their presence on Kingdom was so unlikely it was nearly impossible, and therefore beyond consideration. What made them uneasy was hearing the first sergeant say out loud what they all privately thought—that they were being sent in to punish as well as put down.

Bass broke the disquiet. "You know, the Top tends to put his own spin on things in his unofficial briefings. But he's usually more accurate with his historical facts."

CHAPTER
SEVEN

"High speed on a bad road" was how the Marines described their planetfall maneuver.

They trooped into the Dragons that were already aboard the Essays in the *Grandar Bay* welldeck and strapped themselves in. The shuttles were attached to launch-plungers in the welldeck's overhead. On command to land the landing force, the suction and clamps that held the shuttles to the launch-plunger released their grip, and the tops of the shuttles were slugged with a 100 psi blast of air that ejected them straight away from the ship with a four-g force.

In one second the Essays were three hundred meters away from the ship, and their coxswains fired their main engines. The sudden surge of horizontal power added three g's to the four already in effect. The roar of the engines drowned out the yells the Marines made to equalize pressure on their eardrums. Small rockets on the bottom of the Essays blasted to cancel the downward motion of the entry vehicles; the aft retros fired more strongly than the forward ones to angle them for the main rockets to give them a slight downward thrust. Less than ten seconds after launch, the Essays were already past the 1.5-kilometer-long ship. Only the downward thrust from their main engines kept them from being flung into a higher orbit.

"The shuttle is clear of the ship," the Essays' coxswains reported. "Request permission to commence atmospheric entry."

When permission was granted, each coxswain punched

the button that controlled the topside attitude rockets. The Essays' computers got confirmation from the ship's launch control computer and executed the command. Small vernier rockets above the Essays' noses gave brief thrusts to angle the shuttles downward sharply and convert their orbital velocity of more than 32,000 kilometers per hour into downward speed. Five seconds later the main engines shut off and the Essays went into an unpowered plunge. If their path had been straight down, the Essays would catastrophically impact the planetary surface in less than two minutes. But the glide angle was calculated to take five minutes to reach 50,000 meters above the surface, where wings deployed and the forward thrusters fired to drop speed to something that could be controlled by powered flight.

"High speed on a bad road" was an apt description for the fall from the top of the atmosphere to the beginning of powered flight fifty kilometers above the surface. The fall through the middle thermosphere felt like the Dragon was driving at top speed on a coarsely graveled road, the gravel getting coarser the farther they went. The lower thermosphere eroded the roadway with potholes and bumps; some of the potholes seemed deep enough to swallow the Dragon whole, some of the bumps should have flipped it over. By the time the breaking rockets fired and the wings began to deploy, the shaking and rattling was so hard that the Dragons inside the Essays felt like they were coming apart.

Breaking rockets and deploying wings quickly cut the angle of the dive, and slashed its speed in half by the time the Essays reached the top of the troposphere. When the wings were fully extended, huge flaps extended from them to further decrease the Essays' speed. When the wings finally bit into the thickening air hard enough for controlled flight, the coxswains turned off the breaking rockets, fired up the jets, and maneuvered the craft into a velocity-eating spiral that slowed both their descent and forward motion. At one thousand meters altitude, the coxswains pulled out of the spiral and popped drogue chutes. At two hundred they angled the jets' vernier nozzles downward. Seconds later the shuttles rested on the surface of the ocean, a hundred kilometers off shore.

The coxswains checked that the Dragons were ready, then opened their landing hatches. The Dragons—air-cushioned, light-armored, amphibious vehicles—rose on their cushions and splashed onto the water. They lined up abreast and headed for the horizon and the shore beyond.

That was a combat assault planetfall. The Confederation Army used it when they expected to meet resistance. The Marines used it every time they made planetfall, even on peaceful missions. Everybody else thought only crazy people would ever make a combat assault planetfall when it wasn't necessary.

The Leader could barely restrain his excitement when he was ushered into the presence of the Great Master commanding the operations on the Earthman world. It would be the first time he'd spoken directly to a Great Master, and the honor was much.

The Great Master sat cross-legged on a low chair set on a dais high enough that he could look down on even the tallest of the Large Ones. Five Large Ones were arrayed around the Great Master; one to either side facing front, another behind each of them facing to the side, and a fifth behind him facing the wall to the Great Master's rear. The sheathed sword that lay across the Great Master's thighs had an ornately carved hilt, but the Leader had no doubt its blade was sharp and strong enough to slice through flesh and bone easily.

The Leader approached the dais as he had been instructed, back bowed, eyes on the matting that covered the floor. When he saw the discreet mark woven into the matting's pattern he stopped and lowered himself to his knees. He didn't need a nudge from the chamberlain to tell him he was there. Hands just under his shoulders, he touched his forehead to the matting and waited.

"Lord," the chamberlain barked, "this worthless Leader wishes permission to make a report."

There was a pause before the Great Master growled, "Report."

"Lord Great Master!" In that posture, doubled over and forehead on the mat, it was difficult to speak loudly enough to be heard clearly, but the Leader was happy that he managed so well. "The Earthman Marines have landed!"

"You know this as fact?"

"Yes, Lord Great Master!"

"Raise your face."

The Leader craned his neck to look up at the Great Master, but kept his shoulders low, just above his hands, flat on the matting.

"How do you know the Earthman Marines have landed?"

Speaking in that posture was no easier, but the Leader found it was easier to project his voice. "Lord Great Master, with my own eyes I saw the streaks of their shuttles plummeting from orbit to beyond the horizon. I waited until I saw their amphibious craft speeding toward the beach, then I came directly here."

"How did you come that their surveillance satellites could not track you?"

A thin smile creased the Leader's face. "Lord Great Master, the Earthmen were in too great a hurry to land their Marines. They made planetfall before the surveillance satellites were deployed."

The Great Master barked out a laugh. The Earthman Marines were ashore without knowledge of who they were up against or where they were. He looked at the chamberlain. "You have the coordinates?"

The chamberlain bowed. "Yes, Lord Great Master. They are on their way to Haven."

"Launch Dawn Bird." The Great Master returned his attention to the Leader. "Perhaps you are not worthless. Leave me."

Perhaps not worthless. The Leader exalted at the high praise! He pushed himself to his feet and backed away, back bowed, eyes on the matting.

* * *

Haven, capital city of Kingdom, though less than two centuries old, looked like something out of a history vid about Old Earth's Middle Ages. The entire city seemed to be constructed from native stone and wood—even the avenue that led up to the city was paved with flat stones. Horses—*horses!*—pulled clattering wagons in and out of the gate in the stone curtain wall. That wall was a false front; a palisade wall of tree trunks circled the rest of the city. Most of the buildings visible above the wall appeared to be houses of worship. The tallest was a minaret, though the unfinished bell tower on a Gothic cathedral aspired to top it.

The Marines, unbaptized heathens that they were, weren't granted entrance to Haven. Instead, a troop of Guardian Angels met the lead Dragons and directed them to a large field on the other side of Interstellar City from Haven's walls, where Ambassador Jay Benjamin Spears and Chief-of-Station Prentiss Carlisle met them.

As unfamiliar with the military as Prentiss was, even he realized immediately that the distinguished-looking Marine who was the first man to leave the lead Dragon must be the commander. But not Spears. His face broke into a wide grin as he stepped forward and offered his hand. "Ted, you old rascal, you!" he shouted.

"Jay, you old reprobate!" Brigadier Sturgeon replied. The two embraced and slapped each other hardily on the back.

"I haven't been on station very long, Ted, so all I know is that old Doc Friendly had called for help. I didn't know they were sending in the good old 34th FIST! Damn! How're old Dean and Claypoole?"

Sturgeon laughed. "They're around here somewhere. I thought Creadence was ambassador here, Jay. Damn, it is *good* to see you again!"

"He was recalled just recently, lucky bastard, and I volunteered for the job because I need the money. Oh, excuse me, Ted, this is Prentiss Carlisle, my chief-of-station." Carlisle and Sturgeon shook hands. "Prentiss has only been here a little longer than I. He replaced a man who was killed in an accident."

" 'The Marines have landed and the situation is well in hand.' " Carlisle grinned weakly as he quoted the ancient saying.

"It will be, sir," Sturgeon replied. "How'd your predecessor die?"

Carlisle shrugged. "A vehicular accident, we think. He was out gathering information on the, uh, situation here, and his landcar must have run off the road. He and his driver were both killed."

"Where are the local authorities?" Sturgeon asked. The two Confederation diplomats were the only people in the welcoming committee. Sturgeon hadn't expected pomp and ceremony, but it was normal for representatives of the local government to greet the commander of a Marine force when it made planetfall.

Spears tamped down a grimace before it could appear on his face. "I imagine they're in conference, Ted." Acrimonious haggling was more like it, he thought. The last time they'd deigned to speak to him, it was obvious the theocrats were fighting over how much or little to tell the Marines about the situation. That, and how much of the planet to allow them access to. And how much contact the offworlders could have with their own military. The only thing on which the theocrats seemed to be in agreement was that contact between the Marines and the civilian population should be as limited as possible. But they disagreed on what constituted "as little as possible."

Sturgeon kept his expression neutral and his voice level. It wasn't his position to criticize local governments. "We are here. What do they expect us to do?"

"They said it's my responsibility to quarter you," Spears said, then added apologetically, "But that presents a bit of a problem. Interstellar City isn't big enough to accommodate a FIST and your follow-on reinforcements."

"Jay, we're it." Sturgeon said.

Carlisle swallowed. Suddenly he wished he knew more about the military. For the first time, he looked at Sturgeon, really looked at him. The brigadier's face appeared friendly enough, but there was steel in his expression, and his eyes looked like they never missed any detail of his surroundings. At first glance he seemed relaxed, but Carlisle now noticed an underlying tension, a readiness to move and act on an instant's notice. The Marine leader was a very strong man, accustomed to command and action. He also gave an impression of high intelligence. Carlisle suspected he was more than capable of seeing far beneath surface details. Then the last part of what Sturgeon said registered.

"H-How many men did you bring, Brigadier?" he asked.

"One thousand Marines, with supporting arms, of course."

"Only a thousand men?" he asked.

"Mr. Carlisle, as Ambassador Spears can tell you, a Marine FIST is a most versatile and potent weapon. I assure you, we are more than are needed to deal with a simple peasant rebellion." Before Carlisle could ask what Sturgeon meant by a peasant rebellion, Sturgeon turned to Spears. "Jay, I don't need for you to quarter my Marines. All I need here is an office suite and facilities for my command and control center, say twenty-five of us. The rest of the FIST will be in the field."

"Yup," Spears replied. He turned to Carlisle. "Prentiss, if we were facing a million-man army equipped with the latest weapons, well, the Confederation would've sent us two thousand Marines to do the job." Both he and Sturgeon roared with laughter. Carlisle smiled but his face turned a light shade of red.

"By 'in the field,' I assume you mean on operations?" Prentiss asked.

"That's why we're here, yes." In his peripheral vision Sturgeon noticed a landcar draw up.

"How will you know where to send your Marines?" Prentiss asked. Spears meanwhile was silent, smiling cryptically. He knew enough not to ask such questions.

"That's one reason I wanted to meet the local authorities."

"Well, Ted, you're about to do just that," Spears said.

The landcar stopped and four ornately uniformed men climbed out.

"Mr. Ambassador," the lead, most ornately uniformed soldier said as he approached, "I see the Confederation Marines are arriving."

Spears turned to him and brightened. "Archbishop General Lambsblood! I'm glad to see you."

Lambsblood spared Sturgeon a curious glance, wondering who he was, but kept his attention on the ambassador. "Have you word on when the Marine commander will arrive?"

Sturgeon studied the Kingdomite general during that brief exchange. His uniform was a dusky orange, almost brown tunic over black trousers with silver seam stripes. Gold aiguillettes adorned both shoulders, and an electric blue sash slashed across his chest. A mass of medals was mounted on his left chest, and other ribbons and badges crowded his right. A sidearm in a highly polished holster rode his hip.

"Archbishop General Lambsblood," Spears said without revealing the embarrassment he felt for the Kingdomite commander, "may I present Brigadier Theodosius Sturgeon, Confederation Marine Corps. He is, I might add, the fightin'est goddamned Marine in the Corps."

Lambsblood blanched at the vulgar language the ambassador chose to use. Spears had already gotten off to a bad start with the Kingdomites. As soon as he'd realized how much they hated profanity, he'd started to use it on special occasions, to deflate stuffed shirts in their hierarchy. This was such an occasion, in his view.

Lambsblood blinked, then looked at Sturgeon. The Marine's uniform was dull green, originally designed to blend into the shadows of grassland or forest. Other than the rank insignia on the collar tips of the shirt, the only adornment was a rampant eagle clutching a globe that floated on a starstream, embroidered in black thread on his left shirt pocket. Lambsblood recognized it as the Confederation Marine Corps emblem. What manner of commander is this that he dresses so plainly? Lambsblood wondered. How can he command the respect of his men if he doesn't look like a commander?

"Brigadier," Lambsblood said with a cool but polite nod. The Confederation only sent a brigadier, not a general? he thought. Do they not take our situation seriously?

"General Lambsblood." Sturgeon saluted and held it until Lambsblood returned it.

"You are the Confederation commander for this mission?"

"That's right, sir." Sturgeon smiled inwardly at the dismay Lambsblood wasn't fully successful at keeping off his face.

"And he's a veritable ass-kicker!" Ambassador Spears crowed. Lambsblood blinked again and tried to ignore the ambassador.

"How many days will it take for your force to land and prepare for action?"

"The FIST will all be planetside within an hour. The ground forces will be ready to move out within minutes of the time the last element has landed. The air squadron will take just a little longer to be ready for action." He glanced at his watch; it was 1017 hours local time. Kingdom used an adjusted twenty-four hour clock, even though its rotation period was nearly twenty-five hours standard. Sturgeon's watch was calibrated to Kingdom time. "The entire FIST will be operational by fifteen hours."

"So fast? How few are you?" Lambsblood sharply shook his head. "No. You said *the* FIST. You have only one FIST?"

"That should be more than enough, General."

Lambsblood's face darkened. "Brigadier, I know the reputation of the Confederation Marines. I was a very junior officer the last time the Confederation sent Marines to our aid, so I know that reputation is well-deserved. But the enemy we face has powerful weapons, weapons we've never encountered before." He shook his head and looked away. "They have weapons I've never heard of. They rendered four of my divisions and eight squadrons inoperable in a battle that lasted ten minutes. They can destroy your entire FIST in moments."

Sturgeon nodded. "I understand your concern, General. But the Marines don't stand still. Today's FIST is much more potent than it was a generation ago."

"You are too few," Lambsblood said harshly. "The Confederation has seen fit to waste your lives for nothing. You and your entire force will be killed as soon as you encounter the enemy." He spun on his heel and strode toward his landcar with his retinue in tow. Before they reached it, a soldier jumped from the landcar and raced to the general. He reported, then Lambsblood stood still for a moment, looking off into the distance. The three staff officers exchanged glances and looked anxious. Lambsblood abruptly spun about and marched back to Sturgeon.

"Brigadier," he said as briskly as he'd walked, "you say your Marines are ready. If they are, I have your first mission. I just received a priority message. An outpost of the Lord's Army has been attacked. There are no details available save it sounds as though the outpost may have been wiped out. It's possible that survivors are holding out. How fast can your Marines get there?"

"Where is it?" Sturgeon was signaling for his principal staff to join him even as he asked the question.

Lambsblood grinned wickedly. "Six thousand kilometers almost due west of here. On a mid-ocean island where there had been no previous reports of hostile activity."

"Give me the coordinates." Sturgeon turned to Commander Usner, the FIST operations officer. "Divert the next wave to the coordinates General Lambsblood gives you."

Usner aye-ayed and got on his comm, issuing the orders to divert the wave of six Essays that was already descending to make planetfall. Lambsblood had his staff provide the coordinates.

"See to security," Sturgeon told Commander Daana, the FIST intelligence officer. Then to the Kingdom commander: "Six thousand kilometers? That's the dawn terminator."

Lambsblood agreed. "A dawn attack. Classic."

"Do you want to join us?"

"How many of us do you have room for?"

"Assign a Dragon to them," Sturgeon said to Lieutenant Quaticatl, his aide.

"Aye aye, sir." Quaticatl spoke into his comm unit and a nearby Dragon roared to life and flowed to them on its air cushion. "It can hold twenty combat-ready Marines, sir," he said to Lambsblood.

Lambsblood nodded. He signaled to his communications technician and gestured toward the dropped ramp of the Dragon.

"Jay?" Sturgeon turned to Spears and indicated he could board with the general's entourage.

"Oh, Ted," he drawled, "I don't think so. You almost got me killed the last time, as I recall. No, Prentiss and I will earn our pay the diplomatic way, by sitting on our fat asses and composing flowery goddamned reports back to headquarters."

Lambsblood raised an eyebrow. What kind of people were these two? A commander who dressed like a private soldier, called the ambassador by his *first* name like some old drinking partner, and a Confederation ambassador who—who used the language of a common soldier? He shook his head. What he needed was professional help, not a pair of comedians.

Sturgeon and the necessary members of his staff boarded his Dragon. The Dragons roared into the gaping maw of an Essay.

"Schultz, Mark One! Doyle, infra," Corporal Kerr barked as he slid his magnifier shield into place. It was two minutes since the first Essay of the diverted second wave landed a kilometer from the attacked outpost and its Dragons roared off to approach to within a few hundred meters. The infantrymen were already spreading out in defensive positions around the Kingdomite outpost. Kerr's fire team was near the end of a windbreak treeline half a kilometer from where their Essay had made planetfall. Following Kerr's orders, Corporal Doyle was scanning the landscape before them in the infrared, looking for the heat signals of warm bodies. Lance Corporal Schultz was using his naked eyes. Kerr himself was using the telescopic magnifier shield in his helmet to look farther and see smaller things. Long practice had taught the Marines that the combination of viewing methods was most effective.

An ancient ocean-floor volcano had birthed the island, Trinity. Eons of wind and rain since it went dormant had eroded broken, sharp-edged rock surface into gravel, then sand. Wind- and avian-borne seeds and spores in their turn mulched the sand into dirt. Eventually, lush vegetation had taken hold. The only animate life native to Trinity were insect analogs. Humans had imported all the larger animals that populated it, and they'd imported many, both farm and game. The local economy was the same as the rest of Kingdom, agricultural, though oceanic fish and seaweed farms were as important as the grain, fruit, and vegetable farms on land.

Farmland lined by windbreaks spread out before Kerr and his men. A group of houses and other buildings huddled together a couple of kilometers away. A disproportionate number of the buildings were topped by spires, belfries, or onion domes; a minaret matched the tallest spires. Tendrils of smoke rose from a few of the buildings. A road slashed through the hamlet. One end ran through a break in a tree row exposing boats bobbing gently in the ocean. Even with his magnifier Kerr could see no people in the fields or the beach.

"See anything?" he asked.

Schultz grunted a negative.

"N-Nothing," Doyle stammered. "Shouldn't there be farm animals out there?"

"Chickens, maybe," Kerr said. "They're only growing grain; won't be any cattle or pigs. Nothing bigger than a dog. If you see anything bigger than a dog, speak up."

"R-Right." What would be bigger than a dog other than cattle? Why speak up if he saw cattle? Oh, he realized, they might be human, might be the enemy. The enemy would want to kill him. He wiggled, trying to sink farther into the ground.

Brigadier Sturgeon stood where the Army of the Lord outpost had been and looked at the destruction. During his Marine career he'd seen many 2-D images illustrating the destructiveness of explosive munitions used in the past. He'd even witnessed firsthand what they could do in demonstrations of archaic weapons—and a few instances of their present day use by poorly armed insurgents. But he'd never seen anything like this.

The en route briefing had included a trid of the outpost, so he knew what it looked like before the attack—a substantial building of stone, steel, and wood. From where he stood, there didn't seem to be as much wood scattered about as had gone into the building, and what was there was splinters. The stone was so thoroughly pulverized that much of it had to be in the grainy dust that covered everything. And the steel was . . . shattered was the only word that seemed to convey what had happened to the steel. Strangest of all was the almost total lack of charring. Explosives created heat, blasted out in flame, and started fires. He saw no evidence of fire. It looked as if some unknown force had struck the building from all sides.

"So, Brigadier," Archbishop General Lambsblood said, "what weapon do you think did this?"

Sturgeon could only shake his head. "Where are the soldiers?" he asked. Not only was there no charring, there seemed to be no survivors. Neither were there bodies nor blood, no evidence that the outpost had been manned when it was attacked.

Lambsblood shrugged. "We may find them. Or bits of them. Or maybe we will find nothing." He looked at the surrounding countryside. "We don't always find the remains of our soldiers when an outpost has been destroyed." He paused for a beat, then continued. "There are those who believe these aliens take our soldiers prisoner. Some weaklings think some of our soldiers turn heretic and join the enemy."

He turned hard eyes on the Marine commander. "The images of the demons who have attacked—I cannot believe any Soldiers of the Lord would join with them. And I can more easily believe they eat our missing soldiers than I can believe they hold them prisoner."

Sturgeon looked at him blandly and tried to come up with a way to say what he was thinking that wouldn't offend Lambsblood. "General, when you characterize those who oppose the theocracy as demons, I can accept that as an expression of religious fervor. But 'aliens'? What makes you think they're from off-planet?"

"The images!" Lambsblood snapped. "They're quite clear. We have been attacked by off-planet demons."

"What images do you mean? I haven't been shown any pictures of the rebels."

Lambsblood grew rigid, his face darkened. Then he exploded. "The images your Ambassador Creadence—would the Lord have seen fit to have kept him here—sent with his urgent dispatch! Images that show the hideous form of the demons, images that show their entry craft doing things that no human shuttle can match!" He stopped abruptly and thought. More softly, he continued, "Or did he send the images? If he didn't, that would explain why the Confederation only sent one FIST under the command of a brigadier, rather than an entire army under . . .

"Brigadier Sturgeon, we must return to Haven, to Interstellar City. You must see those images. I don't believe you realize what we are facing here."

CHAPTER
EIGHT

Captain Lewis Conorado observed the other passengers on board the shuttle that was taking them to dock with the SS *Cambria* in orbit around Thorsfinni's World. There were eighteen other people on board. Six of them were members of the Confederation Diplomatic Service's inspector general's office returning from an inspection of the consulate. Three were members of the consulate on reassignment. Five others appeared to be businessmen, and the remaining four were 'Finnis returning to Earth. The diplomats were sitting just aft of Conorado. Their loud talk and laughter somewhat jarred Conorado's nerves, especially when he heard them making disparaging remarks about the 'Finnis. They were so blatant it was evident they did not think the 'Finnis could speak enough English to understand them. Perhaps they just didn't care if the 'Finnis knew they were talking about them. The businessmen, all from Earth, maintained a stiff neutrality.

Someone whispered "bellhop" from somewhere behind him and his companions burst into laughter. Conorado knew they were talking about him. What the hell, he thought, not worth my time to shut him up. But what really got on his nerves was the way they were talking about the 'Finnis on board, one of whom, sporting a handsome mustache, they kept laughing about and calling "old walrus face." In the terminal, before they boarded the shuttle, that particular man had given Conorado a friendly nod and a casual salute, so the captain felt these so-called diplomats were insulting a friend of his.

One of the diplomats, a large man with a florid face and a voice like a foghorn, was making himself particularly obnoxious. The way the others in his party deferred to him, Conorado reflected that he was probably a second or third secretary and used to receiving deferential treatment. In his mind, he contrasted the man with Jayben Spears, the Confederation consul on Wanderjahr, and J. Wellington-Humphreys, who'd come to think so highly of Lance Corporals Dean and Claypoole after they'd rescued her from the mines on Diamunde. He knew there were some decent people in the Diplomatic Service, but there were also those who, because of education and breeding, held themselves above the common citizens of the Confederation's member worlds, the "hoi polloi" and "rubes" of the more "backward" settlements.

Conorado tried to settle back in his seat. The almost physical pain he'd felt at the way he'd parted with Marta had receded to a dull ache. Well, he couldn't think about that anymore. What was it the old song said? "With hearts too full for utterance, with but a silent tear / We dare not look behind us but steadfastly on before." He couldn't remember anymore where he'd heard those lyrics, but they'd stuck with him. They could've been written for a Marine. Well, it was done and he'd have to wait until he got back to patch up their relationship, or learn to deal with bachelorhood again. He had to think ahead now, to what awaited him in Fargo. Damn that woman Hoxey! She must have powerful friends in government to bring charges against him, especially considering that even the chief scientist on her shift, Omer Abraham, had disagreed with the way she abused the Avionians in captivity.

Well, he would have plenty of time to think about his defense on the long trip back to Earth.

The shuttle's coxswain announced they were preparing to dock at the *Cambria* in a few minutes. Be interesting to see what that ship is like, he thought.

The SS *Cambria* was a deep-space cargo craft capable of hauling more than one million metric tons of just about anything. When the cargo bays were used to transport items that required atmosphere, they could develop their own weather in the form of cloud condensation and even rain, in the form of heavy mists. These huge bays were generally used to store raw materials that were impervious to the "weather" or could withstand zero atmosphere conditions. Perishable goods were transported in special shipping containers or in smaller compartments that could be climate controlled as needed.

She was nearly two kilometers in length between bridge and propulsion plant. Those points and the various cargo compartments in between were connected by a horizontal elevator shaft.

On that flight, the *Cambria* had been outward bound from Earth for over a year. She had made a vast swing through Human Space, stopping at dozens of worlds on the way to her terminus, Thorsfinni's World. During the voyage, she had carried just about everything the entrepreneurs and governments of those many worlds could think to order or ship to someone. The *Cambria* and ships like her were a mainstay of the commerce between worlds that was essential to their economic survival.

Now she floated in orbit far above Thorsfinni's surface, her vast cargo holds dark and empty and groaning with the noises of expanding and contracting metals and of fluids being piped through her venting systems, as if she were alive and begging to be fed. And she would be, when they reached Siluria, her only stop on the way back to Earth. There, she would pick up some more passengers and hundreds of thousands of tons of the rich mineral ore mined on that planet. Her owners back on Earth were in a state of near ecstasy over the profits they expected to earn on the voyage, and the members of her crew virtually skipped about their duties in happy anticipation of the huge bonuses they'd make once their pay was settled.

Vast as she was, the *Cambria* required only a crew of ten. A marvel of twenty-fifth-century technology, she was fully automated and required only maintenance and someone to watch over her computer guidance systems. Most of the crew spent their shifts roaming throughout the *Cambria*'s holds and compartments and propulsion plant, checking this, tinkering with that, repairing the occasional minor malfunction, keeping watch on the vessel's hull integrity—or goofing off smoking thule and ogling girlie vids in the bowels of the ship, where her captain and engineer couldn't keep an eye on them.

Supercargo on the *Cambria* lived well. She carried staterooms for a hundred passengers, suitably remote from the crew's quarters, and a full assortment of recreational activities from swimming and exercise rooms to gambling facilities. Medical services were provided by a computerized dispensary that could handle any emergency situation and most acute conditions. For individuals with life-threatening injuries or chronic medical problems the computer system could not handle, there were stasis units to keep patients alive until definitive medical care could be found.

Housekeeping was fully automated in the passenger compartment, and the huge galley prepared excellent meals around the clock. The owners of the *Cambria* made a tidy profit hauling human cargo.

A few more passengers were scheduled to board at Siluria, but even so, the passenger compartments would be far from crowded. Ordinarily this circumstance would lead to an intimate and friendly atmosphere among the passengers, but not on this voyage, not with Mr. Redface and his sycophants. Even before boarding, Conorado had decided to spend most of his time by himself.

As they filed out of the shuttle, the nineteen passengers were greeted warmly by a young woman in a jumpsuit.

"I'm Jennifer Lenfen, ladies and gentlemen. I'm the systems engineer on the *Cambria*, with double duty as purser when we have passengers." She smiled. She was wearing a loose-fitting jumpsuit, the standard work clothes for the ship's crew. The suit did not reveal much of what was inside, but her smile was warm and genuine and it was obvious she was looking forward to dealing with the passengers on this voyage. "Your baggage will be delivered to you once your stateroom assignments have been made. So if you will follow me, I'll lead you to the passengers' galley. The captain will talk to you once we're settled in there."

"What is there to do on this scow, Miss Renfen?" one of the diplomats asked. He was a young man with a wolfish look about him.

"Lenfen, sir," Jennifer corrected him, not missing a beat or losing her smile. "You'll have a full assortment of recreational activities available while on board. Also, when a crew member is available, tours of the ship can be—"

"You're on, honey!" the wolfish young man crowed.

"Tours of the ship can be arranged." She looked straight at the wolfish young man. "Individually or in small groups . . ."

"Individually, Miss Renfen, that's for me!" the young man interjected.

". . . for a gratuity."

"Oh, honey, do I have a 'gratuity' for you!" the young man howled. His companions laughed with him.

"James," Redface said, laughing himself but apparently thinking it wise to rein in his protégé. Miss Lenfen's face flushed and she stumbled over her words, surprised and shocked at the young man's blatant suggestiveness.

"What is your name, sir?" Conorado asked, stepping up to the young diplomat.

"James Palmita," he answered, surprised and taken off guard. He recovered quickly, though, and sneered, "And who in the hell are you, soldier boy?"

Conorado thrust a rigid forefinger into the young man's chest. "James, shut up." Lewis Conorado had just carved out his niche for the rest of the voyage.

The passengers' galley, which was more a restaurant than a dining hall, was built to accommodate fifty diners at a seating. Miss Lenfen led the party to a large table in the center

of the galley and asked everyone to take a seat. Servos rolled
out and began taking orders, much to the delight of the new
arrivals. Conorado ordered a liter of Reindeer ale and was
delighted when it was delivered ice cold. He glanced at the
three 'Finnis, raised his glass in their direction before he
drank.

The diplomats ordered a wild variety of mixed drinks and
aperitifs, things with a twist of that, three jiggers of this,
shaken and mixed just so, but once everyone had been
served, the atmosphere relaxed considerably. Conorado
found himself sitting next to a mousy little woman who had
not joined much in the antics of her companions.

He wiped the suds off his upper lip and turned to the
woman. "My name is Lew Conorado," he said, offering her
his hand.

"Marchia Golden," she answered, but did not take Conorado's hand.

"Where you headed? Back on Earth, I mean? Home
leave?" He kept his hand out for a moment and then awk-
wardly withdrew it.

Marchia Golden did not reply at once, as if considering
whether she should bother to answer the question. "Back to
headquarters. For reassignment."

"Well, Marchia, what do you do? I think it's more than obvious what I do." He laughed.

"I'm an administrative assistant, if you must know."

Conorado cleared his throat. "Well, it's a long voyage,
ma'am, and—" But Marchia Golden had turned abruptly to
one of her coworkers and began a conversation with him.
Wow! Conorado thought. Talk about the social snub! He
shrugged and turned to the man on his left, but the man was
engaged in a deep monologue with another woman diplomat, so he gave up, moved to the other side of the table and
took a seat with the 'Finnis.

A crewman in a dirty jumpsuit walked up to the table and
sat down. He was middle-aged, with several days' growth of
whiskers, and the stub of a cigar jutting out of one side of his

mouth. "I'm the captain," he announced to no one in particular as he ordered a beer from a servo. The table fell silent. This was their captain?

"How do you do, Captain," Redface replied. "I'm Jamison Franks III, second undersecretary of the Confederation embassy on Thorsfinni's World, and these people here are members of the Diplomatic Service." He introduced the IG team. "And we three," he indicated himself, Palmita, and Ms. Golden, "are returning to Earth on reassignment. I have the rank of ambassador."

"Hi," the captain said to the people around him. "My name is Hank Tuit. Welcome to the *Cambria*." He shifted his cigar carefully and took a long drink of his beer. Suds formed a white mustache on his upper lip, which he wiped away carelessly with his hand. He belched. "Hey!" Tuit announced suddenly, looking down the table. "We have a Marine with us! How're you doing, Captain? You must be with 34th FIST?"

"Yessir," Conorado answered, rising from his seat. Tuit waved him back down. "None of that military protocol on this ship, Captain! I had enough of that the forty years I was an officer in the Confederation Navy. I promised myself," he addressed the whole table now, "that when I retired I wouldn't have any protocols anymore, and I don't. When you get back to 34th FIST, Captain, say hello to Gunnery Sergeant Bass for me, would you?"

"You—You know Charlie Bass?" Captain Tuit smiled and took another long swig from his beer.

"Ah, Captain," Franks said, "we'd like to see our staterooms, and may I ask, will anyone be dining with you at your table tonight?"

"Huh? 'Table'? Oh, yeah. No, no. No captain's table on this vessel. I live on the bridge, Mr. Ambassador. I eat there, I sleep there, I even shit there. No, you won't see much of me on this voyage. Unless one of you dies, then I've got to make a report. Otherwise you're on your own.

"Jenny." He turned to Miss Lenfen. "Orient these folks on the passenger compartment and get them into staterooms.

Folks, you're on your own now. Anything you need the rest of this voyage, ask Jenny. You are not permitted outside the passenger compartment unless you're accompanied by a member of my crew. Captain," he turned to Conorado, "join me on the bridge for coffee after Jenny gets you squared away." Carrying his beer with him, Captain Tuit got up to leave, turned his back on his passengers and walked away.

Ambassador Franks stared at his departing back. "Strange old bird," he muttered.

"Best thing the navy ever did was get rid of that old fart," Palmita whispered in a voice loud enough that Tuit and everybody else at the table could hear him, but Tuit ignored the comment and continued out of the dining hall without a backward glance.

Siluria was one of many worlds in Human Space that was not worth colonizing, but its rich ores made it worth exploiting, so two industrial bases had been established there eighty years before to mine the planet's natural resources. The companies that had invested in the enterprise were not interested in wasting any money preserving Siluria's environment. They strip-mined its outer crust and bored dozens of kilometers under its surface to extract priceless cargoes that were then shipped to consumers all over Human Space. About ten thousand men and women labored in the mines of Siluria. The pay was excellent and many of them eagerly renewed their contracts when they expired.

Five who were not going to renew sat in a tiny cabin perched on the rim of a vast pit that was the remnant of a strip mine that had played out years before. The occupants had to shout to make themselves heard above the howl of the frigid wind that buffeted the cabin. That was just what they wanted because their business this night was very private.

A schematic of the SS *Cambria* lay spread before them on the table. "Brothers," their leader was saying, "in three weeks time we strike at last for the Lord." The others muttered "Amen!" to his words. The one speaking was thin with a dark beard and the watery eyes of a fanatic. The four others about the table could have been his brothers, judging by their looks, but they were not related. "You all know what you are to do once we're aboard. We have finished practicing. Each has his duty and each knows just what to do. Until the day of boarding we will spend our free time in prayer and meditation. We must prepare ourselves for paradise." Tears stood out in his eyes as he spoke.

"Amen," the others replied.

"The Unbelievers are sending military forces to our beloved home!" the speaker shouted, as much out of rage as to be heard above the wind. "The leaders of our community have transgressed! They have fallen into the ways of the sinful!"

"We shall show them the wrath of our God!" one of the others shouted.

The leader nodded. "They must be given a Sign. They must be shown the Way! The Lord God has spoken to me, brothers! When we are done, we shall be called home to Him!"

"God be praised!" the others shouted.

One of the men put a small metal container on the table. "The Lord God has favored me with the knowledge of this Secret," he said as he slid the case into the center of the table.

The leader fell silent at the sight of the case but his eyes gleamed. He ran his shaking hands reverently over the surface of the metal. His hands shook not out of fright but with ecstasy. In a voice turned hoarse with emotion he said, "Here—inside this Ark—is the power and the spirit of the universe. Let us pray."

The five men bowed their heads in silent prayer. The metal case, nothing more than the ordinary tool kit of a mining engineer, gleamed softly in the dull light. It contained a thermonuclear bomb.

CHAPTER
NINE

A military base is a dull and cold place to be when the troops are away. For men who don't have their families with them on hardship tours, holidays are an especially bad time too, and Thorsfinni's World was a hardship tour in spades. The single men and those separated from wives and children inevitably turn their thoughts to home. The longer a man stays in the Corps, the more he gets used to family separations and learns that the hardship can be endured with other men in a similar situation, in the spirit of camaraderie that always buoys the spirits of military men far from home.

No combat unit ever deploys at full strength. Men are always on temporary additional duty, ineligible because of physical profiles, because they're off at schools, exempt because of serious family problems, and so on. And when troops deploy, it's a living hell for the men who have to stay behind.

No Marine worth his salt wants to remain in garrison when his unit is out on a combat operation somewhere. Those who are left behind often feel they've been singled out because there's something wrong with them. In the case of 34th FIST, it was true. Colonel Ramadan was being left behind because of his bum leg, and a few other men were recovering from various injuries or suffering from permanent disabilities—men whom the "quarantine" prevented from being discharged and returned home.

But far worse was to be the dependent of a man sent on deployment. All too often when that happened a family's life in the Corps was abruptly ended by a knock on the door and a visit from the chaplain with news of the worst kind. And when tragedy did not intervene, the worry, the loneliness and boredom of the waiting, was too much for some, and weary men returning from some godforsaken hellhole returned home to find their families gone. There was an adage among Marine Corps wives: "We're not in the Service anymore." It was a sharp and cynical statement and it cut in different ways.

Marta Conorado was no stranger to any of this. All the many years of waiting for news of her husband's fate and living without him had hardened her outwardly, but now she had grown weary of life in the Corps. When her children were small, she had the diversion of taking care of them, holding the family together against their father's return. And when he did come home—oh, joy beyond measure! All the anger and pain she felt at their enforced separations would vanish instantly in his arms.

Now, during the first few weeks after her husband's departure, Marta wavered between feeling guilty at what she had said the night he left and feeling righteous anger that she was once more being left in the lurch. She realized that she did not know for sure if she really meant to leave her husband, but that's what she'd said, and there was no way to take the words back; he had left with them ringing in his ears. She comforted herself with the thought that at least he'd be in no danger on that trip, with his company again deployed to some godforsaken hellhole. What could a stupid court-martial do to a man like Lewis Conorado? Maybe, she thought, if the court-martial went against him, he'd at last see the light and take the offer her father had made many times in the past.

Herbius Carmody ran a very successful import-export business. More than once, he had offered Conorado a top position in his firm with the promise of a salary that would make his Marine Corps pay look like peanuts. The old man was serious. Managerial and leadership talent such as Conorado had developed as a Marine officer was hard to come by.

But Conorado had turned him down, politely but flatly, and Marta had always supported him. Her father could never understand it. Marta had always thought she did, but she wasn't so sure anymore.

While Camp Ellis was a ghost town, Mainside, the Confederation Navy base on Thorsfinni's World, thrived with activity. Its clubs and messes were full every night, and during the day the port operation and the naval command headquarters hummed with the life of a base operating at full capacity. The sidewalks at Mainside seemed to vibrate with the sharp salutes of the officers and men going about their duties. When ships of the line came into orbit for a visit, their shuttles discharged eager crewmen anxious to spend money on liberty in New Oslo—the hospitality of the 'Finnis was renowned throughout the Fleet—or even in the enlisted clubs at the base.

While their children were in school, the navy wives at Mainside enjoyed a whirlwind of social events, from card games to shopping sprees in New Oslo. Marta Conorado did not participate in any of that. After obtaining her master's in education and eventually the principalship of a high school off-world, she had met Lew. He'd been on recruiting duty then, but had come to her school not to recruit, but as a guest lecturer in a government seminar. A local politician had also been a member of the discussion panel, and when he began to openly deride the Marine Corps before the senior class, claiming that professional military people were no better than prostitutes, Conorado had shut him down with the simple statement: "Sir, if that is so, next time the enemy comes knocking at your gates, call for a prostitute." Lew had invited her to dinner that night, and she accepted. Since then, as time and circumstances permitted, she had taught in a variety of school systems part-time, but her main focus in life had become her husband and their children.

Yet Marta Conorado was a woman with a high degree of intelligence and lots of good, old-fashioned horse sense. There was little she couldn't figure out on her own. Over the years, for instance, she had taught herself how to repair just about any type of small machine. She had to learn because on Lew's pay they could not easily afford new applicances or the bills required to fix old ones when they broke down.

So Marta did not fit in with the coterie of navy wives who spent their time gossiping, shopping, and having affairs while their men were away. Once, years before, while having lunch with some Marine wives, one of them had commented that her husband would refuse to shave when he was off duty for any length of time. "He tells me, 'I'm off duty and so is my face,' " she said, to the laughter of the other women around the table.

"Well, that's typical of the male of the species," another remarked. "But for a woman, her face is like an officer, it's never off duty! Isn't that so, Marta?"

"Well," Marta answered, "I guess so, but for me, I really don't have to show anyone anything, you know? I'm not in 'show' business."

But despite the fact that Marta Conorado never expended much effort showing the world her face, she was still a handsome woman, even in her fifties. Slim and athletic, not a streak of gray in her auburn hair, she was a smart, confident, healthy woman who didn't need much in the way of beauty aids.

And now, over all her thoughts, hung the chilling knowledge that Lewis had imparted to her about the Skinks and what happened on Society 437. The Marines had dealt with them on that occasion, and she had no doubt they would again, but with the FIST off elsewhere, Marta realized just how vulnerable everyone on the fringes of Human Space really was.

So one night after Lew left for Earth, Marta Conorado decided to go out and get good and drunk.

The motif of the Seven Seas Bar was the old sailing navy of the early twenty-first century. It was a unique and popular feature of the officers' open mess system, if only because the drinks and meals served there were catered by a live serving staff. The waiters and waitresses flitting between tables taking orders were off-duty sailors earning extra pay. They did not seem to mind the unfamiliar and uncomfortable costumes of the old navy the job required, and the patrons loved them.

A huge placard mounted by the entrance to the Seven Seas explained the rules of the club: no headgear could be worn at the bar, under penalty of buying everyone else there a drink; formal dress was only permitted in the dining room; and the tip was set at one percent of the tab. This system had always prevailed at Bronnysund and other primitive outposts, but most naval personnel at Mainside had never been to such places often enough to consider the practice routine.

The Conorados had been to the Seven Seas several times and Marta liked the atmosphere, especially the bar, a long wooden affair where drinkers sat on high chairs and ordered their concoctions from a bartender. Of course, the actual mixing and pouring of the beverages was done by a servo, but the novelty came from being served by a human being dressed in old-fashioned garb. The bar was a dimly lighted, informal place where people could sit together and enjoy quiet conversations. Tobacco and thule were permitted, and the haze of cigarette smoke was said to be part of the bar's attractive ambience.

Marta had only been in the bar area one other time, with her husband, but the place attracted her. She noted on that previous occasion several unaccompanied women, evidently unmarried naval officers, who seemed at home there. She realized that the bar was an ideal place for single people to meet, and on that particular night Marta felt an urge to talk to a stranger, any stranger.

Of the dozen seats at the bar, only three were occupied. Hoping she was not acting too self-consciously, Marta took a seat by herself at the opposite end.

"Good evening, ma'am, my name is Jerry," the bartender said. "What would you like to have?"

Not a drinker, Marta was suddenly nonplussed. "A beer, please?"

"Yes, ma'am, we have . . ." He rattled off the names of several brands of beer. They were mostly incomprehensible to her. But she did recognize one of them.

"Reindeer," she answered as nonchalantly as she could.

"An excellent choice." The bartender was a yeoman first class earning a bit of extra money tending bar, which he had been doing for some time now. He sized Marta up quickly: fiftyish, good facial bones, athletic or at least in good physical shape, married, out by herself, husband with the Fleet. The Seven Seas period atmosphere might be phony and contrived, but Marta Conorado's situation that night was as old as men and the sea.

Marta had drunk Reindeer ale many times before, usually with meals, but she had never particularly liked the brew. But on this night it tasted good to her. She finished her glass and ordered another. The yeoman glanced at her out of the corner of his eye as he added the second beer to her tab. He knew very well what the classy broad wanted, and here he came—a navy aviator dressed in his flight suit.

The lieutenant stood just inside the doorway for a moment, letting his eyes adjust to the dim light. "Excuse me, ma'am, may I take this seat?" he asked as he slid onto the stool next to Marta's.

"Sure," she said. "My name is Marta."

It had been a very hard day at Camp Ellis. Since there was little to do in FIST headquarters, Colonel Ramadan felt obliged to get involved in things that the deputy commander of a Marine FIST would normally not be bothered with, to the great annoyance of the base maintenance personnel, but there was nothing they could do about it. Early in the morning the sewage system had sprung a leak, and Ramadan had spent most of the morning with the engineers trying to get it fixed. When he got back to his office, his system was inundated with messages from Kingdom relayed by Fleet, and although all were routine requests for logistical assistance, he considered acting on them a priority. As a result, it was way after sundown before he'd finished with the chore.

Back in his quarters, Ramadan lighted one of his precious Anniversarios and poured himself a large glass of ale. He looked over his books. One struck his fancy, and he took it to the alcove on the other side of the room, where he did his reading in a comfortable captain's chair. He stretched, sipped from his beer, and read at random from the first page that fell open on his lap:

> This inn was furnished with not a single article that we could either eat or drink; but Mr. Murchison, factor to the Laird of Macleod in Gleneg, sent us a bottle of rum and some sugar . . .

Ramadan smiled to himself. The passage was from James Boswell's *The Journal of a Tour to the Hebrides*, the third edition, the last one to have had the advantage of Boswell's corrections and editions. It was not an original, of course, just a limited editions reprint, but still extremely valuable, and very precious to Ramadan personally. After many years of traveling to the most primitive reaches of Human Space, he often felt he understood how Boswell and Dr. Samuel Johnson had felt on their tour of Scotland in the eighteenth century. Talk about "not a single article that we could either eat or drink"—Colonel Ramadan, as a Marine, had been there, done that.

He suddenly felt a compelling urge for companionship. Carefully, he closed the book and set it aside. The officers' mess would be a dull place tonight, only a few solitary souls seeking a late night snack. No, he required something more lively. He got up and dressed. It would be a long drive, but there was a club on Mainside he liked a lot. He'd spend the evening there.

The airman's name was Lieutenant (jg) Ken Busby and he flew a Raptor. He was already an ace, having shot down the requisite number of Diamundian aircraft during the war there—he'd told Marta all this before his rear end had time to warm the seat he took beside her. That was the campaign

Lew Conorado had fought on the ground, against Marston St. Cyr's tanks, while this Ken was zooming around shooting up a third-rate air force. But she didn't say anything. That evening, Marta did not want to be reminded of her husband.

"Are you a civilian employee here, Marta, or . . . ?" Ken asked. He'd ordered bourbon on the rocks and another beer for her. He left the question hanging because he knew the answer already. He deliberately did not ask if she was married, but had seen the impression on her left ring finger. She'd left the ring home. She wanted to try life without it for the first time in more than twenty years.

"Um," she responded, and Ken was satisfied to let it go.

"Thule?" He offered Marta a cigarette. "It's a Raucher, one of the prime Wanderjahrian brands."

"No thanks, Ken, the beer is enough for me." Marta smiled. "How about you? What's your ship?"

"CSS *Butner*. We're here pending—" He hesitated, for the information was classified. "—a berthing opening, for supplies and refueling, you know."

Marta's heart skipped a beat. She knew that the *Butner* was off to support 34th FIST on wherever it had been sent. If 34th FIST needed the support of a carrier on this operation, it was far more than just a "routine" peacekeeping deployment. Thank God, she thought for the umpteenth time, Lew will be out of this one! Then she kicked herself. She was being selfish: Company L would need him now more than ever, if it were deploying. Then she kicked herself again: Wasn't that the reason their marriage was breaking up? All these deployments? She smiled inwardly, Once a Marine's wife always . . . ? With effort, she suppressed that train of thought.

"How about you, Ken? Where are you staying?"

Ken's heart skipped a beat. Could this be . . . ? "I'm staying at a BOQ here on Mainside. Liberty for a few days, you know? I plan on going into New Oslo tomorrow. Would you—be free?"

"I'm free, Ken. But let me think about it for a while."

Marta regarded the young lieutenant. He was a handsome man—"dashing," was really the word. He had the easygoing, devil-may-care look of the fighter pilot, the kind of man who lived to fly. He wore a scarf about his neck, dark blue with white polka dots. "Are those the colors of your squadron?" she asked.

"Yes!" Ken answered enthusiastically, then launched into an interminable monologue about Attack Squadron 6, the "Blue Devils." When he talked about his flying unit, Ken's face flushed with enthusiasm. He used his hands to illustrate each point, especially when he talked about aircraft performance. It was impossible for Marta not to like the dedicated young flier. She realized he was nervous. This was probably his first attempt to pick up a married woman, or a recently divorced older woman, and she smiled. Ken misinterpreted that as interest in what he was saying about Attack Squadron 6.

"Another drink?" Marta asked, pointing at Ken's nearly empty glass.

"Oh, sure." He ordered another bourbon for himself and a beer for Marta and then rushed on: "But I'm telling you, Marta, this Dickerson guy, he's goddamned crazy! Well, we're all a little crazy, you know, but flying a Raptor at Mach 2 underneath a goddamned bridge!"

Marta found herself laughing with Ken at his stories. She wondered what it would be like to have sex with him. Before either of them realized it, they were holding hands and laughing together. It was the alcohol and the thule, of course, but Marta was beginning to enjoy Ken's company—a lot.

"Good evening, Mrs. Conorado," a deep male voice said from behind them.

Marta whirled around. "Ah, why, good evening, Colonel Ramadan! What a, er, surprise to see you!" She felt as if she were a teenager again and had been just caught masturbating by her father. Her face turned very red, and she hoped in the dim barlight it was not too noticeable.

Ramadan stood with a drink in one hand and a book under the other arm. He smiled.

"Uh, Ken, Lieutenant Busby, this is Colonel Ramadan," Marta said.

"Evening, sir." Ken nodded at Colonel Ramadan. He thought at first the colonel was Marta's husband, then a friend of her husband's. He'd just tried to hit on the wife of a senior Marine officer!

"Evening, Lieutenant, Marta. You enjoying yourselves?"

"Oh, yessir," they both blurted out at the same time.

"Well, excuse me." He nodded at the two of them and walked to a table in a dark corner of the bar.

Marta felt as if she were standing on the edge of a precipice. One step and she'd plunge over. Should she take it? She hesitated. She was not a superstitious woman, but Ramadan's unexpected intervention had been provident. "Ah, Ken, I've got to go," she announced.

"Ah, sure, Marta, sure. I understand. Um, one for the road?"

Marta shook her head no, and finished her beer in one gulp. She kissed Ken lightly on the cheek and walked, not very steadily, out of the bar. Ken shrugged. Just as well, he thought. Well, tomorrow it was on to New Oslo. But he had really liked her. A guy could talk to a woman like Marta. Boy, he thought, some lucky jarhead, to be married to a woman like that!

Back in her apartment, Marta locked the door, shook off her clothes, and stepped into the shower. She turned the water on as hot as she could stand it. She stayed in there for a long time.

CHAPTER
TEN

"Watch my tip, Wing. We're going seventy degrees starboard, take a flyover on that swamp."

"Roger, Lead," the wingman on Raptor Flight 2 replied.

Corporal Rolo Strataslavic, on watch in the squadron's comm shack, heard the voices but didn't register the words. He was too heavily engrossed in the Raptor tech manual he was studying. More than anything else, Strataslavic wanted to get out of headquarters and into the squadron's Raptor section as an electronics tech. There were a lot more high-paying jobs in the civilian world for spacecraft and starcraft electronics techs than there were for comm techs. He knew that experience working on Raptors could help him land one of those jobs when he got out of the Corps in another two years.

Everybody knew he spent his watch time studying, and his superiors approved, though unofficially, of course. It was expected that the men spend work time studying to advance themselves. It was different on a combat deployment, when everybody had to pay close attention to everything because lives were at stake. But Kingdom was hardly a combat op, just a bunch of peasants who could be dealt with by an army military police company, if the damn army could get its act together.

"Wing, cover me, I'm going down to take a closer look at that."

"Roger. Wing orbits." A moment later the wingman exclaimed, "What the hell?"

Corporal Strataslavic didn't notice immediately that the

transmissions from Raptor Flight 2 had ceased. He was immersed in a particularly tricky section on superconductivity.

When he did notice, he started adjusting the comm's controls, thinking something had slipped. He ran a routine ping and got it back—the comm seemed to be working right. Raptor Flight 1 was still coming through on its comm. He flipped frequencies on the two comms. Flight 1 came through loud and clear on 2's comm. Flight 2 didn't come in on 1's. He called 2 but got no response.

Strataslavic punched his own comm and called for the duty officer. He had the comms switched back to their proper frequencies by the time Ensign N!amce entered.

"What'cha got, Strat?" N!amce asked.

"Flight Two's off comm, sir."

"Gimme." N!amce held out a hand, Strataslavic slapped the comm's mike into it.

"Raptor Flight Two, this is Nest. Come in. Over." When he didn't get an immediate reply, he said, "There's a time and a place for fun and games, kiddies. This ain't them. Come in." N!amce had been a grizzled master sergeant when he finally decided to take what he called an early retirement by accepting a commission. He knew too well how Raptor drivers sometimes got lazy, or decided to relieve their boredom by "losing comm" and getting the troops at base all lit up.

"This is N!amce, Raptor Two. Come back or you're mine when you come in." That was no idle threat. Even though every pilot in the squadron held a higher rank than he did, only the squadron commander and sergeant major had more time in the Corps. N!amce had spent decades keeping junior enlisted men in line, and he wasn't shy about applying the same tactics to company-grade officers who messed up. He was also experienced enough not to let the concern show on his face or in his voice when Flight 2 still didn't reply.

"Play it back for me, Strat."

Corporal Strataslavic diddled the controls to replay the last two minutes before comm died.

"So what the hell was it?" N!amce muttered as he pulled

out his own comm and hit the button for the squadron commander's office. "N!amce," he said when the CO's aide answered. "Raptor Flight Two is missing, over—" He glanced at the data flow. "—the Swamp of Perdition."

Ten minutes later Raptor Flight 1 was orbiting over the swamp where Flight 2 had vanished, and a hopper was on its way to FIST headquarters to pick up the recon squad.

It wasn't the largest swamp on Kingdom, but it might have been the most awful. Its animate and its vegetative life were voracious eaters of flesh, and fully omniverous in their tastes. It was almost totally unexplored and, unlike other swamps, no humans—or other creatures of Earth—lived in it. They called it the Swamp of Perdition.

Staff Sergeant Wu, the FIST recon squad leader, stepped softly into the murky water of a sluggish stream. He didn't flinch when the cold water reached his crotch. He eased forward, sliding his feet across the muck of the stream bottom, toward the other bank. This was the most dangerous time, where the water passed his hips, it swirled, making his position visible. Lance Corporal Donat, the recon squad's comm man, stayed behind, covering him until he reached the other side. Then the two continued on opposite sides, stepping on their toes so their heels wouldn't squelch in the mud. With the chameleon shields on their helmets in place, the only sign of their passage was their footprints; they stepped too slowly and cautiously to mark their movement with noise. In the darkness under the swamp's dense canopy, their footprints were visible to only the very sharpest eyes, and the prints rapidly filled in.

Wu hated going in blind like this. The only information he had was that two Raptors from Flight 2 had vanished over a particular spot in this swamp. Cause unknown. Enemy force unknown. Hell, enemy presence unknown, except that two Raptors couldn't spontaneously explode from mechanical failure like the string-of-pearls—the ring of intelligence satellites the navy strung around Kingdom—showed happened to Raptor Flight 2. Well, going in to find out was Recon's job. More often than not Recon went in blind, sometimes even this blind. But no matter how often he had to go in blind, Staff Sergeant Wu still hated it.

The four Marines of recon team one followed another stream a couple of hundred meters to the right of Wu and Donat. Team two was three kilometers to their left. Team three was a third of the way around the swamp in the other direction. Wu allocated three hours for them to go the two kilometers to where they would rendevous, a kilometer from where the two Raptors had vanished. He hoped they weren't rushing so fast that any of them would run into an ambush.

Foliage seemed to drip, and fall lankly from the treelike endemic plants. Mossy growths crawled about trunks. The vegetative life of the swamp looked like it was dead and rotting; it smelled that way too. Fliers cawed in the canopy, insectoids buzzed and flitted about, landed on the men, tasted, found them unpalatable, flitted and buzzed off to find better dining. Crawling things with no legs or short legs slithered over the mud; longer legged creatures squelched through it. Something big splashed into the stream around a bend. Things that lived in the water rippled the surface. Wu saw a carnivorous plant slam its petals shut on a nectar-seeking creature, saw an animal the size of a young child rotting in the snares of another kind of carnivorous plant. He murmured an alert on the all-hands band—there might be larger carnivorous plants. He'd really hate to have a man injured or lost to an ambitious daffodil.

Wu transmitted a situation report every fifteen minutes. The report was always the same: "Situation as before. Continuing." His location was automatically embedded in the transmission. The three team leaders made the same reports to him.

The recon Marines moved slowly, deliberately, deeper into the swamp. They probed every shadow with their infras, light gatherers, and magnifiers, sought to find and examine every place a man could hide. They gauged each step before taking it, never put their full weight on the forward foot until they were sure of it. They sidestepped growth when they could; gently, slowly, moved it aside, and delicately replaced it when they couldn't. They frequently passed within a meter of swamp creatures without disturbing them.

Two hours of that manner of movement will exhaust a normal human being; it will even tire an experienced combat Marine. But the recon Marines had trained for it and were still a long way from needing a second wind.

Two hours in, Staff Sergeant Wu finally found an anomaly. There was a beaten area where a sheen of surface water showed the ground had recently been dry. He toggled the all-hands circuit and told his teams, then switched to the command circuit and reported to FIST headquarters what he'd found and what he was doing about it. He left the command circuit open—if anything happened to him, FIST would need to know immediately. Donat joined Wu while he studied the area with his various vision-enhancing shields and scent detectors. Ten minutes' observation of everything he could see in any format failed to show the presence of any life-form he hadn't already seen in the swamp.

"What does the UPUD show?" he asked Donat.

"Nothing," Donat murmured back.

"Cover me." Wu rose to a crouch and slowly padded in a circle a dozen meters outside the beaten area. His vision shields and scent detectors still didn't pick up anything that didn't belong. Donat didn't warn him of anything from the UPUD. Satisfied that no enemy lurked near, observing the beaten area, he gave the scent detector to Donat and entered it.

Broken swamp growth was mashed into the ground in patches that matched the pattern of growth elsewhere under the trees. It was hard to see surface details through the skim of water in the dimness under the trees, but his shields helped. Up close, the infra showed that an irregularly flattened patch of ground of about three square meters was a degree or two warmer than the surrounding ground, as though a piece of heat-producing machinery had been removed a few hours earlier. Here and there were other, unidentifiable marks on the ground—holes, scrapes, and gouges. He found a few footprints, some shod, some not. Most of them were smaller than his. Two of them didn't quite match, making him think they were made by different individuals; they were more than twice the size of the others. He recorded his observations and burst-transmitted the data to FIST HQ.

Finished, he reported in, "Continuing," then sent the same message on the all-hands circuit. He and Donat moved out as cautiously as before. Maybe more cautiously—now they knew someone else was or had been there.

Brigadier Sturgeon was close to letting his anger show. As if it wasn't bad enough that the images Archbishop General Lambsblood claimed proved the rebels weren't human couldn't be found anywhere, neither Ambassador Spears nor his chief-of-station knew anything about them. A Raptor flight had abruptly exploded without evident cause or threat. And now the FIST recon squad that went in to try to locate whatever might have shot the Raptors down had only found one mystery spot, about which his F2 could tell him nothing more than what the recon squad leader had said in his report from the spot. Sturgeon had the best people and equipment available to the Confederation military, yet he was blind—not to mention that he'd lost people—and he didn't like that one little bit.

Well, Marines don't sit back and pout when things don't go the way they want, they take action, he thought. M Company from the infantry battalion was already in position near the Swamp of Perdition. Sturgeon shook his head at the name, then ignored it.

On the FIST commander's order, the 127 Marines and four navy medical corpsmen of M Company boarded eight Dragons and entered the swamp. Two of the air-cushioned, amphibious Dragons followed each of four streams, headed toward the beaten-down area where the entire recon squad now waited.

From inside the company commander's Dragon, the company's two unmanned aerial vehicle controllers flew their "birds." There was no way to hide the roar of the Dragons' fans, but the birds were camouflaged as large, primitive flying animals indigenous to the swamp so they might not be noticed by any foe who saw them. They flew about a half kilometer ahead of the Dragons, zigging and zagging to cover the front of all four Dragon teams.

Each UAV controller wore a helmet that showed him three views of what the birds could see—normal vision, infra, and amplified light. He could increase or decrease magnification on any of the views he wanted. Sensors on the birds recorded information on chemicals in the air and sent them back, the smells of the swamp—olfactory signals of life-forms. The two Marines filtered the audio pickup to mute the usual insectoid and avian sounds and listened for anything that sounded like voices. Everyone else in the Dragons sat stoically waiting; only the drivers and gunners could see outside; the passengers were blind.

Little more than halfway to the destination, Dragon 3 erupted in a fireball that vaporized parts of it and sent the rest of it spinning out in chunks of metal and flesh. Dragon 4, 3's teammate, jerked forward and to the side in an evasive maneuver that would have thrown its passengers about like dice in a cup if they hadn't been strapped in against just that possibility.

"Evasive action, everybody," Captain Boonstra, the M Company commander, ordered, and followed with, "Report!" He didn't ask who had been on Dragon 3. He knew it was one blaster squad and the assault squad from second platoon. Later he'd have to write letters to the families of those men, but he didn't have the time to think about that now, when he had to give all his concern to his live Marines.

The remaining Dragons transmitted their locations and dispositions, which Boonstra scanned on his heads-up display as he asked for threat data.

"There wasn't any threat warning," reported Corporal Lieuwe, the Dragon 4 commander. "Three just went up!"

"We don't see a damn thing, sir," said Sergeant Kitching, the company's UAV chief. He could see the data coming in from bird two as well as from his own.

The other Dragons also reported no threat warnings or indication of people nearby.

"Dragon Four, withdraw two hundred meters," Boonstra ordered as he reviewed the locations of his Marines and checked that the data was automatically being relayed to the battalion and FIST headquarters. "All dismount. Converge on second platoon. Second platoon, hold your position until the rest of the company arrives." By the time the company assembled around the remains of second platoon, either he'd have a plan of action or higher command would come up with one for him.

Both Brigadier Sturgeon and the infantry battalion commander, Commander van Winkle, were smart enough to let the man on the scene run the show. Sturgeon only asked, "What do you need from me?"

Sturgeon and van Winkle conferred briefly. They were in full agreement that the enemy forces in the swamp must be found and dealt with. Sturgeon ordered van Winkle to get the rest of his battalion in position to sweep through the swamp and the squadron to get all its Raptors into the sky in case the Marines in the mud needed support. He held off on artillery prep fire.

Twenty-three minutes after Dragon 3 inexplicably exploded, M Company began moving in a wave formation through the swamp. First platoon, reinforced by a section from the assault platoon, advanced on a ragged line half a kilometer wide toward the area where Dragon 3 was killed. The company command element, the survivors of second platoon, and the rest of the assault platoon formed the second wave. Third platoon brought up the rear.

First platoon's PFC Gerlach was on the extreme right of the lead wave. He wasn't greatly experienced, had only been with 34th FIST for a few months and had no deployments under his belt. His inexperience and the shock of losing half a platoon all at once made him hyperalert. Had he not been so alert, he might not have looked so carefully through that break in the dripping foliage where he saw a shadow some thirty meters distant. The shadow had a shape and size he hadn't yet seen in the swamp. He stopped and methodically examined it. All his naked eyes showed was a dark blob that might or might not be something. His magnifier shield did nothing more than make the blob bigger. His infras showed a mass the size of a small person, but with a temperature a few degrees below human norm. It was his light gatherer that showed it most clearly.

The shadow resolved into a man-shaped creature lying prone in the mud, facing parallel to the company's movement. The creature was naked and had yellowish skin. It appeared to have slits in its side. The most ominous thing about it was the artifact on its back, tanks of some sort. A hose ran from the tanks to a nozzle it held in its hands.

"I have contact," Gerlach murmured into the squad circuit on his helmet comm. Slowly, cautiously, deliberately, he began to turn around to withdraw. He froze before turning very far. He saw another one. Swiveling only his eyes, he probed the surrounding shadows and saw more. His skin prickled. "They're all around," he murmured into the circuit. They didn't seem to be aware of him yet; he thought he should be able to slip out of the formation fairly easily. Few people who weren't Marines knew how to see a Marine wearing his chameleons and with his chameleon shield in place.

But they were aware of him, they were merely waiting for more Marines to enter the killing zone of the ambush. When the ambush commander realized they had been spotted, he gave the command to open fire. Four of the ambushers aimed the nozzles of their weapons at Gerlach and sprayed a greenish fluid. Two of the streams hit his helmet and melted away the electronics of his comm so that even if he had been able to scream, his voice wouldn't transmit; some of the fluid from the two streams that hit his helmet struck his face and got sucked into his throat when he tried to scream from the pain.

Four other Marines also went down, screaming in agony as the greenish fluid ate into their flesh and dissolved their bones.

"Echelon right!" Captain Boonstra bellowed into the all-hands circuit. "Volley fire by squads!"

First platoon's second squad leader, Sergeant Janackova, with Gerlach and two other men from his squad already down, dove into the mud and was shouting commands at his remaining men before he heard Captain Boonstra's order for squad volley fire.

"Five meters beyond Gerlach!" Janackova called, and seven plasma bolts from as many blasters struck in an irregular line beyond the dead Marine. "Tighten 'em up. Fire!" Seven more bolts bloomed fire that sizzled in the mud and raised a cloud of steam. "Up ten!" The Marines adjusted their aim to hit the ground ten meters beyond the previous shots. "Right five!" The seven Marines fired again, five meters to the right of their previous shots. "Left ten!" They adjusted and fired again. "Up ten, fire for effect." The seven blasters shifted again and rained fire into the area. If anybody was there, they'd be parboiled by the steam if they weren't hit by bolts. The squad would continue the fire until the platoon commander ordered them to shift aim or to cease fire.

More plasma bolts crackled to third squad's flanks, raising shocked clouds of steam from the mud and dank foliage. To their right, blaster bolts were joined by the ripping crackle of an assault gun.

Janackova checked his HUD; the first squad of his own platoon was on his left; a squad from second platoon and a gun from the assault platoon were on the right. He didn't know how the enemy knew to set off their ambush, but they hit so accurately he thought they must have infras. Well, the roiling steam was hot enough to conceal the Marines from infrared vision. Now the enemy would be firing as blindly as they were.

More commands came over the all-hands circuit. The squad from second platoon and the assault gun with it shifted their fire farther to the right. First platoon's assault squad moved up between the two blaster squads, and two squads from the assault platoon moved up behind them.

"First platoon, up and advance briskly," came the voice of Ensign Chinsamy, the platoon commander.

Janackova repeated the command to his men, looked left and right through his infras to make sure they obeyed him and he hadn't lost anybody else, then stepped out at a fast walk into the steam cloud.

The steam a few meters beyond Gerlach's corpse was already dissipated, and the second cloud ten meters past that was also nearly gone. The third cloud, where the fire had been concentrated, was still dense and hot. The ground, so suddenly dried out, crackled and crunched underfoot. The Marines burst through it, almost trotting to get out of the heat. One man in each fire team had his infra screen in place, one his magnifier, and the third used his light gatherer. When they were twenty meters beyond the stream, Sergeant Janackova caught sight of a form running through the trees. He snapped his blaster to his shoulder and fired at it.

He stared in shock when the running form flashed into flame. He'd never heard of such a thing.

The rest of the reinforced platoon opened fire when Janackova shot at the fleeing figure. No unseen bodies flashed into flame.

CHAPTER
ELEVEN

Kilo Company moved into the swamp to the left of M Company. Company L took position to Kilo's right. Three companies abreast, they advanced deeper. The FIST's Raptors orbited a few kilometers away, ready to rain support when needed. Brigadier Sturgeon still held off on the artillery.

Company L advanced in a line of platoons, the platoons in lines of squads. Second squad, third platoon, was the squad on battalion's farthest right. Lance Corporal Schultz had second squad's point. To Schultz's thinking, the extreme right front corner of the battalion advance was the most vulnerable position, the position that required the sharpest, most alert man in the battalion. He believed that he was the sharpest and most alert Marine in the entire FIST. He wanted that position. Nobody was about to say no to Hammer Schultz when he said he wanted the most dangerous position.

Before they started out, Schultz stood motionless for a long moment listening to the sounds of the swamp, then another long moment absorbing its scents. He squatted and listened and smelled. Noises and aromas are marginally different at higher and lower elevations. He wanted to get a range. Satisfied that he had a basic grasp of the sounds and smells of the swamp, enough to allow him to filter out the most mundane of them, he softly said "Ready" into his helmet comm.

A moment later Corporal Kerr's voice came back to him: "Move out."

Schultz stepped through the brush and across a rivulet. Thirty-fourth FIST's infantry battalion began moving deeper into the trackless waste of the Swamp of Perdition.

Light filtered dimly through the thin canopy, creating dark shadows and darkening colors. The dominant tones were the deepest greens of wet foliage and the heavy browns and blacks of water-sodden dirt. Shapes, unless seen up close, were muddled and indistinct, and tended to blend together. Here and there spots of brilliant color signaled "come hither" to pollinating insectoids, or to prey. The air, when it moved, was sluggish, as though too dispirited by its surroundings to waft. The water of the numerous rivulets and streams was more sluggish, seemed too tired to do more than just lay there. It was humid, and the air felt almost thick enough to drink. Fallen foliage slowly rotted on the ground. Mud oozed and slipped underfoot and threatened to tumble the men. Everything emitted aromas, the scents of rot and decay and excretion, a miasma that felt viscous, as though it could be seen and touched, and would cling to flesh, clothing, and equipment. The dank foliage, wet air, and thick mud sopped up sounds, muddied them.

One skilled man can move wraithlike through a swamp, unseen and unheard by its denizens, even his scent lost in the general miasma. One man alone can seep through until he is close enough to an unsuspecting animal to kill it. A few skilled men, three or four or half a dozen, can creep close enough for one of them to kill their prey before it can get away. Four hundred men, no matter how stealthy each one is, cannot move undetected through a swamp. The animals heard them coming. Prey animals fled to the safety of their burrows, or to distance themselves from the threat. Predators realized something bigger and stronger and meaner was coming and got out of its way. Even the carnivorous plant life seemed to sense that it was not dinner time, and furled leaves, closed flowers, withdrew tendrils.

The going for everyone was uncertain. Slip, slide, squish in mud. Tufts of turf tried to trip the unwary. Tangles of tendrils and trailing vines lay in wait to entrap careless feet.

Droopy leaves, twigs, and mossy growths hung in lank sheets to block vision. Streams that moved sluggishly were everywhere, so murky with decaying and decayed matter that the sinkholes on their bottoms couldn't be seen or even felt until stepped into. Small water-dwelling parasites struggled to get through the material of the Marines' uniforms. And there were all those damn insectoids that hadn't yet gotten the word.

Only the flying insectoids thought "banquet" and buzzed and flitted in to dine. It wasn't long before nearly every Marine in the battalion had multiple itching bites from beasties that had managed to get inside his chameleon uniform.

On the right front corner, Schultz ignored the three bites he sustained. He'd been inoculated against all known pathogens, and some itching was simply part of being in the field. His attention remained firmly fixed on his surroundings. Two men back, Corporal Kerr also ignored the itching. Miscellaneous bites were nothing to be concerned with, not unless they infected, and he'd had the same inoculations Schultz had. He was as alert as Schultz, but not all his attention was on his surroundings. As a fire team leader, he had to be fully aware of his men. Normally he would have positioned himself between them, but not this time. He knew Schultz could handle himself and not make mistakes; Corporal Doyle was another matter. Kerr knew he needed to give him close supervision. He used his infra shield more often than he usually would so he could maintain visual contact with Doyle. His eyes constantly flicked to the HUD display he had tacked in the corner of the shield so he could see where Doyle was when he wasn't using his infra.

A lone flitterer wended its way under the chin of Corporal Doyle's helmet and inside the neck of his chameleon shirt to his collarbone, where it settled down to drill a well into the succulent juices of this odd flesh. The juices it siphoned up were just as odd as the flesh, much odder than the flitterer had suspected, and it promptly withdrew its proboscis. Disoriented by the alien nutrients, which were anything but nutritious for it, it wandered about aimlessly for a bit, unable to find its way back out until Doyle slapped his chest and squished it.

Several minutes afterward, between the excruciating itch on his collarbone and horrible thoughts of what that alien insectal ichor must be doing to his tender and all-too-human flesh, Doyle was half driven to distraction and felt himself headed for madness. He forgot to watch where he was stepping and slid, almost fell, when something slipped under his foot.

"Watch your step, Doyle," Kerr's soft voice came to him. "Use your light shield."

"Uh, right," Doyle replied as he regained his balance. He stopped using his infra shield and stayed with the light-gatherer shield so he could see where he was going. He held his blaster by the forestock with his left hand while he scratched at his collarbone and scrubbed at his chest with his right; between his shirt and glove, it was an ineffectual scratching.

The battalion advanced slowly. Some of the slowness was due to the difficulty of movement. Some was in order to maintain formation. The part of the Marines' minds that was aware of the slowness thought it was because of the caution the pointmen and the men on the flanks needed to maintain. The pace was less than a kilometer in a local hour. Such a pace over difficult terrain was exhausting. In the battalion's right front corner, after two hours, Corporal Kerr was running with sweat. He was tired and found his attention wandering. He focused on Doyle and forced himself back to alertness. Doyle was drenched and nearly out of it altogether. He was vaguely aware that he was losing body fluids far faster than he was taking in water. It took everything he had merely to maintain contact with Schultz and find his footing. Schultz was covered with a sheen of perspiration, but his attention and alertness hadn't varied from the sharpness he started out with.

A little more than two kilometers from their starting point, Schultz stopped and lowered himself to one knee. In waves from him, the battalion racheted to a stop.

"What do you have, Hammer?" Kerr asked.

Schultz grunted. What he had was a feeling, an impression. There wasn't a single thing to which he could point and say, "Danger." Not a dimly seen form, not a print in the mud or a newly snapped twig. Not even a fleeting scent or an unexplained sound.

A moment later Gunnery Sergeant Charlie Bass came forward to check out the situation.

"What?" he asked.

Schultz was silent for a few seconds as he continued to study the landscape to his front and his right, wondering how—or whether—to answer the question.

"Skinks," he finally said.

"Where?"

Invisible under his chameleons, Schultz shook his head. "Out there," he murmured.

"Did you see anything? Hear anything?"

Schultz grunted a negative.

"UPUD doesn't show anything, Gunny," Lance Corporal Dupont said.

Bass snarled at him. He didn't want to hear what the UPUD did or did not show. He considered what to say. All reports he'd heard or read said they were up against human rebels. There were no indications they were faced by the fierce, alien beings third platoon had encountered on Waygone. Of course, there *were* those unexplainable weapons. But the Skinks hadn't used anything like them. Still . . .

"If they aren't here, let's move out and find them," Bass finally said. There, he hadn't reprimanded Schultz for invoking a boogeyman nobody else believed in, nor had he even acknowledged the man's belief. In his infra, Schultz rose to his feet and moved forward.

As Bass waited for his position in the platoon column to reach him, he toggled his comm to the company command circuit and reported to Lieutenant Humphrey. Humphrey agreed that he'd done the right thing, and then made his own report to Battalion. Commander van Winkle told him to make sure everybody was alert, then reported to FIST.

Brigadier Sturgeon knew about Schultz's belief that they were up against the Skinks. He was able to follow Schultz's thinking to that conclusion without having to agree with it. On the other hand, the weapon that had killed two of his Raptors and a Dragon wasn't in any human armory he'd ever heard of. So maybe they *were* up against aliens. Elements of his command *had* encountered nonhuman sentiences twice over the past couple of years, so hostile aliens were possible. And any belief that helped his Marines stay alert and alive was all right with him.

When Bass talked with Schultz, he used the circuit that allowed the entire platoon to listen without anyone else being able to break in. Corporal Doyle listened closely. His fatigue vanished, his sweat dried up, his sphincters tightened, and so much adrenaline pumped into his system that a touch would have made him twang like a guitar string. Marines from a war centuries past might have described it as "His pucker factor pegged the meter."

Skinks? Doyle would have said the word out loud if his throat wasn't so tight it wouldn't even let a squeak through. He hadn't been on the mission to Society 437, the planet commonly called Waygone, but once the secret was out, he'd certainly heard about it. Skinks! He'd heard about them. Lots. If he were more imaginative, they would have haunted his dreams. *Skinks!* Such a mild name for ferocious creatures. In his imagination they were more than two and a half meters tall, weighed 250 kilos, spat fire, exhaled corrosion, ate living flesh, breathed water as well as air, and could see chameleoned Marines.

He was partly right. Some of the Skinks were more than two meters tall and weighed more than two hundred kilos. They did breathe water as well as air. They didn't exhale corrosion, though—but they used weapons that shot corrosive acid. As for the rest of it? Doyle's imagination was rich enough to have brought on nightmares.

Suddenly the swamp looked different to Corporal Doyle. Suddenly every shadow held a gigantic, fire-breathing, corrosion exhaling, human-flesh-eating monster that not only could see him, but wanted to kill him. Every cry from a swamp creature was the death rattle of a Marine dying horribly from an encounter with a Skink. Every ripple on the surface of a stream became the trail of a water breather coming to roast him and dissolve his charred remains. Every movement seen in the corner of his eyes was a charging Skink bent on his oblivion.

Doyle's blood pressure rose to forehead-tightening level. His throat constricted until breath couldn't get through to his lungs.

"Get a grip, Doyle," Kerr's voice came over the helmet comm.

Doyle jumped, and his sphincter gave critical ground. "Ah, shit!" he croaked through a throat that also eased.

"Smells like it," Kerr agreed. "Next stream we cross, clean yourself."

Partly disrobe in a stream where Skinks swarmed at him? Was Corporal Kerr crazy?

Unlike Doyle, Kerr *had* been on Waygone and he had fought the Skinks. He knew firsthand how ferocious they were. He also knew their weapons were short-range. A lone Marine with a blaster could take out a lot of Skinks before they got close enough to use their acid-shooting weapons. Unfortunately, the sight lines in the swamp were short enough that the Skinks would be within range before the Marines could see them. Fortunately, the Marines weren't looking for Skinks, they were hunting rebels. There was no evidence of any alien sentience on Kingdom. Except for whatever it was that killed two Raptors and a Dragon—and Schultz's conviction that the Skinks were here.

Schultz, almost preternaturally alert to begin with, became more so, if such a thing was possible. Against a human foe he was imperturbable. He understood humans and the way humans fought. He was a Marine, and he knew the Confederation Marines were the best warriors in the history of mankind. More, he knew that he was among the very best fighters the Marine Corps had. But the Skinks . . .

He thought the Skinks were alien. They didn't live and

fight with the same imperatives humans did. Their base, genetic motives were somehow different. He didn't know in what way they were different, or why they were different. But he remembered the fanaticism with which they'd fought on Waygone, and their fanaticism had combined with their overconfidence and small numbers to allow a lone Marine platoon to defeat them.

The Skinks were on Kingdom in such large numbers that the local armed forces were being slaughtered, along with large numbers of civilians—Schultz lifted his shields and spat; only the most vile soldiers slaughter civilians—and the Confederation had to intervene. To Schultz, the only way to deal with Skinks was to nuke the entire planet, make it uninhabitable. One Marine FIST wasn't enough to defeat them.

Schultz repressed a shiver. He'd been in tight situations before, fights in which many Marines had died. There had even been a few battles he hadn't expected to survive. But he didn't believe he'd ever been in as deadly a position as he was in just then. He thought they were all going to die.

CHAPTER
TWELVE

"Amen," pronounced Increase Harmony, the obligatory benediction completed. He raised his head to the others gathered about the conference table. "The City of God shall prevail," he added.

"God's will," the six men intoned as one.

"We are as merry as men bound for heaven." Harmony smiled.

"That we are, Brother Harmony," Chajim Nishmath agreed, stroking his long white beard thoughtfully. "Brothers," he said, addressing the others, "we have important business to discuss this day and time is perilously short."

The seven men gathered in conference were the leading ministers of the City of God sect. A neo-Puritan movement, the City of God rejected a formal church structure. Each individual congregation or "meeting" was totally independent of the others that loosely composed the sect. Each meeting had its minister, who provided the congregation with spiritual guidance and leadership in formal gatherings for worship, but his tenure was subject to the approval of the congregation and he could be removed by a vote.

The career of a successful minister in a City of God meeting had to be highly political as well as theologically sound—the City of God based its creed strictly upon the literal interpretation of the Authorized Version of the Bible, widely known as the King James Version. Each congregant knew his Bible well from an early age, and any deviation from its teachings on the part of any minister or other congregant was fuel for scandal.

The members of the City of God sect were dour, hard-working, no-nonsense people. They observed no church holidays, dressed plainly always, and, aside from singing psalms, eschewed churchly music of any kind. The City of God was only a minor sect among the many sectarian movements that made up the political life on the Kingdom of Yahweh and His Saints and Their Apostles, but in times of crisis its members were capable of incredible sacrifice and solidarity, and therefore it had survived from the earliest days of settlement on Kingdom.

The seven men around the table were the ministers of large congregations, and they had been leading their flocks successfully for years. As long as they lived and preached, their church would continue to thrive. They would allow nothing to interfere with that. They were survivors. And it was a time for surviving.

"When the Convocation meets tomorrow, we shall remain silent," Jacob Zebulon reminded them. "We shall sit and listen and bide our time, and in the fullness of time the will of the Lord shall be apparent to the Ecumenical Leaders."

The Ecumenical Leaders of Kingdom's sects were meeting the next day in Convocation at Mount Temple to consider the present crisis. The seven ministers would represent the City of God at the Convocation. Mount Temple was a holy place to all the sects on Kingdom, a neutral spot where they could put aside their differences and meet to solve common problems.

"They consider Mount Temple a place free of Satan," Canon Barjona sneered, "but when the sects gather there it is nothing but a temple of the devil!" The others murmured their assent. "I feel unclean even thinking about the apostates who'll be gathered there tomorrow."

"We must be there, brothers," Harmony sighed. "I have discussed with you before my Particular Faith, brothers, that this Convocation will be most significant to the future of our church." A Particular Faith, a carryover from the early days of Puritanism, was a divinely inspired intimation sent to men by God's angels to show them the Way.

"We too have had them, Brother Increase," Elnathan Jones said. "It does not surprise me that the Hand of God has descended upon our elite and opened our eyes to the machinations of Satan and his minions."

"Brothers," Jacob Zebulon intoned, "are the People ready? Are they ready, as the Jews of old, to flee Egypt into the Wilderness?"

"Aye, when the Convocation is concluded, we shall be ready, brother," the others responded. Before the *Cambria* was destroyed and vengeance could descend upon them, the entire congregations of the City of God would be long gone into the wildernesses of Kingdom, to refuges in the vast wastelands of the planet, there to weather the storm that was sure to descend upon them as soon as the news was out that the ship had been destroyed by their men.

"We are going to show them all a thing or two," Eliashub Williams rumbled.

"That we are, Brother Williams! That we are!" Harmony said. "Only the Confederation, in league with the Convocation, could be responsible for these depredations, and you all know, brothers, that the purpose of these incursions is to set Confederation troops among us to destroy us! Well," he shook his fist in direction of Haven, where the sanctuary of Mount Temple was located, "the scales shall be dropped from their eyes and they shall see the truth."

"They'll see it, all right, from every hemisphere on the planet Earth." Williams chuckled.

"Brothers, before we depart here for Mount Temple, let us pray for the souls of our brave brethren who will show the light to the people of Earth. They should already be aboard the *Cambria* and en route to glory."

The seven men bowed their heads and began to recite the Twenty-third Psalm of David.

Bishop Ralphy Bruce Preachintent drummed his fingers impatiently on the tabletop.

"Brother Ralphy Bruce, would you please stop that?" Chairman Shammar asked. Bishop Preachintent had been last year's chairman of the Convocation of Ecumenical Leaders. This year it was the turn of the leader of Kingdom's largest Muslim sect, Ayatollah Jebel Shammar. Ralphy Bruce was included in the select company seated around the conference table because he was the spiritual leader of Kingdom's largest evangelical sect. The other three holy men— Swami Nirmal Bastar, Cardinal Leemus O'Lanners, and the Venerable Muong Bo—represented the largest Hindu, Catholic, and Buddhist sects respectively. Together the five men were the spiritual leaders of three-fifths of Kingdom's population, and since Kingdom was a theocracy, they were also the five most powerful political figures on the planet.

"Need I remind anyone that tomorrow begins the Convocation of Ecumenical Leaders? We must decide now on the strategy we wish to pursue in this time of crisis," Shammar told the others, but he looked straight at Bishop Preachintent as he spoke.

"It is not the dissidents who are responsible for the destruction that has been visited upon us," the Venerable Muong Bo said. "They have neither the forces nor the organization to defeat the Army of God."

"You are right, Venerable," Ayatollah Shammar responded. "It has to be the Confederation itself, brothers."

"Yes, and their goal is the subjugation of our world and the destruction of our sacred beliefs and practices!" Swami Bastar almost shouted. Of all the sects on Kingdom, Bastar's was the most controversial, mainly because it adamantly refused to abandon the ancient practices of its ancestors, which included the immolation of wives on their husbands' funeral pyres.

"Has anyone considered," Ralphy Bruce began, his voice deceptively calm, "that possibly, just possibly, what is happening might be due TO THE WRATH OF A VENGEFUL GOD AS AN EXAMPLE TO US SINNERS?" He shouted the last words at the top of his voice.

The Venerable Muong Bo winced. "No," he responded.

"You are beginning to sound like a minister of the City of God, dear brother Ralphy Bruce." Swami Bastar smiled.

"Hmpf. Well. I just meant that is a possibility, my friends!" Preachintent went back to drumming his fingers on the tabletop.

"Brothers," began Cardinal Leemus O'Lanners, leader of the ultraconservative breakaway Catholic sect known as the Fathers of Padua, "in my Father's house there are many mansions." The others raised their eyebrows slightly. Cardinal O'Lanners was not known for the clarity of his sermons, which were mostly in Latin anyway, the official language of the Fathers. But he was a magnificent specimen of a churchman, in his bright red robes and with his huge patrician nose.

"Well, yes . . . yes. Ahem. Things only happen through the will of Allah, His name be praised." Ayatollah Shammar nodded respectfully at his Buddhist and Hindu colleagues. "But what we have here, I think, is purely a political situation. For many years the Confederation has been dissatisfied with the way we run things on our beloved Kingdom. They are unable, under the rules of their Constitution, to interfere directly in our affairs," he shrugged, "but were we for some reason to ask for their military assistance," he paused, "they would have a foothold on our world. The camel's nose, so to speak, would then be firmly under our tent."

"Well, that is just what we have done!" Preachintent protested. The request for military assistance from the Confederation had been made during his own chairmanship.

"Individually, there are many things we cannot see, but collectively," Shammar shrugged, "our vision is clear."

"Then why didn't any of you speak up during the last Convocation?" Bishop Ralphy Bruce muttered as he went back to drumming his fingers.

"We will give them the foothold they want," Shammar continued. "We will then direct their forces against the sects that have been giving us trouble." He smiled. "We are not without allies in the Confederation. Once the designs of their government are known, we can lobby for a complete withdrawal of their forces. The Confederation government in Fargo may sometimes operate in violation of its own Constitution, but its Congress is jealous of its prerogatives, and the Confederation is a democracy. Policy set by any democratic power is fickle, subject to the whims of the peoples' representatives. If we stick together in this, we can achieve the goal we all have always wanted—the complete destruction of the heretical sects."

"Brothers, I hear you and I will go along with you," Bishop Ralphy Bruce said. "Now, brothers, I know you think I'm just an uneducated country preacher"—the others protested this loudly—"but you have seen the destruction, talked to the survivors! This terror is not the work of Confederation military forces! There is something about what is happening out there that is . . . is . . ."

"Otherworldly?" Shammar interjected. "We all believe in the spiritual, Brother Ralphy Bruce, but I assure you, these attacks are strictly of this world. But if they are a sign from Allah, His name be praised, who is He using as His agent, then? Can you answer me that? What force is the Almighty employing that works like armored fighting vehicles?"

The four men fell silent. Bishop Ralphy Bruce Preachintent stared at his fingers. "I do not know," he answered softly, "and really, neither do any of us."

"The second best thing Creadence did was to get the hell out of here," Jayben Spears, newly arrived ambassador to the Kingdom of Yahweh and His Saints and Their Apostles, told Prentiss Carlisle, his chief-of-station. "And how damned smart was I to take this job, eh?" Spears laughed.

"Well, sir, I didn't get to know him that well. I was only here a month between the time Harly Thorogood died and Ambassador Creadence was transferred."

"Ah . . ." Spears waved his hand and poured them both more Reindeer ale. "I got used to this stuff when I was ambassador to Wanderjahr," he remarked as he poured. "I worked closely with Ted Sturgeon there, as you know. Thirty-fourth FIST is based on Thorsfinni's World, and they drink this animal piss by the gallon. It's pretty good too, once you get by the taste."

"I've got to tell you, sir," Carlisle couldn't suppress a

laugh, "you really stunned old Lambsblood, the way you greeted Brigadier Sturgeon." They both laughed. Carlisle couldn't help remembering the astonished look on the general's face as Ambassador Spears slapped Brigadier Sturgeon on the back and they traded comradely insults like old friends. "Well," Carlisle continued with an effort, "we all thought you were going to retire after Wanderjahr, sir."

"Me too. But let me tell you something, Prentiss—my rank is Diplomatic Service One. Do you know how much a DS1 earns?" Spears laughed. "But I'm retiring after this assignment, that's for goddamned sure!" They drank. "So tell me, Prentiss, what's the take on this—this goddamned rathole? What are the sky pilots down here up to? I got the full intelligence brief before I came out here, but you've been on the ground. What's your view?"

Prentiss shrugged and set his mug down. "Thorogood knew something, sir, but he didn't get a chance to pass it on. But from my short time here, my perspective is that, as usual, the powerful sects are trying to wipe out their lesser competitors. They're the ones who've been destroying these villages. Note that none of the places ravaged belong to any of the dominant sects. So they put the finger on some unspecified rogue member world of the Confederation as the culprit, and call us in to wipe out their main competitors, plus anyone else they don't feel like slaughtering themselves."

"But the so-called Army of God has taken some heavy casualties, Prentiss. That's beyond dispute."

"Yes, sir, but each of these sects has its own military force. The place abounds with small armies. I think the five major sects got together, pooled their resources, and then set the planetary army up to be the fall guys."

"They ambushed their own troops?"

"Yessir. That's the way I see it anyway. Sir, you have to remember, this place is a 'theocracy,' but the only thing these people believe in is power for themselves. They'll do anything to get it and keep it. That's why they're so afraid of dissidents with new ideas. The theocrats, through this Collegium thing—nothing more than a damned inquisition, you ask me—control both the minds and the bodies of their adherents. Then comes along this City of God movement—"

"Neo-Puritans," Spears interrupted.

"Yessir. They really believe the crap they preach, say that for them. But they're crazy. And they're a threat to the ruling sects."

Spears was silent as he sipped his beer. "Well," he said at last, and grinned, "You know what the first best thing was that old Doc Friendly did? He asked for the Marines. Let me tell you, Prentiss, that was the best thing that ever happened to the Kingdom of Yahweh and His Saints and Their Apostles, whether they know it or not. Ever read anything by C. S. Lewis, Prentiss?"

"Can't say I ever heard of him, sir."

"Well, he wrote somewhere—his *Screwtape Letters*, I think—that when the Puritans lost their influence, people ceased to believe in the devil anymore, and that was the best thing that ever happened to the devil. Do you think the devil is operating here on Kingdom, Prentiss?"

"I sure do, sir, and his name is Jebel Shammar."

CHAPTER
THIRTEEN

When contact finally came, it wasn't the battalion's right front corner that made it, it was the center of the formation's rear. All of M Company had followed a stream so sluggish it was nearly stagnant. Some of the Marines waded through it, probing its depths and its banks for anything or anyone hiding in its murkiness. They didn't probe deeply enough through the tangled buttress roots of the trees that lived dangerously atop a deeply undercut section of bank, and so missed what hid there. When the sensors on the sides of the Leader commanding the twenty Fighters who hid within the roots told him the Earthmen were all past, he gave the signal and his Fighters swam into the stream. Some of them stood in the chest-deep water; most slithered up the banks.

Second platoon, which had lost much of its strength so horrendously when Dragon 3 exploded, was rear guard. PFC Zhaque, the rearmost Marine in the column, wasn't experienced enough for walking backward to be second nature for him, the way it was for experienced rear points, so he was facing front when the Skinks came out of hiding and he didn't see them. Lance Corporal Schindigh, the Marine in front of him, on the other hand, was experienced enough to automatically maintain contact with the column and the rear point. Schindingh was also facing forward when the Skinks emerged from the water, but he turned around an instant before the Leader shrilled the command for his Fighters to open fire.

"Behind us!" The sound of Schindigh's voice was

drowned out in the *crack-sizzle* of his blaster as he opened fire on the Skinks. He dove for the ground as he fired, and his gaping jaw slammed shut when he hit—the Skink he'd snap-fired at was hit a glancing blow and flared up in a flash of fire. Schindigh's shock at the sight had popped his mouth open. When it was jarred closed, he bit his tongue hard enough to draw blood. The shock and pain distracted him just long enough for a Skink to point its weapon's nozzle and send a streamer of greenish fluid toward him. He saw it coming in time and rolled out of the way, but more Skinks were spraying in his direction and he was hit by two streams. He screamed.

Zhaque, meanwhile, stood frozen for long seconds before he dropped. Five Skinks fired toward him, and three of their streams hit. He died agonizingly within seconds.

The remaining Marines of M Company's second platoon scrambled to face the threat from their rear. Captain Boonstra, the company commander, raced back to eyeball the situation. As he ran he ordered his other two platoons to maneuver to his flanks. He got there just in time to see a Skink flare up from a blaster hit.

He'd heard that someone flashed like that the first time his company encountered this enemy, but hadn't believed it.

Only two Marines from second platoon were still fighting. Boonstra called for his other two platoons to get into position fast-fast-fast!

Sergeant Janackova and his squad were the first to get on line with the company commander. They couldn't see where the enemy was.

"Range?" Janackova asked into his helmet comm.

"Thirty," Boonstra snapped back.

"Volley, thirty," Janackova ordered his squad. "NOW!" The Marines aimed and fired as one. A line of mud and wet foliage steamed up when the seven bolts hit. "FIRE!" Janackova ordered again. Another seven bolts shot forward, raising more steam and a little black smoke where they hit.

Another squad from M Company's first platoon reached the line and joined in the volley fire. They were greeted by a brilliant flash as another Skink flared into vapor. In another moment all of M Company was on line, volley firing into the swamp to the battalion's rear. There were more flashes from vaporizing Skinks, and the screams of wounded and dying Marines punctuated the firing. Flames began to flicker in the scorched foliage.

When he didn't see any more flashes for fifteen seconds, Boonstra ordered the volleys adjusted to forty meters. Then he ordered, "Scatter fire!" and the Marines ceased their disciplined fire in favor of bolts shot in random patterns.

Soon no more streams of greenish fluid sprayed at them from the front, no more lights flashed. A cloud of steam grew in the canopy as flames from dried foliage licked higher.

"Cease fire!" Boonstra ordered. He studied his company's front while he reported to Commander van Winkle.

The fire team and squad leaders gathered their casualty reports and gave them to their platoon commanders, who relayed the reports to the company command element. Captain Boonstra's heart sank when he got them. Second platoon was dead, only one member of it left uninjured. Half of the survivors of the destroyed Dragon were dead, and the rest were wounded by the acid. Most of the wounded needed immediate evacuation. His other platoons were in better shape, but his company was down to half strength.

"On your feet," he ordered, doing his best to keep the pain of the losses out of his voice. "We're going to sweep that area and look for bodies. If you find anybody alive, try to keep them that way, we need prisoners to question."

The Marines of M Company rose to their feet and cautiously moved back the way they'd come. They found scorched spots where Skinks had flared up, but there were no bodies to be found, much less live ones to be taken prisoner.

"Yessir, that's affirmative," Captain Boonstra reported to Commander van Winkle. "I saw it myself, they flashed into vapor when they were hit."

"You actually saw bodies hit and flare up?"

Boonstra hesitated for a moment. "Nossir, not exactly. I saw the flashes, but I never actually saw one of the enemy."

"So you don't know positively that the—" van Winkle hesitated. Who were they *really* up against? Was it the Skinks Company L's third platoon had encountered on Society 437? What were they doing here? Why did they attack without apparent cause? "—the people you fought were vaporized. The flashes could have been magnesium flares and they dragged off all their dead and wounded." Van Winkle didn't doubt for an instant that the Marines of M Company inflicted casualties on the foe they fought.

"That's right, sir." But Boonstra was convinced that the flashes he'd seen were made by the enemy, whoever they were, vaporizing when they were hit.

"All right. The battalion is continuing into the swamp."

"Aye aye, sir."

"Dragons are on their way to take your casualties out. Catch up with us as soon as they do. And this time make damn sure your rear point is watching the rear. I don't want any more surprises like that one."

In a single afternoon one of his companies was reduced to little more than half strength. In all his years as a Marine, van Winkle had rarely seen a company hit that hard in so short a time.

Four Dragons, almost enough to carry an entire company, arrived. The dead Marines were stacked in one, and the wounded were divided among the other three, where corpsmen kept them stabilized on the way out of the swamp. The remainder of M Company watched the Dragons leave, then hurried to catch up with the rest of the battalion. This time, six alert Marines kept watch on their rear. Halfway to the swamp's edge, with no threat warning, two of the Dragons ferrying casualties to safety erupted.

It wasn't done officially, but word of M Company's firefight and the flashes from the enemy positions quickly filtered through the battalion.

"Skinks," Schultz said on the squad circuit when he heard.

Nobody objected; everyone in third platoon was convinced. Those beings were fanatical fighters with horrible weapons, who attacked for no known reason and never attempted communication.

Most Marines of Company L, however, knew firsthand about one alien sentience, a culture whose existence was kept secret. But *that* sentience's culture, which they'd come across on Avionia, was birdlike, primitive, a thousand years behind human development. It was no threat, and unlikely to ever become one. But the Marines of third platoon had encountered a different sentience, one that *did* attack with neither warning nor reason. The Skinks. And they knew in their bones that they were up against that menace again.

When a wave radiates out from a point and hits something, it reverberates back to everywhere it's already been, but it somehow changes character on the bounce. So it was now. Company L's third platoon took the telling of M Company's firefight and changed it into a fight with Skinks. "Skinks" radiated back through the battalion. And turned to fear.

Kilo Company's rearmost Marines were hyperalert, the last two men in each platoon walking backward to cover their trail—they weren't going to be surprised like M Company. Not to be outdone, the Marines on Kilo Company's left flank were equally alert; they knew that if it was possible, *they'd* hit an enemy unit from the flank. So, uncharacteristically, it was Kilo Company's pointmen who were least alert. The points were slow to recognize as threats the relatively faint, man-sized heat signals their infra shields picked up. By the time one of them remembered that the Skinks were supposed to have a lower body temperature than humans, they were within range.

Again the swamp echoed with the screams of Marines whose flesh was being eaten away. Again steam billowed and rose from mud and wet foliage struck by the plasma bolts of

the Marines' blasters. Once more the darkness of the swamp
was lit by brilliant flashes when plasma bolts struck home.
When it stopped, the Marines found no bodies to show
they'd had an impact on the enemy. Eight Marines from Kilo
Company were down, dead, or hideously wounded.

"Hold where you are," Brigadier Sturgeon ordered Commander van Winkle. He had to evacuate the casualties without losing more Dragons, and he couldn't commit hoppers
for the mission. Not with whoever was in the swamp—he
wasn't yet ready to say they were Skinks—able to kill his
aircraft without warning. What made the situation worse
was that the string-of-pearls satellites weren't providing
the information Sturgeon needed to direct his FIST. The
swamp's canopy was dense enough to block the string-of-
pearls infrared scanning. It picked up his Marines, vaguely,
but didn't show who they were fighting. This was another
datum in favor of Skinks being present; on the ground they
showed up faintly in infrared. Sturgeon was, effectively, operating blind. That blindness was costing Marine lives. It
was time to use his heavy weapons. But where do you shoot
when your target can be hidden anywhere in a large area?

Within minutes the remaining Raptors began using Jericho missiles to clear a path to the infantry battalion's location for Dragons to evacuate the M Company casualties.
Simultaneously, the six guns of the FIST's artillery battery
commenced what was once called "harassment and interdic-
tion" fire to the front and sides of the infantry battalion.
Classic H&I dropped rounds onto routes known or suspected to be used by the enemy to disrupt movement. But
there were no known routes through the Swamp of Perdition,
and the enemy was known to pop up anywhere. The battery
used scatter munitions—rounds that burst open above the
target and scattered large numbers of smaller munitions that
exploded just above the ground. Later, when the infantry
moved out again, the battery would drop delayed action scatter munitions behind the battalion. Those would explode at

random intervals after dropping to the ground, or into the water, or when their built-in motion detectors picked up movement by a man-sized body within the killing radius.

Nobody had any idea of the range of the undetectable weapons that had killed two Raptors and three Dragons, but they hoped they were line of sight. The Raptors stayed behind a row of hills and locked their Jerichos into the string-of-pearls guidance system and fired them into the swamp. Jerichos weren't tactical nukes, but except for the lack of radiation, there wasn't much difference in effect. They were named that because they "brought the walls down." They cleared a half-kilometer-wide swath of swamp of all vegetation and animate life. The barrage stopped only a few hundred meters from the infantry position. The Dragons waited for the temperature in the cleared area to drop to the boiling point of water before they went in. The traumatically dried ground crumbled and crackled under their fans and flew wide in chunks. This time the Dragons carrying the casualties made it back out. Sturgeon ordered the battalion to continue its advance. The artillery battery dropped scatter munitions a safe distance to the front and sides of the infantry.

Corporal Doyle was as frightened as he'd ever been in his life. Check that, he'd *never* been so scared before. Not even when he'd been one of the eight Marines who had to face hordes of fierce warriors on Elneal. That time, nothing seemed to matter because he knew deep inside that he was dead anyway. Besides, he could *see* the hordes of Siad warriors.

Here, though . . . Here he couldn't see anyone. Here, a Skink—they really were Skinks, weren't they?—could be right next to him and he wouldn't know it until the thing popped up and killed him.

M Company had been hit from behind. Doyle knew that. He knew that Kilo Company was hit from the front. He saw a pattern developing—the next attack would happen on Company L's right flank. *He was on the right flank!* That meant the next contact would be on him! And he couldn't and wouldn't see the Skinks until they fired!

Corporal Kerr saw the same pattern. Though he thought the pattern was more happenstance than deliberate, he also expected the next contact to come on the right flank. He was concerned, but not unduly so. His first combat after returning from rehab was against the Skinks on Waygone. He remembered very clearly how the acid from their weapons ate through flesh and bone. But was that more terrible than the plasma bolts fired by the Marines' blasters? Only in kind, not in degree. And their weapons, at least the ones they'd used on Waygone, were short-range—he peered into the swamp—not that the shortness of range mattered much here. The Skinks had been relatively easy to kill—if a blaster hit anywhere on one of them, it went "poof," vaporizing it in a flash of light. As fierce and fanatical fighters as the Skinks were, they weren't hard to beat. The other two companies got hurt as badly as they did because they were surprised by Skinks who were willing to die in their attacks. Third platoon, Kerr was convinced, was more aware of what they were up against and less likely to be taken by surprise.

But what had Kerr concerned was that the Skinks seemed able to sense where the Marines were. He didn't think they saw in the infrared the way the Avionians did, nor did he think their eyes gathered light more efficiently. No, he didn't think it was a visual sense that allowed them to detect the Marines. Neither did he think they used a form of echolocation: they weren't that precise in knowing the Marines' location. The Skinks must have some sort of sixth sense . . .

Kerr shivered.

Lance Corporal Schultz tamped down all thought of who the Skinks were, the hideousness of their weapons, and how they could know where chameleoned Marines were. If he had thought of those things, he would have had to remember how badly the Skinks had shaken him on Waygone. Not that he'd been aware of it at the time; *then* he'd been too busy fighting and staying alive. He hadn't known how badly the Skinks frightened him until Company L was on its way to the quarantined world called Avionia and they were briefed on their mission. When he learned they were on their way to protect aliens from *humans*, his reaction had almost gotten him into serious trouble with Gunny Bass and Top Myer. At that time, he thought all aliens were evil and had to be exterminated. Actual contact with the birdlike sentience on Avionia convinced him otherwise. Or so he thought. Now they were facing Skinks again, and he knew he was up against a fearsome opponent.

Schultz concentrated his awareness on the fact that there were beings in that swamp who wanted him abruptly and violently dead, and if he wanted to remain alive, he had to find and kill them first.

"RIGHT!" The voice that shouted the warning over the platoon circuit was almost drowned out by the *crack-sizzle* of blaster fire that accompanied it.

"Echelon right!" Corporal Kerr shouted. His fire team, still on the point, had continued responsibility for the front even when they faced the danger on their right flank. He dove into the mud under a bush a couple of meters away and swept his blaster from side to side, looking for a target along its barrel as it moved. As he looked he spared a quick glance at his HUD to make sure Doyle was moving to the right of where he'd been. The HUD display showed Doyle taking position almost as sharply as Schultz. Now the three of them were at an angle and could shoot to both the platoon's front and side without having to shoot over each other.

To his right, Kerr heard the cracks of blasters and could see steam rise from blaster strikes on foliage and mud. He thought he saw the fading afterimage of the flash made by a hit Skink.

"Second squad, volley fire, ten meters!" Sergeant Bladon ordered.

Kerr pointed his blaster at a bushy shadow ten meters away, where someone could be hiding, and fired a bolt at it. Steam rose, but there was no answering flash from the bush.

He shifted his aim to the left and fired again. He saw a bolt from Doyle's blaster strike a couple of meters away from his aiming point. Keep it up, Doyle, he thought, you're doing fine.

"Second squad, up five," Bladon ordered. Kerr shifted his aim five meters deeper into the swamp in the disciplined fire pattern the Marines used when they couldn't see what to shoot at.

"Second squad, heads up," Staff Sergeant Hyakowa's voice came over the comm. "Guns are joining you."

"Kerr, I see you," Corporal Stevenson said. "Got you, Chan." The assault squad's second team dropped into place between the two fire teams.

"Where do you want it?" Sergeant Kelly, the assault squad leader, asked.

"Join my volley," Bladon replied. "Second squad, up five."

The bolts from second squad's ten blasters fired deeper into the swamp, but were almost lost to view in the flash-flash-flash of the stream of bolts from the two assault guns as they stitched bolts along the squad's entire front and beyond. There were no answering flares.

"Up five," Bladon ordered.

Twice more they lengthened the range of their volleys without seeing or hearing any indication of a hit foe.

"Cease fire!" came Gunny Bass's command. "Third platoon, cease fire. Report."

"Doyle!" Kerr said.

"H-Here."

"Are you all right?"

"I-I think so."

"How's your batteries?"

"I'm—I'm all right."

"Schultz!"

"Okay. Enough ammo."

"Second fire team, no casualties. Batteries all right."

"Roger, Kerr." The other two fire teams also reported no casualties and sufficient battery power remaining.

"Effect?" Bladon asked.

Kerr hadn't seen sign of damage inflicted on the enemy from his position. Neither had Corporal Chan.

"MacIlargie saw one and shot it before it opened fire," Corporal Linsman reported.

"Hold your position," Bass ordered. "First squad's coming through for a sweep."

A moment later first squad came through second squad's line and advanced into the still-steaming killing zone. When they passed through the steam it blocked them from view, though they maintained constant comm. In fifteen minutes they were back, after finding nothing more than the scorch mark from the Skink MacIlargie had killed.

The battalion's advance resumed.

CHAPTER
FOURTEEN

Lewis Conorado could not sleep. He was thinking about Marta. Always before, their separations had left him missing her and the children terribly for the first few hours. Then, very quickly, he'd be absorbed into the myriad details of commanding his company, and thoughts of his family would sink into the recesses of his consciousness. But this time it was different, because of the anger of their parting, and because there was so little to do on board the *Cambria* to occupy his mind.

The other passengers, it seemed, adjusted quickly to the enforced idleness. Captain Tuit did offer each of them—at their own risk, of course—the opportunity to be placed in stasis for the entire voyage, but all declined. Only the most advanced stasis units were designed to prevent the skeletomuscular problems that sometimes developed after long periods of unconsciousness. The *Cambria*'s units were the old-fashioned kind, designed to stabilize a person who'd experienced severe trauma, and only until definitive medical care was available. None of the passengers on this voyage wanted to risk the months of physical therapy that would be required on Earth to get their atrophied muscles working again. But the *Cambria* carried a vast array of entertainment resources, from physical exercise rooms to virtual reality chambers where her passengers could refight the Battle of Hastings or have sex with anything their fertile imaginations could devise. Most, however, preferred entertaining themselves in the company of their fellow passengers with card games, conversation, tours of the ship's unrestricted areas, and the like.

"The hour is now 3:57 A.M.," a tiny female voice whispered as Conorado wearily turned onto his other side. The onboard computer system, dubbed "Minerva," or "Minnie," by the crew, could sense when the compartment's occupant was awake, but as long as he was physically inside his sleep module, all it would do was softly announce the time. He had considered turning that feature off, but after years of paying very strict attention to the time of day, he realized he'd be uncomfortable not knowing what time it was. He sighed and decided to give up. With a tired groan, Conorado swung his feet onto the floor. As soon as his legs cleared the edge of his bunk, the lights and various utilities went on. "No coffee and turn the music off," he said. The music he'd selected to start each day was "Bonnie Dundee," on the pipes and drums, as once played by the Royal Scots Dragoon Guards.

"Ship's status?" the Minerva asked.

"Not right now." Conorado had set that feature so he would not have to listen to the long recitation of the *Cambria's* operational status. That was required listening for each crew member, but still, when he wanted to know about the ship—which he often did because it was his nature to want to know what was going on around him—all he had to do was ask.

Captain Tuit would be on the bridge, listening to his music and drinking his coffee. Conorado and the old navy man had hit it off immediately, and during the last two weeks they'd spent much time together, reminiscing about past voyages, deployments, and the colorful people they'd known in the Confederation's service. Conorado slipped into his clothing and stepped out of his compartment. As soon as he was through the portal, everything back inside went dead, to lie silent against his return. He turned up the companionway toward the bridge, half a kilometer forward.

A starship in the "night," or the time when most of her crew and passengers would be sleeping, was a fascinating world. He walked slowly along the companionway, savoring the comforting sounds of a vast machine working perfectly.

He stopped suddenly. "When do we reach Siluria, Minnie?" he asked.

"Eight days, standard, Captain Lewis Conorado."

Conorado decided to have some fun with her on the long walk to the bridge. "Are the whatsits and the thingamabobs in order, Minnie?"

"I am sorry, sir, please repeat the question. And, sir? Please call me 'Minerva.' "

Conorado smiled. "What's the price of fish in Denmark, Minnie?"

"Please bear in mind this data is more than one year out of date," Minnie began immediately, "but depending on species and size, the average prices obtained on the Copenhagen market are as follows . . ."

Minnie's voice was soft and feminine and reminded Conorado a bit of Marta. "Thank you," he said when she had finished reeling off the desired information.

"You are welcome, sir. But sir, you asked a question earlier that I was not able to answer for you. Would you please rephrase it so I may be of service to you?"

"Forget it."

"I am sorry, sir, but it is impossible for me to forget anything."

"Okay. When's the last time you got laid, Minnie?" It just popped out.

"I do not understand that question, sir," Minerva responded, a note of perplexity in her voice, "and besides, that was not the one you originally asked."

"I withdraw both questions."

"Thank you so much, sir," she replied. Conorado raised an eyebrow at the response; he thought he heard relief in the damned thing's voice!

Captain Tuit was not in his customary position when Conorado stepped onto the bridge. The only officer present was the systems engineer, Miss Lenfen. "Really, sir," she said as soon as Conorado walked in, "you shouldn't try to confuse Minerva like that."

Conorado mentally kicked himself. He should've known

someone would be monitoring the system. He was embarrassed. "Well, I'm sorry, Miss Lenfen," he smiled, "but I really did want to know when we'll reach Siluria."

Lenfen's cheeks reddened. "Well, I don't mean to sound bitchy, Captain," her cheeks got even redder, "but you know, Minerva's my responsibility and, well, I feel, um, 'proprietary' toward her. Would you like some coffee?"

"Sure. When's Hank, er, Captain Tuit due back?"

Lenfen smiled as she handed Conorado a steaming mug of coffee. "We call him Hank all the time. He's not feeling well and is resting in his stateroom."

"Well, I can't sleep. Mind if I keep you company for a while?" He had not noticed before, but even in her formless jumpsuit, Lenfen was a remarkably pretty woman. "My name is Lewis but I prefer Lew." He held out his hand.

"I'm Jennifer but everyone calls me Jenny." She took his hand.

Her hand in his, Conorado was suddenly and poignantly reminded of his Marta. "Well," he said, squeezing her soft hand briefly and then letting it go, "where are you from?"

Marta Conorado decided to spend a few days in New Oslo. She had not made up her mind what to do about her marriage to Lew. The longer she remained alone in their apartment, the more confused she became. One moment she started to call the flight operations office at Mainside to book herself out on the next Earthbound vessel, but the next instant she wasn't sure she could do it. So she decided to visit New Oslo and forget about everything for a while. The Conorados were not rich by any means, but they had saved, and she could afford to luxuriate for a few days in the finest hotels and restaurants the capital city had to offer. She might even go skiing.

The Family Morale and Recreation office at Mainside had regular flights to New Oslo and other places on Thorsfinni's World, so with little effort Marta was able to book herself out the following morning.

*   *   *

The Trondelag Arms had a nice room available when Marta checked in. She was familiar with New Oslo from when they had lived there. Of the many places the Conorados had been stationed as a family, she liked New Oslo best. The climate, temperate in the summer months, was always bracing, and the 'Finnis, an industrious but fun-loving people, always made good company. Besides, the pace of life in New Oslo was invigorating, everyone intent upon the business of the day, working hard and enjoying it, but then when it came time to relax, they did so vigorously. Just the atmosphere to take her mind off her marital troubles for a while, she thought.

Since her flight arrived in the early afternoon, Marta decided to try a hot bath before dining at her favorite restaurant, the Svalbard. As she soaked she dozed. At one point she thought Lew had come into the room. She awakened with a start. She reflected wryly that she just couldn't get him out of her mind.

The meal was excellent, served with the flair that made the Svalbard one of the prime dining spots in the city.

Outside, she huddled into her furs against the penetrating cold. But she felt warm and content. She had not once thought of Lew during the meal. She started walking back up the street toward her hotel when someone seized her by the arm. Startled, she whirled to see a man, a big man, who began shoving her down the street. His grip tightened and hurt her. She opened her mouth in angry protest.

"Keep quiet and keep moving," the man said in the 'Finni dialect.

During the time she had lived in New Oslo, Marta had picked up quite a bit of the language, but her first reaction to his words, which she understood perfectly, was to blurt out in English, "What the hell . . . ?"

From behind them came shouting. "Halt! Or we will shoot!" Marta assumed it was a police officer. Passersby slipped and slid in the snow to get out of their way, and bystanders shouted and pointed at the pair as they stumbled quickly down the sidewalk and into an alley.

The man only tightened his grip and shoved her along more forcefully. She felt something cold and hard pressed into the flesh just behind her left ear. "Keep moving and keep still," the man said in unaccented English, "or I'll kill you too."

While the City of God sect modeled itself on the Puritans of the seventeenth century, they had no prejudices against the technology of the twenty-fifth century. Entirely the opposite, in fact. The memory of Cotton Mather, one of the most famous of all the American Puritans, was highly revered by the City of God. Mather, a member of the British Royal Society of his day, wrote prolifically on natural science and philosophy and was respected by his non-Puritan contemporaries for his wide-ranging knowledge and active curiosity about the things of the visible world. Subsequent generations came to despise him and Puritanism in general because of what he and they believed about the invisible world, which to Mather and his coreligionists consisted of demons, devils, familiars, and witches, all of which filled the air of New England, whispering into the ears of unsuspecting believers the joys of serving the devil.

While the leaders of the City of God no longer believed in witches, they had a deep and abiding faith in such things as nuclear physics.

The bomb the Army of Zion's team on Siluria had built under the supervision of their leader, Epher Benediction, was a very simple affair but more than capable of rendering the spectacular results he wanted. It was easy to obtain the necessary components on a place like Siluria. That particular device consisted of one kilogram of Plutonium 239 encased in a one-inch-thick sphere or tamper of Uranium 238. The bomb itself was a hollow cylinder containing two elements of fissionable material. Its total weight was a bit more than ten kilograms, or less than twenty-five pounds. Upon detonation, the resulting explosion would be equivalent to thousands of tons of conventional explosive; not much by the standards of the destructive weapons of the day, in fact quite primitive, but set off in the *Cambria*'s propulsion unit, the explosion would light up the night sky of the entire Western Hemisphere of Old Earth. That was what Epher Benediction and his companions wanted.

The five men who were about to sacrifice their lives to destroy the SS *Cambria* boarded her without incident. They carried few bags, but those they did carry were heavy. "We are miners," one named Jesse Gospel told Miss Lenfen, "and we go where the work is, so we're used to carrying all our possessions with us." He smiled broadly through his thick black beard, and Jennifer smiled back warmly. "We have found new jobs on Earth," he concluded. Neither Jennifer nor anyone else on the *Cambria* over the next few days stopped to think that there were no more mining operations on Earth.

CHAPTER
FIFTEEN

For several more hours, the infantry Marines moving deeper into the swamp had no further contact with what nearly all of them by then believed were Skinks. Night fell. Itches that had eased or ceased resumed as new, nocturnal insectoids found their way inside the Marines' uniforms. In the middle distance, night predators stalked and cried, in triumph or frustration. Their prey shrieked death agonies when they were caught, screamed relief or indignation if they escaped.

Commander van Winkle called a halt at sundown. He didn't stop his battalion's advance because his Marines would be blind—their light-gathering shields overcame most of the difficulties of night movement. He stopped because his men were tired and needed to rest. Stopping for the night didn't mean a full bivouac, with everyone in defensive positions and one man in three awake, watching while the others slept. Instead, each of the three companies would have two squads out on patrol. Half of the remaining Marines could sleep while the rest were ready to fight defensively—or go to the aid of the patrols.

"Listen up, second squad," Sergeant Bladon said.

The nine Marines under his command maintained their scattered positions, listening to their squad leader over the squad circuit on their helmet comms. "We've got a short one, we'll only be out there for three hours." Nobody responded with the caveat, "If we don't run into any trouble." They understood that.

"The string-of-pearls picked up something that might be

an anomaly about a klick from here," Bladon continued. "We're going to scope it out."

"Might be an anomaly" was an apt description of the difficulty the string-of-pearls had in detecting and interpreting anything under the swamp's canopy.

"Take a look." Bladon transmitted his HUD map to his squad. Each man examined it in his own display. The map didn't show much; some waterways, their route out and the different route back, a mark for the location of the "might be an anomaly," and three rally points.

The map didn't show paths or animal tracks, didn't show the lesser rills, and the elevation lines were mostly incomplete. There were few landmarks they could use to navigate on. They would be totally dependent on Sergeant Bladon's UPUD, Mark III, to tell them where they were and to find their way back. Nobody liked that—the UPUD communicated with the string-of-pearls, and they knew how much trouble SoP had seeing through the canopy. They were also aware of Gunny Bass's distrust of it, and some of them had been with him when the Mark II had failed. Besides, equipment often failed in hostile environments. And the Swamp of Perdition, with all its water and muck, was definitely a hostile environment.

When he thought they'd had enough time to study the map and its implications, Bladon asked, "Any questions?"

"What's the anomaly?" Doyle asked.

Bladon suppressed a sigh. "We don't know, that's why it's an anomaly. The string-of-pearls saw something that nobody could identify. We're going to find out what it is. Any other questions?" There were none. "Let's move it out."

Without a sound, Schultz rose to his feet and headed out through the company's night perimeter. Everybody knew he'd take the point.

"Me, Chan, Linsman," Bladon said, finishing the patrol route order; he followed second fire team, followed by third, with first bringing up the rear.

They all used their light gatherers; the night was impenetrable without them. Vision was strange, eerie. Distance didn't dim it and there were few deep shadows under foliage; everyplace was equally dark. It affected depth perception—the changes in light intensity and quality that normally gave clues to distance were absent. The ground, what could be seen through the foliage, rippled in shallow swells like the surface of a still ocean. Line of sight was restricted by the denseness of growth; in spots it spiked to forty meters, and was often less than five. The strangeness of vision had little effect on the Marines; all but two of them had combat experience with night vision. Of those two, in Corporal Chan's fire team PFC Longfellow had used the device in Boot Camp training, but that wasn't too far in his past. The one who had trouble with it was Corporal Doyle, whose Boot Camp night-vision training was more than ten years behind him.

Schultz kept the HUD map tacked away in a corner of his vision, and without ever looking directly at it, followed the slowly moving dot that showed Sergeant Bladon's position. As long as the dot was near the line that marked their assigned route, they were close enough on course. Schultz wasn't going to be fanatical about sticking to the route; there were hummocks to go around, thick tangles of growth to bypass, waterways too deep or with bottoms too soft, which needed to be circled. Like any patrol route drawn by someone who hadn't walked the ground, it had stretches that were too difficult or too hazardous. Schultz was cautious and deliberate in his advance.

Mud sucked at their feet, strained to keep them in place, almost like an organism that wanted to hold them, digest them, absorb their nutrients. Prey browsed or foraged closer to a few men than to the entire battalion, predators stalked and cried closer. Water, evaporated from the streams during the day, condensed, slid down twigs and leaves and then plopped to the ground. The night seemed filled with more sounds than during the day. Or maybe the lack of daytime sights caused a subjective increase.

Corporal Doyle was jumpy. All the sounds he didn't understand had him imagining monsters creeping close. Water drops plop-plopped on his helmet like Chinese water torture. His feet *felt* the slime of the mud through his boots. Curiously, he barely noticed the swarming insectoids that had bothered him so much during the day. He kept thinking about the anomaly. Having no idea what it was, it bothered him. Surely *they* had some hint. Was it a structure? Did body heat show up? A heat signature that might indicate an engine of some sort? Was it a blank spot, like the string-of-pearls being blocked? Was it possible to block the multiple sensors and scanners of a string-of-pearls? Surely they knew *something*!

And he couldn't *see* anything! Well, he could *see*, but the light was so strange. It was like walking through a mist with lights coming into it everywhere from so many directions that there was no real point of origin; everything looked exactly the same. Not *exactly* the same—he could distinguish shapes and some colors—but nothing cast shadows, and he couldn't tell where anything was. He had to look at this tree and then past it to that bush and back and at both at the same time to figure out which was closer, which was farther. And then how far away were they and how far from each other? What was going to happen if they got in a firefight and Sergeant Bladon ordered volley fire? How was he supposed to guess how far ten meters was, or twenty or thirty, to put his plasma bolts on line with the others?

Every cry of a night hunter and screech of captured prey made him jump. Small muscles began to twitch involuntarily and his breath came ever more shallow.

If he'd thought it through a little further, Corporal Doyle would have realized that all he had to do with volley fire was aim at a point along the line everyone else was firing on. And if he could see who he was shooting at, he wouldn't have to worry about range because the blaster was a line-of-sight weapon over normal infantry ranges—simply point and shoot and don't worry about making sight adjustments. Besides, as odd as the light might be, he really could see, even better than he could with the unaided eye in the light of swampy day.

They made good time, though the going was difficult. Schultz had to make sure every hollow, every depression he couldn't see into at a distance, was untenanted. He needed to see the back side of every object behind which an enemy could lie in ambush. He had to watch that his footing was firm, that neither he nor the Marines following would slip in loose muck or trod in quicksand. He had to avoid walking on drifted leaves and twigs that might conceal a sinkhole or make unwanted noise. Before entering the water of a rill or stream, he had to assure himself that nobody was opposite, waiting for the Marines to expose themselves. And he couldn't walk through the tangles and sheets of foliage that dangled and dripped from the trees. Somehow, he always found a way that didn't require a path to be hacked or broken.

The HUD showed they were less than fifty meters from the anomaly when Sergeant Bladon called a halt. They were a little more than an hour into the patrol. He spoke softly into his helmet comm.

"Rat, take over. Hammer, you and me take a closer look."

"Aye aye," Corporal Linsman replied, then began his own soft commands to establish a hasty defensive position.

Schultz didn't reply, he simply waited for Bladon to reach him before advancing in a low crouch. The two were crawling by the time they reached their destination. Bladon looked around, checked his HUD, checked the UPUD, looked around again.

"See anything?" he asked.

Schultz grunted softly. He didn't see anything out of what passed for ordinary in the swamp.

After they watched for a few minutes longer, Bladon called in a report. "According to the UPUD, we're at the anomaly. Nothing's here."

"Any marks on the ground to indicate anybody's been there recently?" asked Lieutenant Humphrey, who took the report himself.

"Negative. Looks like nobody's ever been here."

"Set an ambush for half an hour, then come back in."

"Roger," Bladon replied. Then to Schultz, "Let's go." He began to rise to a crouch to head back, stopped when he realized Schultz hadn't moved. "What do you have?"

Schultz didn't reply. Using his infra, Bladon saw Schultz's head slowly rotate, looking around.

Bladon sank back to his knees, one hand on the mud, the other holding his blaster parallel to the ground. He slid his infra into place and scanned his surroundings. No heat signatures showed. He listened and realized it was several minutes since he'd last heard the cries of hunting or hunted animals. He glanced at the UPUD, but it didn't show any movement.

Abruptly, Schultz stood and raised all his shields. He breathed deeply, let the air fill his nostrils, roll across his tongue. He slowly twisted around until he was facing back the way they'd come.

"Skinks," he said, and headed back at a fast walk, gloved hand on his blaster's firing lever.

Bladon didn't ask any questions. If Schultz said there were Skinks behind them, in the direction of the rest of the squad, he wasn't going to doubt him no matter what the UPUD said—Schultz was more likely to be right.

Halfway to the squad's position, Schultz stuck out an arm, and Bladon would have run into it if he hadn't been maintaining proper night movement interval. Schultz slowly swiveled to his right, lowering himself as he did. He raised his left hand and shook it to let the sleeve drop to expose his forearm, then pointed in that direction. Bladon turned to where Schultz pointed and lowered himself to a knee. He looked through his infra.

Twenty meters away, where it formed the apex of an isosceles triangle with him and where he thought the nearest man in the squad was, he picked up a heat signature. It seemed large enough to be a small man, but was too dim for human body temperature.

"Shit," he swore to himself. He'd seen exactly that signature before—on Waygone. It had to be a Skink. He raised his infra and looked through the light gatherer. A Skink was turning, bringing the nozzle of its weapon to bear on him.

"SKINKS!" he shouted, and fired simultaneously.

The Skink flared into vapor. More blasters *crack-sizzled* in the night. His light shield briefly blacked as it was overwhelmed by the flashes of several hit Skinks flaring up.

"Both sides!" Bladon shouted, though he knew his squad was already shooting in all directions. He couldn't see any more Skinks even when he added his magnifier shield to the mix, though he clearly heard their jabbering. He glanced toward Schultz. The big Marine wasn't firing. He slapped his shoulder and the two rose to run to the rest of the squad.

"Coming in!" he shouted. "Kerr, Doyle, it's us!" Then they were with the squad.

"Report!"

Linsman reported that Lance Corporal Rodamour had been splashed by a stream from a Skink weapon, but it was minor and he'd already dug out the acid that was eating into his side. Miraculously, nobody else was injured. The Marines kept up their fire while the reports came in. Their fire was met by more flares from hit Skinks.

One voice rose above the general jabbering that encircled second squad and a whistle sounded. The jabbering cut off, and the only sounds were those of fleeing bodies crashing through brush.

"Where the hell did they come from?"

"Damned if I know," Linsman replied. "We didn't even know they were there until you yelled." He sounded shaken.

Bladon called in his report.

"How many did you get?" Humphrey asked after Bladon told him of his one minor casualty.

"I'm not sure. I saw at least eight or ten flashes."

"Any point in looking for bodies?"

Bladon barked a laugh. Lieutenant Humphrey hadn't been on Waygone, he'd only heard about how even a glancing hit from a plasma bolt made a Skink flash into vapor. Bladon had seen that happen himself.

"None," he replied.

"Right," Humphrey said, almost chagrined that he'd asked such a dumb question. "Return right now."

"Assigned route?"

Humphrey considered the question for a second. "Assigned route," he confirmed. The artillery battery had fires plotted along that route. If second squad needed help on the way back, they could get it.

Probing attacks began around the battalion perimeter while second squad was returning. They were only a hundred meters away when Schultz yelled "SKINKS!" as he dove into the mud and rolled to the side.

A stream of greenish fluid shot through the air where he'd been and just missed Doyle, who toppled to his side as the acid shot past. Kerr leaped forward and landed between Schultz and Doyle in time to see Schultz flare the Skink who'd shot at him.

Kerr saw a faint smear of red in his infra and snapped a bolt at it. A Skink vaporized. More faint smears of red showed up. "Right front!" he said on the squad circuit, and flashed another Skink. On his right he sensed Schultz methodically firing. "Doyle, take them out!" he ordered.

"Where are they? I can't see anything."

"Use your infra. If you don't see a target, fire randomly!"

Doyle began firing randomly to his right front as he slid his infra into place. A bright flash greeted one of his shots and he stopped shooting. "I got one!"

"Keep shooting, there's more where that one came from."

"Oh." Doyle resumed shooting.

Harsh barking sounded to their right front, like a commander issuing orders, organizing his men. Plasma bolts from the Marines in the company perimeter sizzled low overhead.

"Second squad, pull back," Bladon ordered. The bolts from the perimeter were too close and they were in danger of being shot by their own people. "There's a hollow about twenty meters back—head for it."

Still prone, still firing, the ten Marines began crawling backward. Bladon turned around and headed straight for the dip so he could guide his men. It wasn't much shelter, just deep enough to get their torsos below the level of the surrounding mud. It was bottomed with a few inches of water. He used all three shields to see his men and tell them in what direction to crawl. He grabbed the men when they got close and pulled them in.

Corporal Chan was the last one in. He dragged Watson with him. Lance Corporal Watson was dead, hit squarely by two streams of acid.

"Anyone else hit?" Bladon wanted to know.

Again, almost miraculously, nobody else was wounded.

"We must have come up behind them," Bladon said, "and caught them by surprise."

Kerr wondered about that. The Skink that first shot at Schultz was, what, fifteen meters away before it fired? Maybe whatever told the Skinks where the Marines were wasn't as sensitive as he'd thought. Did it have severe distance limitations? The range of the sense had to be more than fifteen meters. On Waygone the Skinks had shot at them at night from thirty or forty meters and come close enough to cause casualties. No human could shoot at a chameleoned Marine at night and consistently hit that close unless he was using an infra. Maybe the Skink had to hold off until it had a sight line?

Kerr stopped thinking about it long enough to snap off a round at a smear of red that showed in his infra. Instantly, the nine Marines in the hollow opened fire. Three flashes brightened the night as three Skinks vaporized.

The roughly circular hollow was only ten meters or so in diameter, the Marines dangerously bunched along its lip. One good spray from the flank would hit most of them.

"Third fire team, move to the right flank," Bladon ordered. "First fire team, left flank, put someone on our rear. Second team, spread out!"

The Marines crab-crawled, firing as they scuttled. They were still too close together, but one lucky spray wouldn't hit as many of them, and the flanks and rear were covered. Fire continued from the company perimeter. The bolts that made it as far as the hollow were high enough that second squad wasn't in immediate danger from them. Harsh voices shouted above the *crack-sizzle* of the blaster fire and the jabbering of the Skinks. It sounded like they were getting organized for an assault on the hollow. Bladon looked at the UPUD. It showed large numbers of bodies moving around the hollow. He called in a situation report.

Lieutenant Humphrey signed off after getting Sergeant Bladon's report and called out on the company command circuit.

"Bladon thinks they're organizing to overrun his squad," Humphrey told his platoon commanders and platoon sergeants. They could all hear firing and the Skink voices. Heavy fire sounded from the positions of the other two companies, but the only shooting Company L was doing was in the direction of third platoon's second squad. The Skink voices were all in that direction, and sounded closer to the isolated squad than to the perimeter. "We have to send someone out there to help them."

"Those are my people, Skipper," Gunnery Sergeant Bass said immediately. "I have to go."

"Charlie, you only have one blaster squad and your gun squad. That's not enough, we don't know how many of them are between us and your squad."

"It's enough if we hit them fast and hard. They probably won't expect us. We can break through and bring my people back before they can organize to do anything about us."

"Skipper," interjected Lieutenant Rokmonov, the assault platoon commander, "I've got a very pissed-off section leader breathing down my neck. He wants to take a squad outside the perimeter and raise some hell."

"That would give me a lot more fire power than a full-strength blaster platoon," Bass added before Humphrey could nix the idea.

There wasn't time for further discussion, and Humphrey was reluctant to pull a platoon from a different part of the perimeter.

"Do it," he ordered. "Rokmonov, place a section to cover third platoon's sector."

It only took two minutes for third platoon to get ready for its rush and for Staff Sergeant daCruz to arrive with a squad from his section. Fire and voices rose toward a crescendo at second squad's position.

Bass made sure the assault squad with its heavy gun was on the platoon circuit, then gave the order. "Nothing fancy, people, this is a roundhouse blow. We go out at the double and don't stop for anything. Hold your fire for my command unless you see a target. Kill anyone and anything that isn't a Marine. Ready?" He didn't ask for questions. "Let's go!"

Twenty-four Marines ran on line toward second squad's position. The rate of fire and the alien shouts there were furious. As he ran, Bass radioed to Bladon that they were on their way. He no sooner said that than a swarm of dim red smears showed on his infra.

"THIRD PLATOON, FIRE!" he shouted loud enough that he didn't need his helmet comm. "Second squad, get down!" He opened fire.

The assault squad set up its gun and fired into the midst of the Skinks massed before second squad's hollow. The night lit up with the flashes of so many dying Skinks, the Marines had to raise their light gatherers. The *crack-sizzle* of blasters combined with the whine of the assault gun to drown out all other noises.

"Second squad, on me!" Bass shouted as he flared three charging Skinks before they could get off shots of their own.

"Squad leaders, make sure you've got everybody, then withdraw," Bass ordered as soon as second squad joined him. He didn't comment on the body his infra showed one Marine carrying, or the irregular gaits of several of the others.

"On the double, people; Mama doesn't want us staying out all night."

They ran.

*   *   *

"Oh, man, did you see that?" Lance Corporal Claypoole said excitedly. "It was like a fireworks show out there! Our weapons were the Roman candles and their flashes were the bursting stars!" His adrenaline was still pumping.

Lance Corporal Dean just stared at him. It had been horrendous. There were so many Skinks out there that if third platoon hadn't caught them by such complete surprise, the slaughter would have gone the other way. His adrenaline had stopped pumping and he was feeling the letdown.

"You're lucky you're not in my fire team," Corporal Pasquin snarled.

"What do you mean?" Claypoole asked, grinning.

"You're so damn dumb that if you were in my fire team I'd just have to smack you upside the head. You're not, so I can't. That's Corporal Dornhofer's job." Pasquin reached out and thumped the back of Dean's helmet.

"Ow! Wha'd you hit me for?" Dean yelped.

"Because you're listening to that dumb turd. Besides, you're mine and I'm allowed to."

"Good thing you didn't hit my favorite turd, Pasquin," Dornhofer snarled as he rapped his knuckles against Claypoole's helmet. "I'd have to hurt you bad if you did."

Pasquin laughed. "Yeah? You and what army?"

Dornhofer leaned close, jutting his jaw. "Ain't nothing no damn army can do a Marine corporal worth his salt can't do better by his lonesome."

"Now now, children," said Sergeant Ratliff, first squad leader, "play nice or you don't get any cookies with your bedtime milk."

The two corporals looked at him indignantly, then leaned in close together.

"One of these days we have to do something about him," Dornhofer whispered.

"Yeah," Pasquin whispered back. "Sergeants. Promote a corporal to sergeant and he looses all humanity. They need to be taught some humility once in a while."

PFC Godenov, the third man in Pasquin's fire team,

laughed to himself through the entire exchange. PFC Hayes, Dornhofer's third man, on only his second deployment and in his first real combat, looked on wide-eyed.

The mood in second squad wasn't so high. Watson was dead, and Linsman, Rodamour, and Kerr had wounds. Longfellow needed to be evacuated. The corpsmen wanted to evacuate Schultz, but the big man leveled his blaster at them and told them it was his arm, not a leg, he could walk, so patch him up well enough to stay with the squad. The corpsmen complied. They knew Schultz would respond to the battalion surgeon the same way, so there wasn't any point in sending him to the battalion aid station.

Fighting continued around the perimeters of the other two companies, but Company L's area was quiet.

"I think your second squad broke up an assault on us," Top Myer said. He sipped the steaming caf he was sharing with the third platoon commander in the company command post. Bass had already debriefed on second squad's patrol and his own rescue mission.

Gunny Bass listened to the fighting around the other two companies. "I think you're right," he agreed. "That's one reason we send patrols out when we're in night positions." He blew on his caf and wished again that Myer hadn't served so much time on ship's complement—he'd gotten used to navy coffee and brewed his own the same way. As near as Bass was able to figure out, the navy made coffee from the sludge that remained behind after they scrubbed old paint from their ships.

"Gutsy thing you did then, charging out there with an understrength platoon."

"They're my people, Top. No way I could abandon them."

Myer nodded. That was a big part of what made Charlie Bass such a good commander—he took care of his people. The Corps needed more officers like that. Now if only he could convince him to accept a commission.

"Just because they aren't hitting us now doesn't mean they're not going to later," Myer said.

"Got that right. I'll make sure my people are ready." Bass poured out the dregs of his caf and left the company command post.

Myer stared at the space Bass had just occupied and sipped at his caf. Yes indeed, that Charlie Bass would make a fine FIST commander someday. If only he'd let the Corps turn him into an officer.

CHAPTER
SIXTEEN

Lew Conorado considered the five men who boarded the *Cambria* at Siluria a bit odd but not so out of the ordinary that he had reason to think them suspicious. They just did not act like miners. It was his experience that men who made their living in danger's way were garrulous and lived hard when off duty. Such men were loud, raw, and earthy, like Marines. These men were not like that. They spoke politely when spoken to but never initiated a conversation and kept largely to themselves.

That the miners were religious men was evident at the first meal served in the common dining area. They sat together in a far corner of the galley and before they ate their simple meal, held hands as they said grace over their food. The antique ritual caused some brief comment among the other diners at first, but by the second day the other passengers had taken to ignoring the five strangers, which seemed to suit the five just fine.

It took several days to load the *Cambria*'s holds. Conorado spent much of the time on the bridge, observing the operations. Hundreds of lighters soared up from the planet's surface to unload cargo into the ship's yawning bays. The passengers were allowed to visit Siluria's surface if they wanted to, but Conorado was content to stay on board. Besides, the crew, especially its young systems engineer, Jennifer Lenfen, were required to remain at their stations until the loading was completed, and Conorado felt a need to be near her.

Their chance meeting on the bridge that night before the

ship reached Siluria had developed into a sort of friendship. They had even taken to eating their meals together when Jennifer was off duty. The more time he spent with the young technician, the more he liked her. Besides, when he was with her, his own problems, marital and official, receded a bit and he was actually able to relax and enjoy himself.

"I wanted to join the navy after college," she told him at lunch the second day after making the jump into hyperspace from Siluria, "but my family is not very well off. This job pays more, and between contracts I have plenty of time to spend with my folks and sisters and brothers."

"How many in your family?" Conorado asked.

"Nine of us. I'm number seven." Conorado raised an eyebrow and said something about how he'd have liked to have had a family that size.

"Well," she responded, "old traditions die slowly. The Chinese have always favored large families, especially if the kids are boys. But I haven't done badly for a girl."

"Where do you come from?"

"My ancestors were among the original settlers on T'ai Chung at the end of the last century, but I got my engineering and computer science degrees at M'Jumba University on Carhart's World."

Conorado smiled. "I don't know T'ai Chung, probably because you don't have any need for a Marine expeditionary force there, which is just as well. M'Jumba's a good school, I've heard. A professor of history there helped us out once with some badly needed advice. It was on the Diamundian Incursion. Do you know about that operation?"

"I remember reading about it. Who was the professor?"

"Jere . . . Jere . . ."

"Benjamin! Yes, I had him for an elective course!" She sat up and snapped her fingers. "Old Jere Benjamin! Golly, he was a character! But could he teach! We all loved the old bird. What's he doing now?"

Conorado hesitated a moment. "He passed away, Jenny," he answered softly. At the look of real sorrow that crossed the young technician's face, Conorado wished he'd lied and said he didn't know what had happened to the professor. "Well, there was heavy fighting on Diamunde, and unfortunately Professor Benjamin was killed. It was quick and he really was a brave man, Jenny, as brave as any of my Marines." He was not about to tell her that Professor Benjamin had been tortured to death by Marston St. Cyr. "I'm really sorry, Jenny, I wish—"

"Oh," she sighed, "that's okay, Lew. It was just unexpected news, that's all. Besides, who'd ever have thought the two of us would meet like this and that we'd have these common points of interest?" She was quiet for a moment and then brightened again. "Say, Lew! Have you gone on a tour of the ship yet? I'm scheduled to take some of the diplomatic personnel out tomorrow. Would you like to come along?"

"Not only yes, but hell, yes! as we say in the Corps! You just tell me when and where and what the uniform is and I'll be there!"

Jennifer laid a hand softly on Conorado's forearm, "Lew, I want you to come along, and thanks for taking the time to sit with me and talk like this." She wanted to rush on and say something awkward like, "I've never met a man like you before!" but she was not that stupid. "We're assembling on the bridge at four hours tomorrow."

Conorado laughed. He had almost blurted out what he was really thinking: that he couldn't think of anyone he'd rather take a tour of the ship with than Jennifer Lenfen. But he would never embarrass a woman like Jennifer. Instead he said, "I have nothing else on my schedule for tomorrow that can't be moved to another day. I'll wear my utilities."

Conorado whistled softly as he walked back to his stateroom. This trip to perdition—or whatever fate awaited him back on Earth—was not turning out to be half as bad as he'd anticipated.

A car was waiting about a hundred meters up the alley.

"Who are you?" the man asked as he shoved Marta along.

"My name is Conorado and I am the wife of a Confederation Marine officer," she answered. "And who are you?"

"Ah?" the man responded. "That is excellent! Excellent!" He pushed her toward the car but did not give his own name. The foul stink of the vehicle's internal combustion engine brought tears to Marta's eyes and she began to cough. The driver shoved open the rear door from inside. From the main street behind them several men appeared, running, weapons drawn.

"Halt or we shoot!" one yelled in Norse.

"You shoot, I kill the woman! She is the wife of a Confederation Marine officer," the big man yelled back. Holding Marta firmly by the hair, he twisted her around so the policemen could see her face before he roughly shoved her into the back of the car. He slid in beside her. Looking out the back window, Marta saw the police hesitate for a moment and then run quickly back out into the main street. The driver gunned the engine, and they were off down the alleyway before the doors were fully closed.

"Did you get him?" the driver asked as she guided the vehicle out of the alley into another main thoroughfare and directly into a heavy stream of traffic. Despite the squealing of brakes and desperate maneuvering of the other drivers, she weaved in and out of the traffic expertly. She saw an opening and raced for it, pressing her passengers into the backseat as the car accelerated.

"I got him, but he wasn't alone. There were people with him."

"Goddamnit, Bengt! Did they recognize you?"

"No. I wore the mask."

"Who's the woman?"

It was clear to Marta that he'd not planned to take a hostage after whatever it was he'd done. He just snatched the first vulnerable person he'd seen on the street. "I am Marta Conorado, wife of Captain Lewis Conorado, Confederation Marine Corps!" she shouted over the roar of the car's laboring engine. "It's just my luck," she added in Norse, "to be kidnapped by a couple of morons who can't even pull off a—a—job without fucking it up!"

"Oh?" the man called Bengt responded as he shoved the gun into her ribs and fired.

Jennifer Lenfen was surprised so many of the passengers showed up for her tour of the *Cambria*. All five of the grim men who'd boarded at Siluria were there, as well as Jamison Franks and several of his staff, including James Palmita, who never took his eyes off her. None of the others seemed to notice or care, so it was with a sense of relief that she went to stand beside Lew Conorado when he finally showed up.

"Gentlemen," she began, "welcome to the bridge of the starship *Cambria*. I am going to introduce you to the crew on duty up here and explain how the bridge of a starship operates. Then we will tour the ship. Along the way you'll meet other members of our crew. Please get to know them. Every one of us is dedicated to serving you while you are a passenger on this vessel."

"You can 'serve' me anytime, baby," Palmita muttered.

The five miners seemed particularly interested as Jennifer explained the workings of the bridge. She was surprised at how intelligent their questions were and gratified by the interest they expressed when she explained her own responsibilities. She had no way to know, but one of the miners, who introduced himself as Epher Gospel, actually knew quite a bit about starship navigation, and another, Lordsday Sabbath, was, like Jennifer, a computer systems engineer.

"Miss," one of the miners said, "we had the obligatory emergency evacuation orientation when we came aboard, but would it be possible to see one of the lifecraft on our tour today?"

Jennifer was caught off guard by the question. "Well, yes, sir, we can, we can, but you know, spaceway regulations only require that passengers be briefed on a ship's evacuation plan. The crew is responsible for the lifecraft, and it is not necessary that you even see one for us to get you inside in the most unlikely event—I assure you—that they are needed. Even if we were holed many times for whatever the cause, the *Cambria* has a self-sealing system that can immediately—"

"Yes, miss, I understand that, but just curious. I would just like to peek inside a lifecraft." Several of his companions nodded their agreement.

"Yeah, Jenny," Palmita added with a grin, "let's you and me climb inside one of those things and make a breakaway."

Jennifer studiously ignored Palmita. The grin quickly faded from his face at the glare Conorado gave him.

"Gentlemen," she addressed the miners, "certainly we'll take a look inside one of our lifecraft. Now, are we ready to board shuttles and visit the first of the *Cambria*'s five cargo modules? They are all full of the ore we loaded on Siluria, over one million metric tons of it, destined for the refineries of Luna. We will conclude the tour at the propulsion plant. All told, it will take us about five hours to make the circuit." She clapped her hands eagerly. "Is everyone ready?" she asked. Conorado smiled. She was acting just like an activity director on a cruise ship, inviting everyone to a game of shuffleboard.

"Lead on, Miss Lenfen, and damned be he who cries, 'Hold, enough!' " Jamison Franks III said with a dramatic flourish and a bow.

Palmita laughed. "I got up real early this morning, just for you, Jenny."

Colonel Ramadan unglued his eyes and looked at the time: 0315 hours! "Goddamn," he muttered as he punched the comm unit. "Ramadan here."

"Sir, Ensign Joannides, staff duty officer, naval district HQ. Sorry to wake you up, but top priority message from New Oslo, a relay from the embassy. You'll need your visuals."

Ramadan punched a button and the ensign's image appeared on his screen. "Who's it from, Ensign?"

Ensign Joannides hesitated a moment. "Well, it's the chief

of the New Oslo police department, sir. Looks like one of your dependents has been, er, kidnapped."

"Put him on."

The image of a middle-aged man appeared on the tiny screen beside Ramadan's bed. "Agder Vest, here, Colonel, chief of the New Oslo police department. I apologize for waking you at dis hour, sir." Vest's prematurely gray hair was closely cropped, as was the moustache that graced his upper lip. He had the face of a man who had spent much time out of doors, and a chin that jutted forward, projecting the image of a man familiar with the exercise of authority.

"What's up, Chief?"

"May I show you a picture one of my men took just a few hours ago?" A picture of a woman, blurry at first but quickly resolving into the unmistakable image of Marta Conorado, filled the screen.

"That is Marta Conorado, the wife of one of my company commanders. Is she all right?" Ramadan asked.

"As far as ve know right now, yes, Colonel. But I have the unfortunate duty to report to you, sir, dat she has evidently been kidnapped. Iss eder her husband or family available?"

"Her husband's on deployment right now, Chief, and their kids are also in the service. What can I do to help?"

"Can you come to New Oslo, den?"

"I'll be there as quickly as a flight can be arranged. Chief, I have to talk to the navy now."

"Ve vill be waiting. I vill gif you a full briefing when you get here. But for right now, a man committed a murder here and took Mrs. Conorado as his hostage. Ve vill get her back, Colonel, and thank you."

The face of Ensign Joannides immediately replaced Chief Vest's image. "Ensign, patch me through to the admiral."

Joannides hesitated. "Right now, sir?" he asked.

So typical of the squids, Ramadan thought: wake up a Marine anytime, but the navy brass needed its sleep. "Yes, Ensign, right goddamned now. Oh, Ensign, one more thing. Find out which medical clinic Mrs. Conorado used. I'll need both her health and dental records."

*   *   *

Whatever Bengt had shot into Marta, it was not fatal. She slumped in her seat, totally paralyzed and half comatose. She was aware of the movements of the landcar as it sped along, and she could hear her captors talking, but the words made no sense to her. Gradually, feeling began to creep back into her extremities, and at the same time her head began to clear. From the way the car bounced and jerked, they had to be traveling over an unimproved road, but she could not sit upright and look out the window because her hands and feet were securely tied. She began to cough spasmodically.

"Ah, the Marine wife is back with us!" Bengt exclaimed. "You are very lucky, madam, that I did not fire the wrong chamber into you back there. Otherwise—poof! No more hostage!"

"Wh-Where are we?" Marta managed to croak.

"Well, we are far, far from New Oslo, and thanks to my dear Kiruna, we have successfully eluded the police. We are taking you to a safe place, from which we will make a successful escape to a hideaway in the southern hemisphere. You will not accompany us, unfortunately."

"Kill her now and get it over with," Kiruna said from the driver's module. She turned and looked at Marta. Her skin was very white and she had strikingly blue eyes. Her closely cropped hair was so pale it looked white in the dim light—night was coming on—and it framed a sharp face with high cheekbones and a small mouth.

"Not yet, my dear. We may still need this beautiful lady." Bengt stroked Marta's hair. That brought a snarl from the driver. Bengt quickly removed his hand.

Marta calculated. It had been a good two hours before sunset when she left the restaurant. She had checked her watch. They'd been driving at a rapid pace, and at a hundred kilometers an hour average speed, that would put them some distance from the city. But what direction? She tried to call up in her memory a map of the surrounding terrain. Her ears popped. North! They had to have driven north, which would put them deep into the Thorvald Mountains! Some of the peaks were over three thousand meters high, she recalled, and except for a few resort villages, the range was largely uninhabited. The slopes of the mountains were also heavily forested. The pair must have some kind of aircraft hidden away somewhere they were going to use to escape.

At last the car came to a stop. Bengt got out and with one arm pulled Marta bodily outside. It was snowing and it was cold. As he dragged her out of the car, her expensive new coat snagged on something and ripped. Her head banged against the door frame and then she was lying in snow half a meter deep. Bengt began dragging her still-bound body through the snow. Marta realized she wasn't dressed to escape in such weather. Cold snow packed itself between her neck and the collar of her coat as Bengt dragged her along. He dragged her up some steps, they paused, a door opened, and he threw her inside an unheated room. Bengt slammed the door behind them and began fiddling with the unit's power console.

As Marta lay there, sensation and full consciousness gradually returned and she began taking stock of her surroundings. The room was bare except for a few chairs and closets or storage compartments built into its walls. The floor was of wood and the walls were paneled in wood, giving the room a rustic look. Marta assumed it was a hunting lodge of some sort.

The door banged open, allowing a swirl of ice cold air into the cabin. Kiruna stomped in, cursing.

"Is the car well-hidden?"

Kiruna only snorted. "You should have left the power on," she told Bengt as she took off her parka.

"I told you, I wanted the place to look deserted while we were away. It'll only take a few minutes to warm it up."

"The snow is falling very hard now and there is a wind. Our tracks are almost covered, and with the car in the shed, it will be impossible for anyone to spot us."

"Good," Bengt replied. He took off his parka and threw it into one of the chairs. He opened a closet, and a small wet bar emerged from its recesses. "Let us refresh ourselves," he said.

Marta was able to follow most of their conversation. Bengt and Kiruna toasted one another and then embraced and kissed long and passionately. Kiruna glanced at Marta over Bengt's shoulder. "Kill her now," she said, nodding at Marta.

"Not quite yet, my dear. We may still need her."

"Well," Marta replied from where she lay on the floor, "since you're going to kill me anyway, would you mind telling me what it is you did? And how about at least untying my legs and letting me sit up instead of keeping me on the floor like this?"

Bengt shrugged, untangled himself from Kiruna's embrace and bent over Marta. "There was this businessman, a baron of the fishing industries, who someone wanted out of the way. Kiruna and I take care of such matters." He produced a knife and cut the bonds about her feet, lifted her up and set her into a chair. "It was just your very bad luck you were in the wrong place and that my target was not alone, as he was supposed to be."

Marta's hands had been tied in front of her. She braced herself on the arms of her chair, tensed her abdomen and kicked Bengt in the groin. He staggered back with an "Ooof!" then stepped in quickly between her legs and, holding her still bound arms with one hand, jabbed the blade of the knife into her left nostril and sliced it open. He stepped back quickly, breathing hard. "I like a feisty woman," he said in English. Marta was too stunned to resist further as Bengt retied her feet. "You are too good to waste," Bengt said in English, "so before you die, I am going to put you to good use. And, Mrs. Marine, give me any more trouble and you will die most slowly, I promise."

"What did you say? What did you say?" Kiruna shouted.

"I told her that tomorrow we will kill her," Bengt lied.

Blood dribbled down across Marta's mouth and dripped from her chin. Despite the burning pain and humiliation, she realized Kiruna could not understand English and that Bengt didn't want her to know what he had just said. Even in her pain and desperation, Marta Conorado realized that fact might somehow be used to her advantage.

The *Cambria*'s cargo holds were a fascinating place, cavernous even when filled to capacity. The cargo bulkheads loomed over the tourists, who filed gingerly along the narrow companionways between them, dwarfed and awed by their size and the knowledge that thousands of tons of raw ore sat poised behind the thin steel bulkheads. From inside the compartments came an occasional rumble as tons of ore shifted position in the artificial gravity, adding a deep bass to the constant creaks and pop and ping as the metal adjusted to changes in the ship's attitude and temperature. The *Cambria*'s gyroscopic and ventilating systems worked quite well, but no system yet devised could possibly maintain a uniform temperature throughout such a vast expanse as the ship's cargo holds.

The tourists all wore water-repellent gear to protect them from the constant drizzle and the occasional actual rainfall that formed from condensation up high near the "roofs" of the bays. "The environment is a lot drier in the propulsion unit aft," Jennifer told her guests, "so please bear with the weather until we get there. Over here," she turned to one of the miners, "is one of our lifecraft. Would you like to look inside?"

Conorado and one of the miners followed Jennifer inside. She was explaining the operation of the unit to them when someone outside asked a question. "Excuse me, I'll be right back," she said.

There were thirteen lifecraft onboard the *Cambria*. Each had a capacity of ten people. That provided emergency escape vehicles for the ship's crew, a full load of passengers, plus two additional craft for insurance against breakdowns and damage to any of the other craft. While none of the craft had Beamspace capability, each could support its passengers for months and each was equipped with several hyperspace drones that could be dispatched to report its location to rescuers or other ships under way. The immutable law of the spaceways, as on the high seas of Earth in the days of maritime navigation, was that any ship learning another was in distress had to go to its aid.

As Conorado admired the interior of the lifecraft, he did not notice the miner placing a small, buttonlike object on the pilot's console.

"Hope we never have to use these," Conorado said to the miner.

The miner smiled. "I am sure we won't," he said. Within the hour the small object, which contained a highly corrosive substance, would completely and quietly destroy the craft's controls. He carried enough of the devices to cripple the remaining twelve vehicles. By the time the tour was over there would be no escape from the doomed starship.

Suddenly, from somewhere outside, there came the sound of raised and angry voices. Conorado glanced at the miner, who shrugged. Then he recognized Jennifer's voice, although he couldn't make out what she was saying. She cried out in pain. Conorado flung himself through the lifecraft's portal into the companionway. In the dim light he could not see any of the other passengers.

"Conflict! There is human conflict in the ship!" Minerva bellowed. "There is conflict in sector . . ." Conorado did not pay any attention to the rest of the warning. He ran toward the noise of scuffling and heavy breathing coming from an inspection station just down the companionway, in the forward direction of the ship. Inside the recess, Palmita, one hand caressing Jennifer's buttocks, had her against the bulkhead and was pressing his lips tightly against her cheek. Conorado hit him on the side of his head with the full force of his fist.

Dazed but not down, Palmita released Jennifer and staggered into the companionway. Freed from Palmita's grasp, Jennifer slumped against the bulkhead. Conorado stepped in and braced her. "Lew," she gasped, "that—that bastard!" At that point Palmita danced in and drove his fist hard into

Conorado's left kidney. Holding on to Jennifer, Conorado sank to his knees, wracked by pain so intense he thought he'd vomit.

"Okay, bellhop! Come on, come on, let's have it out! Right here! Right now!" Palmita danced lightly on his feet in the center of the companionway. A thin stream of blood dripped down his left cheek from the blow Conorado had given him, but it did not appear to be bothering him. He was young, he was lithe, and he was in good condition.

Conorado discovered very quickly that the man could fight. Warily, still in great pain, Conorado straightened up. Palmita whirled in and delivered several blows and kicks, one opening a cut above Conorado's right eye and the other to his midsection, which doubled him up again. Palmita danced back lightly, like a prizefighter, "Come on, come on, lover boy! Get up and get some more!"

"Conflict! Human conflict!" Minerva blared.

Lewis Conorado knew three basic things about hand-to-hand: get your opponent on the ground, never let him get on your back, and fight dirty. Palmita was proving deadly, but only because Conorado had been trying to fight back by the same rules. He rushed Palmita, grabbed him around the waist, and shoved him back along the companionway. Palmita pedaled desperately to keep his balance while raining chops to the back and sides of Conorado's head, but he went down with a crash and Conorado was on top. He grabbed Palmita's hair with his right hand and smashed the back of his head on the deck plating so hard he scraped his own knuckles. Then he gouged the thumb of his left hand into Palmita's right eye while squeezing him as tightly with his legs as he could. Palmita flailed and screamed as Conorado's hands turned red with his blood.

"Stop this at once! Stop it! I order you, stop this!" Ambassador Franks shouted. He and the rest of the tourists stood filling the companionway aft, gawking at the pair. One of the 'Finnis, a big man with a tobacco-stained yellow beard, grinned fiercely and nodded his head in approval.

"He tried to rape me," Jennifer said, stepping up to the ambassador.

Franks thought she meant Conorado had assaulted her. "Captain! I am going to ask Captain Tuit to put you under arrest! What kind of a man—"

"No, goddamnit! It was him! It was that goddamned Palmita, not Captain Conorado!" Jennifer shouted, pointing a rigid finger at the diplomatic officer, who now stood panting, one hand over his bloodied eye.

"Sir, I was only trying to kiss her! I thought she liked me! Then all this screaming," Palmita shouted.

"Well . . ."

"Excuse me." The miner who'd been with Conorado in the lifecraft stepped up. "I am Epher Benediction. The captain is right. I saw the whole thing. This man was forcing his attentions upon the young lady."

"Well . . ." Franks began. "Well, ahem! Miss, if you wish to make a formal complaint against Mr. Palmita—"

"Just keep the sonofabitch away from me the rest of this voyage," Jennifer hissed.

"Well, then, I suggest these gentlemen see to their wounds and we call the tour off for now and return to our quarters."

"Just a minute, sir," Conorado interjected, glaring at Ambassador Franks. "You wanted to put me in irons when you thought I'd assaulted Miss Lenfen, but now that it's your man in the dock all you want to do is call off the tour? I say what's good for me is good for him too."

"Captain, this matter is concluded," Franks answered, and turned to go.

Conorado laid a restraining hand on the ambassador's shoulder. "Not so quick; I have something more to say to you."

"Get your hand off of me, sir!" Franks said.

Conorado pointed at Palmita with a forefinger and then he waved it under the ambassador's nose. "You're not in my chain of command, Ambassador. Both of you listen to me. Carefully. If that man over there ever tries anything like this again, if he even *says* anything to Miss Lenfen, I will perform a radical operation on him that will not even leave enough meat for him to jerk off with. Do you understand me? And then I'll make *personal* inquiries into the effectiveness of his chain of command."

"Awriiight, belay all that nonsense down there," Captain Tuit broke in. "You two see to your wounds and then report to me on the bridge. You too, Lenfen, and you also, Mr. Benediction. Anybody goes to the brig on this ship, it'll be on my order, and since we haven't got a brig, I'll put all of yer asses in stasis the rest of this voyage and then when we get to Earth you can forget about kissing and learn how to walk all over again. For the rest of you, I apologize. We'll arrange to continue your tour another time."

The passengers filed on by Conorado, some patting him on the shoulder as they passed. He and Jennifer stood there for a moment before following them.

"Captain." It was the miner who called himself Epher Benediction. He stood there extending his hand. "You are a brave and honorable man. The Bible teaches us that courage and honor are valuable qualities. The Lord shall welcome a man like you."

"Thanks, Epher." They shook hands warmly. "But forgive me, I hope the Lord will keep me around a while longer." Conorado grinned.

"Only the Lord knows the day of our death." Epher grinned back. Under other circumstances, Conorado would have found that grin very disturbing.

CHAPTER
SEVENTEEN

All fighting stopped a couple of hours before dawn. Brigadier Sturgeon didn't go to sleep with the coming of quiet, though; he stayed in contact with his battalion and squadron commanders and kept his F2 and F3 shops busy analyzing incoming data from the string-of-pearls, planning what to do next. At daybreak he had the squadron's Raptors once again clear a path through the swamp for Dragons to bring out the casualties. They made it without incident. There was a distressing number of casualties—fifty-eight dead and well over a hundred wounded; the exact number was uncertain because many wounded Marines refused to be evacuated—in addition to the two Raptors and three Dragons killed by weapons he couldn't identify. In his years as a FIST commander, he'd lost so many Marines killed or wounded on only one other deployment—the war on Diamunde—and it had taken weeks in that war for casualties to mount so high. Equipment, tactics, and medical treatment had reached a point where Marines simply didn't suffer so many casualties anymore.

Sturgeon was by then convinced that they were fighting the same kind of Skinks a platoon from Company L had encountered on Society 437. Who were the Skinks? Where did they come from? As far as General Aguilano had been able to find out, Society 437 was the only known contact with them. If the Assistant Commandant of the Marine Corps couldn't ferret out other contacts, there probably hadn't been any. Why did they attack humans without at least attempting communication?

He shunted the questions aside. All they would do was raise more unanswerable questions. His infantrymen were in trouble and he had to get them out of that swamp.

The string-of-pearls still couldn't find the Skinks, not a trace. The navy techs and analysts working on the data in orbit still had no idea what that possible anomaly might have been, where the squad sent to check it out had found nothing—and then had been cut off and almost overrun. All he had to go on were the reports from Commander van Winkle, and those didn't tell him enough to make any intelligent command decisions.

Well, he was a Marine. When in doubt, be decisive.

His choices were to continue through or to pull out the same way they'd come in. The Marines wouldn't like pressing forward; that was what they were doing when they were getting hurt. But pulling back over ground they'd already covered would feel like retreat, and that could be catastrophic for morale. He might not have the information he needed to make intelligent command decisions, but deciding which way to go was easy. Press forward. That way was shorter anyway. The battalion had advanced more than halfway through the swamp during the previous day. He issued the order and had both the squadron and the battery stand by to give support.

"Saddle up, people, we're moving out." Staff Sergeant Hyakowa's voice came loud and clear into the helmet comm of every member of third platoon. "Saddle up!"

There was general grumbling at the order, but none that wasn't totally routine for tired men trying to ignore the life-threatening aspect of where they were and what they were doing. None of them wanted to be there; certainly none of them wanted to get up and go into further danger. But they knew it was more dangerous to stay where they were, and the only way out was to go through more of what they'd already been through.

"We're continuing through the swamp," Hyakowa said. "Same order of movement as yesterday."

Shouted objections greeted that announcement. Continuing through the swamp meant going through more of what they'd already gone through.

"Secure that, people," Hyakowa snapped. "Forward is the short way. Back is farther. Do you want to get out of this swamp or not?"

The objections quieted. They wanted to get out, they just didn't want to walk it. But there was no other way.

Schultz flexed his left arm, willing the traumatized tissue to loosen up. He ignored the pain as adhesions broke and blood tried to seep past the artificial skin that covered the wound. He took his position, sniffed the air, listened to the sounds, got himself ready to give far worse than the Skinks could give back.

Doyle looked around fearfully, terrified of continuing the march through the swamp.

Kerr scuttled over to make sure Schultz was all right. On his return he checked Doyle to make sure he had everything he was supposed to and his blaster was loaded and functional. Then the signal came to move out. Kerr was glad he'd been so busy with his men that he didn't have the time to worry about how he was doing himself. The action the night before, when the squad was cut off, left him with a stronger feeling of mortality than he'd had since his first contact after he returned from convalescence. He'd gotten over it quickly enough that time; this time it was gnawing at him.

Word had finally spread through the insectoid world that the massive herd migrating through its territory wasn't an ambulatory banquet, so few of the Marines were bitten or stung, and most of their itching was residual from the previous day and night. Even the walking came a little easier. The land sloped gently, almost imperceptably, up toward the mountains from which its water flowed. The muck underfoot became less clingy, firmer, gave their boots better traction. Water moved less sluggishly, less often lay in sheets on the ground, and stream beds were better defined. Vegetation was hung in fewer lank sheets and tangles, sight lines were lengthened. They were heading through more swamp, but it wasn't as depressing as it had been; spirits rose. Especially when they didn't have any contact for the first several hours. But all things end. Especially the good ones.

The battalion was almost at the far side of the swamp. The leftmost platoon of Kilo Company had already broken into an arm of open land that poked into the swamp. With firmer ground in which to dig their roots, trees grew taller. Grasses hopscotched under them to grow in scattered clumps where sunlight managed to filter to the ground. It was as dark as ever under the trees, but colors began to appear where light did come through. The air was freshening from its swampy rankness.

Schultz froze. He could never afterward remember what made him freeze, he simply knew a threat was nearby. While he was still deciding if immediate action was necessary, Doyle, who sensed the nearness of the end of the swamp and wasn't paying attention to Schultz, blundered into him. The two fell, and that saved Schultz's life. As he hit the ground, Schultz very clearly heard the sharp crack of something supersonic pass through the space he'd just occupied.

"Thanks," he rumbled in surprise and rolled away. In the instant, he thought Doyle saw whatever was coming and deliberately tackled him to save his life.

Doyle also heard the crack but didn't understand what it meant. He wanted to raise his head and look around, but when his infra showed Schultz hugging the ground, he realized raising his head might be a good way to lose it. He scrambled for cover.

"*Right!*" Kerr shouted, and dove to the ground. Behind him the rest of second squad hit the mud and faced their right, firing blindly into the swamp.

No greenish streams of viscous fluid shot at the Marines. Supersonic cracks shot overhead, faster and faster, until in seconds they crescendoed in a skull-splitting whine. Leaves and branches, sliced through by whatever was being shot at them, cascaded down. Trees toppled in front of them, their trunks cut through.

"Where are they?" someone shouted.

"There!" someone shouted back.

Sergeant Bladon couldn't see where the hellish fire came from, nor did his UPUD show anything. He did the only thing he could. *"Volley fire, thirty!"* he shouted. "Fire!" On the platoon command circuit he heard Gunny Bass order the gun squad to move into position to help second squad. Bass ordered first squad to move back and swing to what was now second squad's right side.

The eight blasters of second squad put out a ragged line of plasma bolts that struck the mud thirty meters distant.

"Volley fire, up ten!" Bladon ordered as soon as he saw his squad's fire was on line. The bolts from the squad's eight blasters hit foliage and ground deeper in the swamp. The two guns added their rapid fire. A curtain of steam rose from the frying mud.

"Up ten!" Bladon ordered. The squad's fire, even with the guns added to it, seemed to have no effect on the enemy's rate of fire.

"Third platoon, volley fire, sixty!" Bass shouted over the all-hands circuit. First squad was on line by them and added fire from its blasters.

Kerr couldn't see sixty meters through the steam rising from the overheated mud. He guessed where it was and fired a bolt. He shifted aim to his right and fired again, shifted left and fired. Again and again he shifted, trying to draw a stippled line in the mud sixty meters away. What the hell kind of weapons were they using? He'd never seen or even heard of weapons like this.

"Third platoon, up ten!" Bass commanded. They fired deeper.

Felled trees smoldered, tongues of flame flickering up from them from repeated blaster hits. Trees crackled and popped from the abruptly heated fluids in their trunks and some split. The crashes of felled trees in the killing zone between the Marines and their ambushers became more frequent. Trees toppled behind them. The ground shook. *Things* hit the mud in front of them, behind them, between them, pulverized the ground where they hit, exploded flesh and bone when they found their targets.

A tremendous crash came from first squad's area. Someone screamed briefly.

"Who was that?" Bass demanded.

The volume of blaster fire increased as first platoon arrived on third platoon's left flank with one section from the assault platoon. A moment later second platoon and the other assault section reached their right flank and joined in.

"*Company L! Volley fire, seventy!*" Lieutenant Humphrey ordered on the company all-hands circuit. Where the hell are they? he wondered. Sightlines were thirty meters, rarely more than fifty. Volley fire at seventy meters over flat land should have been killing just about everything up to double that distance, yet everything his company was throwing out had no effect on the enemy's fire. There was no way anyone could be in that range and be able to put out directed fire. He heard the fire from his company slowly slacken and saw holes open in the coverage.

Two minutes into the firefight, Surveillance Radar Analyst Third Class Auperson on the *Grandar Bay* shouted, "Chief, take a look. You're not going to believe this."

"What'cha got, Auperson," Chief Nome asked as he leaned over Auperson's shoulder to look at his displays. He blinked.

"You're right, I don't believe that." Without turning his head he called, "Sir! Over here. Are those jarheads down there in trouble?"

Lieutenant (jg) McPherson, the string-of-pearls watch officer, raised a "wait one" finger; he was talking on his headset. He joined Nome and Auperson as he wrapped up the conversation. "The Marines are screaming for data. What do you have?"

Nome pointed. McPherson looked at the display. "Hot damn, that's it!" He got back onto his headset and reported. "Those coordinates the Marines are at—there's a swath of swamp being torn apart between them and an area eight hundred meters to their east northeast. Looks like mad bull-dozers at work." He rattled off the coordinates of the north-eastern edge of the area, then said, "Aye aye, sir, I'll keep on top of it." Fascinated, he kept his eyes glued to the display. He couldn't imagine what kind of weapon would wreak the destruction he was watching.

"That's the report, sir, but it's not possible," said Lieutenant Quaticatl when Brigadier Sturgeon looked up after reading the string-of-pearls report.

"Possible or not, it's all we've got," Sturgeon replied. "Three!"

"Sir?" Commander Usner replied. He had also just finished reading the report.

"Work with air. Box those coordinates. I want the heaviest hit possible there, and I want it now."

"Aye aye, sir." Usner got on the open comm link to the squadron's operations officer and fed him the information. "The brigadier wants it five minutes ago," he finished. He nodded, satisfied with the response of the squadron's S3.

"Sir," he reported to his commander, "half of the Raptors are orbiting within range now and will fire with Jerichos as soon as they're pointed in the right direction. The other half are fueled, loaded, and launching. They'll be on station in five minutes."

"Good," Sturgeon grunted. His brow was deeply furrowed. He looked into someplace only he could see. What the hell kind of weapons were the Skinks using?

Thirty seconds after getting their fire orders, the four orbiting Raptors lined up, pointing their noses at the Swamp of Perdition, and hovered while they locked their Jerichos in with the string-of-pearls guidance system. Then they let rip in six waves of eight missiles. They turned about and headed back to base to refuel and rearm. Two minutes into their return they wiggled their wings at the other four Raptors and got wiggles back. Fifteen minutes after firing they were back on station awaiting another fire mission.

*   *   *

"Cease fire! Cease fire!" the commands rang out. The mind-numbing whine had stopped, mud no longer pulverized, no more flesh and bone exploded. *"Report!"* Casualty counts came in. M Company had been pinned down, unable to maneuver to join in the fight. It lost three more Marines killed. Two had limbs blown off, but corpsmen reached them in time to stanch the bleeding and stick them in stasis bags to stabilize them until they reached the hospital. Kilo Company lost four men while maneuvering to Company L's right flank, and another six once they joined the fighting. The assault company had lost two full squads, a third of its strength, when their guns were hit by *things*.

In Company L, Sergeant Bladon was down. Something had torn off his right arm midway between the elbow and wrist. First squad's Lance Corporal Van Impe was crushed by a toppled tree; PFCs Godenov and Hayes were wounded. In second squad, Lance Corporal Rodamour, wounded the night before, was killed. So were Corporal Stevenson and PFC Gimbel in the gun squad. First platoon lost five men, dead or mangled; second platoon lost six.

Commander van Winkle didn't give his Marines time to dwell on their casualties. As soon as the battalion surgeon informed him that he was able to gather the wounded and dead, van Winkle ordered the battalion to get on line and sweep toward the enemy position.

There wasn't any mud in front of third platoon for the first 150 meters. It had all been baked into dirt by the plasma bolts from their blasters and bigger guns. The dirt was pitted and pounded into dust by the Skink weapons. They had to step or climb over trees; hardly any were left standing. Many of the downed trees—and a few of the standing ones—were smoldering or burning. Those, the Marines walked around. That first 150 meters looked like it had been hit by a swarm of tornadoes accompanied by lightning strikes, but there were none of the scorch marks left behind by dying Skinks.

Beyond the first 150 meters, the swarm of tornadoes continued its rampage, but had been abandoned by the lightning.

"H-Have you ever seen anything like this?" Doyle asked. Schultz grunted a negative. Kerr softly said, "Never."

Corporal Linsman, now the acting squad leader, had but didn't mention it. He once saw a forest after a twenty ton meteorite had exploded in the atmosphere above it. This looked like that, except that had covered hundreds of square kilometers. This devastation was a band a couple of hundred meters wide. A couple of hundred meters wide, but how long? He had heard the explosions of the missiles, but couldn't judge their distance. There was too much other noise, and the sound echoed off and was muffled by the trees. He could see a lot farther than he should have been able to in this swamp. In the distance a black cloud rose from the swamp. What the hell are the Skinks using? he wondered.

A little more than seven hundred meters from where they'd lain to futilely return fire, they reached the closest Jericho hit. The fire started by the missiles was almost completely burned out. Most of the trees had been reduced to embers and charred bits. They continued through. A box three hundred meters on a side had been hit by Jerichos. The area between there and the Marines' former position had been devastated, but the Skink position, if that was really where they'd been, was obliterated. A few badly charred spikes stood up where trees had been, most of the wood and vegetation that had been there reduced to embers and charcoal. There was no chance of finding bodies or even Skink scorch marks.

"Hey, Dorny, look at this," Claypoole shouted.

"What do you have?" Corporal Dornhofer asked as he trotted over.

"Damned if I know, but it used to be something."

It was a mess of metal, some bent totally out of shape, some sagged from too much heat. Parts of it had completely melted and puddled.

"You're right," Dornhofer said when he saw it, "it used to

be something. But what?" He squatted and used the magnifier shield to look at it more closely. "Rabbit, I've got something," he said on the squad command circuit.

"Show yourself," Sergeant Ratliff replied.

Dornhofer raised an arm so his camouflage sleeve slid down to expose his flesh and said, "Coming up."

"Too small for a vehicle," the first squad leader said when he saw it. "Must have been a weapon of some kind."

"Yeah, but what kind?" Claypoole asked.

"The kind that was shooting at us, that's what kind."

Gunny Bass joined them. "Don't touch anything," he said as soon as he saw it. "The navy forensic people might be able to figure out what it used to be."

"You really think so?" Ratliff asked. He looked dubiously at the twisted, half-melted metal.

"I think they maybe really can. Really. Maybe," Bass said.

The battalion spent the rest of the day searching the swamp in the vicinity of the fight but found nothing. No bodies, no scorch marks, no equipment or weapons. Best of all, nobody shot at them. They moved out of the swamp at dusk. In the morning they went back in and swept south, parallel to the route they'd taken north. They found no sign of anybody, nobody shot at them. It appeared that the Swamp of Perdition was cleared of enemy forces.

Thirty-fourth FIST's infantry battalion returned to its encampment outside Interstellar City to lick its wounds and begin to heal.

CHAPTER
EIGHTEEN

Although not a member of any recognized sect, Conrad Milch was a quiet, reserved, and intensely religious man. As a propulsion engineer all his working life, he had a profound sense of nature's most elemental forces harnessed in the power plants of starships such as the *Cambria*. He reasoned that if man could capture the energy of the stars and put it to work for him, then how much more awesome was the Power that had created mankind.

Milch was enormously content on that particular voyage because the *Cambria*'s chief engineer, a besotted Scot who thought only about his impending retirement, had left the supervision of the ship's drives almost totally in the humble young man's capable hands. Milch spent most of his waking hours ensconced far in the aft reaches of the enormous ship, monitoring the wonders of the Beam drive. He knew little about drive theory, but he knew the drive's components and he could keep them working at peak efficiency. He would happily have stood all the watches by himself; Captain Tuit demanded he eat and sleep to keep his body functioning properly and his mind sharp enough to do his exacting work.

When Conrad Milch was away from his drives, he felt no interest in the other onboard operations or the activities of the crew and their passengers—until the miners from Siluria boarded the *Cambria*. One day as he passed through one of the recreation rooms on the way to the crew's quarters, he saw them holding hands, obviously deep in meditation or prayer. Now there was something he could relate to! He often spent the long hours of his watches contemplating the irresistible potency of his engines and yearning to be one with the omnipotence of the universe.

When the men appeared to be finished with their prayers, Conrad approached them timidly.

"What do you do on this ship?" one of them asked after Conrad's clumsy attempt at introductions.

"I'm a Beam drive engineer," he answered proudly. The men looked at each other and then smiled. "Do you say your prayers often?" he asked. Conrad was embarrassed by the question even as it left his lips; he should not intrude on strangers.

One of them looked up at him intently and then replied, "Engineer Milch, all men seek to rejoin the spirit of God, the Creator. While in these bodies, we can do that only through prayer and the reading of scripture. I believe, brothers," he addressed the other men, "that God has sent this man to us."

Conrad felt a sudden rush of recognition! Yes! He understood that! "Well . . ." he began in confusion, not daring to tell such obviously holy men what he was thinking.

"Brother Milch," another of the miners said, smiling fiercely through his thick black beard, "won't you join us?" The miners shifted around the table to make an open space for Conrad. Gingerly, he sat down. Yes, he thought in exultation, I will be one with God! These men know the Way! He smiled at them and they smiled back.

Lew Conorado lay in his stateroom, preparing for the jump out of Beamspace. In only a little while the long voyage would be over and he'd be facing the rigors of his courtmartial. For the bulk of the voyage he'd been able to put his problems behind him, distracted for the most part by the relationship that had developed between Jennifer Lenfen and himself. But now his mind whirled. He knew he had done the right thing on Avionia Station, but Dr. Hoxey must have built a strong case against him. Otherwise the government would never have gone to the expense of bringing him all the way back from the far reaches of Human Space to face trial.

Under naval regulations, Conorado could ask for anyone he wanted to defend him—another Marine officer, a civilian lawyer, anyone. But who would he pick? He knew no one back on Earth well enough to ask for such an important service. He would probably just let the Corps pick someone. His basic defense would be that he did the right thing as a Marine officer and as a moral human being to free the aliens Hoxey had imprisoned in her lab. He was certain he could build a strong case on that argument alone.

And on top of all that, he and Palmita had to face Captain Tuit after the jump. They were in for an expert ass-chewing. Conorado smiled. If only the judge would turn out to be like the old navy man who in a short while would take a chunk out of his behind.

And then there was Jennifer. The worst thing about the relationship that had developed between them was that she reminded him so much of Marta when his wife was her age. The similarity was so strong that there were brief, poignant moments when he actually mistook Jennifer for Marta. And that made him feel guilty because Marta was alone back on Thorsfinni's World, the woman who had borne him beautiful children, the woman who had faithfully shared some of the best years of her life with him. Lewis Conorado loved his Marta unstintingly.

Jennifer had asked him about Marta, and he'd told her honestly that their marriage was, just then, on the rocks. She also asked him why he was returning to Earth, and he'd lied. Jennifer had accepted the fact that he was married, had been for a long time, and she had told him frankly she didn't care why the Corps was calling him back to headquarters.

"But Lew," she said one day, "I know enough about bureaucracies to know they don't call middle managers all the way across Human Space without a reason. You're in some kind of trouble. You don't have to tell me what it is because I don't care. I just hope you come through it okay."

How in the hell did I get myself into this mess? he thought. He would probably have killed Palmita that morning if no one had intervened. He'd attacked the man with the same degree of determination and ferocity he would have used had the woman been Marta instead of Jennifer. And that was the problem: he thought he loved Jennifer as much as he loved his wife.

Jennifer Lenfen had her own thoughts on the subject. All the crew were at their stations, waiting for the captain to give the command to initiate the jump. Her duties were minimal since the computer systems were all functioning perfectly, but she had her station on the bridge just the same. Just my luck, she was thinking as they waited for Captain Tuit to give the command, that the only man I'd die for is married. Jennifer Lenfen already knew Lewis Conorado well enough to realize he'd never give up his marriage on his own. Even if he didn't love her—and she knew he did—he would never be the one to break the bond. The ache she felt for him seemed like a great big hole through the center of her guts, and it was wonderful. She blinked. A tear ran down her cheek. Goddamnit, she thought, I hope the others aren't watching! She smiled inwardly and relaxed because, despite her youth and inexperience, she knew that true love was boundless—and not jealous.

Just before the *Cambria* made the transition from Beamspace, Conorado wondered what Marta was doing at that moment.

The New Oslo police headquarters was a depressingly modern and spartan place. The officers were neatly dressed, efficient, and polite. At that time of the year—deep winter in that hemisphere—they all wore thick black turtleneck sweaters. The men all sported short haircuts, and those who had facial hair kept it neatly trimmed; the few female officers Colonel Ramadan observed as he walked through the corridors to the chief's office bobbed their hair neatly. They all looked dedicated, but to Ramadan there was something ineffably "garrison" about the New Oslo police force. He had to wonder how they'd operate in the field. He was soon to find out.

"Colonel!" Agdar Vest, the police chief, greeted Ramadan warmly as he entered his office. "So good of you to come to help us out on dis case! I hope Inspector Hamnes briefed you on vat ve know so far about the Conorado woman's kidnapping?"

Ramadan nodded. Inspector Hamnes, a man of about sixty with a neatly trimmed mustache, was in charge of the operation to rescue Marta Conorado. He had given Ramadan all the information at his disposal on the ride from the aerial port to the headquarters.

"These two—Bengt Trondelag and Kiruna Rena—are professional assassins, Colonel," Hamnes had told him. "They are very good, and ve have not been able to gather the evidence ve need to tie dem to the murders ve know they have committed—until now, that is. By taking Mrs. Conorado hostage, they have given us the best witness ve'll ever have. But they are ruthless people, and now they are desperate as well, and I am afraid they will keep Mrs. Conorado alive only so long as she can serve them as a hostage. They must kill her, you see. And the worst part of it is, ve don't know where they are in the mountains."

The New Oslo police did not follow the pair into the mountains because they thought they had a more reliable and less intrusive method for keeping track of them. They sent a surveillance drone on their trail instead, an absolutely reliable and safe tracking method. "Unfortunately," Hamnes had said, "the weather in the mountains deteriorated so quickly we could not continue the surveillance."

Ramadan thought of the razzle-dazzle technologies sold to the Corps that didn't work in a pinch, but it was slight comfort knowing others had the same problems. "So what will you do, Inspector?" Ramadan had asked, his heart sinking.

Hamnes shrugged. "When the weather clears a little, ve vill go in after dem. Your Mrs. Conorado is certainly dead if ve don't. The chances are not good if ve do find dem in time. But ve must act because there is the slight chance that way ve can save her."

Now, Chief Vest asked, "Haf you brought Mrs. Conorado's medical and dental records, Colonel?" Conorado handed over the crystals. "I vill see dese are returned. I'll gif dem now to forensics." He sighed. "I hope, Colonel, ve vill not haf to use dem, but I must warn you, sir, Mrs. Conorado's position is desperate. Already the snow in de mountains is to a depth of three meters, and vinter has only just begun up dere. If dey make good dere escape, ve may never find her."

"Yeah," Ramadan sighed, "and we don't have the slightest idea where they are."

"Brother Conrad?"

Conrad Milch looked up from his reading of the Book of Revelation and smiled. "Brother Benediction." He stood, and they embraced warmly.

"Brother Conrad, I would like to ask you if Brother Revelation and I might have one last tour of the ship's power plant."

"But—But we're due to dock at Luna in two days. Everyone's preparing to disembark." Milch frowned. "I do not relish our parting, Brother Revelation. You and your brothers have opened my eyes to so much! I wonder if we may stay in touch—"

Benediction lay his hand softly on Conrad's shoulder. "This may be the last time we can commune directly with the wonderful Power, Brother Conrad. It would make our eventual parting so much sweeter if this one last time you could oblige us." They needed Conrad because the shuttle between the last cargo bay and the power plant would not operate unless a certified crew member logged on with his voice and palm prints.

Conrad thought. "I go on duty in fifteen minutes. Why, of course, Brother Benediction, I'd be delighted to take you down once more."

Epher Benediction, the bomb maker, smiled.

The five "soldiers" of the Army of Zion had studied detailed plans of the *Cambria*'s layout for weeks before they boarded her. They had rehearsed their moves endlessly, until each man knew what he was to do. During the entire voyage, not one had spoken to any of his comrades about the mission. They did not need to. Each man's duty, along with a schematic of the ship, was burned into his memory. Thus nobody on board the ship suspected them of being anything more than a group of eccentric laboring men, because there was no possibility either the ship's crew or passengers might overhear anything. Since their luggage was not searched, the bomb's components lay stashed safely in their staterooms.

The plan was very simple. Two days before docking at Luna Station, they would seize the ship. Benediction and Revelation would assemble the bomb in the power plant, while Gospel, Lordsday, and Merab secured the crew and passengers and locked them into their compartments. At the same time, the destructive devices planted in the lifecraft and on the navigation console on the bridge would detonate, making sure the ship's Earthward inertia was maintained and sealing everyone on board, to die in the explosion that would be timed to occur when the ship blew up. Lordsday, the systems engineer, would use the ship's computer to transmit the Army of Zion's message to the world, which would watch in horror as the cargo, worth trillions, the crew, passengers, and Army of Zion all went up in one glorious nuclear detonation between Earth and the moon.

Conrad asked Epher what was in the two cases he and Increase Revelation were carrying, and was satisfied to learn they contained sacraments. "We would like you to join us in our last service aboard this ship," Increase said. "It will be a fitting tribute to the ending of this long voyage."

"Too bad the others won't join us," Conrad said as he stepped into the shuttle.

"Oh, they are holding their own service elsewhere," Revelation said.

"In another section of the ship," Benediction added.

As they rode the shuttle toward the *Cambria*'s power

plant, Conrad rattled on and on about his readings in the Bible. He was particularly struck by the seventh verse of Chapter Twenty-two of Revelation: "Behold, I come quickly."

"Yes, Brother Conrad, He will come quickly," Benediction intoned somberly from just behind where Milch was sitting in the tiny shuttle car. "Maybe even today."

"In a blaze of glorious light, I bet!" Conrad enthused.

"Yes, yes, I am sure," Benediction responded, raising his eyebrows at Revelation. They smiled.

The shuttle docked at last and its hatches popped open. Conrad stepped out, followed by his two passengers.

"Conrad, you ass, what the hell is this?" the assistant engineer on duty barked. "Damnit, we have to start the god-damned power-down sequence and you're bringing tourists down here?"

Epher Benediction sat his case carefully on the deck, drew a hand weapon and shot the man in the forehead. Blood, brains, and bone splattered over his instrument console.

Conrad gaped. Increase Revelation, standing just behind him, placed the muzzle of his own weapon at the back of the engineer's head and fired. Conrad's gray matter splattered over the opposite bulkhead of the power plant. The two bodies flopped and thudded on the floor for a moment before lying still, tendrils of blood forming into pools on the deck plates.

"What a mess," Epher Benediction sighed as he shifted to avoid a long rivulet of blood creeping toward where he stood. He began to unpack the bomb.

Jennifer Lenfen, Lewis Conorado, and James Palmita stood in a loose semicircle around Captain Hank Tuit's command chair.

"I've looked into what went on down there this morning, Palmita, and you were out of line," Tuit began.

"Captain, I am a diplomat and I have immunity from—"

"Not while you're on my ship, sonny."

"Then when we get to Luna—"

"You ain't getting' off my ship when we get to Luna, not until I say so! And when and if you do get off this ship, you're going off with your tail on fire, boy." He turned to Conorado. "And you, Captain. Don't you think I know what you and Lenfen have been up to? Your conduct as an officer and a married man has been disgraceful. It's been the talk of the ship, goddamnit! I'da let it go, until you two idiots started beating each other up in front of everyone." The three stood silently in front of him. Jennifer hung her head; Conorado just stared at a point an inch above the captain's head; Palmita glared at the captain with his one good eye. Inwardly, Tuit smiled. Conorado had done a job on that boy! It'd be months before that eye could be replaced.

"Okay, Jennifer, what should I do to our 'diplomat' here?"

"Sir?"

"Well, you're the 'offended' party, girl! Do you want me to turn him over to the port authority on Luna for—for—oh, aggravated sexual assault or whatever? Come on, come on, speak up! We dock in two days!"

Jennifer's face turned red. She was sorry the incident had happened, but at the same time she was proud of Conorado for having defended her. "I just want to forget about it all, sir," she stammered.

"What? What did you say, Lenfen?"

"He's lost his eye. That's enough, Captain. I won't press any charges."

"Oh, you won't, huh?" Tuit leaned back in his chair. He picked up the stogie he'd been smoking and puffed on it assiduously, producing a fine cloud of blue smoke. He regarded the three balefully through the cloud. It was clear to them that he was enjoying this. "Well, it's my decision anyway. And I haven't made it yet. I'll let you know after we've docked. In the meantime, you three," he jabbed the glowing cigar end at them, "will, I repeat, will have no contact with each other. Now there's one more thing—"

"Emergency, emergency! Attention all personnel!" Min-

erva shrieked. *"Fire on board! Fire on board! There are fires in the lifecraft! Repeat; fires in the lifecraft! Sealing all compartments and initiating suppression sequences!"*

Jennifer leaped to her console; Tuit was right behind her, knocking both Conorado and Palmita out of the way.

Dense, acrid smoke began spiraling up from a spot on the navigator's console. The crew member on duty there leaped backward to avoid the superheated droplets that began to splutter away from the glowing ball affixed to the console. It grew in size as he stared at it.

Palmita shoved the man aside and grabbed the glowing ball in his hand. He shrieked in agony as the stuff burned through the fingers of his hand, exposing the bones. He shook his hand violently to get rid of the stuff and a big glob dropped onto his chest, where it instantly ate through his shirt. He screamed terribly and beat at the glowing spot. This only caused the substance to spread from his chest to his hands and arms. He fell to the deck, writhing in agony. A crewman dashed over with an extinguisher, but the substance continued to burn its way through Palmita's flesh. He went silent at last, but only after Conorado grabbed the extinguisher and smashed it several times onto Palmita's head. After a few seconds the stuff burned completely through his body and several millimeters into the steel plating of the deck underneath him before dying out.

"I guess—I guess I'll let that boy off after all," Tuit whispered.

"Navigation's out," the navigator reported. "There was enough of that stuff left to burn through."

"No function at all?" Tuit asked.

The navigator checked his instruments. "We have some lateral vernier jets still operating, Captain, but that's all."

"What the hell is going on?" Tuit whispered. Then: "Minnie! Damage report!"

"All fires extinguished, Captain. Hull integrity maintained at one hundred percent. Lifecraft propulsion systems destroyed. Captain? Two of the crew in the power plant are no longer operational."

"What?"

"They are dead, sir. They were killed by two passengers."

"Give me video, Minnie!"

"The video system in the plant has been disabled."

"Jennifer, send a distress message to all ships and stations—"

"That is not permitted, Captain," Sabbath Lordsday said from the bridge hatch.

"Captain!" Minerva shouted. *"There are armed intruders on your bridge!"*

CHAPTER
NINETEEN

"I think you did it, Ted."

Brigadier Sturgeon slowly nodded. "It does appear possible, Jay," he agreed. It was evening and the two of them, Brigadier Sturgeon and Ambassador Spears, along with the chief-of-station, Prentiss Carlisle, were relaxing over drinks in Spears's quarters.

Spears cocked an eyebrow. He'd heard a hint of doubt in Sturgeon's tone. "It's been a week since you beat them in the swamp, and there have been no more contacts by your Marines, or reports from anywhere on Kingdom. According to Archbishop General Lambsblood, they never went this long without raiding *somewhere* before." Spears said "they" because he wasn't yet ready to concede that "they" weren't rebels.

Carlisle kept quiet. He did believe "they" were aliens, but didn't feel like making a point of it with his boss with an outsider present, no matter how well his boss and the outsider seemed to know each other.

"That's not all," Spears said with a grimace. "I had a command audience with Ayatollah Jebel Shammar this morning—you know, the chairman of Convocation of Ecumenical Leaders. The old boy's unhappy. The Convocation met yesterday and demanded to know why an infidel army is still garrisoned on Kingdom after it defeated the 'demons.' I wasn't able to convince him it's a good idea for you to be here until we can be positive the threat is over. He demanded that you depart immediately."

Sturgeon leaned back for a moment in thought. As commander of the expeditionary force it was up to him to decide when the mission was complete. The *Grandar Bay* would remain in orbit until he ordered his Marines back aboard or until a higher authority gave him orders to pull his Marines out. He straightened and said briskly, "We don't know how many of them there were, how many might still be out there, or where they came from. For all we know, they're just sitting back, waiting for complacency to set in before striking again. Is it really safe for us to leave now?"

Spears nodded. "I agree with you, Ted. The Convocation is making a serious mistake, a potentially disastrous one, if they send you away before you're convinced the threat is past. But they're adamant. As the ranking Confederation officer present, I have no choice but to require you to comply with the Convocation's wishes."

"Fools!" Carlisle snorted. He glanced at the other two. "Not you, them. Kingdom was just invaded by an off-world force," finally saying what he'd been holding back. "Even if you Marines did totally defeat the invaders, who's to say that wasn't just a preliminary raid? For all we know, a larger force is on its way right now. Instead of sending you away, they should be requesting a navy shield to stop an invasion fleet, and an army force planetside to combat anybody who gets through the blockade."

"Very good thinking," Sturgeon said. "My thoughts are much the same. Whoever they are, wherever they came from, that fight in the swamp isn't the end of it. Battle has been engaged. It hasn't been ended." He shrugged. "The complicator is, we have no idea whether they want to take and hold Kingdom, or if they have other designs that will have them striking elsewhere next."

Spears chose to ignore the implications of what Sturgeon and Carlisle had said. He didn't want to get into a discussion about the origin of whoever "they" were. "Regardless of what might well be excellent military considerations, the fact remains that the Convocation demands that 34th FIST leave."

Sturgeon gave a wry smile. "A sign of a good guest is

being ready to leave when you're no longer welcome. I'd prefer sticking around for a couple more months, but . . ."

"You don't have to leave tomorrow, of course. Take your time." Spears grimaced. "They need to have their noses tweaked." He took a drink. "They also want the string-of-pearls gone."

Sturgeon's smile became less wry. "They're afraid we'll find out things about how they run their world that'll shock and offend the rest of the Confederation."

Carlisle barked out a laugh. "It doesn't take spy satellites to do that."

"True believers are the same throughout all of human time and space," Sturgeon said. "It's their way or be damned. The biggest difference among them is whether they first try to convert those who don't agree or simply kill them. But that's not a problem my FIST can address."

Spears sensed a reluctance in Sturgeon, a powerful desire to remain. "I've seen your Marines," he said. "They seem unhappy."

Indeed, morale had suffered in the infantry battalion. Even though the FIST won the fight in the swamp, it was the Raptors that won it while the infantry suffered the casualties. Sturgeon kept them busy enough that they had neither the time nor energy to dwell on their loss, but constant patrolling without result wasn't actually a morale builder.

"There's no place on Kingdom where they can vent," Spears went on. "They need to raise some hell, get drunk, and get laid."

"They do," Sturgeon agreed. "They can't do that here, but they can back at Camp Ellis." He sighed. Spears was right. The Convocation demanded that they leave. Since they weren't actively engaged with the enemy and had no proof the enemy was still present, he knew he had no choice.

"I'll order my people to saddle up and the *Grandar Bay* to pull in its string-of-pearls. You can tell the Ayatollah we'll be gone in a few days."

"He'll want to know why it takes a few days to leave when you arrived in a matter of hours," Carlisle said.

Sturgeon looked at him levelly. "When we arrived, we had to be ready for immediate action. We don't have that same time pressure now. We can take enough time to make sure we leave in good order."

The Great Master was old. The covers of his gill slits had partially atrophied from lack of use since the last time he breathed water. When he chuckled, the sound rasped from his sides as well as from his mouth. No one dared say where he could hear it—or hear of it—that they found the rasping disturbing. The Great Master knew the underlings found it disturbing, so he chuckled more frequently than he would have had he not rasped. It was good to keep underlings disturbed and frightened—it made it easier to keep them firmly under his control.

The Earthman Marines were departing. His scouts reported the jubilation displayed by the Marine fighters as they boarded their shuttles. He looked forward to reports of their dashed hopes when they discovered they were not leaving after all, that they had to face more death at the hands of *his* Fighters.

"Launch Moonlight Stroll," he rumbled.

"It is done, Great Master." The Over Master in command of that phase of the operation bowed low and backed away from the Grand Master's presense.

Hetman Bulba looked out over the fields of his host, saw his people working them, and knew they were good. Most of the vegetables were already harvested. In a few more days it would be time to harvest the grain. This harvest was so rich they could stint on their tithing and the Convocation would never guess.

As soon as the grains were reaped, they would celebrate. In his mind he already smelled beeves roasting over fire pits. Already he could taste the fresh baked breads and pastries the women of his host would bake. He thought of the fresh beer he would drink. And the women. Ah, the women!

Yes, the valley of the Pripyat—he was glad he'd led his

host to this place. It would do for another two years, then he would lead the Yar host of the Kzakh to a new land. Just then, the Pripyat was as near to Paradise as he wished to imagine.

He turned his pony and gazed at the village. His chest swelled as it always did when he saw what his people had built in so short a time. It was not only their own houses and silos and craft shops that made him proud, but the magnificent church with its colorful onion domes, and the priest house, which equaled his own in size and splendor. God smiled on the Yar when he caused Bulba to be made hetman. Hetman Bulba would see to it that the priest celebrated a fine High Mass to begin the harvest celebrations. Everyone would receive the bread and wine of Our Savior's body and blood. Then to the beeves and the bread and the squash. And the beer and the women. Ah, the women!

Distant cries and rifle shots came to his ears, and he turned his pony toward them.

The raid into the valley of the nomads was commanded by a Senior Master. Under him were four Masters, a dozen Leaders, and more than two hundred Fighters. It was small enough a force that a senior among the Masters could have been in command, but there were strictures the Over Master was most concerned about, so he deemed a Senior Master should command the raid. Even lacking swamps and caves, infiltrating the valley was child's play. The nomad guards, prancing so proudly on their ponies, presented no obstacle to the Senior Master and his force. The guards' eyes were set on the horizon; they could easily see anyone who approached on horseback or walked openly across the hills. They paid scant attention to the small copses that dotted the hills and the valley floor, and almost none to the narrow streamlets that drained those hills into the river. Had he chosen to, the Senior Master could have led his raiders down the river, and the nomads would be none the wiser until his Fighters arose in their midst. But the strictures could be better met if he came from the side of the valley and struck the outskirts of the settlement first.

The Senior Master smiled when he considered the confusion and fear his Fighters were about to unleash on these transplanted Earthmen. He briefly studied the data display his aide held before him, tapped a spot on the schematic, and said, "Now."

Fifteen dun-uniformed Fighters hunkered in the shadows of a copse. They watched a group of mounted Earthmen parading nearby and waited patiently for their Leader's order. If he commanded them to kill the Earthmen, they would do so immediately. If he did not so command, they would remain patiently hunkered until he ordered them to do otherwise. The Fighters didn't mind—they were bred to have little will of their own.

The Leader watched almost as patiently. He did have will of his own, but he knew well how limited was his freedom to act in the absence of orders. The order for which he waited came at last. He looked at the passing parade and saw that the nomads were already almost within range of his Fighters' weapons. He shrilled a command, and the Fighters bounded to their feet and ran in pursuit of the nomads.

One of the nomads heard the Leader's shrill command. He didn't recognize the sharp sound as the cry of a bird or beast of the Pripyat valley, so he casually looked back. The sight of the racing men who didn't quite look like men startled him, so he didn't react immediately. When he did, it was to ask one of the other riders, "Who do you think they are?"

By then the Fighters were in range of the rearmost nomads, and the Leader blew a signal on his whistle. The Fighters pointed the nozzles of their weapons at the nomads and fired. The rearmost nomads screamed surprised agony when the greenish fluid hit them, and fell from their mounts as the ponies reared and bucked and fled in their pain.

The rest of the horsemen scattered forward several meters before they spun about to face the unexpected danger. They would have laughed at the small manlike figures with tanks on their backs and hoses in their hands had not their own companions been writhing in agony in the grass—those who were moving at all. They snapped their rifles to their shoulders and fired. Six of the strange manlings tumbled to the grass, but the others continued their charge, firing as they ran. The horsemen fired again and again, but by then the strange creatures were close enough for their weapons to reach, and their fields of fire were very effectively laid out.

In seconds the horsemen were all down, dead or dying. The Leader snapped a command, and his six remaining Fighters ran back to the copse to await his next order. Careful not to burn himself, the Leader went about the area of the fight setting fire to the grass. Then he raced to the copse, led his Fighters to a nearby streamlet, and followed it back into the hills.

Hetman Bulba heeled his pony to a gallop and began shouting as soon as he saw the fighting, but the fight was over before he'd covered much more than fifty meters. He looked about and saw a score of men converging on him or on the fight. He hoped they reached it before the fire spread so they could get the wounded and the dead away from the flames. Whether they did or not, he needed them to go with him in pursuit of the bandits. His pony faltered and almost fell when a brilliant flash flared up in the burning grass, but he managed to keep control of the animal so it retained its balance. More flares went up, so fast he couldn't get an exact count, but more than half a dozen.

The fire spread rapidly after the flashes.

The Senior Master allowed himself a brief smile of satisfaction at the chaos growing around the grass fire, then spoke into his communicator. Two kilometers distant, another Leader led twenty Fighters in an attack against the Earthmen working the fields. Once they killed the workers, the Leader fired the ripening grain. At the same time, a Master and thirty Fighters triggered an ambush on a band of horsemen speeding to the first attack. When those horsemen were dead, the Master fired the grass in which their bodies and those of several Fighters lay. Another Master with a Leader and forty Fighters assaulted the settlement. They killed half of the Earthmen and fired the church and priest house, then withdrew.

The Senior Master granted himself another slight smile when he received the reports. So far he'd committed fewer than half of his force and suffered no more than twenty dead. Fifty or more of the nomads were cremated in the fires. Phase one of the raid was complete. Now to wait for the strictures, then commit phase two, in which the Yar host of the Kzakh would die.

At the same time, a thousand kilometers away, another farming community was attacked by a force of two hundred. This attack was also in two phases, with a pause between them. Three hundred Skinks attacked a mining community in yet a third remote location. The miners fought valiantly enough to cancel the pause between the two phases, but to no avail. Like the farmers, the miners all died most horribly. Skinks rampaged through a mountain monastery and destroyed sacred relics and tomes, a loss many felt was greater than the lives of the monks. Isolated homesteads were leveled in so many locations, it would be a month before the full extent of the slaughter was known. The Army of the Lord outpost in a provincial town was massacred. That massacre was followed by almost complete slaughter of the citizens. The town was burned to the ground.

"What do you mean, we're going planetside?" PFC MacIlargie demanded. "We're going back to Camp Ellis."

"I mean we get aboard the Dragons and go 'high speed on a rocky road,' that's what I mean," Corporal Linsman said.

"Back down to Kingdom?"

"Back down to Kingdom."

Corporal Doyle looked around the squad. They'd started with ten Marines. Now there were seven—and four of the seven were hobbled by wounds. How could they go back? And the rest of the platoon wasn't in any better shape. The whole company was pretty badly shot up. Why were they going back?

Corporal Kerr looked uncomfortable but said nothing and checked his men—mostly Doyle; Schultz didn't need much checking. Schultz seemed to be his normal, quietly ready self on the verge of a planetfall.

Corporal Chan closed his eyes for a moment. He remembered Waygone, where all the Skinks had been in one place. He'd hoped that was true this time as well. It looked like he thought wrong. He gathered himself and asked PFC Longfellow, his lone remaining man, how his wound felt.

"Good enough, I guess," Longfellow said. It hurt like hell, but he wasn't about to say so, not when others had been wounded so much worse.

Linsman looked at Kerr. "You're number one now, you know."

Kerr nodded. He was next in line to take over as acting squad leader if Linsman was killed or badly wounded.

Linsman looked at Chan and said, "You take MacIlargie."

"What?" MacIlargie yelped. "What's the matter, don't you like me anymore?"

"I never did like you." He looked at him. "I'm acting squad leader. That leaves you as the only man left in the fire team. Chan's shorthanded. Go with him."

MacIlargie swore. Well, at least if he was with Chan, two members of that fire team were all right—neither he nor the corporal had been wounded. In Kerr's fire team only Doyle was whole, and he wasn't all that much use on a good day.

The Marines were somber as they boarded the Dragons waiting in the Essays for the return planetside.

Archbishop General Lambsblood glowered at the oncoming Dragons. He'd hoped the Marines had destroyed the demons. Instead, they'd merely crushed one coven. How many more were out there? There hadn't been enough Marines to begin with; now there were fewer. His own Soldiers of the Lord, numerous as they were, were no match for the demons. The Marine commander *had* to call for reinforcements, call for an entire army. All he could hope for was that the Army of the Lord and these few Confederation Marines could survive until that army arrived. If Brigadier Sturgeon hadn't already requested the reinforcements . . . Lambsblood sighed. If he hadn't, they were all damned. He didn't even glance at Ambassador Spears or Chief-of-Staff Carlisle, who stood talking next to him.

The lead Dragons pulled up. Brigadier Sturgeon was one of the first Marines out. He marched directly to the trio.

"Mister Ambassador, General . . ." He nodded at Carlisle. "My operations people are already working on the information you provided. As soon as my squadron is operational, my infantrymen will search for the enemy near these strikes." He took two sheets of paper from Lieutenant Quaticatl and handed them to Lambsblood and Spears.

Spears merely glanced at the paper and handed it to Carlisle. Lambsblood shook with barely restrained fury.

"Ted"—Spears's voice was strained—"this is no good. They hit too many places simultaneously. There must be too many of them. You don't have enough Marines to find them all."

A corner of Sturgeon's mouth twitched in what could have been the beginning of a smile. "I hope the Skink commander agrees with you. An awful lot of opposition commanders over the centuries who thought that way found out the hard way they were wrong."

Lambsblood couldn't hold back any longer. *"You fool!"* he erupted. "Hubris! Do you know the word? The arrogance that goes before a fall. I only have partial reports, but a rough tally indicates that there were at least—let me emphasize that, *at least*—ten thousand demons involved in those monstrous attacks. *Ten thousand!* How many Marines do you have left? Nine hundred? They have weapons that can kill your aircraft and armor before they even know there's a threat. They have weapons they can use against your infantry at a greater range than your infantry weapons can effectively fire. How long do you think your Marines can hold out against them?"

"General," Sturgeon replied in a calm voice, "we don't have to go against all ten thousand at once. The reports indicate they are widely dispersed. My Marines can find them and defeat them in detail."

Lambsblood snorted. "This," he shook the sheet of paper, "tells me you plan to strike in five different locations. They will defeat *you* in detail."

"Not today they won't."

Quaticatl leaned forward to whisper to Sturgeon. Sturgeon listened, then said briskly, "General, Mr. Ambassador, if you will excuse me, my squadron is ready. I have a FIST to fight." He walked rapidly to the command post, which was already set up.

CHAPTER TWENTY

"Mr. Ambassador? Mr. Ambassador?"

"Huh?" Jay Benjamin Spears started awake to find his station chief gently shaking his shoulder. Spears wiped a thin rivulet of spittle out of his beard and sat upright in his chair. An old-fashioned book lay facedown in his lap. "Damn!" he muttered, picking it up. "Never lay a book down like that, Prentiss, ruins the spine."

Prentiss Carlisle smiled. He was getting used to Spears's eccentricities, one of which was that for relaxation he read old books, really old books, printed on paper and bound between covers, the pages woven into "signatures," as Spears called them. Carlisle learned quickly not to call the pages "pages," but instead "leaves," and he knew from Spears's lectures that leaves had two sides, "recto" and "verso." "It is slovenly to call them 'pages,' my dear Prentiss," Spears had commented one night after several beers.

"You should've been a librarian, Mr. Ambassador," Carlisle said.

"Eh? And missed this life of adventure?"

It was obvious to Carlisle that Spears had wanted to go with Brigadier Sturgeon but declined because he thought his duty as a diplomat required him to remain behind in Interstellar City. But now something interesting had come up. "Sir, an urgent message from the naval ship in orbit. Seems—"

"Prentiss, you should read this volume. Very interesting!" Spears handed his station chief a leather-bound book. "It's hideously rare, although only a twentieth-century facsimile of the original edition of 1692."

"Twentieth century?" Carlislie asked. Carefully, he picked up the book and opened it to the title page. Spears had told him that "title page" was correct, not "title leaf." Carlisle had decided he'd never understand the arcane nomenclature of printed books. "*The Wonders of the Invisible World*," he read, "by Cotton Mather." He read on silently. "Yes, I've heard of those witchcraft trials and this Mather. He was a clergyman, wasn't he? One of the prosecutors?"

Spears took the book back and placed it gently on a side table. "No, he was an explicator of the whole affair. I am reading this, Prentiss, to get a better idea of what motivates the City of God sect, the neo-Puritans. They hearken back to their seventeenth century roots, you know, especially the Puritans of seventeenth-century New England America. They fascinate me, and of all the sects represented here on Kingdom, I think they are the most interesting and possibly the most sincere. What's the message, Prentiss?"

Back to business. "It's from the captain of the navy vessel in orbit, sir. For the past several days they've observed through their string-of-pearls sort of a one-way, um, 'migration' from several of the larger towns into the vicinity of the Achor Marshes along the Sea of Gerizim."

" 'Migration,' did you say?"

"Yessir. There's been no traffic in the opposite direction."

"Ah. Which cities are involved?"

Carlisle consulted the reader he held in one hand. "New Salem, New Dedham, New Stoneham . . ."

Spears perked up immediately. Now here was something interesting! "Those towns belong to the City of God," he said, holding out his hand for the reader. He scanned the message. "And he reports much traffic toward Gerizim but none coming back? Has anyone attempted to contact the people in those towns?"

"Well, no, sir. I'd have asked the brigadier to dispatch a drone but he's on the other side of the world and, well, I didn't want to share this just now with the Council. Not until we'd had a chance to evaluate what's going on."

"Excellent! Very good judgment, Prentiss." Spears stood up and began pacing, hands behind his back. "Well, Prentiss, that's the question: What the hell is going on?"

"Some kind of religious retreat, perhaps?"

Spears snorted. "Neither of us has been at our posts very long, Prentiss, but one thing you should know about the City of God, they don't have 'retreats,' religious holidays, 'feast' days, none of that. They live simple, dress simple, and look simple. Some ungenerous souls who do not understand them say they think simple too. If these people are moving, there's a reason, and it's long-term, not for the goddamned weekend. Well, New Salem is about a hundred kilometers south southwest of here. Get a car."

"Er, a car, sir?"

"Yes, Prentiss, a car. We're going to New Salem. We are going to use the oldest method of intelligence gathering known to spying, otherwise called 'diplomacy.' If anybody's still there, we'll just ask them what's up. If not, we'll look around, maybe follow their trail. Come on, come on, Prentiss, there are still six hours to sundown."

"But, sir, it could be, uh, dangerous? I mean, there are these terrible attacks going on, and who knows what's brewing among the sects? We could very well wind up in the middle of some internecine feud . . ." Carlisle's voice trailed off. He looked helplessly at Spears.

Spears nodded once. "You're quite right, Prentiss, of course. How shortsighted of me. Get a car and some guns. I'm driving."

Consort Brattle blew a strand of loose hair out of her face and wiped her forehead with the back of her hand. The packing was almost complete. She straightened up. The Brattles did not own much, aside from the furnishings inside their home, most of which they were leaving behind in New Salem, but still, the storage compartment of their landcar was already packed full. Fortunately, the livestock had all been taken on before, in the care of the village's unmarried men. And the harvest was done for this year, so if the stay at Gerizim turned out to be a long one, they would have food and could get in a new planting before the next growing season.

"Comfort?" she called to her twenty-year-old daughter.

"Yes, Mother?"

"Take this box of your father's reading crystals to the car, would you? Where's Samuel?" Samuel Brattle was her fourteen-year-old son, an obedient lad but sometimes easily distracted. The whole idea of moving the village to the Sea of Gerizim had been distracting enough to everyone in New Salem, but especially the boys around Samuel's age, none of whom could wait to get under way. Besides, during the trip and for many days afterward there'd be no school. But for the adults in New Salem the move was troublesome. The Ministers of the City of God expected new persecutions, and had convinced the sect's individual congregations that moving to the remote shores of Lake Gerizim and consolidating their population would offer them better protection.

"Sam is saying good-bye to the neighbors," Comfort replied. Dutifully, she took the box of crystals from her mother and started for the landcar.

The Brattles would be the last family to leave New Salem. Zechariah, Consort's husband, as mayor of New Salem had the responsibility of making sure the village was clear and everything left behind secured against the inhabitants' eventual return. He and Samuel would go to each house before leaving, to make sure all the doors and windows were secured. Once the current emergency was over, the Ministers had promised, they would return to their homes, so each house was ordered to be safely locked and all the chattels that could not be transported to the camp along the Sea of Gerizim safely stored away inside them.

"Consort," Zechariah called from the stairs leading to the upper floor where the sleeping compartments were, "call in the children. We must seek a blessing before we leave."

Zechariah Brattle was a big man, well over six feet tall, but sinewy, not an ounce of fat on his large-boned frame. New Salem was a farming community, and although the City of God believed in using whatever technology was available to earn their bread, farming on Kingdom was laborious and hard, and Zechariah Brattle's lean, rock-hard muscles reflected a lifetime in the fields. But he was a gentle and peaceable man.

Some calling brought Samuel inside, and the four of them stood in the sparsely furnished living room.

Zechariah raised a big hand over his family. "Loved ones, we Brattles have lived in New Salem for over two hundred years. We have worked hard and lived well off our labor and we have kept faith with the Lord. Our labors have been rewarded and we have been protected. But the world is in turmoil today. The Ministers fear we shall be attacked. Wars have come to Kingdom before, but now the Ministers fear persecution, and that is why we must leave our homes. But I have met with wonderful things this day." He beamed down at his wife and children. "In the forenoon, while I was at prayer, pleading the sacrifice of my Lord Jesus Christ for my family, I began to feel the blessed breezes of a particular faith, blowing from Heaven upon my mind. I began to see the clear road before us—led on, as the Children of Israel in olden times were led on by the same good Hand that bestowed life and blessings upon us and our brethren. Samuel! Are you listening? Pay attention now."

Zechariah smiled down at his son and went on: "Whereupon, I begged of the Lord that He would by His good Spirit incline me to exemplary courage in our journey and permit us again to obtain such favor as to have the good things with us, as in our former circumstances. Let us pray:

"The Tabernacles of the Just
   The Voice of joy afford,
And of Salvation, strongly works
   The right hand of the Lord,

We shall not die, but live, and shall
The Works of God declare.
The Lord did sorely chasten us,
But us from Death did spare.

"Amen."

"Father, will those Marines come here after we're gone?"
Samuel asked.

Zechariah looked askance at his son. The boy was bright,
good at his studies, but his fascination with military subjects
and adventure stories was a trifle worrying to his father, who
was afraid the boy was subject to frivolity. "I know we are
leaving in only a few minutes, Samuel, but yesterday Master
Roxbury gave you an assignment. Is it finished?"

"Yes, Father," Samuel answered, surprised that his father
had asked him such a question. "It was to translate the first
seventy-four lines of Virgil's *Aeneid*. 'I sing of arms and the
man,' " he said, quoting the famous opening line of the
poem.

"It's *a* man, Samuel, *a* man."

"Ah, yes, Father, *a* man," Samuel replied, exasperation in
his voice. "But Father, I have been reading a history of the
Confederation Marine Corps' campaigns, and I must say, it
is more interesting than Caesar's *Commentaries*. We read
them last year."

"More interesting, Samuel?" his father asked.

"Well, sir, as interesting. And a lot easier to read. No
translation required."

Zechariah raised an eyebrow. He knew his son's moods
and he knew what the next question would be, so he answered it now. "We study Latin because to understand the
Bible you must study it in its original translations, and besides, the Fathers, chief among them the Mathers, were La-
tinists and excellent Greek and Hebrew scholars as well, so
that is why we study those languages today. Now time is of
the essence, Samuel, we must go."

"But Father," Comfort interrupted, "will the Marines
come to this part of Kingdom? I've seen them on Samuel's

reader, and they are indeed handsome men and a lot more interesting than the young gentlemen we have around here."

"Comfort!" her mother admonished.

"Well, Mother, you know perfectly well that Simeon Lawson's been making goo-goo eyes at me. One of those offworld Marines might make a good husband for an eligible young woman. Like me."

Zechariah knew his daughter well too. He blew out his cheeks in feigned exasperation. "Comfort, your little jokes try our patience. Now as to Marines, I do not know if they will ever come here. They are at present on the other side of the world, I hear. And you know there is widespread talk they are part of the problems we have been experiencing on Kingdom lately. I do not believe it myself, but respectable people think so. Now Comfort, Samuel, listen to me: to be a Marine is not a bad thing. Any man who devotes himself to the protection of others is blessed in the eyes of the Lord. If these Marines come, they come; if they don't, they don't, and that's it.

"Now are there any more questions?" There were none. Zechariah looked at his family and smiled. "Sam, let's check the doors. Consort, fire up the car." He gave a small box of reading crystals to his daughter. "Comfort, you hold this. These are the town records, all the way back to the first settlement in New Salem. Hold 'em tight. All right," he clapped his big hands together briskly, "we've given God His due, now let's roll them out!"

The road to New Salem was unimproved. Trailing a long cloud of dust, Spears stopped on a ridge above the town. The dust swirled around them. "Nothing like the element of surprise," Carlisle commented dryly.

Spears chuckled. "We're in City of God territory now, Prentiss. They don't believe in spending money on improving the roads, not the ones to the other territories, because they really don't want visitors."

"Since I've met all the other so-called leaders, can't say I blame them."

Spears held up a finger. "Now you're catching on, Prentiss. Well, the place looks deserted. Let's see how good our optics are." He tapped some commands into the system, and the screen mounted on the floor between them filled with a close-up of the main street. He ordered the system to scan slowly. "Looks like everything is totally buttoned up."

"Not even a piece of paper in the street," Carlisle observed. "I don't think we're going to find anybody to talk to down there. I don't like it."

"Neither do I, Prentiss." Spears fingered the handgun he carried in a shoulder harness. Spears knew very well that if the village had been attacked, the handguns would be useless against the weapons the mysterious aggressors had been using, but the mere presence of the puny weapons was at least comforting. "Jim, are you getting all this?" he asked the communications technician monitoring them back at Interstellar City.

"Yessir," Jim Chang answered. "Transmission is very clear, Mr. Ambassador."

"Okay, Jim. Prentiss? Shall we visit the ghost town of New Salem?"

The City of God did not share its demographics with the other sects, so the exact population of its towns and cities was not known. But New Salem, judging by the number of homes located there, could not have had a population much in excess of five thousand. It was one of the smaller of the sect's towns. Altogether, the City of God was estimated to consist of a little more than 200,000 adherents.

The farmers of New Salem lived in the town, not in their fields, which stretched for tens of thousands of hectares in every direction. During the harvest they would camp in the fields until the work was done, but the life of the community was in the town. None of the community or commercial buildings in the town was identified. They did not need signs, because everyone knew where everything was in the town, and while the City of God believed in being hospitable to visitors and wayfarers, they did not feel it necessary to advertise. In fact, although the sect believed it was every man's duty to work hard and prosper, advertising one's trade, or success at that trade, was considered too brash, too commercial, for the vow of simplicity the sect required of its members.

So Spears and Carlisle stood in the empty main street and scratched their heads. Only the church—or meeting house, as it was called—was recognizable to them. And that was only because they knew enough about the sect to recognize the structure: it was the biggest building in town. "Let's try there first," Carlisle suggested.

They trudged up the dusty street, then Spears abruptly stopped. "Look at this building here, on the left, Prentiss. See those big doors? That must be a garage or a machine shop. I want to look through the window for a moment." Inside there was a vast empty space, dimly lighted. The floor was concrete and stained with lubricants. Spears nodded and flicked on his hand communicator. "Jim," he said to the technician back at Interstellar City, "have the navy give us a complete run of its close-up surveillance of the movement toward the Sea of Gerizim. I want to see what was in those convoys." He turned to Carlisle. "Prentiss, there is a reason for all this at this particular time. I think it's very important that we find out."

"You think the City of God knows something we don't?"

"Precisely. They've taken everything of importance that could be moved, including all the heavy machinery and mountings that used to be inside here. I bet if we look inside the houses we might find some furniture left behind, but everything they need to reestablish themselves seems to have been taken with them. Now what do they know that we don't?"

"Fear of the attacks?"

"Possibly." Spears thought for a moment. "They are certain they will be attacked by someone. Prentiss, we've heard the rumors that the sects think we're behind these depredations. We know that's ridiculous. The raiders are using weapons nobody's ever heard of before. But the attacks have been random so far. No one particular sect has been attacked. Now why would the City of God think they in particular are in for trouble?"

"All this fear of this, fear of that, is making me nervous." Carlisle chuckled.

Spears looked intently at his station chief. "Prentiss, I think you have good reason to be nervous. Come on, let's bust into city hall." He nodded toward the meeting house at the end of the street.

The Confederation of Human Worlds ambassador to the Kingdom of Yahweh and His Saints and Their Apostles drew his handgun and blasted the lock off the front door to the meeting house. The report of his gun echoed loudly through the empty street. He kicked the doors open and walked inside. Aside from the pews on the ground floor and some office furniture in the rooms above, the place was also empty.

They stood outside on the steps and looked down the main street. At the far end stood their car. "I think we should have driven up here, sir," Carlisle said nervously. "It's a long walk back to the car." He shaded his eyes and looked through the rays of the sinking sun. "Dark in another hour."

"We're not responsible, the sects are not responsible, so who or what's causing all the trouble here?" Spears said, almost thinking out loud. "You've heard the rumors we're not alone in Human Space, haven't you, Prentiss?"

"Yes." That thought had occurred to him.

"That's what we're up against here, I know it." Spears smacked a fist into the palm of his hand. The smack echoed in the gathering shadows. Carlisle looked about nervously. Suddenly, he did not want to draw attention to himself. "But these bastards," he nodded at the meeting house behind them, "are up to something too, and whatever it is, it'll only complicate things even more around here." Spears laughed. "By God, Prentiss, I think I'm actually beginning to enjoy this assignment!"

"Enjoy being scared shitless, which is what I am right now? It'll be full dark long before we get back to Interstellar City," Carlisle added.

"I know, Prentiss, I know. Well, we've seen enough. Let us

make like the shepherd, Prentiss, and get the flock outta here."

Since the Sea of Gerizim was well within the boundaries of the territory occupied by the City of God, moving the Faithful there posed no problem of real estate acquisition. The hills above the Achor Marshes were riddled with deep limestone caverns, and they had been prepared as an alternate capital many years before, during one of the many factional wars that had marred the history of human relations of Kingdom. All the Ministers had to do was plan the logistics of the move, and that had been done long before the five terrorists were dispatched to Siluria.

"Reminds me of the catacombs of ancient Rome, Increase," Eliashub Williams remarked, standing deep underground in one of the caverns.

"That is fitting, Brother Williams," Increase Harmony responded. "The power system will be operating by tomorrow at the latest. Dry this place out a bit. The stores are in order?"

"Yes and no. Some of the more perishable goods have deteriorated since they were placed in here many years ago, but the construction is still solid and the water supply is excellent."

Someone approached them out of the darkness. "Ah, Brother Jones! What is the word from above?"

"The Lord is with us. The campsites in the oak groves are prepared, and if we are here until the next growing season, we can plant the land on the mesa. The soil up there is perfect, and above 200,000 hectares are available. I would say all is on schedule, brothers," Elnathan Jones replied. He flicked his own light off as he came within the circle illuminated by the other two. "The last families have already moved into the camps. The temporary shelters are up and we should get through the winter very comfortably."

"As soon as word comes that Brother Epher and his men have been successful, we shall move our people down here. The *Cambria* should be entering Earth's solar system within the next forty-eight hours. Say two months from now the news will reach us? I'm leaving for Haven tomorrow, to attend to our affairs among the Ecumenical Leaders. I guess I'll be in the center of the storm when it breaks." Harmony smiled.

"We met in council, Brother Jones, and selected you for that grave duty, but I know the Hand of the Lord guided us," Harmony said. "Are we ready, brothers?" The other two nodded. "Then let us go above, join the other Ministers and repair to our respective congregations, to tell them what is about to happen."

Each congregation moved into its reserved spot in the vast oak forest in the hills above the sea and waited for its respective religious leader to join them. For the villagers of New Salem, that was the Reverend Mr. Resolution Bolton. Bolton was a small man with a powerful voice whose preaching, whether at regular meetings or days of thanksgiving or public fasting, funerals or baptisms, was enjoyed by all. As a man of great scriptural learning who spoke plainly, lived plainly, and loved his congregation, he was greatly respected by the people of New Salem.

"Can everyone hear me?" Bolton inquired. The people of New Salem were crowded under a vast temporary shelter but the acoustics were perfect. Assured that his words would be heard, the Reverend Mr. Bolton asked for God's blessing on their meeting. Then he stood on the dais for a long moment, staring pensively at his feet, as if—wonder of wonders!—he was at a loss for words. When he spoke, his voice was husky with emotion. At his first words, the entire gathering went completely silent, except for the occasional cry of a baby or a child's exclamation, which were quickly silenced by anxious parents.

"I have just come from a meeting with the Ministers of the City of God. I have momentous and terrible news to reveal. Friends, our community of spirits is in danger from several quarters, and it is right that we have taken this refuge, but the worst danger is that which we are about to bring upon ourselves." He told them about the impending destruction of the cargo ship, the SS *Cambria*, and how the Ministers hoped that would focus public attention on what they believed was the Confederation's covert attack against the people of Kingdom.

The congregants of New Salem remained silent for a brief moment after they'd taken in the news. Zechariah Brattle was the first to come to his feet, the time-honored signal that he had something to say to the congregation. "I am a peaceable man," he began in a voice almost as powerful as that of the Reverend Mr. Bolton. "But this—this scheme is murder!" His voice thundered on the word. "I will have no part of it!"

"It is the decision of the Ministers," another man said, "and it is too late to stop it. We must hold together, no matter what comes!"

"I disagree!" a woman in the far back of the crowd shouted. "We are under no authority but that of our own community and our individual consciences! Under the covenant of our church, I request we vote to withdraw our congregation from the City of God."

Pandemonium broke loose. The Reverend Mr. Bolton called for order and after a time it was restored. "Friends, the Ministers conceived this plan under the inspiration of a particular faith, and they believe it was revealed to them by God. You know that our God is a harsh taskmaster at times. However, I remind you that as we are all human beings, we can be deceived, by Satan, by other men, and by ourselves. I happen to agree with Brother Brattle, and since Sister Hannah Flood has moved—as it is her right to move—that we vote on accepting this decision, I second it. Since there are so many of us here, we will dispense with the secret ballot. Those in favor of the plan, remain seated, everyone else step outside, please. I will have the deacons count those inside first, and then those outside will be numbered one by one as they return."

The shuffling and moving about took some time. The Brattles, along with numerous other families, stood in the trees outside and waited for the count to be finished.

Zechariah looked about. From where he stood he could see that the congregation was going to vote to support the Ministers. "If that happens," he told Consort, "we leave. Do you support me?"

"Yes, Zechariah, I do."

He turned to his children. "We also, Father."

Zechariah nodded. " 'Particular faiths,' " he snorted. "Lately there've been far too many of them, and they all seem to support whatever bullshit the Ministers want to put over on us."

"Including the one you had about this move, Father?" Comfort asked.

"That was different—" He laughed. "Well, as the Reverend Mr. Bolton said, daughter, we sometimes fool ourselves."

"Zechariah is right," a woman said in the shadows next to where they were standing. It was Hannah Flood. In the dim light she stood there like a vast mountain, surrounded by her five children. Some years before, her husband had fallen into a cultivating machine during harvest. Since then, with the help of her neighbors and her own determination, she had carried on. "If you leave, Zechariah, we will go with you."

"They're calling us back in, Father. The count inside must be over," Samuel reported. The Brattles, along with the other families that had been standing outside, filed slowly back into the meeting hall. Each person over the age of twenty-one was counted by men standing at the doors. Then the votes were tallied.

"Friends," the Reverend Bolton announced at last, "the count is decisive. One thousand nine hundred and fifty-three adults have voted to confirm the decision of the Ministers, against 872 who did not. Those who voted against are free to leave if they wish. I want it known for the record that I voted against the plan, but I am staying, because that is my duty. This meeting is adjourned."

The Brattles trooped outside. "Consort, Sam, Comfort, get the car and get packed. We're leaving tonight. I'm going to find Reverend Bolton and turn the town records over to him. I guess I'm finished being mayor of New Salem too. Oh, Comfort, find Hannah and her family and tell them and anybody else you can find who wants to go that we're leaving soon."

The Reverend Mr. Bolton lay prostrate in his tent, seeking divine guidance. Zechariah waited patiently until he was finished. Bolton's face was flushed and his cheeks tearstained as he at last got to his feet. "Zach, this thing the Ministers have done is evil and the Lord shall punish us for it."

"Here are the town records, Reverend." Zechariah handed over the crystals. The two men were of the same age and had known each other all their lives. "I admire you for staying behind. Maybe you'll be the one righteous man for whom the Lord will spare this Sodom."

"Zach, I admire you for your principles. I'll join you when the crisis is over." The two men embraced warmly.

The Brattles and the several other families that had decided to leave the congregation were only a few kilometers down the road back to New Salem when the Skinks struck the encampment.

CHAPTER
TWENTY-ONE

Ollie Buskerud shook hands diffidently with Colonel Ramadan, "At your service, Colonel," he squeaked. He nodded at Chief Vest and Inspector Hamnes. "I will be your guide," he added.

Ramadan looked carefully at Buskerud. The man was short and weather-beaten. He sported a neatly trimmed Van Dyke beard and wore thick spectacles. Genetic engineering hadn't yet become a standard procedure on Thorsfinni's World, so most of the people had to go through life with birth defects like astigmatism. Buskerud's handshake was too limp for Ramadan's liking and his voice had the effect on him of fingernails scraping down a blackboard. The Marine officer hoped his expression did not reveal what he was thinking just now.

"Mr. Buskerud knows the Thorvalds better than anybody else, Colonel," Chief Vest said. "He will identify the most likely locations for a camp and we will visit them all. Inspector Hamnes will coordinate the operation, and I hope you will assist him."

"Delighted, Mr. Buskerud," Ramadan said without conviction.

"As am I, Colonel." The little man bowed. Ramadan also noted, with some dismay, that he had very bad teeth. Mentally he shook his head. He'd just been around Marines too long.

"We have set up a temporary operations center in the basement, gentlemen," Hamnes said. "We will coordinate the operation from there. If you would come this way, we'll get started." He nodded at his superior and ushered the men out the door.

The operations center was in an overheated and brightly lighted but too small room beside the building's basement power plant. The plant was a fossil-fuel affair that required constant attendance and reeked. A man in dirty overalls cursed and muttered about the furnace, with its incessant clanking and banging.

"This is the best we can do," Hamnes said as they entered the makeshift operations center. Several police officers who had been sitting there got out of their chairs, and Hamnes introduced Ramadan and Buskerud to them. "These officers will head the special action teams we will send to the campsites Mr. Buskerud will identify for us. Gentlemen," he said, turning to address the officers, "this will be a long and difficult operation. Please be seated and let's get organized."

The plan Hamnes had come up with was very simple and involved a hundred officers in ten teams. The ten men in the operations center were the team leaders. All the officers selected were trained in special weapons and tactics. They would reach the camps by air or by ground transport—depending on the weather and terrain conditions—secure their respective areas, and search them. If nothing was found, they would deploy to the next site on the list until all the possible sites had been covered. Buskerud's knowledge of the mountains would be vital to the operation because he knew all the most likely refuge spots, as well as permanent sites, which included a few private homes, all of which would be closed up during the winter.

"Time is against us," Hamnes told the officers. "As soon as the weather breaks, the kidnappers will try for the coast, I am sure, and when they are safely away, Mrs. Conorado will be of no more use to them. Before they can do that, we must find her, gentlemen."

"Now, Mr. Buskerud, Colonel Ramadan, and I will coordinate your deployments from here. Remember who you are dealing with, gentlemen, and use whatever force is necessary to subdue them without causing harm to Mrs. Conorado. You all know that the general orders of this department call for negotiations in every hostage situation. That will not work here, gentlemen. Neutralize the bad guys and rescue the hostage, it's that simple. If you can't stop the bad guys, rescue the hostage; we'll get them later. The weather service will be giving us fifteen minute updates. We'll be in touch with all of you constantly. Mr. Buskerud?"

Ollie Buskerud came to the front of the room. He nodded at the technician in his booth at the rear, and a huge map of the Thorvalds appeared on one wall. "All the permanent and temporary campsites in the range are marked," he told the policemen. "All the private homes are marked." As he spoke, the sites appeared on the map in different colors. "I suggest you hit the permanent sites first because in this weather I don't think your fugitives would be dumb enough to camp in the open with nothing but sleeping bags, or pitch a tent, for that matter. But remember, this map is not complete. Any structure put up within the last year or so would not appear here. We have asked the Confederation Navy," he nodded at Ramadan, "to assist with their geosynchronous surveillance satellites. If the weather clears for only an instant, their infrared capability might be of great help to us. But remember to keep us always apprised of your exact location. We don't want to get you mixed up with potential targets."

"What kind of ground transportation will you be using?" Ramadan asked Hamnes.

The inspector shrugged. "We have snow cats—heavy duty commercial vehicles used to haul cargo like timber. They are powerful but slow, but they will do the job good enough."

"Could you use a Dragon?" Ramadan asked.

"Dragon?"

"Armored All-Surface Assault Landing Craft, Air Cushioned. The Marines basic ground vehicle."

"Ah! Can you get us one?"

"Maybe. We had several deadlined in the motor pool back at Camp Ellis, when 34th FIST deployed. I think for this operation I could get the base mechanics to put one back on line and ship it out here. It's worth a try. Dragons can go anywhere."

"How long would it take to get one here?" a policeman asked.

"If I call right now and they can get one in working order, maybe eight hours. Will the storm hold that long?"

"The weather service thinks so. But Colonel, if 34th FIST is deployed, where from do you get the crew to drive this Dragon?"

"You're looking at it," Colonel Ramadan answered.

Sabbath Lordsday, followed closely by Jesse Gospel and Joshua Merab, all holding weapons at the ready, stepped onto the *Cambria*'s bridge. "Please stand very still and do not interfere," Lordsday said. "Captain Tuit, Miss Lenfen, Captain Conorado, kindly step over there by the navigator's station and do not move until I tell you."

"Just what in the hell do you think you're doing, goddamnit!" Tuit shouted.

Lordsday motioned with the barrel of his blaster. "Move, Captain, or I will kill you. I will kill everyone on this bridge, on this ship, if you don't do precisely what I ask." Lordsday spoke in a calm, conversational tone of voice and smiled. It was evident he meant just what he said. Slowly, the trio moved over to the navigator's console and stood there, hands raised. Conorado noticed that two of the "miners" were missing.

"Brother Gospel." Lordsday nodded toward Jesse Gospel.

A tall, angular man, Gospel stepped briskly up to Jennifer Lenfen's station. He withdrew a case from a pocket and popped out a crystal, which he inserted into a port. "Your computer now belongs to me," he said. "Minerva?"

"Yes, Brother Gospel?" Minerva answered.

"Send the message."

"The message is sent, Brother Gospel."

Gospel looked up from the console and grinned. "This is a wonderful program I have written," he said to Jennifer. "I have overridden all your safeguards and installed my own password. You commercial people are too free with descriptions of the systems you use on your ships." He typed some commands on the keyboard. "Brother Lordsday, the course is set and cannot be altered. It will take us to three thousand kilometers above the Earth's surface over the Western hemisphere. It will be nighttime when we arrive at that point in, um, precisely forty-seven hours, eighteen minutes, twenty-two seconds. And," he added, smiling at Captain Tuit, "you cannot possibly alter course manually because," he nodded at the navigation console, "we have taken care of that."

"Good!" Lordsday pronounced.

"What about my men in the propulsion unit?" Tuit asked.

"They do not matter, Captain."

"What 'message' did you send?" Jennifer asked Gospel.

"To the President of the Confederation of Worlds!" he answered. "Informing her that we have taken over this ship in protest—"

"Stop!" Lordsday commanded. "No more! They do not need to know any more. Now, Brother Gospel, have the computer tell the crew and passengers to report to the passenger dining area for an emergency meeting. You," he gestured at his four prisoners, "will come with Joshua and me, and when you are all gathered in the dining room I will explain everything to you. Captain Conorado, I know what you are thinking."

"I'm thinking what any Marine would think in a situation like this, mister," Conorado answered.

"I know." Lordsday smiled tightly. "But stop it. Even if you were able to jump us and take our guns, this ship will still proceed to its destination. There is no way you can alter its course. Now, all of you, we are going to the dining area. Please do not try anything foolish on the way."

The thirteen other passengers and eight remaining crewmen stood and sat about the dining room expectantly.

"This ship is now under my control," Lordsday announced. "After this meeting you will proceed to your respective staterooms and remain there until our mission is complete."

"And just what is that 'mission,' sir?" Ambassador Franks asked. "And just who are you?"

"I am a soldier in the Army of Zion," Lordsday answered. "My mission is to send a message to your Confederation. Obey my orders and you will not be harmed. Interfere with our mission and you will die."

"Where are Conrad and Bernstein?" one of the crewmen asked, looking around for the engineers.

"They no longer matter," Lordsday answered.

"You goddamned sonofabitch!" Captain Tuit shouted. "You killed my men and you're a lying bastard! You're going to kill us too! What the hell are you up to? This is a god-damned cargo ship, you can't hijack it!"

"Captain, Captain," Lordsday admonished quietly, "you should not take the Lord's name in vain. Proceed now to your suites in an orderly manner. All will become clear to you in time."

"Jenny," Conorado whispered to Lenfen at his side, "they're going to kill us. Stay in your room until I come for you."

"Lew," she whispered back, "it'll be too dangerous! What can one man do anyway?"

"Watch me," Conorado whispered.

"Now that we are alone, my dear, shouldn't we get to know one another better?" Bengt said. He had pulled Marta's pants down to her knees, as far as they would go while she was still sitting with her legs bound at the ankles.

"Kiruna will be back any minute!" Marta gasped as he ran his ice cold hands over her buttocks. Bengt only snorted. One hand crept up between her shoulder blades. She felt like throwing up. "Untie my hands. If you promise not to hurt me I'll be quiet," Marta wheezed, her breath taken away by the filthy probing of Bengt's cold fingers.

Bengt paused and looked up into Marta's face. "You dare

to cross me, Mrs. Marine, and I will kill you." He placed the tip of his knife under Marta's chin and pressed the blade into her flesh. She gasped and tried to wrench her head away from the point but Bengt kept pressing until blood welled out of the wound. He laughed, and tumbled her out of the chair onto her stomach, where he cut the ropes binding her hands behind her back. Pinning Marta's legs with his knees, Bengt wrenched her pants as far down as he could and began running his hands over her exposed backside. Her hands free now, Marta tried to lever herself up off the stone-cold floor, but Bengt forced her back down with one hand. "Ah, my pretty," he whispered, his breath hot on the back of her neck, "let us make love face-to-face." He grabbed her shoulder and began to roll Marta onto her back.

Kiruna slammed a chair onto the top of Bengt's head. He fell halfway across Marta's prostrate body, and Kiruna hit him again. Then she dragged Bengt off Marta and, breathing heavily, brought the chair down on her shoulders. The force of the blow stunned Marta and slammed her back down on the floor. Screaming inarticulately in Norse, Kiruna jumped on Marta's back and began pulling her hair.

"Bitch!" Kiruna screamed in English. "You want fucking my man? I fucking fuck you fucking good!" She tried to slam Marta's head into the floor. Marta braced her neck as much as she could and attempted to get her arms underneath her body to lever herself up enough to try to roll over on her back. Her hand closed over something hard. Bengt's knife!

Kiruna raked her nails over Marta's face, clawing and screaming in English and Norse. "Pretty—no—more—I—finish—" Kiruna shouted. To get at Marta's face, Kiruna flipped her on her back, and as Marta rolled over she drove the blade straight into Kiruna's face. The knife slammed almost effortlessly right into Kiruna's left eyeball—up to the hilt. Kiruna Rena, professional hit woman, was dead before her body collapsed on top of Marta.

Marta lay on the floor for a moment, too stunned to react, her breath coming in hissing gasps. At last her heart stopped its pounding inside her chest and she found the strength to roll out from under Kiruna's body. Using Bengt's blood-stained knife, she cut the ropes around her ankles. She threw the knife as far from her as she could and, pulling her pants up, got shakily to her feet. Bengt lay unconscious in a pool of blood seeping from several deep gashes on his head. Quickly, she threw on her coat and stumbled toward the open door. Already, driven snow was piling up inside the cabin. She stepped out into the raging storm. Whatever dangers nature had in store for her, Marta thought, could not be worse than what lay behind her in that cabin.

In her rush to get away, she neglected to don either gloves or headgear.

"Madam President," Glecko Malaka began gravely, "I have just received the most dreadful communication."

Madam President Chang-Sturdevant looked up from her reader and regarded her chief of staff balefully. He was standing here personally, so the news was very bad indeed. But with Glecko, all news was bad anyway. "Here is a transcript of a most extraordinary message the communications staff has just received from what appear to be terrorists aboard a cargo ship, the SS *Cambria*, even now en route to Earth's orbit where—" His voice faltered. "—where they are going to blow it up!"

Madam Chang-Sturdevant took the palm reader Malaka offered and looked at it. "Glecko, what in the world is this nonsense?"

The message read:

> WE ARE THE ARMY OF ZION, THE SWORD OF THE CITY OF GOD.
>
> MOST HONORED MADAM CHANG-STURDEVANT, PRESIDENT OF THE CONFEDERATION OF WORLDS, GREETINGS AND MAY THE BLESSING OF OUR LORD AND SAVIOR, JESUS CHRIST, BE UPON YOU ALWAYS!
>
> WE MAKE THE FOLLOWING TESTAMENT:
>
> WHEREAS THE EVIL OF SATAN IS NOT TURNED AWAY, BUT HIS HAND IS STRETCHED OUT AGAINST GOD'S PEOPLE IN

MANIFOLD JUDGMENTS, PARTICULARLY IN DRAWING OUT PERSECUTIONS AGAINST THEM AND MORE ESPECIALLY RESPECTING OURSELVES IN OUR PROVINCE OF KINGDOM, DIMINISHING OUR SUBSTANCE, CUTTING SHORT OUR HARVEST, BLASTING OUR MOST PROMISING UNDERTAKINGS, AND IN MORE WAYS THAN ONE ACCOMPLISHING THE UNSETTLING OF US, AND BY HIS MORE IMMEDIATE HAND SNATCHING AWAY MANY OF OUR EMBRACES BY SUDDEN AND VIOLENT DEATHS EVEN AT THIS TIME WHEN THE SWORD IS DEVOURING SO MANY BOTH AT HOME AND ABROAD, AND THAT AFTER MANY DAYS OF PUBLIC AND SOLEMN ADDRESSING OF THE LORD FOR SURCREASE OF THESE HIDEOUS EVILS, AND ALTHOUGH CONSIDERING THE MANY SINS PREVAILING IN THE MIDST OF US, WE CANNOT BUT CONCLUDE THAT THE LORD GOD OUR MASTER HAS PERMITTED THESE DISASTERS TO BE ACCOMPLISHED AGAINST US FOR A REASON.

"Jesus H. Christ, get on with it!" Chang-Sturdevant muttered.

DOUBTLESS THERE ARE SOME PARTICULAR SINS ABOUT WHICH GOD IS ANGRY WITH OUR ISRAEL THAT HAVE NOT BEEN DULY SEEN AND EXTIRPATED BY US, ABOUT WHICH GOD EXPECTS TO BE SOUGHT, AND IT IS EVIDENT THAT CHIEF AMONG THEM HAS BEEN OUR DOCILITY AND INACTION IN THE FACE OF THE OVERPOWERING EVIL THAT EMANATES FROM YOUR GOVERNMENT, MADAM PRESIDENT! THE INCURSION OF YOUR MINIONS UPON OUR PLANTATIONS IS AN INTOLERABLE AFFRONT TO GOD AND HIS CHOSEN PEOPLE! THAT YOUR GOVERNMENT HAS CHOSEN TO INTRUDE UPON US IN THIS SLY AND COVERT WAY, PRETENDING TO EXTEND THE HAND OF FRIENDSHIP TO OUR PEOPLE WHILE HOLDING A SWORD OVER US, IS THE VERY MARK OF SATAN, AND WERE IT KNOWN AMONG RIGHTEOUS AND HONORABLE MEN, THEY WOULD RISE UP AS ONE AND DEMAND THAT YOU INSTANTLY WITHDRAW YOUR DETESTABLE OPPRESSORS FROM OUR LANDS AND PROVINCES.

THEREFORE, WE MUST NOW SET ASIDE THE PATIENCE
AND MERCY OF OUR LORD JESUS CHRIST AND TAKE UP THE
SWORD OF JEHOVAH. IT IS WITH THE GREATEST SADNESS
WE NOW INFORM YOUR EXCELLENCY THAT WE HAVE BEEN
FORCED TO SEIZE THE CARGO SHIP, SS CAMBRIA, THE
PROPERTY OF THE SEWALL SHIPPING COMPANY, ITS CARGO,
CREW, AND PASSENGERS. CAST THEN YOUR EYES TOWARD
THE NIGHT SKY AND WITNESS THE ANGER OF THE LORD!
REVELATION 10:18

Madam Chang-Sturdevant blew out her cheeks and
looked up at her chief of staff. "Long-winded bastards,
aren't they? What's the quote from the Book of Revelation?"

" 'By these three was the third part of men killed, by the
fire, and by the smoke and by the brimstone, which issued
out of their mouths.' That's why I think they plan to blow her
up, ma'am."

"Yes, and seems to me they plan to blow her up so everyone'll know about it. And they're going to do it when it's
night in this hemisphere. It's eight hours now, so it'll be either tonight or tomorrow. We need to know where that ship
is now and how far it is from Earth's orbit, and I want to
know who's on board her and what she's carrying."

"The navy's checking now to get a fix on her position,
ma'am, and I have some of that information. She's carrying
a full load of ore from the mines on Siluria—it's worth trillions. If she goes up, Sewall may well be bankrupted,
ma'am, and you know the effect that could have on the economy. Sewall gave us a partial list of passengers, but since it
was made up months ago, we can't be sure it's complete.
Ambassador Jamison Franks III and his team were to have
been picked up on Thorsfinni's World."

"Oh, that's perfectly delightful!" Madam Chang-
Sturdevant banged her fist angrily. Jamison Franks was well-
known in the political world of the Confederation since he
came from a prominent family that contributed liberally to
various parties, chief among them the one Madam Chang-
Sturdevant represented. "We don't have much time, Glecko.

Assemble my cabinet. Make sure the Combined Chiefs are there, especially whatshisname, the Chief of Naval Operations."

"It is already being done, ma'am."

"Has anyone tried to contact the *Cambria*?"

"Yes, ma'am. They are not responding."

Madam Chang-Sturdevant shook her head in exasperation. "So there'll be no negotiations." She grimaced. "Well, find out all you can about this Army of—of—what do they call themselves, the Army of Zion? And find out what the hell we're doing on—on Kingdom, did they say? Christ, I remember something about that place in a meeting months ago now, but damned if I can remember the circumstances. Find out why these guys are upset with us." She stood up. "Okay, let's get to the war room."

Admiral Joseph K. C. B. Porter, Confederation Chief of Naval Operations, ran a hand nervously over his enormous muttonchop whiskers and looked at his reader again. "Madam President, we have a fix on the *Cambria*. She's approximately seventeen hours out of Earth orbit, given her present course and speed, which seem fixed. It gets dark in this hemisphere at this season beginning at about nineteen hours on the eastern seaboard, so it'll be full dark here at Fargo by twenty-one hours tonight. If they really intend to blow the *Cambria* up, they're going to do it sometime tonight. It's nine hours now. We don't have much time to react."

"Can we react?" Chang-Sturdevant asked. All eyes turned to Admiral Porter, who was not enjoying the attention.

"Yes, ma'am, we can have a ship at her location in two hours. But a rescue operation might be very chancy. If they've rigged the ship with explosives and intend to immolate themselves along with her, we could lose a navy ship and its entire crew."

"Well, gentlemen, my chief of staff informs me we have a break. The damned fools—this Army of Zion, as they call themselves—neglected to send their message to anybody but us." She paused.

"How does that give us a break, ma'am?" a cabinet officer asked.

"Simple. Since the rest of the world doesn't know what's going on, we can minimize the embarrassment of being ridiculed by these fanatics by striking first. It'll be bad news for Sewall and Lloyds, but I think we can work out some subsidies that'll keep the company and its insurers afloat until they can make up the losses. We can find an explanation for the disaster that'll satisfy public opinion."

"Madam President, are you saying that . . . ?" Admiral Porter shifted uncomfortably in his seat.

"I am saying, gentlemen, that we dispatch a destroyer to the position of the SS *Cambria* and blast it out of space before the fanatics do it for us, in front of half the world, to the utter embarrassment of this administration and the frustration of our foreign policy, which demands that we deploy our military forces whenever and wherever they are needed. I am not going to stand for a bunch of crazies dictating to my government. The damned fools who took over the *Cambria* screwed up when they didn't send their message to the goddamned press. We have to act quickly and decisively before they realize their mistake, before they execute their threat." There was utter silence in the war room.

"Gentlemen, the passengers and crew on that ship are doomed no matter what. I believe—we believe—this Army of Zion intends to immolate itself along with them. I will not risk the entire crew of a navy ship to attempt a rescue." Madam Chang-Sturdevant turned to Admiral Porter, who unconsciously was slumping as far down in his chair as possible, as if that would excuse him from what he knew was coming. "Admiral," the President of the Confederation Council of Worlds said calmly, with complete confidence in her voice, "give the order."

Captain Lewis Conorado, Confederation Marine Corps, lay in his bunk thinking. There was no doubt in his mind that the fanatics who'd taken control of the ship were going to kill them all. Otherwise, why sabotage the navigation system and the lifecraft? Nobody, not even the terrorists themselves, was going to get off the *Cambria* alive. Conorado knew he had to act. He had to do something, no matter how desperate. It was not in his nature to sit by when threatened.

There were three of them in the main part of the ship and two more in the propulsion unit. The three he had seen were all armed with military hand-blasters. If he could just get one of the bastards, he'd have a chance at the rest of them. But then what? Evidently they were going to set off some kind of bomb in the propulsion unit, and when it went, everything else would go too. So suppose he somehow could overpower the three men up here. How could he get to the ones in the power plant before they set off the bomb? Probably it was already set to go off, so if he did succeed in eliminating all five of the terrorists, how could he defuse the damned bomb? What a prizefight, and he was the underdog!

Okay, okay, Conorado told himself, think it through, take it one step, one round, at a time. First step: get the three up here. How? He suddenly sat bolt upright in his bed, grinning, and swung his legs to the deck.

Round one to the Marine?

CHAPTER
TWENTY-TWO

The hours crept slowly by for the three men in the makeshift police operations center. Hamnes and Buskerud stayed constantly on the radio and vid hookups with the teams as they laboriously went from site to site, approaching cautiously and effecting traumatic entry into the cabins. Not a few citizens were terribly surprised to be interrupted at their long winter's pastimes as heavily armed men burst into their bedrooms.

Colonel Ramadan had already smoked two of his precious Anniversarios and shared a third, cut into equal halves, between Hamnes and Buskerud. After the one he had just popped into his mouth, he would be out until he got back to Camp Ellis.

"How many more sites do we have to search in those mountains?" Ramadan asked.

Buskerud shook his head. "Lots, Colonel. We have only just begun."

"Well, the cops are sure on duty, but where in the hell is the Dragon?" Ramadan groused, looking at his watch again for the umpteenth time. "They should've been here an hour ago! Inspector, how's the weather holding?"

Inspector Hamnes finished talking to a team chief who had just come up with another dry hole and turned to Ramadan. "We're in luck there, Colonel. The weather report has been revised. The storm will last at least until morning. And when the sun finally rises, we'll have surveillance over every square meter of those mountains, especially on the routes leading to the sea. Do not worry, Colonel, we will get them." He went back to talking to the teams.

"This is an exceptionally good cigar, Colonel," Buskerud said, holding up his half of the Anniversario admiringly. "I compliment you on your judgment in smoking materials."

"And I on your taste, Ollie," Ramadan answered, bowing slightly toward the little man. Colonel Ramadan had decided that if Ollie Buskerud appreciated a fine cigar, he couldn't be all that bad. And he was indefatigable in his work, constantly plotting the sites to be searched, expertly guiding the teams to their targets.

"Your embassy is on the line at last, Colonel! I think your Dragon is down," Inspector Hamnes announced.

"Gentlemen," Ramadan said as he slipped quickly into his foul weather gear, "I'll be back within the hour."

It had been a long, long time since Colonel Israel Ramadan had driven a Dragon. The entire instrument panel seemed to have changed since his days as an enlisted man, but the power-up sequence had remained the same. The mechanic who had driven the Dragon to the embassy compound from the spaceport only shrugged when Ramadan refused his offer to continue as driver. The commander of the Marine security detachment at the embassy raised his eyebrows in astonishment as the colonel mounted the ramp and buttoned up the Dragon, even after his offer to go along had been politely refused. But he was a captain and Ramadan was a bull colonel. The captain discreetly closed his eyes as Ramadan unskillfully slewed the Dragon through the main gate, knocking over a pillar as the behemoth slid out into the late afternoon traffic. The mechanic laughed outright but he shut up immediately at a withering glance from the officer.

Ramadan plowed along at twenty kilometers per hour, happily reliving his youth in the driver's seat, but he quickly regained his confidence and the Dragon picked up speed. A huge cloud of blown snow marked its passage down the streets of New Oslo. Drivers pulled to the curb to let him pass and pedestrians gaped in wonder as the monster roared along.

"We have a break!" Inspector Hamnes shouted as Ramadan clomped back into the command center. The inspector looked up and paused. Ramadan's face was flushed bright red and his face split from ear to ear with an enormous grin. "Colonel, you look twenty years younger than you did an hour ago!" the inspector exclaimed.

"I feel younger!" Ramadan exclaimed. "Been a long time since I drove a Dragon! Man, do we have a powerhouse there! What's up?"

"Your satellite surveillance got an infrared signal from a remote chateau, Colonel," Buskerud answered. "The owners are in the city and they say there should not be anybody in there. We think it might be the kidnappers." His face too was flushed with excitement. "Best of all, Colonel, none of the teams in the field can get up there for a long time. That means *we* get to go in!"

"Huh? Inspector Hamnes?" Ramadan turned to the policeman.

"Yes, Colonel, Ollie and I have discussed the situation. Your arrival is absolutely fortuitous. We have three aircraft down due to mechanical failure. None of the other teams is close enough to get to this site today. The break in the cloud cover was only temporary. The storm has in fact increased in its fury. Only land vehicles could make it up there now, and none of the teams is close enough to a road to get through. You and Ollie must go."

"Then give me a gun and we're off," Ramadan said.

Captain Conorado rummaged through his luggage until he found it. The antique pistol was almost small enough to hide comfortably in the palm of his hand. He examined it closely now because he'd had no time to look at it when Dean and Claypoole had presented him with the thing back in Lima Company's orderly room. In fact, had he thought about it at the time, he wouldn't have bothered to pack the weapon in the first place.

It had a detachable magazine that fit snugly into a well in

the butt. He pressed the stud on the right side of the grip and the magazine popped out. The magazine was spring loaded. There was a spot of rust on it. Rust on a weapon? Conorado smiled to himself as he thumbed seven tiny cartridges out onto his bed. He'd be sure to remind those lads about their dreadful lack of maintenance, giving him a rusty weapon, even if it might save his and everybody else's life on the ship!

Conorado was familiar with the projectile weapons the Siad warriors had used on Elneal, so the tiny pistol held no mystery for him. He just wondered if seven rounds of .32 caliber ammunition would be enough to bring down three full-grown, determined men. Well, this particular pistol had worked well enough on Wanderjahr. Claypoole had killed a man with it at close range, shot him in the head, so it would do the job here—if he didn't miss.

Conorado knew that in any kind of face-off with firearms, the first shot was the one that counted; not necessarily the size or power of the bullet fired, but where it hit the opponent. The central nervous system would be best. Disabling that would bring a man down instantly. A bullet in the heart or an artery would kill a man but not necessarily prevent him from getting off a shot of his own even after being hit. But Conorado realized if he couldn't get a head shot, he'd have to shoot at the center of mass, the chest. And how many bullets would it take to bring down a man with a gun like this? Two? If he could only get one of the three men on the bridge alone, he was sure he could bring him down with the tiny pistol and take his more potent blaster. Then he'd have a fighting chance!

He reinserted the empty magazine, worked the slide, and dry-fired the pistol several times to get the feel of it. The action was smooth and it did not take much pressure on the trigger to trip the hammer when it was all the way down. If he cocked the hammer first, the gun would fire with almost no pressure at all on the trigger. There was a lever on the left side of the gun's slide; when he pressed it downward, it de-

cocked the hammer. As far as he could tell, that was the only
safety device. He fiddled with the empty pistol for a while,
then reloaded the magazine, pulled the slide back, and put
the gun into battery. He decocked the weapon. He was ready.
He would shoot his man at very close range, less than a
meter, so aiming should be no problem. He wondered how
much noise the gun would make when it fired. So long as it
fired, that did not matter.

Conorado stood up and slipped the loaded pistol into a
pocket of his coveralls. How would he get to his first man?
"Important information" for their leader? What? What kind
of information could he possibly dream up that'd get him on
the bridge and make one of the terrorists let his guard down
for only a second? He'd think of something. But wait a second! As soon as he brought his man down, that goddamned
computer would sound the alarm, like it did when the terrorists killed the engineers in the propulsion plant! He took
a deep breath. Oh-kaaaay, he'd have to get all three of them
at the same time. He'd have to get to the bridge or wherever
the three of them were congregating. That'd mean two quick
pops apiece and one bullet left over for emergencies. Now
what kind of cover story could he come up with to get that
close to all three of them? Think! Think! he told himself.
Conorado sighed. I don't have a chance, he thought. Then:
What the hell? They won't be expecting an attack and I'll
hurt them at least, and by God I'll go down fighting!

Conorado smiled. At least he wouldn't be facing that kan-
garoo court at the end of this voyage! He shook his head,
squared his shoulders, and stepped out into the companionway.

Ramadan drove the Dragon while Buskerud navigated. In
places the road into the mountains disappeared completely
under heavy snow cover, and as they drove higher and
higher, Ramadan began to worry about running off the
roadway and over one of the dizzying cliffs that fell away
into deep gorges. "Do not vorry, Colonel, I knows de vay!"

Buskerud crowed happily as he monitored the terrain through the Dragon's onboard navigation system. "Ah, dis is a wunnerful machine, Colonel, wunnerful!"

"You ain't seen nothing yet!" Ramadan answered over the tactical net. "Watch me take out that peak over there!"

"No, no, Colonel! No!" Buskerud protested, not sure whether Ramadan was joking or not. "Dere is good chance of big landslide! Besides, de vay sound carries in dese mountains, firing your gun could warn de peoples at the chalet. Ve are only a few kilometers from dere now."

"All right. You tell me when to park this thing and we'll go take a look-see."

After about twenty more minutes of climbing they reached a pass between two peaks where Buskerud indicated Ramadan should pull over to the side of the road, which had been exposed at that spot by the gale-force wind howling down between the peaks. The visibility there was greatly reduced by blown snow.

Buskerud opened an equipment bag he'd brought with him and took out snowshoes. "Ve vill need dese, Colonel. The chalet is in de forest on de leeward side ov de mountain, so da snow vill be very deep dere. Alzo, be absolutely sure dere iss no exposed skin on your face, or it vill freeze in dis weather." They shrugged into heavy parkas and strapped on the snowshoes. Ramadan showed Buskerud how to use the tactical headgear he provided from the Dragon's equipment locker.

"We'll need this to communicate in that weather," he said. Then he showed Buskerud how to operate the shoulder-fired blaster he gave him from the onboard weapons locker. "I will walk the point," Ramadan said. "You guide me from a few paces behind and be ready to support me if we run into any hostile fire. Handling these blasters through gloves will be awkward, but just remember, do not touch the firing lever until you are ready to shoot and sure of your target. And don't forget, Ollie, I'll be in front of your muzzle." He grinned and slapped Buskerud on the back. "Ready?" Buskerud nodded, and then Ramadan lowered the Dragon's ramp. A cloud of windblown snow gusted into the Dragon as they stomped down the ramp and onto the road.

"Go left, Colonel," Buskerud said into his throat mike. "Dere is a path about thirty meters behind vere ve are parked. You vill see it as an opening in de trees. De chalet is about half a kilometer back in de voods."

They slogged into the lee of the mountain and suddenly the wind died away. Under the trees, heavily laden with snow, it was so quiet the men could hear their snowshoes crunching on the frozen crust beneath them. But each breath burned with the cold, and visibility under the trees was almost zero because of the fine mist created by the ice crystals suspended in the air. "De trees vill thin out ven ve get near to de chalet, Colonel, and den de vind vill pick up again, so be careful."

Ramadan guessed from the level of the snow packed up against the trees that it was at least two meters deep where they were. In time Ramadan began to sweat beneath his parka, but he paced himself carefully. The temperature under the trees had to be way below freezing, but out of the wind there was not a chill factor to deal with. Although the air burned fiercely as he sucked it in, he knew his body would heat it sufficiently by the time it got to his lungs so it would not do any damage. Long strings of ice began to form around the opening in his face mask, the frozen condensation of his breath. The trees began to thin. "Are we near the chalet yet?" he asked.

"Yes," Buskerud answered.

The wind picked up again, and suddenly Ramadan could make out in a clearing to his front a rustic building buried almost to its eaves in snow. "There it is," he whispered. He crouched beside the nearest tree. Buskerud came up and knelt beside him. They were silent for a few moments, catching their breath. A gust of wind howled across the clearing, swirling a cloud of snow that temporarily obscured the chalet. Ramadan put his arm around Buskerud's shoulders. "I'm going in first," he said, "when the next gust comes along. You cover me from here. Any fire from that house, you return it at once. Otherwise, come on up when I get to the front of the building. Have you been in touch with Hamnes?"

"Yes, Colonel, all along, as you showed me how to do with dis communications system."

"Okay. Soon as I move out you tell him we're going in and he should back us up as soon as there's a team available that can get up to this pass. But Ollie, we're on our own. Any resistance and we'll have to fight. Ready?"

"Ready, Colonel." Ollie Buskerud was familiar with danger. He had survived landslides, deadly falls, unexpected winter storms, and seen many other men die in the mountains. But he had never killed anyone. He checked the safety on his blaster. It was off. He clicked it on and off several times, to be sure it had not frozen in the safe position. He held the weapon carefully, as Ramadan had showed him, at what he called the "high ready" position, butt under his right armpit, muzzle held up at about thirty degrees above his midsection, ready to employ the weapon from the shoulder or the hip in a 180-degree arc from where he crouched.

Ramadan disappeared into the next gust of wind, and before the snow had blown away, the colonel was nearly at the cabin door. Buskerud started after him. His breath sounded harsh in his ears as he shuffled quickly along on the top of the hard-frozen snow. "We are going in!" he announced over the command net, confident that the Dragon's system would relay his words immediately to Inspector Hamnes back in New Oslo. "Send backup," he half shouted. Hamnes knew precisely where the pair were from the GPS devices they carried that connected them to the string-of-pearls in orbit.

"None available!" Hamnes answered immediately. "Not until the storm clears. Be careful. Keep in touch with me, Ollie!"

Ramadan stepped lightly on the porch. The goddamned door was open! He slammed through with his shoulder and rolled immediately to his right once inside, his blaster at the ready. "Ollie! Ollie!" he shouted over the tactical net. "Get in here right now!"

*   *   *

"Attention on the bridge!" Minerva screamed. "There is a passenger in the companionway! There is a passenger loose on the ship! It is Captain Lewis Conorado! Attention on the bridge!"

I'm in for it now, Conorado thought as he hurried along the passageway. A figure suddenly appeared before him. It was the man called Merab or something. He leveled his hand-blaster at Conorado and ordered him to return to his stateroom.

Conorado raised his hands and stopped. "I must talk to your leader," he pleaded.

"No! Return to your place at once or I will shoot."

"Listen! I have something to tell you. It's very important. Please, I must talk to your leader. Look, I'm unarmed. I represent no threat to you." He could feel the tiny bulk of the pistol in his right pocket as he spoke.

"What?"

"I am not a Marine officer. I'm an intelligence agent planted on board this ship. We know what it is you are going to do but I was not quick enough to stop you. There are weapons cached on the ship, and my men and I were to use them against you. But you have to understand, my superiors expected a message from me hours ago, assuring them you had been neutralized. When that message was not sent, they instituted Plan B." Conorado was thinking fast now. What the hell would Plan B consist of anyway?

"Plan B?" Merab asked.

"Yes. The Confederation has dispatched a cruiser to destroy this vessel. They cannot afford to be embarrassed by you. They are going to sacrifice all of us to avoid that. We only have a few minutes before the strike. I must talk to your leader right now!"

Merab hesitated, then said, "Very well, come with me." He motioned Conorado forward with his blaster, keeping as far away from the Marine as he could when Conorado walked past him toward the bridge.

Conorado stepped onto the bridge first. Sabbath Lordsday

whirled around in the captain's chair. "What is the captain doing here?"

"Brother Sabbath, this man has important news I thought you should hear," Merab said. The third terrorist who had been at the ship's computer console stepped toward Conorado.

It was now or never. Pulling out the tiny pistol, Conorado spun halfway around and shot Merab in the neck. The discharge made a loud crack, and the pistol recoiled sharply in Conorado's hand. Merab staggered backward, one hand clapped to his left external carotid artery. Conorado then swung toward Lordsday in the captain's chair and shot him full in the face. The round entered Lordsday's left nostril and lodged in his frontal sinus; not a fatal wound, but extremely painful and bloody. Lordsday clapped his hands to his face and staggered out of the chair, where he sprawled on the deck, shrieking in agony. Conorado whirled and faced the third terrorist, the one called Jesse Gospel, and shot him in the chest three times from very close range. Gospel swung his blaster up toward Conorado, and Conorado, taking aim over the pistol's tiny sights, shot him once more in the chest. Gospel staggered and then collapsed to the deck, his eyes rolling into the back of his head.

Conorado let out his breath. The whole scene had not lasted more than five seconds. Lordsday was on his knees, gasping, *"Unnng, unnng, unnnnnnnng,"* but he had drawn his blaster and was pointing it straight at Conorado. Without hesitating, Conorado fired. The tiny bullet entered Lordsday's forehead. His eyes went wide for an instant before he pitched forward on the deck, stone dead. Conorado had aimed instinctively and fired without thinking. He looked down in surprise at the pistol in his hand, its slide locked back on the empty magazine. After the first shot, he hadn't noticed the thing going off or the recoil.

Now he was acutely aware of Minerva shrieking an alarm: "Brother Lordsday, Brother Lordsday!" the computer voice screamed. "People on the bridge are out of order! All available crew report to the bridge immediately! Repeat—"

"Minerva! Shut up, will you?" Conorado shouted. He stepped over to where Merab lay. He was still alive. His face had turned a sickly white and the blood spurting through his fingers was coming in weak streams now, but he was trying to say something, working his lips silently.

"I do not understand that command," Minerva whined.

Conorado ignored her. He knelt beside Merab. "Listen, you, it's all over. I want the password to the computer system. Give it to me. Now."

"Our Father . . ." Merab gasped. He looked at Conorado desperately. "Would you . . . ?" he asked. Conorado took his free hand and recited the Lord's Prayer with the dying man. Merab smiled weakly. "God bless you," he said, and died.

"Brother Lordsday, please give me commands. I do not understand 'Shut up,' " Minerva reported.

Conorado sighed and stood up. His legs were like rubber as the effects of the adrenaline that had pumped him up during the fight began to wear off. The hand holding the gun was shaking. He dropped the empty magazine and let the slide go forward. Dean and Claypoole, he thought, shaking his head. What a pair. He wondered idly where he could get some more bullets for the antique firearm and then dropped it back into his pocket. He reached down and picked up one of the blasters. He put the safety on.

Lewis Conorado, Captain, CMC, looked over the bridge. The deck was splattered with blood. His own bloody footprints were everywhere. It had been a long, long time since he had killed anyone up close. Well, he'd had no choice. He asked aloud, "Now what?" But Minerva remained silent.

A body lay sprawled on the floor of the cabin. It was freezing cold inside, and Ramadan's breath came through his face mask in white clouds of condensation. "Oh, my God," he whispered. He rolled the body over. A frozen tendril of blood stretched down the woman's face from a wound in her eye. "Oh, thank God!" Ramadan almost shouted when he saw that she was not Marta Conorado.

Buskerud clattered through the door behind him, his

snowshoes making a racket on the wooden floor. "Is it . . . ?"
he asked, a sinking feeling in his guts.

"No, no," Ramadan shouted, straightening up. "It's not
Marta. Where—"

"Colonel, der is a path in da snow! Two peoples! Dey haf
gone oud dere. Quick! De vind is covering it up!" Buskerud
pointed out the door with one arm. "But Colonel, be careful.
Dat way iss a drop off, maybe one thousand meters into da
Ume River valley. I be right behind you!"

Ramadan pushed past Buskerud back out into the storm.
Sure enough, there was a faint trail in the snow leading away
from the cabin. Already the wind was covering it.

Marta had never felt such pain as she did then on the exposed parts of her face and ears. She flung an arm across her
face to block out some of the wind-driven snow, but there
was nothing she could do about her ears, which quickly
began to burn in the fierce subzero cold. Her hair flapped
about her head in frozen dreadlocks. The fingers on her right
hand began to hurt excruciatingly. She buried them in a
pocket and flung her left arm across her face as she staggered onward. Within a few meters of the cabin, which she
could not even see anymore through the blizzard, she began
to tire. In some places the snow was up to her chest. She
stumbled and fell many times. Her breath came in ragged
gasps and the air burned like fire as she eagerly sucked it in.
She fell again and lay facedown in the snow. Ah, the burning pain was subsiding! It was so good to rest. How far had
she come from the cabin? A good ways, she thought. They
would never find her out here. In the back of her mind somewhere she realized she would die if she didn't get under
cover, but she didn't care. She just wanted to rest, to sleep,
to dream. Oh, how wonderful to rest. She thought of her
children and Lewis and wondered, idly, what they were
doing right now. Camilla, her daughter, she took after Lewis
in so many ways.

"Bitch!" Bengt screamed. He grabbed Marta by the hair
and pulled her out of the snow. "You are not going to die so

easy, bitch! I'm taking you back to the cabin. You'll varm up and den—den I vill use you and use you, and ven I am done wid you, I vill kill you, Mrs. Marine goddamned cunt, slow, painful you die, and I enjoys everytink I gonna do to you!"

Incongruously, Marta noted that his perfect English inflection had vanished now that he was mad. Boy, she thought, half amused, I have really pissed this guy off! She didn't care what he would do to her once they were back in the cabin—at least it would be warm! She laughed, or at least she thought she did, remembering a poem she'd once heard about a man who froze to death in the Arctic only to be revived when his partner tried to cremate him in an oven. Sam Magee, that was his name!

Bengt began dragging Marta around to the left, back toward the cabin, when he screamed suddenly and just as suddenly let go of her. Marta slumped back into the snow. Bengt's high-pitched screaming diminished very quickly and then died away completely. She had no idea what had happened to him, and she didn't care. Marta sank back into the snow and lost consciousness.

Colonel Ramadan never would have found Marta Conorado if it hadn't been for her hand sticking up out of the snow bank where Bengt had left her. He stumbled forward and began pawing at the snow covering her body.

Buskerud came up behind him and laid a gloved hand on his shoulder as Ramadan furiously brushed snow away from Marta's still form. "Goddamnit, Ollie, help me! We've got to get her out of here!"

"Colonel, Colonel," Buskerud insisted. "Look. Look."

"What? What?" Ramadan looked up in annoyance at the guide.

Buskerud gestured at the ground in front of where Marta lay. At that moment the wind died away and the swirling clouds of snow subsided. Ramadan gasped as he looked out across a vast empty space, the valley of the Ume, only a handbreadth from where Marta was lying. "C'mon, Ollie, we've got to get her back to the cabin! Give me a hand!"

They uncovered Marta and lifted her up. Ramadan took

off his gloves and began rubbing her face. "She's like ice, Ollie!" he gasped. Buskerud bent close over the pair to shelter them from the wind, which had picked up again.

"She vill haf bad frostbite," Buskerud said. "Does she live?"

Ramadan mentally kicked himself for not trying to get a pulse. He lay two fingers along the carotid just under her jaw and put his ear close to her mouth. Yes! A pulse, weak, but a pulse! He breathed on her lips and continued rubbing her face while calling her name as loud as he could in the rushing wind.

Marta's eyes fluttered open and she looked up at the ice-ringed, snow-blown face of Colonel Israel Ramadan. "Lewis," she muttered, "I'm so glad you've come home!"

CHAPTER
TWENTY-THREE

Captain Tuit was the first crewman on the bridge after it became clear that Conorado had somehow secured it from the terrorists. "What? What happened up here?" He gaped at the bodies and the blood. He looked up at Conorado, who slumped in the captain's chair. "Lew, I knew you were a fighter, but—but how the hell did you pull this off?"

Conorado gestured vaguely at the bodies. "I had an ace in the hole, Hank. The bridge is now yours again, Captain." He stepped out of the chair, indicating Captain Tuit should occupy it.

"Lot of good that'd do, Lew. They wiped out the navigation system and took control of Minerva. The only thing I can do with this ship now is fire the goddamned verniers." He ran a hand nervously through his hair.

"Can we communicate with the two back in the propulsion unit?" Conorado asked.

"Yes," Jennifer answered. She and two other crew members had just arrived on the bridge. "We have a telephone hookup that is independent of Minerva."

"That's right," Tuit said, punching a button on the console by his command chair. "I'm putting this conversation on the speaker so you can all hear what these guys have to say." He waited several seconds before someone picked up the instrument on the other end.

"Brother Lordsday?" Increase Revelation asked tentatively.

"Hell no, this is Captain Tuit speaking. What in the hell are you two up to back there?"

There was a brief pause. "I am Increase Revelation, Captain. Please let me speak to Brother Lordsday."

"I got news for you, asshole, a real 'increase' in your 'revelation.' Your buddies are dead. Now disarm that goddamned bomb you got back there and get your tails up here so I won't have to come back there and kick them for you."

"Are the brothers dead?" There was another long pause. "The bomb cannot be disarmed, Captain. It is set to go off when we are precisely at the proper point. We are armed and we are prepared to hold this place until our work is done. But even if you get by us, Captain, you cannot disarm the bomb."

"And when, may I ask, will it go off?"

"You may ask, Captain, but I will not tell you."

"Now you listen here, you bowel-lurking little piece of turd slime—"

"Captain. Please. Instead of wasting time and breath cursing me, look to your eternal soul, for shortly, very shortly, we will all stand before our Creator. We will not talk again in this life. May God bless you all."

Tuit shrugged and set the instrument back into its holder. "Lew, you're one hell of a man to have stacked these guys up like this, but looks like we're finished."

"Guess that means we don't get no bonuses this trip," one of the crewmen interjected. The remark was so out of context everyone was forced to laugh, despite the desperation of their predicament.

Ambassador Franks came onto the bridge, took in the carnage, and asked, "Who did this?"

"I did, Mr. Ambassador," Conorado answered.

"Figures," Franks said. "Congratulations, Captain. At least we won't go up without a fight." He walked over to Conorado and extended his hand. "Now where do we stand?"

Tuit filled the ambassador in. "If we could fight our way in there and eject the bomb somehow, wouldn't that save us?"

"If we had a lifecraft that worked, maybe we could shoot

it off into space, after sacrificing more lives to get into the propulsion unit, and it might just go off far enough away that we wouldn't go up with it, Mr. Ambassador. But all our lifecraft have been disabled," Tuit said. "We could bust in, find the bomb, and eject it outside the hull, but all it'd do would be to match vector with the ship."

"There is one possibility," Jennifer said. All heads turned in her direction. She hesitated. "Well, the vernier jets still work and—"

"Jenny, what good are they to us now?" Tuit asked.

"Well, Captain, if we could get one powerful burst out of them that would put the ship into a spin and then somehow, uh, well, detach the propulsion unit from the rest of the ship—detach it at just the right point in the arc, like a rock in a slingshot—"

"Cap'n," the navigator broke in, "she's got a point! The verniers are supposed to be used only for making slight course adjustments, as when docking," he explained to Ambassador Franks, "but if I can get one sustained burst out of all of them at the same time, it might just work. But all we're going to get is one goddamned chance. At the most I might get twenty seconds of thrust out of them. We're stern abeam to the moon now. I calculate it'll take fifteen seconds of sustained thrust to swing this crate around so she's bow on. Soon's the moon begins to appear in the bow viewing screens, we separate the propulsion unit. By then we should have generated enough centrifugal force to start carrying it away toward its apogee. That'll really mess up their schedule."

Everyone's attention now turned to Jennifer Lenfen. "Jenny, hurry it up," Tuit said. "I don't think we've got much time left."

"Well, each lifecraft has a small explosive charge set to detonate when the craft is launched, you know, to propel it free of the ship's gravitational orbit. I was thinking, if we can gather together a few of the charges, hook them up into a sequence with a fuse of some sort, we can—"

"Goddamnit, girl, set the charges off with enough explosive force to separate the propulsion unit from the rest of the ship! Time it precisely so it goes off at the arc of the ship's swing when we start the verniers, and it'll act like a stone thrown from a slingshot!" Captain Tuit stepped up to Jennifer, put his arms around her and kissed her.

By now the rest of the crew had gathered on the bridge. "Okay, here's how I'll work it. Everyone'll suit up prior to the blast. Passengers and crew not engaged in navigation or setting off the charges will secure the lifecraft. They'll provide some extra protection when the big bomb goes off. Navigator and I will remain on the bridge." He looked at Conorado. "Lew, I don't suppose you know anything about demolitions, do you?"

Conorado smiled. " 'If it absolutely, positively has to be destroyed overnight, send in the Marines,' " he quoted the old adage.

"Lew, it'll be a very dangerous operation. Whoever sets that thing off could go up with it. You'll have to be suited up for the operation. If a fragment penetrates your suit, you'll boil away like—"

"I know, Hank. I'll need a lot of wire or cable and a power source and some stuff to make a detonator. I'll also need a volunteer to assist me."

"I volunteer," Jennifer said without hesitation.

"No!" Both Conorado and Tuit shouted at the same time.

"It was my idea and I want to be the volunteer," she said with determination.

"I should go too," the navigator spoke up forcefully.

"No, absolutely not, Clem," Jennifer said. "Your job is critical. Only you can handle the verniers well enough to spin this old crate around. It's my idea, I want to go."

"Me too," another crewman who'd just come onto the bridge spoke up.

"Bob! You're the only engineer I have left—" Captain Tuit began.

The engineer, Bob Storer, held up a hand. He was an older, husky individual with a military-style haircut. "I can help with the placement of the charges, Hank, and I can rig the detonation system Captain Conorado will need to set the charges off. And besides that, Captain, you don't need a god-damned engineer on this ship anymore."

Tuit was silent for a moment. "Okay," he said, "the three of you get to work."

The three quickly collected the propulsion charges from the ten lifecraft nearest the bridge and passenger compartments.

"These are set off electronically from the pilot's console using a 1.5 amp system," Storer explained. "I should be able to rig an electrical firing system to set them off in a series, using, say, three hundred meters of eighteen-gauge copper wire."

Jennifer looked at Conorado and raised her eyebrows. "Glad we did bring you along, Bob," she said.

"Okay, Bob, but we'll need a dual firing system in case there's a misfire on the first try. That'll require two completely independent electrical systems, both of them capable of firing the charges. That will mean two detonators in each charge so that the firing of either circuit will detonate all the charges. Can you set it up?"

"Sure," Storer replied. "We have two lifecraft we didn't raid, considering number thirteen is in the propulsion unit, so I'll use the propellant from one of those to rig the second set of detonators."

Conorado hefted one of the propulsion charges. "Well, I'll be—this is composition military stuff, Tetrytol, .75 kilograms per charge. Jesu, the detonation velocity of this stuff has got to be up somewhere near seven thousand meters a second! The navy uses compressed air to launch Essays. This stuff is powerful and dangerous. One good thing, though—they've got one set of built-in detonators. That'll make your job a bit easier, Bob."

"Well, the navy launches all the time," Jennifer said. "We only do it once, and when we're on our way, we don't intend to come back."

"It's amazing what salvage crews can do these days," Bob added.

Conorado let out a little laugh. "Good thing for us you civilians are so far behind the times. Bob, since we can't access the computer, what do you remember about the structure of the conduit that connects the last storage compartment with the propulsion unit? What's it made of?"

"Molycarbondum. It has the tensile strength of structural steel but one hundredth the weight."

"So in reality we're dealing with structural steel," Conorado said. "All right. That's something I understand. How much of it will we have to blow up to separate the conduit? I need to know how many struts we'll need to cut through and the area of the flanges and webs to calculate how much of this stuff we'll need."

"There are five struts to a section," Storer said, "but hell, I don't have any idea what the area of the flanges and webs is."

"Then let's get everything together and go back and measure the flanges and webs and set this damned stuff off," Conorado said.

The total area of the flange and web for one strut came out to 58.5 square centimeters. Conorado calculated in his head. "I'm a bit rusty on this stuff, but I think we'll need 1.5 kilograms to separate each strut. So we use all ten of these charges and we should be in business. Ah, one more thing. Distance. Depending on the size of the charge, you've got to put a certain distance between yourself and the explosion to avoid going up with the stuff. That's a minimum of 274 meters on charges up to twelve kilograms. Can we set this thing off from that distance, Bob?"

"I don't have enough wire! I had to double what I did have to make up the dual electrical firing systems. I could strip some more, but how much time do we have before that thing goes off?"

Conorado hesitated. "I don't know, but we've got to figure it'll go off any minute now. Hell, we can't be more than an hour away from Luna's orbit, and the damned thing's probably timed to go off for maximum visual effect on the people watching from Earth. Okay. We'll do it from right inside the storage bay. We can stack cargo between us and the blast." He turned to Jennifer. "You keep in touch with the bridge, Jenny. Tell them we're going to set the charges now and they should get ready to fire the jets on my command. We'll suit up and secure ourselves once the charges are in place and ready to be fired."

Both men were perspiring profusely before they finished rigging the charges. Meanwhile, using a front loader, Jennifer had stacked cargo containers in the form of a small square inside which they could fire the charges and expect some protection from the blast. They knew that as soon as the charges detonated, Minerva would automatically initiate emergency procedures to seal off the damaged compartment from the rest of the ship.

They crouched in the makeshift shelter. Conorado nodded at Jennifer, who was in touch with the bridge and her companions via the voice mike in her suit.

"Fire when ready, Captain!" She paused. "The verniers have been fired!"

"Mark!" Conorado shouted. Storer, a gloved hand paused above the detonator switch, began to count the seconds. They would mark the seconds, and if, due to a comm failure, the bridge did not give the signal to detonate the charges after fifteen seconds, they would set them off anyway.

At first there was no sensation of movement at all, but after five seconds the ship began to swing to her port. Ten seconds into the count the maneuver had become so pronounced the three bombers felt themselves pulled hard to the starboard quarter.

At precisely fifteen seconds into the maneuver Jennifer screamed "Fire!" The explosion was much more powerful than expected.

Lieutenant Commander Willa Stanton, on the bridge of the fast frigate CNSS *Sergeant Major Richard Banks*, had the *Cambria* in view. She had been told that terrorists had taken over the ship, murdered its crew and passengers, and were going to use it as a huge bomb to destroy Luna Station. She did not question her orders when given the assignment to destroy the *Cambria*, but what Fleet did not know was that Commander Stanton had once served under retired navy captain Tuit and she was well aware that he was captain of that vessel. Her feelings about her orders were mixed. What if Tuit and his people were still alive? she asked herself. Was there any other way to avoid disaster?

"Any success getting through to her?" she asked her communications officer. She had been told that Fleet had been trying for some time with no success to reach the *Cambria*, but Commander Stanton thought they might get a response now that her ship was close enough to have been detected by the cargo ship's sensors.

"None, Captain. They've taken control of her communications system; otherwise, her computers are programmed to respond to emergency messages."

"How long would it take to break the code and get through?"

"I've been trying, Captain—"

He's a 4.0 officer! Commander Stanton thought.

"—but it'll be too late before our system can break through. Fleet's cryptanalysts could do it in no time," he added wistfully.

Commander Stanton wondered again why Fleet had not already done just that. There were things about this mission that didn't make sense to her. Her orders to destroy the cargo ship were clear and apparently legitimate. But she did not quite believe the story she had been given. And she knew her orders came from much higher up than CNO or even the Combined Chiefs. That ship was worth trillions. Were the people on board really dead? Were they infected with some dreadful alien plague? Had they been taken over by something?

Commander Stanton's executive officer frowned. "Our orders are to shoot her, Captain, not try to talk them down," he reminded her.

Commander Stanton sighed. "Gunnery officer, are we in range?"

"Aye, Captain, in range."

"Very well. Prepare to fire main battery."

"Aye, Captain, main battery prepared to fire."

"Hey!" the exec exclaimed. "What was that?"

A small bright flash erupted on the *Banks*'s viewscreens.

"She's separated into two fragments!" he exclaimed. "Captain, that was a damned explosion! The smaller of the two fragments appears to be her propulsion unit."

Commander Stanton stared at the screen for a moment. "Guns! Are you following what's going on?"

"Aye, Captain, the target is in two parts now."

"Lock on the smaller fragment."

"Aye, target locked on."

"Fire!"

The *Cambria*'s propulsion unit disappeared in a very big flash.

"Secure your battery."

"Aye, battery secured."

"XO, prepare a boarding party, two volunteers only, and take the con. I'm going to board that vessel."

"Captain, you can't do that! Our orders are to destroy that vessel, not board her!"

"I'm the officer on the scene and it's my decision to board her. Get cracking."

"Aye aye, Captain," the XO reluctantly conceded. He turned to the chief of the boat. "Chief, prepare a boarding party to consist of the captain and two volunteers."

"Aye aye, sir, prepare boarding party! I volunteer," the chief, a grizzled old boatswain, added immediately.

"XO," Commander Stanton laid a hand on his arm, "if I give the word, douse the *Cambria* immediately. Hank Tuit's captain of that vessel. I served under him as an ensign thirty years ago. If there's any chance he's still alive, I'm going to find out. I have score to settle with that old bastard." She grinned up at her executive officer. "I'll settle up with the navy afterward."

*   *   *

The first blast shook the *Cambria* forcefully but did not damage any of her structure forward of the sternmost storage area. Minerva went into apoplexy, however, shutting off the damaged area and reporting damage loudly to "Brother Lordsday." When he did not respond, the system went dead again.

Captain Tuit ordered everyone to remain suited until he was sure there would be no secondary blast from the propulsion unit. Then he saw the bolt that lanced out from the *Banks*'s main battery. Again Minerva went wild, but after only a few seconds it was obvious there was no structural damage to the surviving part of the ship and her life support system was still functioning.

"Did the bomb go off?" the navigator asked, a hand to his head where he had slammed it into his console. The hand came away bloody.

"No, didn't you see that? We've been fired on by a navy ship! I've seen it often enough to know! A goddamned frigate! What the hell?" He was both wildly elated and deadly certain they would be next.

Ambassador Franks, awkward in his spacesuit, staggered onto the bridge. "Captain, what is happening? Are we safe?" His voice sounded high and tinny over the suit's communication system.

"I thought I told everyone to stay in place until I gave the word it was safe to unsuit?" Captain Tuit shouted. All he needed now was a damned civilian blundering around on his bridge.

"Sorry, Captain, but I—"

"Forget it," Tuit relented. He'd need all the help he could get in the next few minutes. "The ship is all right, but I've got to find out what happened to Conorado's team," he said. "Conorado! Jennifer! Bob! Come in!" he said into his throat mike. There was no answer.

"Conorado's emergency transponder is functioning, Captain!" the navigator shouted. "It's down in what's left of Compartment Five!" Maybe that's all that's functioning, he thought. That there were no signals from the other two transponders was not encouraging. But he left these thoughts unsaid.

"We can seal off Compartment Four and then go into Compartment Five and retrieve the, er, bring them back in . . ." Tuit's voice trailed off. He doubted anyone survived the first explosion, much less the second one. Tuit turned to Franks. "Mr. Ambassador, can you work the comm unit here? Sit down at the con and I'll show you. I'm leaving you in charge on the bridge, sir."

"This is highly irregular, Captain!" Franks responded, but he eagerly sat in Tuit's command chair.

"Mr. Ambassador," Tuit said dryly, "everything's 'highly irregular' about this voyage. I need you to keep in constant touch with us. I'm going to take all my crew to the fourth storage compartment, recover Captain Conorado, see if anybody survived the blast. You keep your eye on the viewscreen there. We might have visitors. Let me know if you see or hear anything. Don't be worried, this ship ain't gonna drift into anything, and if she does, there's not a god-damned thing anybody can do about it."

" 'Visitors'?" Franks repeated, looking askance at Tuit.

"Can't explain now, sir. You have the con." Tuit reseated his headpiece, gestured at his navigator, and then clomped off the bridge.

Well, Ambassador Franks thought, I've got the con! "Steward!" he said to the empty air, "bring me a martini, please. Extra dry."

Compartment Five was a shambles of ruined superstruc-ture, loose cabling, and debris. All the ore and the entire hundred meters of the stern portion of the compartment was gone. "It's all out there." A crewman gestured toward the gaping hole that was now the "stern" of the *Cambria*. Tons of ore and other debris, mixed with what was left of the propulsion unit, floated in a long trail behind the ship. "Geez," another said, "that's gonna cost Sewall millions!"

They located Conorado in a cargo supervisor's station, pinned under debris. He was unconscious but his suit had withstood the explosions. "Let's get him to the infirmary," Tuit ordered. "Give me a line. I'm going out there to see if I can find Jenny and Bob."

"Captain!" Minerva broke into the net. "I have a message for you from the captain of the CNSS *Sergeant Major Richard Banks*!"

"Goddamn," one of the crew said, "they must've deciphered the password those bastards set on her!"

"Good to have you back, Minerva," Tuit said to the computer. He did not feel ridiculous to be talking to a machine as if it were a person. At that particular moment he felt Minerva was human, and he was glad to have her back on line. "What's the message?"

"Captain!" Franks's voice came up on Tuit's comm unit. "Somebody's knocking at the door!"

"That's the message, Captain," Minerva answered.

CHAPTER
TWENTY-FOUR

The last thing Conorado remembered was Jennifer shouting "Fire!" and then the world went dark for him until he awoke in the *Cambria's* infirmary, Hank Tuit standing over him, peering down anxiously into his face.

"Lew? Lew, can you hear me?"

"Yeah. Hank, did we do it?"

"You did it, old jarhead, you sure did it." Tuit's face broke into a broad smile.

"Jennifer? Bob?"

Another face appeared, a middle-aged female. "Hi, I'm Commander Stanton of the fast frigate CNSS *Sergeant Major Richard Banks*. How're you doing, Marine?"

Conorado smiled back at her. "I've never been so glad to see a squid—excuse me, ma'am, I mean a sailor—in my life. What about Jennifer and Bob, Commander?" She said nothing. He turned to Tuit. "Hank?" An anxious note crept into Conorado's voice. He was beginning to have that old, bad feeling again, one he'd had many times before after a firefight.

"Well," Captain Tuitt responded, "we're looking for them, Lew."

The sinking feeling in the pit of Conorado's stomach took a turn for the worse: Tuit didn't look at him as he spoke. "Help me up, will you?" he asked. He groaned as Stanton and Tuit lifted him into a sitting position on the examination table.

"Minerva says you're okay, Lew, just bruised and concussed," Tuit said, trying to sound bright and optimistic.

"How long's it been since I went out?"

"Some hours," Commander Stanton answered. "I have several rescue crews searching this entire quadrant for survivors. Those blasts were quite violent."

" 'Blasts,' did you say?"

Commander Stanton explained the sequence of events. "The blast you set off is what knocked you into the cargo supervisor's kiosk and probably saved your life. It was our blast, unfortunately, that emptied the ore in Compartment Five that your bomb weakened. Your friends went with it."

"My boy! My boy!" Ambassador Franks bustled into the infirmary, his arms outstretched toward Conorado. "I have never witnessed such bravery! Such ingenuity in a desperate spot! I'll see to it that the commandant—the President herself—knows what you and those two unfortunate souls—" He went silent at the angry glance Tuit gave him.

Conorado looked at Tuit. "Hank, they're dead, aren't they?"

"Yeah, most likely. Their emergency transponders are not working. Their suits were punctured. You know what that means. We're looking for what's left of them."

Jennifer Lenfen dead? Killed volunteering for something dangerous in order to save others. And that engineer, Bob Storer, he had family. "They went out like Marines," Conorado muttered.

"Captain, I am sorry," Franks said, "very sorry. But you are a hero, my boy. You and your friends, heroes. You saved all of us. I promise you," he held a finger up, "that the world is going to know about the sacrifices that were made on this voyage."

"Folks, would you leave me alone for a while?" Conorado asked. "I'm not feeling too chipper just now."

They filed out of the infirmary. Franks returned to his suite to prepare for evacuation from the *Cambria* to the *Banks*, leaving Tuit and Stanton alone in the companionway.

"Most of your cargo can be recovered," Stanton said. "All in all, you came through this in almost one piece."

"How the devil did you get on to us like that?" Tuit asked.

Stanton told him.

"Hmm. Commander, seems you might have exceeded your orders a bit there, huh?" Tuit smiled.

"Maybe. Fleet might try to get my ass, but you know something—that ambassador, Franks? I think he'll stick up for what I did."

"Franks? Damnit, Commander, he'll have to stand in line, and I'm gonna be first on that one!" They both laughed. Tuit put his arm around Stanton's shoulder. "I know you, don't I? When we get back on the ground and all this is settled, can I buy you dinner?"

"Yes to both questions, Captain! Do you remember, oh, thirty years ago now, an 'incident' on St. Brendan's World? You commanded a transport then, the *Oregon*, and I was Officer of the Day in port at New Cobh. I was an ensign at the time."

Tuit smacked his forehead. "Yes! There was a disturbance in a bar and you left your station to—"

"Yes. And when I got to the place, I found our guys getting beat up by the local police, so the shore party and I—"

"Waded into them! And you all wound up in the local jail! How could I have forgotten that?" He started to laugh.

"Well, Captain, you chewed a big chunk out of my behind but you never made out a report. I really screwed up. Any other commander would've hung me out to dry. You saved my career by handling it yourself. I've never forgotten that."

"Aw, hell, only what a good commander does when a good officer screws up. Besides, you were young, trying to prove yourself, and you had that goddamned nasty old chief bosun with you that night, what the hell was his name . . . ?"

Commander Stanton leaned over and kissed Tuit on the cheek. "I've wanted to do that for thirty years and say again, thanks."

The old score was now settled.

The survivors of the *Cambria* had not even disembarked from the *Banks* before orders arrived from the Ministry of Justice that all of them, passengers and crew, were to be confined at Luna Station until Confederation representatives could debrief them on the incident. The crew of the *Banks* was denied shore liberty and placed under the same restriction. That did not prevent the two old sailors, Tuit and Stanton, from having dinner the first night at Luna Station—and breakfast and lunch too.

On the third day two very official-looking men assembled the *Cambria* survivors in a small theater on a sublevel of the station. "We are from the Ministry of Justice," one of them announced. "You do not need to know our names. This same briefing is being given right now to the crew of the *Banks*. Once we are done here today, your onward transportation will be ready to take you all home.

"Now we want you to listen very carefully to what we have to say." The room was deathly silent. "You are to speak to no one about what happened on the Sewall Company's cargo ship, the SS *Cambria*. If asked, passengers, you will say something went wrong with the power plant. You don't know what, it happened so fast. Captain Tuit, you and your crew will say that your reactor malfunctioned. You lost four of your crew trying to save it. Since none of your engineers survived, nobody knows precisely what went wrong. Your computer logs have been adjusted. The propulsion unit blew up before the problem was fully diagnosed. If anyone presses you for information, the matter is under investigation by the Ministry of Interstellar Navigation and Commerce. You are unable to comment. Some of you will be asked by the press or even by relatives of the crew who died in the explosion. Refer any inquiries to the ministry."

"What the hell about the five sonsabitches—" Tuit shouted.

The speaker waved a hand. "They did not exist. I repeat, they did not exist. Your passenger manifest does not show them on board your vessel, Captain. Am I making myself clear?"

A murmur went through the small group. "I am Ambassador Jamison Franks III, Inspector General—"

"We know who you are, sir," the second man said coldly, unimpressed.

"I am going to make a full report on this incident to my superiors, gentlemen. And I am going to single out Captain Lewis Conorado and two members of the crew for their courage and sacrifice—"

"I appreciate what those people did, sir," the first man interrupted, "but there will be no report of any kind. I am sorry, truly, but that is the way it is going to be. This incident is a matter of Confederation security, and any of you who ignore what you have been told this afternoon will be subject to prosecution."

"I will send a message to my superiors in the diplomatic service and we will see—"

"Ambassador Franks, sit down! If you send any such message I will arrest you immediately."

Franks sat down.

"Now," the first man continued, "I have statements prepared for all of you to sign. By signing, you acknowledge that you understand what I have just told you and will keep your silence on this matter. Please step forward one at a time and we will be finished. Ambassador Franks, you first, please."

Conorado was getting used to this sort of thing. He signed without comment. "There's someone here to see you, Captain," one of the men said.

Two military policemen stepped into the theater. "Captain Lewis Conorado?" one, a gunnery sergeant, asked.

Conorado knew what was coming next. "Yes, Gunny."

"Captain, you are under arrest. Please come with us."

The quarters they put Conorado up in at Camp Darby, a military installation on the outskirts of Fargo, were comfortable but not luxurious. He was on his own recognizance and free to roam the post but otherwise considered under arrest of quarters until the trial was over.

A young navy lieutenant, Aldo Heintges, had been assigned as Conorado's counsel. Heintges had reddish-brown hair and boyish freckles on his face. He reminded Conorado of Lance Corporal Dean. Their first meeting, on the eve of the trial, went well.

"Captain," Heintges explained when they met, "this trial is being conducted by the civil authority. But since its subject remains so highly classified, the court's venue has been established here at Camp Darby. Otherwise we'd all be going downtown. And also because the subject is so highly classified, it won't be a jury trial. There'll be one judge sitting on the bench and he will hear our arguments."

"Yes, and that's why the trial's taking place in the comm facility: high security, no windows, no crowds. I'm thankful for one thing though: since all this is so hush-hush, I won't have an MP escort everywhere I go. Do you know the judge?"

"By reputation. His name is Stefan Epstein. He's a no-nonsense type of guy, hard but fair. You may remember the war crimes tribunals after the revolution on Munhango? That was a highly emotionally charged trial, and Epstein was the chief judge of the tribunal. He proceeded strictly on the basis of facts and hard evidence, and while the panel's decisions displeased those who wanted hangings, they stood up to judicial review. It'll be just him, and no jury."

"Goddamn, Lieutenant, no jury? I saw the list of witnesses the other side's calling. Hoxey's whole staff, the entire damned shift is going to be called as witnesses against me!"

"One thing, Captain. You and I are going to spend a lot of time together in the coming days and we're going to get to know each other very well. Please call me Aldo?"

"Call me Lew." They shook hands across the table in the tiny office Heintges had been given to work out of.

"To answer your question, Lew, you've got to remember that her shift is now in rotation, so all those people are available. Now, I talked to General Cazombi and Agent Nast. They've been subpoenaed as witnesses for the defense, and they're here. You'll see them tomorrow. Anyway, I think on cross-examination Hoxey's witnesses will turn out to be good ones for you. Also, I have the sworn statements the judge advocate took from your men back at Camp Ellis. I'll introduce those on your behalf and the judge will consider them. Captain, look. You did the right thing. I think I can get this whole mess tossed out."

"Damn," Conorado muttered, "the bitch tried to get her hands on Owen, our mascot, to—to—vivisect him!" He shook his head. "Who's Hoxey's lawyer?"

"A pair of prize assholes, Lew. They're Bureau of Human Habitability Exploration and Investigation lawyers. Hoc Vinces is the lead lawyer and his partner is a woman named Drellia Fortescue. They hate the military, as do a lot of the people who inhabit BHHEI." He smiled. "That's just another reason we refer to them as 'Behind.' "

"Well, some of them aren't that bad, Aldo. Hoxey's husband, for instance. Strange match there." He shook his head.

"I get that impression too, but beware of these shysters. They'll pull every legal trick in the book to make you look bad. They're good at that. I've never gone up against them myself, but I know them by reputation. You're better off without a jury trial because Epstein won't be swayed by any theatrics or legal maneuvers." He paused a moment. "Look, Lew, I've got to tell you this. You are entitled to your own consul. I was appointed by the navy to defend you, and I want to, but you can pick anyone you'd like to do the job. I'm not a prize trial lawyer. Oh, I've done plenty of court-martials, but I went into the navy as soon as I passed my bar exams. This'll be my first time in a civil court on a criminal case. You need to know that."

"I 'preciate that, Aldo. I've sat on general courts-martial boards."

"If you pick a civilian counsel, you'll have to pay—"

"Yes. But I can pick anybody, can't I? I mean, I don't have to pick a lawyer, even."

"Yes, but I strongly advise you, pick a good lawyer."

"Aldo, I've got a lawyer and I think he's a good one—you. But I want someone else on my side when we go into court."

Heintges blushed. "Thanks, Lew. I got myself a damned fine client, if you want to know. So who you got in mind to join us?"

"Name's Hank Tuit."

CHAPTER
TWENTY-FIVE

"What kind of monsters did this?"

"Don't touch anyone, they might be booby-trapped," Gunnery Sergeant Bass warned.

Third platoon was at a convent in the middle of a forest. Unlike the other places the Skinks had raided, the buildings here were intact, the livestock alive, nothing was burned. Only the people were dead. Seventy-three nuns and two handymen were in the convent's courtyard. Most of them had been killed by bladed weapons; only a few had their flesh eaten by the acid guns. Drag marks indicated they'd been shot down while trying to run away. There was no evidence of the horrible weapons the Skinks had used during the fight in the Swamp of Perdition.

The bodies were all naked. The two male bodies and six female were arranged in an obscene tangle. The rest of them were sexually mutilated, many with breasts cut off or lower bellies cut open. Many were laid in grotesque positions. The Skinks had taken time to lay out a tableau, one they obviously knew would offend and sicken.

Bass tore his eyes away from the awful sight and snapped into the all-hands circuit, "Secure this area."

Staff Sergeant Hyakowa took advantage of the order to leave the courtyard. "First squad, northeast; second squad, southwest," he said into the all-hands circuit as he went. His voice rasped, his throat constricted and raw. "Gun, into the bell tower."

"Get me the Skipper," Bass said to Lance Corporal Dupont, the platoon communications man.

269

Dupont had trouble finding his voice to make the call.

Bass took the UPUD's handset to report what they'd found and to request that local authorities be dispatched to deal with it. When he handed it back, he felt like he should wash his hands. At least the radio worked so far, even if he didn't trust any other part of the Mark III.

"God's will, I cannot look on it," said First Acolyte Wanderer, averting his eyes from the carnage in the courtyard. Bass had his shields raised so his face was visible, but the rest of him was invisible to the Kingdomite officer. Wanderer's gaze jumped about, everywhere but at the bodies and at Bass. He found speaking with what appeared to be a disembodied face too unnerving.

The deacon who arrived with the company of the Army of the Lord, to make sure they weren't contaminated by the off-world heathens, seemed struck dumb by the sight.

" 'God's will,' you have to," Bass snapped. "These are your people, your holy women." He paused to take a deep, calming breath. "Listen, we respect your beliefs, even though your beliefs portray us as little better than devils. I have no idea of what your customs are, how you treat the bodies of murdered people, how you handle the bodies of holy women. I don't want to do anything to defile them . . ."

"Defile? You speak of defilement? Have you looked on them? They have already been defiled—by demons! That mortal clay is beyond redemption."

Bass moved close to the young officer and dropped his voice. "I'm taking my Marines and going out to see if we can find where the Skinks who did this went. The women are yours. You take care of them. If I find out you left them like this, you best hope you never see me again."

"You threaten an officer of the Lord?" demanded the deacon, who had gotten past his shock and was suddenly next to them. He stared sharply at Bass's hovering face.

Bass looked at the deacon. If he hadn't known he was a minister of some sort, he wouldn't have guessed. The man wore a standard army field uniform. His collar emblem may have been a religious symbol, but it wasn't one Bass recognized.

"No," he said coldly, "I do not threaten him. I advise him. You're a holy man. You know the rules, the procedures, the ceremonies for the dead. You see to it that those bodies are properly cared for. And do it reverently." He slid his chameleon shield into place and said into his helmet comm, "Third platoon, saddle up and assemble on the south side."

The deacon swallowed when Bass's face vanished. The officer blanched. Bass didn't warn him about booby traps. He thought the man didn't need anything else to discourage him from dealing with the carnage.

"That way." Schultz raised his arm to let his sleeve slide down and pointed a few degrees off due south. That was where the Skinks went when they left the convent.

"Did you send anybody out there?" Bass asked Hyakowa.

"About half a klick," the platoon sergeant replied. "The trail continued."

"Line 'em up and let's follow. I want a fire team out about seventy-five meters on each flank."

"Aye aye, boss." Hyakowa issued the marching orders on the platoon command circuit.

Bass looked into the forest while the platoon prepared to move out. It was the local equivalent of a temperate zone deciduous forest. Some of the trees strongly resembled Earth oaks he'd seen in nature preserves in a number of worlds. He briefly wondered if the Kingdomites had imported and planted real oaks. More important than thinking about the trees, though, was the Skinks. Until now third platoon, which had more contact with them than anybody else, had only encountered them in or near swamps. He didn't need to bring up a map to know that the nearest swamp or wetlands was more than a hundred kilometers from the convent. All of the strikes the Skinks had made while the Marines were embarking on the *Grandar Bay* were some distance from swamps. Maybe they weren't all that dependent on water to function. He wondered why they had held off for a week after the battle in the swamp before they struck again. Was it coincidence that they launched all those raids while the Marines were boarding ship, or was it deliberate? If it was deliberate, what was their motivation?

"Ready any time you say, boss," Hyakowa said, interrupting his ruminations.

Bass toggled on the all-hands circuit. "Look alive, people. These Skinks might be smarter and tougher than we ever guessed. Move out."

It was an old growth forest. The trees were large and separated widely enough so their branches didn't meet to form a full canopy. There was a lot of undergrowth, except under the biggest, most thickly leafed trees. The trail was easy to follow; the Skinks hadn't been interested in passing unnoticed.

Schultz, on the point as usual, was mildly surprised that the Skinks were so careless in their passage. It was as though they were encouraging pursuit. He could only think of two reasons: to lead the pursuers into an ambush; to lead the pursuers away from something more important. He was *here*, not someplace else, so *here* was his concern. He watched the trail carefully, alert for any sign that it slackened, as though fewer bodies were making it. He also watched ahead as far as he could make out for sign that the creatures they followed had turned aside to double back and set an ambush. He didn't lead the platoon along the same track the Skinks had taken, but parallel to it. An easily followed path was too likely to be booby-trapped. He and the Marines behind him left a far less visible trail than the Skinks had.

Two or three hundred meters beyond where the patrol had gone, a small river crossed the Skinks' trail. The trail didn't resume on the other side of the river.

"We have to check it out," Bass said. "First squad, go upstream, second squad go downstream. If you don't see sign of them coming out in two klicks, cross over and come back checking the other side." Through his infra he watched the two squads leave. He didn't feel comfortable about splitting the platoon, but it was the fastest way to check out where the Skinks might have left the river.

"What are you thinking?" Hyakowa asked.

"I'm thinking they're trying to screw with our minds."

"I imagine you're right."

"They're messing with us," Schultz rumbled when second squad was halfway back to its starting point.

"What do you mean?" Kerr asked.

"They stayed in the river."

"How do you know?"

"Mind fuck."

"How can you be sure?"

Schultz grunted. It was obvious to him that the Skinks were playing games with the Marines, working on their psyches.

"You think they just kept going?"

Schultz grunted.

"They're trying to put us on edge and keep us there?" It wasn't really a question; Kerr was extrapolating from what Schultz said. It fit with what Gunny Bass had said, that the Skinks might be smarter than they guessed. It didn't take much thought for him to realize that if he were the commander of an outmatched unit in enemy territory, he'd want to do things to keep his opponent unsettled. After a big fight, let them think they'd won, then hit again while they were withdrawing. The withdrawing force would think it was over. Their morale might go down if they suddenly had to go back and fight again—especially if they'd suffered significant casualties in gaining what they thought was victory, which 34th FIST had. But why not hit the withdrawing forces, injure them while they were less alert and able to fight back?

That was one more question to add to who they were, where they came from, and why they always attacked without attempting to communicate.

* * *

Bass already knew the squads had found nothing before they returned. He radioed his report to Lieutenant Humphrey.

"What do you think is the most likely direction they went?" Humphrey asked.

"Downstream. According to this map, the river gets pretty narrow upstream and the land gets rocky."

"I agree. Follow downstream about ten klicks. Stay in close touch."

"Aye aye."

As soon as the platoon was reassembled, Bass called, "Squad leaders up."

In a moment the three squad leaders joined him and Hyakowa. They all slid their shields up so they could see each other's faces. Dupont kept watching the display on the UPUD, Mark III. Bass did his best to ignore the damn thing.

"It's more likely they went downstream than up," he told the squad leaders. They nodded agreement. "So we're going downstream too. About ten klicks. We'll get picked up there. If that damn thing," he jerked a thumb at the UPUD, "gives us anything near an accurate position. First squad, right bank. Second squad, left. One gun with each squad. Questions?" There weren't any. "Let's do it."

They didn't find where the Skinks left the river, all they found was that the forest continued and the river got bigger. Then the platoon was dispatched to the site of another Skink raid.

The Great Master chuckled as he listened to the reports, his breath rasping. Operation Blossoming Blood was proceeding precisely as planned. The Earthman Marines were scattered in increasingly small segments throughout the populated areas of this world they called "Kingdom," always racing to places his forces had already raided and departed. Any time he chose, he could have his forces lie in ambush and destroy the Marines piecemeal. But he did not choose to destroy them—yet.

"Continue Blossoming Blood," he ordered, and his breath rasped through his gill slits as he chuckled again.

The doorway through which the monk ushered them was wide enough for Brigadier Sturgeon and Ambassador Spears to walk side by side. It was Sturgeon's first time inside Temple Mount. Previously, his only contacts with the leading council had been through either Ambassador Spears or Archbishop General Lambsblood. The two Confederation representatives joined Lambsblood, who stood in front of the massive conference table facing the five spiritual leaders, who sat like a panel of judges. They bowed, Sturgeon's bow shallower and brisker than Spears's. The five seated leaders each had a cup near his hand. No one came forward to offer refreshment to the standing men.

Ayatollah Jebel Shammar, seated in the middle of the quintet, glowered at them from under bushy eyebrows and drummed his fingers impatiently on the tabletop. Swami Nirmal Bastar sat sternly to the right of Shammar. The Venerable Muong Bo, on his left, looked somehow disapproving in his inscrutability. Cardinal Leemus O'Lanners, resplendent in his scarlet robes, looked like he should be in the middle instead of the plainly dressed Ayatollah. Bishop Ralphy Bruce Preachintent sat at the opposite end of the row. Unlike the others, Ralphy Bruce directed his disapproval at Shammar's drumming fingers. A secretary sat ready with stylus and paper behind each principal.

Ayatollah Shammar ceased his finger-drumming long enough to intone, "The demons increase their depredations. You have done naught to deliver us from them."

Sturgeon ignored the obvious accusation in Shammar's tone. "Revered One, the raiders strike in widely scattered locations. By the time we learn about their raids and reach the sites, they're already gone."

"You spy on us from the sky, yet you never see them in time!"

"We don't spy on you, Revered One," Spears said. "The

Confederation's string-of-pearls is looking for the raiders, but there aren't enough analysts on the ship to spot all movement. They cannot be expected to spot every raid in time. Eventually they will spot raiders before they launch one of their attacks." He was well aware that were there enough analysts to examine all the data; the accusation of spying could well be accurate.

Shammar slammed the palms of both hands onto the tabletop. "Eventually is not soon enough!" he thundered. "The demons murder the Faithful and mutilate their bodies. They destroy our crops and kine. They must be stopped!"

"Revered One," Spears said in his most diplomatic voice, "Brigadier Sturgeon assures me his Marines can be more effective than they are, but you must allow them to move out of their Interstellar City camp."

"I *do* allow them to leave!" Shammar thundered. "Every time the demons raid they have leave to pursue them!"

Spears shook his head. "Revered One, it's too late then."

"Sir," Sturgeon broke in, "none of the raids are in the vicinity of Haven. By the time my Marines can reach them, the raiders are long gone. We need your—"

"You have suborbitals," Swami Bastar interrupted. "They can move your soldiers anywhere on Kingdom within an hour and a half. Your encampment is close enough." The blaze in his eyes made Sturgeon think of Siva, the ancient Hindu god of destruction.

"Sir, that hour and a half is more than the raiders need to do their killing and make good their escape. Especially when my *Marines* aren't informed of the raid until several hours afterward." He used the subtlety of emphasis to indicate that there was a difference between soldiers and Marines.

"Would you then be getting to the site those several hours earlier if your *soldiers* were stationed closer?" Cardinal O'Lanners asked blandly, returning the emphasis. He drank from his cup and signaled for an attendant to refill it.

"No, Eminence, it wouldn't get my Marines there those many hours earlier. But it could put us in a better position to learn about the raids early enough to intercept the raiders."

Shammar held up a hand to stop anyone from speaking further. He rolled his eyes up in momentary thought, then flicked his fingers and said, "Leave us."

Spears bowed, Sturgeon nodded. Lambsblood bowed lowest and left the room with them.

"We wait here," Lambsblood murmured when the door of the council chamber closed behind them.

"What do you think they're talking about?" Sturgeon asked.

"I think they know they have to do something they do not want to do," the Kingdomite commander replied.

A few moments later the door opened again and a scribe beckoned them to reenter.

Ayatollah Shammar peered at them for a long moment over steepled fingers. The expressions of the others were unreadable.

"Your point is well taken," he finally said. "But we cannot let infidels loose amongst our Faithful to spread their heinous apostasy. We have garrisons a hundred men strong throughout our lands. You may station up to ten of your soldiers with each garrison. When the garrison commander hears of a raid, he will lead your soldiers to it for immediate action."

Spears cocked an eye at Sturgeon. He knew the Marine wouldn't like the implications of that.

Sturgeon restrained a smile; he'd been hoping for something like this. "Revered One, I thank you. My Marines have considerable experience commanding indigenous troops."

Shammar's eyes looked like they should have been firing lightning, and Swami Bastar's visage, even more than before, invoked the image of Siva. Even Venerable Moung Bo's inscrutability seemed threatening.

"What?" Bishop Ralphy Bruce squawked. "You can't— can't—" He stopped to gather himself, but Cardinal O'Lanners cut him off.

"Sure and you wouldn't be thinking your heathens can be allowed to command our Soldiers of the Lord, now would you?"

"Your Eminence, when Confederation Marines operate

with local forces, the Marines always have military command. Let me say that again," he hurried on, "*military* command. We will do nothing whatsoever to impede or intefere with whatever reasonable measure you take to protect your soldiers from any supposed 'apostasy.' "

Spears read the laughter under Sturgeon's final statement. Experienced diplomat that he was, he kept his own expression neutral.

Shammar's steepled fingers went white from the sudden pressure he exerted on them.

Sturgeon turned to Lambsblood. "With all due respect, sir, Confederation Marines have vastly more experience and combat skills than any planetary military. And the Confederation Marines are both well-schooled and experienced in working with planetary forces. We always leave a local military more capable than it was when we arrived."

"I am aware of the value of the training, Brigadier. The last time Confederation Marines were deployed to Kingdom, the Army of the Lord received invaluable training. But command—"

"Yessir, command," Sturgeon said. "Even if I were willing to entrust the lives of my Marines to local command, I am forbidden to do so by Confederation Marine Corps standard operational proceedure. I'm simply not allowed to. Archbishop General," he said in a placating tone, "Marines have been training and leading local forces since before humanity went to the stars. We know what we're doing."

Lambsblood said nothing, but his expression as he turned his face from Sturgeon to his own leaders made it plain that he was unwilling to hand over command of even one Soldier of the Lord to the off-world Marines.

"Command is out of the question," Ayatollah Shammar said. He again flicked his fingers at them, and they left the chamber. The audience was over.

Over the next four days seven more settlements and two additional army outposts were lost to Skink raids. In each instance, the Marines didn't find out until too long afterward to catch the raiders.

*   *   *

"Archbishop General Lambsblood," Ayatollah Shammar intoned when the Kingdomite commander and the two Confederation representatives were again summoned, "the Army of the Lord shall closely oversee the dispersal of the off-world Marines and their assumption of *military* command. The Army of the Lord will treble the number of chaplains assigned to each unit so involved. Leave us."

Lambsblood's face went pale, but he bowed his head and said, "Thy will be done."

Outside the conference room, Lambsblood said to Spears, "Your military headquarters will be contacted by my operations staff to make the necessary arrangements." He didn't look at the Marine.

CHAPTER
TWENTY-SIX

Lance Corporal Schultz glowered. This was the kind of assignment he most detested. "I'm a lance corporal," he growled, "not an NCO. I follow. I fight. No leader. That's the deal."

"I know that, Hammer," Charlie Bass said patiently. "And I'm not asking you to be a leader. If I wanted you to be a leader, I'd give you Marines to lead. I need you to help Corporal Kerr and Corporal Doyle teach these amateurs," he indicated the nearby platoon of Soldiers of the Lord, "how to patrol and fight." The Kingdomite soldiers were doing their best to not look at the two heads that hovered in midair a few meters from the formation.

Schultz glanced at the sword-shaped pin in Bass's exposed hand. "That's their sergeant's collar insignia. You want me to wear it."

Bass shook his head. "It's a 'sword's' rank insignia," he said. "A 'sword' is not the same as a Marine sergeant. Do you think I'd give a Kingdomite sword command of a Marine squad?"

"You did this before," Schultz rumbled. On Wanderjahr the Marines had been integrated into the feldpolizei as commissioned and noncommissioned officers. Schultz, a career lance corporal, had been made an acting section leader in the feldpolizei—the equivalent of a squad leader. He'd hated that assignment.

"And you did a very good job training the feldpolizei. I expect you to do the same kind of job training the Kingdomites." Bass groped for the invisible collar of Schultz's chameleon shirt and pinned the sword emblem on it.

A Soldier of the Lord fainted at the sight of disembodied hands pinning the emblem in midair below a hovering head.

Schultz looked like he wanted to kill somebody. Preferably starting with the Kingdomite platoon.

Corporal Doyle broke off from admiring his own newly pinned-on Kingdomite rank insignia to cast a concerned glance at Schultz. He hadn't been with third platoon on the Wanderjahr deployment and knew only vaguely how Schultz had reacted to the assignment.

Corporal Kerr ignored the byplay between Bass and Schultz. He was more concerned with the three ministers the Army of the Lord had posted with the platoon. He was concerned that before the mission was over those three men might pose problems even more serious for the Marines than the Skinks presented.

First Acolyte Fakir sat most uncomfortably in a very unaccustomed place—the wrong side of his own field desk. The one-armed man who sat opposite, in Fakir's own chair, wore the doubled cross of a lesser imam on one collar point of his drab green shirt. Lesser imam was the proper rank of a company commander in the Army of the Lord. Should the Army of the Lord assign a lesser imam to take command of the 157th Defense Garrison, the command position Fakir had been filling for several months now, he could fully understand and accept it. And then beg forgiveness from God for the jealousy and rage he would feel at not himself being granted promotion to lesser imam. But the one-armed man who sat in *his* chair, on *his* side of *his* desk, who had just assumed command of *his* company, also wore, on the collar point that did not have the doubled cross of a lesser imam, the three chevrons and crossed blasters of a Confederation Marine Corps sergeant, a rank equivalent to sword, a squad leader. This First Acolyte Fakir did not fully understand, nor could he fully accept it. How had he offended God that he and his company should be placed under the command of a mere enlisted man—and a one-armed enlisted man at that? Outside the office, other Marines, men with ranks equal to subsword and ordinary soldiers, had assumed all of the command and leadership positions in the company.

"Acolyte, I can understand if you're unhappy about our situation here. I'm not happy about being returned to duty before my arm's been regenerated either." Sergeant Bladon lifted the stump of his missing arm. "If it's too long before the regeneration process starts, the arm that grows here won't be as good as the arm that I lost. *You* lose some pride for a short period of time." He looked at the stump. "*I* stand to lose something more." He ignored the monk who sat to Fakir's right and slightly behind him.

"Lesser Imam," Fakir said, "I didn't realize I said anything to indicate any unhappiness with a brave soldier such as yourself being in command."

Bladon stared at him with a coldness that made the acolyte shiver. "We're starting off wrong," he said in a voice as cold as his gaze. "My men and I are not 'soldiers,' we are Marines, and you will address us as such. There is a very significant difference between soldiers and Marines. This is something you will learn very well in the coming days."

Fakir wanted to clear his throat and run a finger around his suddenly too tight collar, to wipe the beads of persperation from his brow, but he didn't dare. This acting lesser imam might in fact have only the equivalent rank of a sword, but in manner he might have been a colonel deacon, a personage to be obeyed instantly.

"As for the rest of what you said," Bladon continued more conversationally, "you don't have to say anything for me to know you're unhappy. You're an officer in a class-bound army, in a strongly hierarchical society—your unhappiness shows in your face." Bladon made to fold his arms on the desk and lean forward on them, flinched when he put weight on the stump, sat straighter. "But you have to understand something. I and all of my men have training in leadership for the units we will be commanding. Even more important than that, most of my Marines and I have experience in training and leading planetary forces. We know what we're doing. Also, all of us have faced the Skinks." He lifted his stump to drive the point home. He paused for a moment, then decided it was pointless to keep secret the fact that this wasn't the first appearance of the Skinks. "Most of us have faced them elsewhere—and defeated them. We are the best people in all of Human Space to train your people in how to fight them, and the best qualified to lead you against the Skinks."

Fakir cleared his throat. "Lesser Imam"—he couldn't bring himself to say "sir"—"I doubt neither your abilities nor your qualifications."

"Of course not," Bladon said dryly. "Now, to business. We—this entire company—need to be able to respond immediately to a report anywhere in our assigned area, this thousand-square-kilometer area." He turned on a map projection and studied it. The map showed ten small settlements and a number of isolated homesteads. "What kind of communications do you have with those villages?"

"Lesser Imam?"

"How do they get in touch with you if they need help?"

"Our headquarters notifies us." He sounded as if the thought of the villages making contact on their own was an alien concept.

"Not good enough. By the time they contact your headquarters and your HQ notifies us, the Skinks will be gone." He glanced sharply at Fakir. "How do they contact your HQ?"

"The village headman radios the district town, and the district council decides whether the military needs to be called. If so, they notify headquarters and headquarters calls us."

Bladon shook his head sharply. "Even worse. That process takes entirely too long. Do those villages have your frequency?"

"Lesser Imam?" Fakir looked confused; the question was too bizarre. "The village headmen have no need for our frequency."

"They do now. I want you to contact every village immediately and instruct them to call here if they are attacked. Do those isolated homesteads have radios?"

"I can't do that, I haven't the authority!" He looked at the monk for guidance.

Bladon leaned toward Fakir and gave him a hard look. He ignored the pain in his stump. "This is not a religious matter, Acolyte," he snapped. "All the authority you need is right here." He tapped his chest. "I order you to do it. You will do it. You will do it right now. If you don't like it, or if you think it will get you in trouble with your HQ, report to them. *After* you have obeyed my order." He looked directly at the minister when he said the last.

Fakir blanched, but headquarters was distant in both space and time, and this off-world Marine was right here and right now. He jumped to his feet and hurried to obey the order. The monk followed more leisurely.

"And every one of the isolated homesteads that has a radio," Bladon called after him. Alone at last, he allowed himself to grimace at the pain in his stump, and at the phantom pain and itching in his missing arm. He looked at where his arm should have been and wondered if he'd get the regeneration treatment in time. Fakir's lack of communication with the villagers flashed through his mind, and he wondered if the Army of the Lord was worth training and leading, whether even the damn planet was worth saving from the Skinks, worth the Marines who had already died or been maimed.

He made a face and pulled himself together. Even if he didn't like the local government, there was no reason for him to condemn the people to the Skinks. Besides, he was a Marine, he went where he was sent and did his job to the best of his abilities. Nobody ever said he had to like any particular assignment. He glanced at his stump again. Neither had anyone promised he'd finish his time in the Corps whole in body.

"Lesser Imam," Fakir said, interrupting his thoughts, "the settlements have been notified. We are in the process of notifying the farmsteads as well."

"Good. Now we need to work out a reaction plan. Then I'll tell you about the training program we have." He gestured for Fakir to come in and resume his seat.

The monk entered behind the young officer.

None of the other commissioned and noncommissioned officers of the 157th Defense Garrison reacted any better to being under the command of off-worlders. Most of them attempted to resist.

"Acolyte, I must insist!" Second Acolyte Balashir was confident he could overawe the off-worlder who, despite the gilded cross he wore on his invisible collar, was really only a subsword. After all, the simple fact that he was a duly commissioned officer demonstrated his superiority over a mere subsword given a sham "temporary" commission. "My soldiers know how to patrol. We know our territory from patrolling it constantly. We can go wherever we want whenever we choose, and none can find or stop us."

Corporal Kerr idly scratched at his chameleon shirt over the place on his chest that should have born a scar from the time he was almost killed. "You're sure of that?" he asked.

"Surety is not the question. I *know* it."

Kerr looked down to where he knew the hand holding his helmet was, then abruptly lifted it and put it on. He slid the chameleon shield into place, flipped up his collar point to make the gilded cross vanish, and stepped back and to the side. Balashir started when the tall man he was addressing disappeared.

"I'm in arm's reach," Kerr said. "Touch me." He side-stepped and took two paces forward, behind Balashir, who was groping at where he'd been.

"That's not where I'm at," Kerr snapped.

Balashir spun around.

"You're looking in the wrong direction," Kerr said from yet another place.

"What are you doing?" Balashir demanded. "This is a child's game. If you have a point, make it."

"The point is," Kerr said, back in his starting place, his invisible helmet again off and hanging at the end of his invisible arm, "I was standing out in the open, in arm's reach of you, and you couldn't see me. The Skinks can see me at a distance in a forest or a swamp. I don't know how they do it, we've never found any evidence that they have infrared vision equipment. If they can see a man who you can't, what makes you think they won't see you?"

Balashir swallowed. No one had told him the demons could see invisible men. "Is it possible to patrol so they can't see us?"

Kerr slowly shook his head. "No. But it is possible to patrol in such a manner that you have a chance of spotting them before they kill you. It's possible to patrol in a way that won't allow them to kill all of you before you have a chance to fight back. If you start paying less attention to the fact that in the Confederation Marines I'm a corporal, and more attention to the fact that I've fought in campaigns on a dozen or more worlds—that the weakest foe I've fought was better trained, better led, and better armed than the toughest peasant revolt you've ever faced—then I can teach you things that just might keep you and your men alive."

Balashir looked wonderingly at Kerr. Even if this sub-sword was exaggerating his experience, his knowledge of combat might in fact be superior to his own. "I will instruct my men to obey you as they would me in their training," he said. But he thought, Who has command when we fight is another matter.

*   *   *

Some members of the 157th Defense Garrison had an easier time than others accepting the off-worlders' command. Sword Santa Jesus Maria took one look at the glare emitted from the eyes in the face that hovered too far above the ground in front of his reinforced squad and resolved to do absolutely nothing to rouse the man's ire.

"I don't want to be in this position," Schultz growled at Maria and his soldiers. "I don't want to be on this silly assed excuse for a world. I want to kill Skinks. You *will* do what I tell you to. You *will* do it when I tell you to. You *will* do it the way I train you. If you prevent me from killing Skinks, I *will* kill you."

Sword Santa Jesus Maria, a career soldier decorated three times for heroism in combat, struggled to control his shaking. This Marine frightened him more than any heretic he'd ever fought.

"I'm going to teach you how to shoot."

Nobody protested that they already knew how to shoot. Schultz taught them by example, and used far fewer words than he already had. He made them believe they needed to learn how to shoot.

A few of the officers and noncoms thought it would be beneficial to bring the Marines under their own command: Marines were supposed to be superior fighters, and should prove to be excellent examples to their own men. Sword Sriyjava was one who thought so once he saw the uncertainty in the face of the Marine who was supposed to assume command.

"Sword Doyle, I welcome you," he said effusively. "A fine soldier such as yourself is a most welcome addition to the 157th Defense Garrison. I hardly welcome you into my squad."

"Ah, thank you. Thank you." Corporal Doyle was pleased that the nervousness he felt didn't come through in his voice. "Don't bother to introduce everybody right now, I'll get to know all of you soon enough." He hoped he would. "The first thing I need to know is the chain of command within the squad."

"Absolutely, Sword! As experienced as you surely are, and bearing as you do the acting rank of sword, I have absolutely no qualms whatsoever, and neither do my men, at making you my second in command." A few of the soldiers in the ranks snickered behind their hands.

Doyle blinked. "Ah, maybe you didn't get the word?" he said hesitantly. "I'm supposed to be in command. You're *my* second."

"But Sword Doyle, surely you instantly recognize the folly in that. You do not know my men. You do not know the land. You do not know the people here!" He slapped his chest. "I know them intimately. It is absurd to expect an off-worlder to come in and take command." One or two of the soldiers laughed out loud.

Doyle wished he had the quiet command presence of Corporal Kerr, or that he could inspire fear in people the way Lance Corporal Schultz did. He didn't and he couldn't, but he had to take command from Sword Sriyjava anyway. And he had to do it in a way that didn't turn these soldiers against him.

"Sword Sriyjava," he said slowly, "do you normally disobey orders from Army of the Lord high command?"

Sriyjava assumed the look of an innocent falsely accused. "Never! The Army of the Lord high command speaks with the voice of the Convocation. All Soldiers of the Lord are constrained to obey its orders as we would obey the word of Allah."

"The order to place Marines in command positions came from your high command."

Sriyjava nodded and stepped closer. "Sword Doyle," he said in a low, conspiratorial tone, "we will reach an accommodation. We can show you in command, while I—who know the men, the land, and the people—am actually in charge." The soldiers behind him exchanged knowing glances.

Doyle sighed. He'd felt silly in making his preparations to assume command of this squad, but more than half expected a confrontation, and he'd come prepared to impress them. He stepped back and peeled off his chameleon shirt to reveal the dress scarlet tunic he wore under it.

"Do you know what these are?" he asked, running his fingers along the two rows of medals on his left chest. "These," he indicated the six medals on the bottom row, "are the Confederation Marine Corps Expeditionary Medal and campaign medals. The Expeditionary Medal, you will notice, has two comets on it to indicate I've been awarded it three times. That's eight times I've gone to different worlds on a combat deployment." These soldiers didn't need to know that he'd been a clerk on all those expeditions and campaigns, that he was on his first deployment as an infantryman. Anyway, he'd get around to the time he fought. "This," he indicated the leftmost of the two medals on the top row, "is the Marine Good Conduct Medal, with two comets for subsequent awards. Right, I've been a Marine for more than twelve years, I've got experience. These," the three ribbons on his right chest, "are unit citations. You'll notice they have gold comets on them, meaning I've been awarded each more than once. This," he saved the best for last and lifted the star hanging from the ribbon in the superior position on his left chest, "is the Bronze Star with Comet for bravery in combat."

A couple of the soldiers in the ranks gasped. They'd heard about the Confederation Marines Bronze Star. So had Sword Sriyjava. None of them laughed; he had their complete attention.

"I was awarded it for being one of eight Marines on patrol on a world called Elneal. We ran into, ah . . . let's say a whole lot of armed men who wanted us dead. A lot of them died before they backed off and let us walk out of the Martac Waste—and all eight of us *did* walk out." He paused and took a deep breath. "Do you know what you would have gotten if your entire defense garrison ran into the people we ran into? You would have gotten a lot of buzzards picking at your bones, that's what."

The soldiers looked sheepishly at each other, or at the ground, or into the distance, anywhere but at Corporal Doyle. He'd made the impression he wanted to make. Now to see if he could live up to it.

CHAPTER
TWENTY-SEVEN

"Are you crazy?" Hank Tuit shouted. "Not only no, but hell no!" The vidscreen went dead.

Conorado turned to Aldo and shrugged. "I tried."

"It's late. Call him back in the morning. Give him the night to think it over," Heintges suggested.

The vidscreen beeped. It was Tuit calling back. "Lewis, are you serious?"

"Yes, Hank. I want you in the courtroom with Aldo. I want somebody with me I can trust to support me. This thing could get ugly. I need a friend with me."

"Lew, I've sat on court-martials before, but never in civil court with professional shysters. Hell, man, I just lost my ship! You want me to 'stand by' you? I can't even keep my command, much less help you out in a court of law!"

"Captain Tuit," Heintges broke in, "the trial starts tomorrow. I'm going to ask for a continuance until you can be cleared to go into court with us. I also want to subpoena other witnesses. All this will take a few days. Will you be available? Look, sir—"

"Call me Hank."

"Okay, Hank; call me Aldo. Hank, Lew's right. Come on with us. I'll do all the finagling, prepare the briefs, and plead the case, all the lawyerly stuff. But you can provide moral support that I can't. Besides, as we get going, you might be surprised. Lew's told me about you. I think you and Judge Epstein might hit it off. He's a man of few words but they're to the point, like yours."

"I'm a man of no words," Tuit answered. "But, well, Sewall's in an uproar just now so I suppose it'll be some time before they give me another assignment, if they give me another one. All right. What do I do now?"

"Just wait until we get back to you. As I said, it'll take a few days, but with your background, a clearance should be no problem. After court tomorrow I'll see the staff judge advocate and request you be assigned to the case as Lew's personal attorney. It's irregular, but so is this whole damned case. I'll ask first off that the case be dismissed. I've read the BHHEI charter and it seems to me it's clear that experimentation on sentient alien beings is prohibited. If that doesn't work, I'll ask for a continuance. The other side's had months to prepare its case. I only today met Lew, and haven't yet had a chance to interview his witnesses. I'm sure Judge Epstein will give us all the time we need.

"And Hank, remember, Lew is being charged with a very serious crime, a violation of Title 18 of the Confederation Code—of interfering with and disrupting a scientific investigation being conducted by an agency of the government. The maximum penalty is life in prison. If Lew is found guilty, Hoxey's lawyers will ask for the maximum. No matter what he gets, if Lew's found guilty, that's the end of his career. If he wants you on his team, he deserves you."

"Very good."

"Hank?" Conorado leaned into the screen. "Here's lookin' at you!" he raised a schooner of ale and toasted Tuit's image.

"Lew, you're living too damned good for a mere jarhead officer!"

Camp Darby was an army installation. Back when humanity was confined to one world, it had been used as a transmitter facility for communications from the Chief of Staff to army units worldwide. But with the advent of the Beam drive and the interstellar deployment of army units, the camp's role had greatly diminished and it came to be used as a housing area and a morale and welfare center for army personnel stationed in and around Fargo. The post commander, an army colonel, had no idea of the case brought against Conorado, but he'd been ordered to cooperate fully with the Ministry of Justice, so he spared no effort to accommodate his guests.

The communications facility, which had not been used in years and was scheduled for conversion to a commissary store, was temporarily converted into a courtroom. Since the hearings would be closed, military police were posted inside the main entrance and outside the door to the judge's chambers, but not outside the building, so as to draw as little attention to the proceedings as possible. Aldo Heintges advised Conorado to wear civilian clothes, not his uniform.

The witnesses would wait in a large anteroom until called by the lone bailiff who'd been cleared to officiate at the proceedings. He would also be the recorder and clerk of the court, sitting in a corner of the judge's chambers where he'd operate a vid unit, mark exhibits, and escort and swear witnesses as they were called.

Conorado, Heintges, General Cazombi, and Agent Nast sat on one side of the anteroom. The two officers were in their dress uniforms. Hoxey, her two lawyers, and several members of her shift—including the unctuous and cowering Dannul Graag, Hoxey's administration officer, and the supercilious Dr. B. Proteus Gurselfanks, her laryngopathologist—sat on the other side. Dr. Omer Abraham, C Shift's chief scientist, was there too. He nodded surreptitiously at Conorado and then quickly looked away in embarrassment. "There's our chief witness for the defense," Conorado whispered to Heintges.

But Conorado was shocked to see Hoxey again. She had aged. Still, she stared at him with burning eyes. Clearly, her attitude was that he had thwarted her and must suffer for it.

"Plaintiff, respondent, and respective counsel, please enter the judge's chambers," the bailiff announced, holding open the door to Judge Epstein's makeshift chambers.

"We won't be more than ten minutes," Heintges whispered to Cazombi and Nast. "Stay out of trouble while we're in there. We'll all have lunch together when the judge dismisses us for the day."

Judge Epstein sat behind a battered old desk. He was dressed in casual street clothes. A group of chairs was arranged on each side of the room for the respective parties to the case. "All right, this court is now in session," Epstein said. "Be seated." He gestured at the chairs. "Ladies and gentlemen, this case is most unusual, and as you all know, classified ultrasecret, although I don't understand for one goddamned minute why." He glared at the lawyers. "Now I don't want this thing to drag on and on, understand? Make your pleadings, present your evidence and witnesses, and conduct your examinations with dispatch. Nobody's watching, there are no reputations to be made here, and I've seen it all so don't try to impress me. All right, who's who here?"

The lawyers introduced themselves.

"Okay. How do you plead, Captain Conorado?" the judge asked.

Conorado stood. "Not guilty, Your Honor."

"Your Honor . . ." Heintges stood. "We ask that you dismiss this case. I introduce as Exhibit A the Bureau of Human Habitability Exploration and Investigation charter. Section 108–2 clearly states that vivisection of sentient alien beings is prohibited."

"Your Honor . . ." Hoc Vinces jumped to his feet. "Defense is referring to paragraph 22b of Section 108–2. It is our contention that it does not specifically and categorically prohibit medical and scientific examination of alien beings, sentient or otherwise. It does authorize examinations."

"Your Honor, the word used in the charter is 'examination,' " Heintges said. "Examining a specimen of any kind is different from experimenting on one, especially one that is sentient."

Judge Epstein studied the charter for a while. He sighed and addressed Heintges. "Consul, I find the wording vague and open to interpretation. Motion denied."

"Then, Your Honor, I ask the court for a continuance."

Epstein looked annoyed. "Why?"

"I have not had a chance to prepare my witnesses, Your

Honor. And I plan to subpoena more witnesses. I haven't had sufficient time to do that. Besides, Captain Conorado only arrived here yesterday. And he has asked for another person to join us as coconsul. It'll take some time to get him cleared."

The woman sitting with Hoxey—her coconsul Drellia Fortescue—whispered something to Hoc Vinces and stood up. "We object, Your Honor!" Hoxey's lawyers were extremely well-dressed. Fortescue was slightly overweight, blond but frumpy, yet her voice was deep and sexy; Vinces was thin and dark-haired, clean-shaven, but his beard, which would have been thick and black if he'd let it grow, gave his cheeks a permanently bluish, four o'clock tinge.

"These other witnesses include the former director of our agency. Lieutenant Heintges is grasping at straws here," Fortescue continued, "trying every tactic he can to delay this court from getting down to its appointed duty."

"Well, counsel, seems to me defense's request is reasonable enough," Judge Epstein responded. "Balls of fire, Drellia, why wasn't Heintges given the time he needs to prepare his case anyway? Am I dealing with amateurs here?"

"Sir, plaintiff is not well. We feel the continuation of this case for any reason would be detrimental to her health. Besides, the facts in this case are very simple. The defense does not need extra time to prepare his witnesses. And frankly, Your Honor, the defense's request to add another person to his team just seems to us a ploy to further delay the proceedings."

"What's wrong with your client?"

Fortescue looked sympathetically at Hoxey, who slumped in her chair, glowering at Conorado. "Dr. Hoxey is suffering from exhaustion, Your Honor. The preparation for this trial, not to mention the traumatic events that the respondent precipitated at Avionia Station, have severely undermined her health."

"Well, Dr. Hoxey, are you healthy enough to sit through this trial?" Epstein asked.

Hoxey rose to her feet. Conorado was surprised to see that she had to lean on the table for support. "Yes, Your Honor," she rasped.

"Lieutenant?"

"Your Honor, Captain Conorado is charged with a very serious crime," Heintges said. "His entire life is at stake here. I must point out that he has spent his entire adult life defending the citizens of this Confederation and—"

"Captain Conorado," Judge Epstein interrupted, "I've read your file. I wouldn't object if my own son were to serve under an officer like you. But," he addressed Heintges, "come to the point."

"He deserves every chance to defend himself. My respected colleagues," Heintges nodded at Vinces and Fortescue, "have had plenty of time to prepare, while I have not. And I would respectfully add, sir, that the facts in this case are not as simple as Ms. Fortescue implies they are."

"Who's your cocounsel going to be, Lieutenant? Anybody I know?"

"A retired navy commander, sir, named Henry Tuit."

Judge Epstein's eyebrows arched in surprise and Vinces laughed outright. Vinces stood up. "Your Honor, this is a farce! Tuit is the man who just lost a valuable cargo ship. Only a crazy man would ask a fool like that to—"

"Enough of that! Is this Tuit the same man who's been in the news recently?"

"Yes, Your Honor."

"And your client wishes this man to join him as counsel?"

"Yes, Your Honor, as is his right."

"I know, I know. How long will it take to get him cleared?"

"Your Honor, he's a former navy officer who had the highest clearances. I will ask the staff judge advocate to hurry up the clearance process. I would ask the court for five days, no more. I also ask the court to grant a travel dispensation for my client. I want him to accompany me to the staff judge advocate's office this morning."

Judge Epstein drummed his fingers on his desk. "Okay. Bailiff, call in the witnesses." The little room was severely crowded by the time everyone had crowded in. "I am going to adjourn this court to give the defense more time to prepare. I am not going to sequester you, although I understand, Captain Conorado, that your military superiors have in effect restricted you to the confines of Camp Darby for the duration of this trial. But I remind you all about the rules of secrecy that cover these proceedings. You all know what they entail, so I don't have to enjoin you to discuss these hearings with no one but your counsel." He slammed his fist down on the desktop. "This court is now adjourned until 0700 hours next Thursday."

Filing out of the judge's chambers, Hoxey stumbled and would have fallen had Abraham not caught her. "Old girl really looks on her last legs," Nast whispered.

"Understand Abraham married her back a little while ago," General Cazombi commented.

"No accounting for affairs of the heart," Nast responded.

"Well, I really must've stepped on her teat," Conorado said. "I'll go to my grave believing I had no choice, but still, I feel sorry for her."

Heintges took his party aside. "Lew and I are going to the SJA's office right now. Can we all meet back at my office at say 1300 hours, have lunch together there? The place has been screened, so we can talk about the case without fear of compromising security. We've got a lot of work to do before next Thursday."

Nast nodded his assent. "We aren't going very far," he remarked, "since they've put us all up here at Darby until the trial's over." He looked at Cazombi. "How's your quarters, General?"

"Adequate," Cazombi replied. "Lew, keep a stiff upper. We'll get you out of this. See you all at lunch."

The staff judge advocate was a red-faced army colonel. "Request denied!" he thundered, his face growing even redder. "I have never heard of anything so stupid! Are you crazy, Captain, to make a demand on the legal system like this?"

Heintges was about to say something but Conorado laid a hand on his arm. "Colonel, I am sick and goddamned tired of people calling me crazy. Now, either you get Tuit cleared to sit as my coconsul or I fire Lieutenant Heintges here, and when a new lawyer is appointed for me, I fire him too, and so on until either Hoxey or I die of old age."

"Well—Well," the colonel blustered, "I didn't mean to say you're mentally unbalanced, Captain, excuse me. It's just that this request is a bit, uh, unusual, you might say."

"He's perfectly within his rights," Heintges added.

"Yes. Well, I'll have him here as soon as possible."

Lunch for the quartet consisted of sandwiches ordered from the Camp Darby post exchange. They took their time eating, although Aldo kept reminding them of all the work that lay ahead. At 1700 hours General Cazombi broke out a bottle of bourbon and they drank it in paper cups.

General Cazombi told the first story, an adventure he'd had when he'd been a lieutenant many years before. Conorado reciprocated. Nast and then Heintges contributed their own tales. By 1800 they were well into the bottle.

"How's Claypoole?" Nast asked Conorado.

"Huh? You know Claypoole?" Conorado asked, astonished.

"Well, I probably shouldn't tell you this, but to hell with it. Yeah. Remember when he and Dean were sent off on special TAD, as 'Marine security detail' on a survey ship?" He told Conorado about what had happened on Havanagas. The captain sat openmouthed as Nast related the story.

"Well, I'll be a shithouse mouse!" he exclaimed when Nast was done. "And Claypoole broke your nose?" Conorado laughed.

Nast laughed and fingered his nose. "Yep. Not that I didn't deserve it."

"Well, Thom, let me tell you something about Claypoole. He just saved my ass." Then, remembering the injunction about discussing what had happened on the *Cambria*, he changed the subject. Apparently, Nast and the others had had enough to drink at that point that nobody noticed.

At 1900 hours, much to everybody's surprise, there was a knock on the door.

"Well, gentlemen," Hank Tuit said as he entered the room and took in what was going on, "I lose my ship, get set up to put my best friend in jail, and now I'm in with a bunch of drunks. Anything left in that bottle for a guest?"

Conorado introduced Tuit.

"That was fast!" Heintges said. "Close the door, we've got a lot of work to do."

Tuit glanced around the room, taking in the mess, pretending to be offended by what he saw. "Yeah," he commented sourly, "looks like you been at it all afternoon too."

"You ain't seen nothing yet, Hank," General Cazombi said, a slight twitch to the right side of his face indicating he was enormously pleased with his surroundings. He pulled another bottle of bourbon out of his briefcase. "Never go anywhere without my medicinal medicaments."

"We really should get down to work, now that Hank's here," Aldo said.

"Eh, take it easy, Aldo, the night's young and we've got until next goddamned week," Conorado said. "You gotta get to know Hank better before we start talking business."

" 'Get to work' my ass!" Nast said. "Who the hell can do any work after all the bourbon we've had to drink? May as well get plastered. Hell, it may be the last time old Lew here'll have a chance to lift one with friends. They don't have bourbon on Darkside, Lew!"

Everyone laughed except Conorado.

"Hey, Lew, they don't have seegars up there either!" Tuit said. "But we do here!" He pulled a box out of his pocket and produced five Anniversarios No. 2, which he passed out.

"Gawdamn," General Cazombi said, "that's nearly a month's pay for a general!"

"Two months' pay for a mere captain," Conorado said, taking one and biting off the end.

"General, I am a civilian now," Tuit said, "so I get my pay as a ship's master and a retirement stipend from old Mother Navy."

"Don't call me 'General,' Hank. It's Al, short for Alistair. Tell us what happened to your ship."

Tuit became serious. "Bad accident, Al. Lew was with me. Hadn't been for him, neither of us would be here now."

"Hadn't been for Claypoole and Dean, neither of us would be here now," Conorado added. Then he realized he'd said too much. He exchanged a guilty look with Tuit, which General Cazombi caught.

"Okay, boys, what really happened? We heard the news about your propulsion unit going critical and all that crap. Never believed a word of it. Give us the scoop, this office is secure." Cazombi blew out a large cloud of smoke and sipped from his cup.

Tuit and Conorado exchanged glances again. Tuit shrugged. "What the hell," he said. "If anybody's listening, get fucked." He told them what had happened.

"So that's what you meant when you said Dean and Claypoole had saved your life," Nast said.

"Lew," Heintges said, "if we could only make that story public, nobody in his right mind would find you guilty of breaking the law on Avionia Station." He sighed. "But we can't make it public."

"So let's kill this bottle," Tuit suggested, "and we'll worry about our heads in the morning, while Lew worries about his ass, but tonight we don't worry about nuttin'."

The next thing Conorado knew, Aldo Heintges was shaking him awake. He could remember leaving Aldo's office in the early morning hours, staggering down the darkened streets of the main post at Camp Darby to the bachelor officer's quarters and undressing, but he didn't recall going to sleep.

"Gawdamn," he muttered, "my mouth tastes like a whole regiment of Siad warriors marched their horses through it. What the hell's up, Aldo?"

"Hoxey's dead."

Conorado sat straight up in his bed. *"What!"*

"She died last night, Lew. Judge Epstein wants to see us all in the courtroom at ten hours, and it's eight hours now. Let's get moving."

"Dead?"

"Yes, she died sometime last night, while we were carousing."

"Well—how?"

"Lew, I don't know. But I think you're off the hook. Look, a couple days ago I subpoenaed the former chief of BHHEI, Dr. Blossom Enderly. Her sworn statement just came in this morning." He held up a crystal. "She couldn't make it in person for her own health reasons, but it's your ticket home. Now get dressed and let's get moving."

Everyone sat quietly in the anteroom to Judge Epstein's chambers. Conorado noticed that Dr. Abraham was missing. That was understandable. Nobody had much to say to anybody else. The bailiff emerged from the judge's chambers and summoned everyone into the court. "Ladies and gentlemen," he announced, "court is now in session, the Honorable Stefan Epstein presiding."

Judge Epstein addressed the court: "I have called you all in here this morning because I am going to conclude this trial today, one way or another. I know it's cramped here in my chambers, but please bear with me.

"Counsel for the plaintiffs, I understand Dr. Hoxey passed away last evening. You have my condolences."

"That is correct, Your Honor. She died of heart failure, apparently. Dr. Hoxey has been ill for some time, brought on by the traumatic events precipitated by the respondent—"

"That's enough, counsel."

"Yes, Your Honor." Vinces blushed. "But BHHEI believes a serious crime was committed, and I request that the court continue this trial to a conclusion."

"Lieutenant Heintges?"

"Your Honor, may I introduce retired navy captain Henry Tuit, my coconsul?" Tuit stood. Judge Epstein nodded at the bailiff recorder. "He just got in last night, Your Honor."

"Looks like it," Judge Epstein murmured dryly. "Gotta be the fastest case of granting a clearance on record. The *Cambria* was your ship, wasn't it, Captain? Sewall's gonna take a bath on that one. You'll have to tell me all about it when this business is over." Tuit managed a sickly grin.

"Sir, I move that the court dismiss the charges against Captain Conorado," Heintges continued. "I have here a sworn statement from the former chief of the Bureau for Human Habitability Exploration and Investigation that fully clears my client of these charges. She was chief during the time this alleged crime was committed."

"We haven't seen that!" Vinces protested.

"Now you will see it," the judge said. "Bailiff, introduce this crystal as Exhibit B and then put it on the reader so everyone can see it."

Dr. Enderly's face appeared on the screen. She identified herself, said something about how long she had been chief of BHHEI, and then: "I have reviewed the statements presented to me by Lieutenant Aldo Heintges on behalf of his client, Captain Lewis Conorado, Confederation Marine Corps. I have this to say: As head of the BHHEI, I never authorized experimentation of the kind described in these statements, and if Dr. Thelma Hoxey was performing experiments of this nature, they were in direct contravention of the bureau's charter, as I understood the charter, and all the rules of common human decency. Instead of putting this Marine officer on trial, he should be thanked for what he did on Avionia Station."

The judge's chambers were totally silent after Enderly's statement was over.

"Your Honor," Vinces said, "Dr. Enderly is retired and her health is very fragile. I ask the court to consider that in evaluating her statements."

"I suppose you're going to say something like that about me, because Thelma died last night?" a voice said from the back of the room as Dr. Omer Abraham stepped inside. "Your Honor, I loved my wife, but what she did to those Avionians was wrong." Abraham walked down the short aisle between the chairs and stood before Judge Epstein's desk. His face was haggard and his eyes red-rimmed but he stood with his back straight and his fists clenched by his sides. "I opposed those hideous experiments from the start, and Thelma and I argued about it continuously. It was wrong. The Avionians are sentient beings, not animals, and what she ordered done to them in the name of 'science' wouldn't be permitted on an animal, much less a creature with a soul. The captain was right to stop it. But I should have done that myself long before he ever came along. I should be on trial here for not doing the decent thing, not Captain Conorado, who had the guts to do it himself. I had to come here to tell you that this morning, sir. I had to." Abraham seemed to wilt after he finished speaking. He just stood there looking at the judge in silence.

"Sit down, Doctor," Judge Epstein said softly. Vinces was about to protest but Epstein silenced him with a wave of his hand. "Mr. Vinces, Ms. Fortescue, I order you to return to BHHEI forthwith and rewrite that agency's charter to specifically prohibit experimentation of any kind on any alien being with an intelligence level above that of a tomato. You will submit it to this court within two weeks for review and approval. This case is dismissed," he announced, slamming his hand on his desk.

Outside the building, Conorado caught up with Dr. Abraham and laid a hand on his shoulder. "I am very sorry about Dr. Hoxey, sir. I'm sorry she passed on and I am sorry if what I did contributed to that in any way."

"Captain, thank you. Thelma was a hard person to get to know but once you did . . ." He shrugged. "I appreciate what you did on the station, Captain. Thelma was wrong, that's all there is to it."

"Thank you, Doctor. And thanks for coming down here this morning. That took some real courage." They shook hands.

"Well, Lew, when do you head back to 34th FIST?" Tuit asked when Conorado rejoined the others.

"Soon as I can, but not before I take care of some unfinished business, Hank."

"And what might that be?"

"I'm going to see Jennifer Lenfen's parents."

"Right. I'll go with you," Tuit responded, clapping Conorado on the back.

CHAPTER
TWENTY-EIGHT

"Lesser Imam, Lesser Imam!" First Acolyte Fakir burst into what had been his office, which, now that he shared it, he mostly avoided. He waved a flimsy in his hand.

Acting Lesser Imam Bladon looked up from the training plan he and his fire team leaders were reviewing. "First Acolyte," he calmly acknowledged, though Fakir's excitement indicated pending action.

"Lesser Imam, the demons are striking Blessing Waters at this time." He thrust the flimsy at Bladon.

Still calm on the outside, Bladon took the flimsy and scanned it. The noted time of receipt showed the message was only two minutes old. Place of transmission verified it came from the village of Blessing Waters. The message itself was terse: "Demons are attacking. Help us ere we all die."

That was it.

Bladon stood. "Rat, inform Platoon and see if the string-of-pearls shows anything. Kerr, get our people ready to move out. Chan, get transport. First Acolyte, have your people assemble in the courtyard, ready to move. I want us on the way within five minutes." He was talking to himself on the last sentence, because each man to whom he gave an order left the office immediately.

Two minutes after Fakir ran in with the message, the last Soldiers of the Lord were scrambling into the company formation, urged on by the Marines. The garrison's armored personnel carriers were manned and rumbling to life. Corporal "Rat" Linsman was intently studying the data flow the *Grandar Bay* was transmitting to his UPUD, Mark III.

"Report!" Bladon commanded before he even reached his position in front of the company.

"First platoon," PFC MacIlargie eagle-eyed a late arriver, "all present and accounted for!"

"Second platoon, ready to mount up," Corporal Kerr announced.

"Third platoon?" Corporal Chan was running to his position from the APCs.

"Third platoon, all present!" PFC Longfellow shouted.

"Transport!" Bladon cried.

Chan, now in place in front of his platoon, glanced at the APCs. "Transport ready," he replied.

"Mount up!"

Under the direction of the Marines, the soldiers of the 157th Defense Garrison boarded their assigned vehicles in much better order than they would have a few days earlier.

"Listen up, don't interrupt," Bladon said over the squad circuit as he and Linsman headed toward their APC. He wanted his Marines to know everything they could. "Got anything?" he asked Linsman.

"Looks like it's still in progress," Linsman answered without taking his eyes from the UPUD display.

"How many are there and what's their disposition?" The two Marines boarded the APC and strapped themselves in.

Linsman shook his head. "Can't tell, Skinks don't show up well in infrared. Take a look." He tapped a button to switch the display from numerical data to visual and handed the UPUD to Bladon. "I think all those red spots are civilians."

"Report," Bladon ordered as he accepted the UPUD.

In a moment all the Marines reported their soldiers were aboard the APCs and strapped in.

"Move out," he ordered on the company command circuit.

In the Army of the Lord, the command officers and religious officers of a defense garrison company were tied into a comm net—enlisted men, even noncommissioned officers, weren't. The APCs jerked and moved out to form in three parallel lines, tracks and wheels rumbling over the ground as they picked up speed. Conversation inside them was impossible except over the helmet comms.

Bladon studied the display for a moment, then swore under his breath. They had to go in blind. All he could do was see where the red dots were, what direction they ran in—the ones that ran rather than trying to hide—and try to extrapolate from that where the Skinks were. No way to tell how many there were, or whether any of them were actually chasing the fleeing civilians.

"What's that?" he asked.

Linsman looked at the display. A dot, larger and brighter than the dots he interpreted as civilians, had entered the display. He took the UPUD and tapped the button to resume the numerical data flow.

"Shit," he swore. "It's a vehicle. String-of-pearls says it doesn't return an IFF signal."

"Must be one of theirs," Bladon murmured.

Linsman nodded. "Think they've got that armor-killer weapon?" he asked.

"It's possible." Bladon thought about it. Nobody knew what the range of that weapon was, or at least he didn't. It had fired at them at eight hundred meters in the Swamp of Perdition. They didn't know how far away it was when it killed the Dragons. He toggled on his HUD map and set it to a scale that showed the garrison, the village, and their position. To reach the village, they had to cross over a row of small hills—the map labled them "Martyrs Mounts"—that ran at a tangential angle to their line of approach. The hills were two kilometers from the village, and they were still five klicks from the hills.

"There are three of them now," Linsman said. "Headed into the village center."

Fakir was on a different APC. Bladon toggled to the command frequency to talk to him. He told Fakir which map he was using and updated him on what was happening in the village. Then he told him to have the vehicles keep the Martyrs Mounts between them and the village until they were as close to it as they could get, and he gave Fakir the coordinates. That was where they'd dismount. Only then did he report the presence of vehicles to third platoon headquarters and request instructions.

The APCs pitched as they turned onto their new vector.

The Marines ordered the soldiers to spread out and stay below the crest of the hills. They themselves went the rest of the way to where they could observe.

Blessing Waters was home to four hundred people, five hundred if the outlying households were included. Corporal Doyle counted five spires, a minaret, and an onion dome that he assumed was also a place of worship. He wondered how so few people could support so many temples. A movement caught his eye, and he forgot all about the ways of the religious; a vehicle crashed through a house on the fringe of town, shattering it. He looked more widely and spotted two more armored vehicles smashing through the village. One of the steeples toppled as he watched.

Armored vehicles. On Diamunde six FISTs went up against several armored divisions to kick open the door for the army, but he had been the company's chief clerk and didn't participate in the combat. But he'd heard about it, and he was the one who processed the casualty reports.

There was armor down there. He gripped his blaster and felt sick—they didn't have weapons that could defeat armor. Even the Army of the Lord APCs only had antipersonnel weapons; they'd never had to fight armor. If the Skinks spotted the Marines on the hills and came after them, they wouldn't be able to defend themselves. Doyle fought down the bile that rose; it wouldn't do to let the soldiers he was supposed to be leading know it—they had to think he was confident and competent.

On Diamunde, Lance Corporal Schultz had been in the thick of the fighting, even managed to take out a tank with his blaster. Not directly, though. He was trying to burn through the turret hatch when a crewman opened a forward hatch to take *him* out. He had flamed that crewman, then jammed his blaster through the open hatch before anyone inside could close it and fired until he'd killed the crew and melted the tank's electronics. But Schultz harbored no delusions about being able to kill one of the Skink armored vehicles with only his blaster. These three scared him more than the divisions of tanks he'd faced on Diamunde.

Corporal Kerr missed that action because he was still recuperating. But he knew they needed weapons they didn't have to defeat these tanks.

As soon as Acting Lesser Imam Bladon visually confirmed that the vehicles were armor, he reported to third platoon. Gunny Bass replied that Raptors were orbiting on ready station and he'd get them headed his way.

Bladon watched the scene a klick and a half away and swore to himself in a constant stream. He didn't dare move his company in until the tanks were dead. Through his magnifier shield he could make out dun-colored figures here and there, dartng in and out of view. They seemed to be running about randomly, searching and pursuing. Bodies lay flung about, dead civilians. He was afraid that by the time he and his troops got to the village, most of the civilians would be dead.

"One-five-seven, this is your Bluebird of Happiness," a voice interrupted Bladon's swearing. "I have you on visual. That is you, isn't it?"

"Bluebird, stand by for confirm," Bladon said. He turned around, used his infra to make sure nobody was in his line of sight, and fired his blaster downhill.

"Ooh-ee, One-five-seven, that's a mighty pretty shoulder flame you've got there."

Bladon felt relief. "Visual confirmed," he said. He hadn't told the Bluebird pilot what he was using as a visual signal; the pilot had to identify it and wait for his confirmation. That way no enemy could confuse the pilot by using the same signal to give a false position.

"I show three vehicles in the town," the pilot said. "That what you need taken care of?"

"That's affirmative, Bluebird. All the good guys are near my confirm. Be careful, civilians are getting slaughtered by the bad guys."

"Roger that, One-five-seven. I'm using the SOP to guide our goodies. The squids get the blame if any noncombatants get hit."

"You're wasting time, Bluebird. Civilians are getting killed."

"Roger, Marine. As soon as we're lined up." While Bluebird lead was talking, he and his wingman had locked their missiles' guidance systems into the string-of-pearls. They punched in their designated targets, pointed their noses toward the Martyrs Mounts, then they each fired two missiles that swooped up over the hills and arrowed at the village. Guided by the ring of surveillance satellites, they altered vector and sped toward the rampaging tanks. One missile struck close enough to tear the treads off its target and nearly knock it onto its side. Another hit the engine compartment of its target and killed it. The third tank took a direct hit on its turret and erupted. The final missile made a radical, last instant course correction and plunged into the side of the crippled tank, killing it.

"Bluebird of Happiness, paint three tanks on your forehead," Bladon said, barely suppressing a cheer. "If I ever run into you in a civilian bar, I owe you and your wingman a drink or three."

"Damn! Why is it every time I go on an infantry support mission the mud commander is enlisted and can't buy me a drink in the officers club?" Bluebird said. "Hey, you ever go for a commission, I'll buy you a drink in the O-club." Then more seriously, "Listen, One-five-seven, we've got more missiles, we just refueled, and mom isn't expecting us for dinner right away. Want us to stick around just in case?"

"I'd love to have your company, Bluebird. Here are my command and all-hands freqs." Bladon sent them. Now the two Raptors could monitor what the troops on the ground were doing and not have to wait for a call if they needed help in a hurry.

Bladon switched to the all-hands frequency. "Saddle up, we're moving in. Contingency Charlie." Contingency Charlie had the APCs moving in support of the infantry.

"If they've got one of those weapons," Kerr said on the squad circuit, "they'll start taking out the APCs."

"That's right," Bladon replied. "We can save the infantry if they do." His map showed irregularities in the ground that the infantry could use to avoid the line of sight to the Skinks.

The 157th Defense Garrison got on line and moved over the hills. Once on the flat, the Marines urged them into a trot. The APCs rumbled along, dispersed between squads. They had covered half the distance before the Skinks who had gathered around the nearest killed tank became aware of them. There were a few seconds of apparent confusion among the Skinks, then they began to run into the ruined village.

"Flame them!" Bladon shouted.

The Marines dropped into firing positions and took careful aim. Their fusillade was rewarded with several flashes from vaporizing Skinks. Then no more Skinks were in sight. The Soldiers of the Lord were impressed by both the range and accuracy of the Marines' fire.

"Move out!" Bladon ordered on the all-hands circuit. "Double time!"

They all sprinted forward.

"Lesser Imam," Fakir panted into the command circuit, "shouldn't we board the APCs? We can catch them better in the vehicles than on foot."

"We stay spread out," Bladon replied. There was still a chance the Skinks had that weapon, and he didn't want to risk losing half a platoon to one shot.

But the Skinks didn't have that weapon, whatever it was. Or chose not to use it. The Marines and their charges ran through the village and into a forest beyond it without seeing any more Skinks. They continued into the forest for half a kilometer before Gunny Bass ordered them to turn back and see what they could do for the civilian survivors.

Blessing Waters was thoroughly devastated. More than a quarter of the buildings were knocked down and many others had received damage, some severe, from the three tanks. Bladon assigned Linsman to set a platoon in defensive positions between the village and the forest, and observation posts on other possible approaches. Then he had the rest of the company gather the injured people in one place, where he and the rest of the Marines used their knives to dig any still-active acid out of their wounds. Once the wounded were gathered for care, Bladon set the soldiers to work gathering corpses near the village graveyard for burial. The Marines did their best to ignore the screams and whimpers of the wounded, and the wails of the survivors crying over their dead. Of four hundred residents, more than half had been killed in the raid. When visitors from the outlying homesteads were included, there were nearly three hundred fatalities.

The Skinks didn't return.

Second squad wasn't unique in having problems integrating into command and leadership positions with the Army of the Lord's Defense Garrisons. A hundred kilometers from the 157th, first squad had difficulties.

"Acting Lesser Imam," Friar Acolyte Archangel Raphael said from the doorway of the office of the commander of the 241st Defense Garrison.

Sergeant Ratliff looked up from the contingency operation plans he and Lesser Imam Yasith, the garrison's regular commander, were refining. He didn't like Friar Acolyte Archangel Raphael, who constantly interjected himself into strictly military matters.

"I bring a message for Lesser Imam Yasith. It has to do with danger to the Faithful."

"Come." Ratliff didn't have the patience to grant the priest any more than the bare minimum of courtesy a commander owed to an obstreperous subordinate.

Archangel Raphael entered the office and thrust a flimsy at Yasith.

The Kingdomite read it quickly and handed it to Ratliff. "We need to move fast," he said.

Ratliff read the brief message. It was from the village of Kibbutz Aviv, which was under attack. The message was five minutes old. It had been received in the room directly outside the commander's office.

"Form up the garrison for immediate movement," Ratliff told Yasith. As he brushed past Archangel Raphael he said, "This message is five minutes old. That's not acceptable. People—your people—are dying." He got on his comm and began issuing orders to his Marines as he made his way to the parade ground outside of the garrison compound.

Archangel Raphael scurried to keep up. "It was necessary for me to confirm the message," he said harshly.

"Confirmation is a military responsibility. We would already be on the way if you'd given me that message as soon as it came in."

"What if you arrived and the message was false? The Faithful of Kibbutz Aviv would be at risk of heretical contamination."

Ratliff spun about abruptly, and the priest almost fell to avoid running into him.

"You were so concerned about the remote possibility someone might hear something you disagree with that you chose to let people die. We have minimum contact with the villagers when we go in; that's one of our Rules of Engagement. The people who die because we were delayed, their deaths are on your soul. Their deaths are your sin."

"Heathen!" Archangel Raphael shrilled. "It is no one's sin to die resisting heresy!"

But Ratliff was already striding to the parade ground and didn't listen. He had a counterattack to mount.

Within two minutes the entire 241st Defense Garrison and the Marines who commanded and led it were aboard APCs, headed for Kibbutz Aviv. They were in sight of the village, re-formed on line and charging at top speed into open farmland when the APC on the line's left flank went into a dip in the ground and didn't come out.

Ratliff was studying the situation on his UPUD's visual display when he saw the APC suddenly stop. "Runner Eleven, report," he said into the company command circuit. There was no reply. Who did he have in Eleven? PFC Hayes, that's right. He switched to the squad circuit. "Hayes, sound off. What's happening?"

No reply. Hayes's ID bracelet telltale didn't show when Ratliff switched the UPUD display to show the Marines' locations.

Still on the squad circuit, he said, "Dorny, Rock, check it out. Everybody else, keep moving." *Damn*, not only was he half blind, he was going to hit an unknown number of Skinks with an understrength company.

"We've got trouble," Corporal Dornhofer reported. *"God-damn! Skinks all over the place!"* Ratliff heard Dornhofer order the two APCs to maneuver to where the infantrymen could dismount.

"We're coming, give us directions!" Ratliff shouted. He deployed the APCs according to Dornhofer's report and had the troops dismount seventy-five meters from the dip. Dornhofer, Claypoole, and their Kingdomites were already on foot, firing desperately at hoards of Skinks that were attacking from the other side of the dip. He couldn't see the APC from where he was—it was too deep.

"Pasquin, loop left, get on their flank," Ratliff ordered. "Juice, move to your right and lay down a base of fire."

On the right side, Corporal "Juice" Goudanis and PFC Quick quickly had their platoon move forward and fire into the mass of Skinks. The *crack-sizzle* of the Marine blasters mingled with the louder rat-a-tat of the Kingdomites' fléchette rifles. Skinks flared into vapor, hit by plasma bolts, and others sprayed blood from bodies rent by the miniature darts from the fléchette rifles.

On the left, Pasquin and Dean tried to maintain order in the platoon they herded through the wheat, galloping to a flanking position.

Ratliff demanded that the UPUD focus on the immediate area of the firefight. After a moment, the display view jerked and adjusted to a larger scale that encompassed a square five hundred meters on a side. He looked closely and could barely make out the infrared signatures of the Skinks. There seemed to be hundreds of them.

By then Pasquin, Dean, and the second platoon were in their flanking position, pouring enfilade fire into the Skinks. So many of them flared, it looked like scattered lights were strobing at close but irregular intervals in the wheat. More Skinks yet were shredded by fléchettes.

A whistle shrilled a complex pattern that was taken up by other whistles. Ratliff's jaw dropped at the response of the Skinks to the whistles. They jumped up and ran into the trees to their rear, but many delayed their flight to start fires in the field. They didn't attempt to take their wounded and dead, they set the fires next to them. The bodies flashed and helped spread the flames.

"Up and at 'em!" Goudanis bellowed. "Don't let them get away!" He leaped to his feet and led the third platoon in a race into the trees after the fleeing Skinks. The trees were closer to his platoon's position than the rest of the field where they had fought.

"Juice, hold your position!" Ratliff shouted into the squad circuit.

"But—"

"No 'but.' Stop and drop!"

Goudanis called for the platoon to drop in place. He didn't give the order quite soon enough. The trees, now thirty meters away, were suddenly alive with streams of greenish fluid shooting at the exposed men in range. The Marines and Kindgomites were where the Skinks wanted them to be—in range of the hellish weapons.

"Dorny, give them support! Pasquin, maneuver to where you can support them. Juice, pull back!"

First platoon began firing over the heads of the prone third platoon. Flashes lit up inside the trees. In a moment Pasquin and Dean had maneuvered second platoon to where it could help. The men of third platoon were crawling backward. In that section of the wheat field the screams of wounded and frightened men almost overwhelmed the din of blaster and rifle fire.

Then they were out of range, at least those men who weren't dead or too badly wounded to crawl. More flashes lit up in the trees, the Skinks torching their own casualties.

"They're inhuman!" Dean gasped. "They're killing their own."

"What, didn't you know they aren't human?" Pasquin retorted. "Can't expect them to be like us."

"You know what I mean," Dean snapped back.

Flames flickered in the underbrush, but the flashes in the trees weren't enough to start a forest fire.

"Report," Ratliff ordered as soon as it was clear the fighting was over for the moment.

Dornhofer replied that he and Claypoole were all right, but seven of their Kingdomites were down—three dead, two dying, and two with lesser but disabling wounds. But it appeared that everyone in Runner 11 was dead; he hadn't had an opportunity to inspect it yet.

Pasquin reported that second platoon was all present, no casulaties.

PFC Quick, sounding close to breakdown, said Corporal Goudanis was down, maybe dead. He wasn't sure how many Kingdomites were down other than to say a lot of them.

"Pasquin, take over third platoon. Report as soon as you can," Ratliff ordered. "Dorny, let's check out Runner Eleven."

The APC at the bottom of the dip looked like it had been submerged in a bath of sulfuric acid and forgotten about. Its entire surface was pitted, fully eaten through in a number of places, so it resembled a block of particularly holey Swiss cheese gone to mold. Green goo still ate at it in spots. Shards of its treads dangled from the sprocket wheels, the tires completely gone.

"My God," Dornhofer whispered.

"It looks like every Skink who could get in range opened up on it," Ratliff said. "Let's get that hatch open and see if anyone's still alive in there." He didn't have much hope of that.

The surface around the hatch was still too damp for them to risk touching it. Ratliff raised all shields except the infra and looked through a hole next to the hatch. He saw a lot of bodies in infrared, but the signatures were dimming. "Anybody alive?" he asked, and got only an echo for answer.

"Let's use this," Dornhofer said. He held a fléchette rifle dropped by one of his Kingdomites, jammed it into a hole where the acid had eaten through alongside the hatch. Using the barrel as a lever, he forced the hatch open then jumped back to avoid a puddle of acid that flowed out.

The two Marines looked in with their light gatherers and looked away quickly. None of the fifteen men inside was alive.

"Now what?" Dornhofer asked dully.

"We have to deal with this later," Ratliff replied, and turned away. "Pasquin, what's happening with third platoon?"

"Goudanis is still alive, but barely. I think we got all the active acid cut out of him. He needs a hospital, right now. We're still bringing in the casualites. All I can say is, third lost too many men to function as a platoon."

Ratliff sighed. "Let me know when you know more."

"Aye aye."

"You know, we came out here for a reason," Ratliff said to Dornhofer.

"How can I forget?" Dornhofer answered dryly, looking at the APC in which one of his Marines and a third of his platoon had died.

They climbed out of the dip and Ratliff studied his UPUD display. The red dots that showed the civilians weren't jittering in flight anymore. Most of them were stationary, the dots in motion moving slowly. "Allah's balls," he swore. "I think they lured us into an ambush and took off from the village as soon as we walked into their killing zone." A blow from behind staggered him.

"Heathen! Blasphemer!" Friar Acolyte Archangel Raphael shrieked at him. "How many Soldiers of the Lord died this day because God in his mercy set the demons upon you for blaspheming his name?"

Ratliff took a long step to stand chest-to-chest with the religious officer. "No 'demons' were set on us by any god because of my speech," he said, his voice ominously low. "If you hadn't delayed giving me that message, we might have been through here before their ambush was ready." He knew that wasn't true, the ambush was probably in place before the attack on the village began.

His hands clenched into fists, and his right elbow was cocked. Dornhofer grabbed his arm.

"Leave him alone. He's a fanatic, you can't talk to him. We've got a job to do, let's do it, Marine."

Ratliff glared at Dornhofer, but he uncocked his arm and unclenched his fists. He turned from the priest and headed for the APCs. He issued orders as he went.

"Pasquin, leave Dean in command of third platoon. Mount second platoon on the APCs. Dornhofer, mount up first platoon. We're continuing to the village. Dean, get the casualties on APCs and return to the garrison." He reported to Gunny Bass as they headed for the village and again when they got there.

The Skinks were gone from Kibbutz Aviv by the time the 241st Defense Garrison reached it. Physical damage was less than at Blessing Waters and the casualties were fewer. Ratliff was right, the Skinks had withdrawn from the village as soon as the ambush was sprung.

CHAPTER
TWENTY-NINE

A diminutive, fragile-looking female knelt gracefully at the feet of the Great Master and delicately poured a steaming liquid into a handleless cup that sat on a low, lacquered table by his feet. The pouring done, she bowed low to touch her forehead to the matting that covered the floor. A sprig of pastel flowers, carefully packaged in a fluted vase for its long journey from Home was the only other object on the table. The Great Master picked up the cup with a grace that belied his fierce mien and sipped. His eyes closed and his face glowed with ecstasy. He spoke briefly to the female, his voice the rumbling of water rushing over rocks. The female murmured a few words of reply, her voice the sound of a babbling brook. The female appeared to bow even lower than she already was, then gracefully rose and backed away with her gaze fixed on the floor by her feet.

The Great Master sat cross-legged on a thick mat at one end of the large subterranean room. He wore his ceremonial robe with its rectangles of golden metal plate. A ceremonial sword lay across his lap. The sword, sheathed in precious wood that curved slightly with the curve of the blade, was as nonfunctional for combat as his armor.

Two Large Ones sat close to the Great Master's rear, one more to either side. A fifth Large One sat with his back to the Great Master's back. The armor the bodyguards wore was fully functional, as were the unsheathed swords they held. Ten more Large Ones sat cross-legged around the sides of the room, unsheathed swords across their laps.

In its center, the room was filled with Over Masters and

the more senior of the Senior Masters. They sat in open ranks on thinner mats than that of the Great Master. Their armor, like the armor of the bodyguards, was functional; their swords, like that of the Great Master, were sheathed. No acid guns were in evidence, but hidden behind screens at the tops of the walls, four acid guns were trained on the Masters.

With the Great Master served and approving, several females entered the room. They shuffled from the tightness of the ankle-length robes. Each carried a small, stub-legged table. The tables each held two small cups and a pot, steam rising from the pot spouts. The females gracefully knelt, each between two Masters, and set the tables down where the Master to either side could easily reach it. They poured from the pot into the cups, bowed low, then rose gracefully and exited. The female who served the Great Master returned with her pot freshly filled and knelt between his knee and the table, her head bowed low.

The Great Master took another sip from his tiny cup, replaced it on the table, and the female at his knee refilled it. Finally, he looked out at the assembled Over Masters and most senior of the Senior Masters. They bowed so their foreheads nearly touched the mats in front of their folded legs, then sipped from their own cups. All beamed and grunted pleasure.

The Great Master leaned forward with one elbow resting on a knee. His eyes shone with the glory of a true believer proved right. He spoke, his voice the sound of breakers crashing on a rocky shore.

"Phase one of the Grand Master's plan has gone as I expected it to. The Earthman Marines are scattered among the small outposts of the army of the pond-scum Earthmen who infest this mudball. The Earthman Marines have suffered severe casualties at the hands of our Fighters. The army of these pond scum has suffered even more severe casualties, their morale is nearly gone. The Earthmen in their towns and villages are terrified. Many of the survivors are fleeing to the presumed safety of cities and the garrisons of the pond-scum soldiers. They flee even from towns and villages we haven't struck. The Earthmen are in near total disarray."

He grinned the grin of a predator about to pounce on a doomed prey animal. "It is now time to commence phase two. Only it will be my phase two. When I call in the second wave," his voice became the crash and rumble of an earthquake, "they will arrive in time to help us celebrate our great victory over the Earthman Marines!"

The Over Masters and more senior of the Senior Masters roared back their eagerness for phase two.

Brigadier Sturgeon scrolled through the medium scale situation map, studying each part as it was projected in the wall display, looking for a pattern to the Skink raids. He couldn't find one. There were no groupings of raids, no patch where they looked like they might radiate from one location. He missed Colonel Ramadan—his chief of staff was better than he was at picking out certain patterns of enemy action.

"Speak up if you think you see anything," he told his staff. He thought it probably wasn't necessary for him to say that, but he couldn't take the risk that someone might see something and assume wrongly that he already had. None of the assembled officers said anything immediately. It wasn't until halfway through the next rotation through the map that Captain Shadeh, the personnel officer, spoke up.

"Sir?" Shadeh, the F1 personnel officer, waited for Sturgeon's nod before continuing. "They seem to be widening the range of the raids, as though they intend to spread us thinner and thinner."

Sturgeon hit a sequence of buttons and the map changed to show the entire area of operation. A series of tiny red lights blinked on, changed to yellow, were replaced by a different scattering of red lights, changed to green as the new red lights became yellow and were replaced by yet more red lights. Greens became gray and stayed that color as additional red lights demoted earlier reds to yellows and yellows to greens.

"It looks like you're right," he said, glancing at Shadeh.

"Trust the F1 to come up with a pattern that affects personnel disposition."

Shadeh smiled grimly.

"Anybody see anything that looks like it can indicate a starting point?" He looked at Commander Daana, the intelligence officer.

"Nossir," the F2 said. "The latest computer analysis says a random pattern generator is behind it. So far it hasn't been able to come up with a logarithm to duplicate it."

"Any other ideas anybody?"

Commander Usner, the operations officer, leaned back and crossed his arms over his chest. "Sir, an idea is niggling at the back of my mind. In some ways this is a reversal of the classic guerrilla campaign."

"Explain."

"Sir, the classic guerrilla campaign begins with small acts of terrorism and small hit-and-run hits on military targets to, let's say, cause 'a death of a thousand cuts' and damage morale. Over time it builds up to conventional force engagements. What happened when we made planetfall? First they gave us a sample of their strength by hitting a remote garrison. When we first encountered them it was in a major engagement. We won that one, but at a dear cost. We don't know how badly we hurt them, but there must have been enough of them left over for them to defeat us if they massed. They didn't. Instead they went to terroristic hit-and-run raids. They're hitting villages, hard. When we show up, they run before we can engage them—except when they've got an ambush set. Then they seem to fight us until we have to withdraw or until they're dead. They've convinced the people that neither the government nor the army can protect them." He made a sour face. "People in the outlying areas have no confidence in us. The army is losing its confidence in us. Even the theocracy is beginning to accuse us of incompetence."

"Following your logic, their next step is minor terroristic acts."

"Possible. They haven't conducted any raids for the past

three days. That *could* mean they've given up. But maybe they've been stretching us out, wearing us out, damaging the morale of the army, in order to set us up for something big."

Sturgeon looked back at the map. The ever-increasing lights showed no slacking of frequency. "The way they vaporize when they're hit with a plasma bolt," he shook his head, "we can't tell how many of them we've killed. Either they're losing much of their strength and exhausting their surviving soldiers, or they have a very substantial number of them—they certainly give no indication of a desire to conserve their lives. In the first case, they can't continue much longer, they won't have enough troops to carry on, and we go into a mopping up action. In the latter, we may not be enough to deal with them." He looked at his staff. "Do any of you believe they're near the end?"

They all shook their heads.

"Suggestions?"

"Draw up a contingency plan in case they are setting us up for a big hit," Usner said.

"Do it."

"Aye aye, sir."

"Anybody else?"

"Sir, I believe our Marines are too thinly spread," Shadeh said. "Every squad reports conflict with the local unit command structure. It wouldn't take a very large Skink force to overrun any of those garrisons. A battalion could probably do it fairly easily. I'd like to see our Marines consolidated."

Sturgeon shook his head. "While I sympathize and might even agree with you on that, if we pulled out of the garrisons, it would have an even more traumatic effect on the Army of the Lord than their losses and inability to close with the Skinks has."

Shadeh nodded. The brigadier was right on that point. Still, it was liable to cost many more Marines their lives.

"Anyone else? Four, I haven't heard from you."

"Sir, logistics are in fine shape," Captain West said. "As for what to do, I'm thoroughly baffled. The Skinks don't seem to think like we do." He looked embarrassed at that.

The Skinks weren't human, were they? It wasn't realistic to expect them to think like humans.

"Dismissed," Sturgeon said, and turned off the map.

When he was alone, he settled back in his chair and thought. A FIST commander always had to be prepared for the worst. The worst almost never happened, of course, but a commander who wasn't prepared for it lost the battle if it did happen. The worst here was that the Skinks were so strong they could continue raiding and fighting until 34th FIST was so worn down it was no longer functional—if the Skinks didn't do something to totally destroy the FIST. The only thing he could think of to deal with this worst was more Marines. First he needed to replace his losses. He shook his head. Not even in the war on Diamunde had 34th FIST suffered such heavy casualties. Beyond replacements, this situation could call for an additional FIST. But how could he request another FIST? As far as anybody on Earth knew, the problem on Kingdom was a peasant rebellion. The existence of the Skinks—or any alien sentience—was a closely held state secret. He couldn't request another FIST. Back at the Heptagon they'd think he'd lost it, was no longer fit to command. The most they'd do is send someone to replace *him*.

There was only one person he could go to who wouldn't think he'd lost his mind or his courage, and that would mean bypassing the chain of command. He picked up his comm unit and punched in Ambassador Spears's code.

"Thanks for seeing me on such short notice, Jay," Sturgeon said as he entered the den in Spears's quarters.

"Absolutely no problem," Spears said as he led Sturgeon to a comfortable chair. "I always have time to see a distinguished Marine. Especially one I've been through the mill with. Refreshment? I'm drinking tea myself. Sencha, grown locally from the descendants of shrubs imported from Japan."

"Thank you. Tea sounds excellent."

Spears busied himself for a moment, setting a cup for Sturgeon and ceremoniously pouring the tea, then sat. "Now,

Brigadier, to what do I owe the pleasure of your company? Judging by your grave expression, I assume this isn't a purely social call."

"I'm afraid you're right, Jay. Do you have a back channel for getting private messages to Earth?"

Spears laughed. "As many decades as I've spent in the diplomatic realm? Ted, I have more ways of getting messages to anybody than the Minister of State does. How can I help you?"

"I need to get a message to the Assistant Commandant of the Marine Corps."

Spears looked at him curiously. "Don't you have your own channels for that?"

Sturgeon took a deep breath. He'd spent too many years at the bosom of Mother Corps; what he needed to do now violated basic principles of his beliefs. "Yes, but the message would take too long to get to him via regular channels. And it might not reach him at all."

"It's about the Skinks, isn't it?"

Sturgeon nodded.

"And the Heptagon doesn't know they exist, and some functionary will see the message and decide you've gone around the bend, so the assistant commandant may never get a message from you if you say 'Skinks.' "

"Right again."

"But why the assistant commandant? Why not the commandant himself?"

"Because General Aguilano is probably the only person in the entire Marine Corps outside 34th FIST who knows about the Skinks. If he knows what's really happening here, he'll see to it that the appropriate action is taken. I cannot count on anyone else in the entire Confederation military taking this situation seriously."

Spears tipped his head back and thought. Abruptly he sat up straight again. "I have a friend at State who has a cousin on the staff at Headquarters, Marine Corps." He grinned. "A *civilian* employee, so there won't be any problem with the military chain of command. Compose your message. I'll write a chatty letter to my friend at State, and include your message with an urgent request that it be delivered most expeditiously. A diplomatic pouch is going out tomorrow. I'll include my letter and your message."

Sturgeon looked uncertain. "Are you sure your friend will do it?"

Spears laughed. "My friend is a career diplomatic bureaucrat. Thumbing his nose at military protocol is the most natural thing in the world for him."

And just as natural, there was another problem Sturgeon had to deal with mere hours after the diplomatic pouch was dispatched via Beamspace drone.

"YOU FAILED!" Ayatollah Jebel Shammar thundered. "You bring your infidels and your ideas of Shaitan to our holy land and you fail to exorcize the demons who torment us!"

"Revered One—"

"SILENCE!" Shammar cut Ambassador Spears off. "I speak not to you, but to this alleged military commander! He is the one who has failed. You are but a gnat buzzing about Mohammed's sacred nose, and you will remain silent until commanded to speak." He looked at Sturgeon, daring him to claim anything other than failure.

"Revered One," Sturgeon said in a calm, firm voice, "we have not failed. The Skinks are wily and numerous. There is no discernable pattern to their raids, so we can't anticipate them. They run before we reach the villages they attack, so we cannot fight them when we arrive. But when we do make contact, we defeat them. Their casualties have been horrendous."

"Yet they continue to ravage the Faithful!" He slapped the top of the massive table hard enough to cause his teacup to splash out a few drops. "We are of the belief that the demons stepped up their depredations against God's people when you arrived. A motion is before the Convocation of Ecumenical Leaders to demand the immediate removal from the Kingdom of Yahweh and His Saints and Their Apostles of all infidels other than those few necessary to maintain needed contact with the Confederation of Human Worlds. It will pass when the Convocation meets tomorrow. You and your soldiers will be on board your ship and leaving our space by Haven's nightfall tomorrow."

"With all due respect, Revered One, I am under the orders of the President and Congress of the Confederation of Human Worlds. They ordered 34th FIST to deploy to the Kingdom of Yahweh and His Saints and Their Apostles to conduct military operations to a successful conclusion. The last time you wanted us to leave, it appeared that the mission was concluded. We now know the operations have not been successfully concluded. I am not at liberty to remove my FIST from this world without express orders from my commander in chief or the Confederation's properly designated representative."

Sturgeon's reply caught Spears unprepared, but he was diplomatic enough not to let the surprise show on his face. He, Jay Benjamin Spears, was the properly designated representative of the Confederation President and Congress on Kingdom. He, with sufficient cause, had full authority to order 34th FIST to leave Kingdom. A ruling by the Convocation demanding that the Marines leave was sufficient cause. Spears was certain Sturgeon knew that; the Marine was taking a considerable risk if he was attempting to bluff these five men.

"I care not for your Confederation!" Shammar roared, pounding the table and splashing out more of his tea. "You have failed miserably, and the Faithful suffer the consequences. I desire and command that you and your infidels quit this world! We shall find a way through our faith to exorcise these demons."

Sturgeon couldn't help but catch Shammar's use of the first person singular pronoun. Was Shammar alone in this thinking, and using the force of his fury to bull the others into reluctant agreement? He calmly looked at the other members of the leadership council. Swami Bastar's expression reflected one of the more vengeful of the ancient Hindu gods. No help there. Cardinal Leemus O'Lanners could have been Ignatius Loyola's chief Inquisitor; he fiddled with his teacup, drank deeply from it, signed for a refill. The Venerable Muong Bo looked more ready to do violence than a Buddhist prelate should. Only Bishop Ralphy Bruce Preach-intent seemed uncomfortable with the proceedings, with a leavening of fear underlying his discomfort. Bishop Ralphy Bruce might be the chink in their front he needed to reverse the decision.

"And the rest of you?" Sturgeon asked. "Do you agree?"

Swami Baster held up a long-nailed finger. "You have failed," he said.

The Venerable Muong Bo composed his face into an expression of sublime serenity. "Violence is not the Way," he said softly. "You are creatures of violence."

Cardinal O'Lanners drank down his cup again, signaled for an attendant to refill it, quaffed again. The liquid the attendant poured didn't look like the tea in the cups before the other four prelates. "Holy Mother Church holds exorcism to be a very serious matter," he said. "We would be using it only in matters of demonic possession. I cannot believe that anyone—or anyplace—on Kingdom is demonically possessed. Though certainly these 'demons' do exist and destroy our people and property."

"Now—Now wait just—just a minute here," Bishop Ralphy Bruce stammered. "We've been invaded by someone who . . . someone nobody seems to know anything about. We can't beat them off by ourselves. Hell and damnation, that's why we asked for Confederation help in the first place! We can't do it. Ayatollah, these are flesh and blood creatures . . . Well, they're physical, whether they're flesh and blood like us or not. Exorcism won't work. They need to be fought with physical weapons. We don't have the weapons. The Army of the Lord can't stand against them. Except when the Marines are leading them. The army has never beaten any of them by itself." He glanced apologetically at Lambs-blood. "If we send the Confederation Marines away, we're all going to *die*! We need *more* Marines, not none!"

Before Shammar could react, a saffron-robed cleric with shaven head and clasped hands padded into the room, shuffled to Shammar's shoulder, and bent to whisper in his ear. The Ayatollah's already livid face turned nearly purple as he listened to the whispers. The message given, he imperiously flicked his fingers and the cleric shuffled away.

"The demons dare attack Haven! Can you do naught?" he demanded of Sturgeon.

"By your leave, Revered One." Sturgeon gave a small bow and left the room without waiting to be dismissed. It was time for the FIST's "cooks and bakers" to join battle.

CHAPTER
THIRTY

The suborbital flight from Fargo to Falls Church International Airport in Virginia took two hours. Coming in from the west, the morning sun gleamed brilliantly off the huge inland sea where the District of Columbia and the state of Maryland had once been, before the Second American Civil War. The ancient city of Falls Church, founded in 1690, had become a resort town. The Lenfens lived in a condo on the forty-first floor of the Skyline Drive Complex, only five kilometers from the beach.

"I appreciate your coming, gentlemen," Jennifer's mother said as she greeted them at the door. "My daughter often mentioned you, Mr. Tuit—and she also mentioned you, Captain Conorado." Conorado exchanged a glance with Tuit. When did Jennifer ever have a chance to mention him to her mother? he wondered. "Please come in and have some refreshment."

"Thank you, Mrs. Lenfen," Tuit said.

"Please, calling me 'Mrs.' makes me sound so old." Jennifer's mother laughed. "Call me Homa—that's what everyone else calls me." Above a hundred, Mrs. Lenfen bore a remarkable resemblance to her daughter, and as he watched her, Conorado felt a powerful wave of sadness come over him. He'd often heard people say that if you wanted to know what a woman would look like in old age, just observe her mother. If poor Jennifer had lived to her mother's age, she'd still have been an attractive woman.

A young man in his thirties stood as the pair entered the living room. "This is Charles, gentlemen, Jennifer's youngest brother. The other children are spread out all over the place, with their own careers and families, and as you may know, my husband has been dead for some while now. My other sons and daughters would have liked to meet you and talk to you, but they couldn't make it on such short notice. Charles is a student at George Mason University, not far from here, so," she smiled whimsically, "he lives at home and avoids the distractions and temptations of university life."

They shook hands with Charles, an intense young man who did not smile. "How did my sister really die?" he asked even before the visitors were seated.

"Charles!" his mother admonished. "Well, we are interested in how our Jenny died, but," she glared at her son, "not before you have refreshed yourselves." She poured hot tea from an ancient porcelain teapot.

Tuit sipped carefully from his teacup. He set it down just as carefully before he spoke. "Mrs. Lenfen, er, Homa," he began, "your daughter was one of the bravest and brightest young officers ever to serve under me, in the navy or in the merchant marine." He looked first into Mrs. Lenfen's face and then to Charles. The old lady smiled and nodded, but Charles's face showed no expression. Tuit thought, They know something's fishy here. He glanced at Conorado, who nodded and set his own cup down.

"We aren't going to bullshit you—" Conorado's face turned red and he grimaced. "Excuse me, Mrs. Lenfen, that just slipped out."

Mrs. Lenfen smiled. "Captain, you are no diplomat. That's one reason my daughter liked you so much."

Again Conorado was puzzled by the old woman's remarks. How could she know anything about what was between himself and her daughter?

"I think they're lying, Mother," Charles said softly.

Mrs. Lenfen silenced her son with a wave of her hand. "Tell us what you can, gentlemen."

"All we are at liberty to tell you, Homa," Tuit said, "is that Jennifer volunteered for a very dangerous mission, the success of which saved all our lives and most of my ship. It did involve an, uh, 'incident' in the propulsion unit of the *Cambria*, which did explode. She was killed in that explosion. The incident was much more complicated than that, but that is all we're at liberty to say. I can only add this: Jennifer's courage saved my life too."

Mrs. Lenfen turned to Conorado. "Have you anything to add to this, Captain?"

"No, ma'am. We are not allowed to tell you more."

"And what were you to my sister?" Charles asked abruptly, his eyes blazing.

"We became friends, Charles."

"Captain Conorado, did you know Jennifer kept a diary? It was among her personal effects." Mrs. Lenfen reached inside her blouse and took out a small leather-bound book, which she offered to Conorado. There were tears in the old woman's eyes. Conorado took the book but could not bring himself to open it. "She was so old-fashioned, you know, a systems engineer who insisted on writing in a paper diary, of all things. She brushed at a tear. "Someone's ripped out the last pages. It ends with her description of your fight with that man . . ."

Conorado cleared his throat. "Palmita."

Mrs. Lenfen nodded. "Yes. Read what she wrote."

"N-No." He turned the book, unopened, in his hands. He felt embarrassment and a nasty lump in his throat. "I can't open it. I don't want to read it, Mrs. Lenfen." He handed it back.

"You were her hero," Charles commented cynically. His mother looked at him sharply.

"Mrs. Lenfen, let me put it to you this way. Jennifer to me was somewhere—somewhere between my wife and my daughter. I'm going back to my wife, Mrs. Lenfen. I always was going back to her, and Jenny knew that. I was—"

"You were her goddamned knight, that's the way she put it, an old-fashioned hero on a white horse," Charles screamed. He stood suddenly, clenching his fists in anger, and stomped out of the room.

"Yes, Captain, you were Jenny's 'knight,' that's how she thought of you. Please forgive Charles. He was very close to his sister. We'll never get over that she's gone." Mrs. Lenfen paused. "But you military men know death, what it does when someone you care for dies or is killed. We old women know it too. That's a sad lesson young Charles will have to learn." She stood, indicating the interview was over. "Again, gentlemen, thank you very much for coming to see me. You didn't have to, I know. Captain Conorado," she turned to him and held out her hand, "you will always be welcome in my home, and if things had turned out differently, I'd have been proud to have had a son-in-law like you."

"Whew!" Tuit let out his breath once they were in the elevator. "I didn't have any idea Jenny kept a diary. It could've been embarrassing if we'd tried to bluff the old girl."

"Hank, she reminded me of Jennifer."

"Oh." Tuit's face reddened. "Sorry, Lew. Just a dumb old scow boat captain shooting his mouth off there."

Conorado smiled and clapped Tuit on the shoulder. Outside, they stepped into the bright sunlight. "Where to now, Hank?"

"Oh, I'm back to Fargo. See if Sewall's got another ship for me or if I go into retirement. How 'bout you, Lew?"

"Back to 34th FIST. My place is with them. Let's take the tube to the port and, as the shepherd said, get the flock out of here."

"Hey!" someone called from behind them. It was Charles Lenfen. He came straight up to Conorado. "You screwed my sister, you bastard! All this crap about 'knights' and 'heroes' and stuff! All you wanted was a warm woman on a long voyage, you—"

Conorado reached out and grabbed the young man by his shirtfront. "You are beginning to piss me off, Charles. What was between your sister and me was our business and not yours. Now you get out of my face or by God I'll wipe off the front of this building with you." He let Charles go and stepped back, breathing hard. Charles just stood there, his mouth working but no words coming out. Suddenly, Conorado relented. "God forgive me, Charles, I did love your sister! It was just like she wrote. But Charles, nobody can be a 'knight' without a princess. Jennifer was my princess."

Charles Lenfen slowly folded to the ground, weeping. Conorado sighed. "Come on, come on, Charles," he said softly, lifting him up. He laid a hand on the sobbing man's shoulder. "Charles, I don't mean to be harsh, but be a man. Get over what's happened and get on with your life."

"But we don't even have a body to bury, Captain," Charles sobbed.

Conorado tapped Charles on the chest above the heart. "You don't need a body, a monument. She'll always be here. I have about two hundred souls in there, Charles. Jenny's number 201. Come over here with me." He led Charles to some benches surrounding a small garden with a fountain in its center. Conorado motioned for Tuit to leave them alone.

"Charles, what I'm about to tell you now is breaking the law, but I'm going to tell you anyway." When he finished, he stood up. "Charles, you or your family, if I can ever help you in any way, you know where to find me. Time to go." He held out his hand.

"Captain, thanks. I appreciate what you've shared with me. I—I apologize for—"

"Don't mention it."

"Won't you and Captain Tuit stay with us for a while? Maybe stay for dinner with Mother and me?"

"Thanks, Charles. But we have ships to catch, and I'm going home."

"And where is that for you, sir?"

Conorado hesitated. "Home is where they have to take you in when you get there, and for me that's 34th FIST."

Admiral Joseph K. C. B. Porter, Chairman of the Combined Chiefs of Staff, snarled his displeasure. "Goddamned Marines!" he thundered. "Always charging in somewhere, always blasting their chops about how goddamned ready to fight they are, but let them get their tails in a hard place and they scream for the army." He drummed his fingers on his desk. "And besides, we go sending combat units all over the place, the existence of these," he gestured with a hand but did not mention Skinks, "will become common knowledge. You and I both know that is ultrasecret. I cannot authorize this without much, much higher authority."

"Well, it's not exactly the army they're asking for, sir," the Combined Chiefs operations officer, the C3, an army major general, protested. "The officer on the scene, this Brigadier Sturgeon, has only asked the commandant to release another FIST to support him on this—this—" He consulted his reader. "—Kingdom. Sir, his report is pretty grim."

"I've read it. Over who's authority was the request forwarded to us?"

"The deputy commandant, sir, General Aguilano. He's acting in the temporary absence of the commandant, who's on travel this whole month."

"You see! You see!" Porter slammed his fist on his desk, "There they go again, passing the buck up the chain, putting the goddamned monkey on my back! I haven't forgotten what happened to Wimbush, when that Aguilano commanded the ground forces on Diamunde! Oh, nosiree. Oh, yes, he's the guy who screwed up on Diamunde and then got old Wimbush axed over the whole affair. Well, they ain't getting this old salt."

"How high should we send this request then, Admiral?"

"To the goddamned President!" Porter thundered. "First we go into the tank with it next meeting of the chiefs, then once I get their recommendation—I'm not taking sole responsibility for this—I'll take it to her with our advice. That's the way it works."

"But, sir, that'll take time. The chiefs won't meet again until next week and—"

"Goddamned right, C3! Next regularly scheduled meeting is soon enough. I won't call an emergency session for something like this!"

"—and the Marines have asked for an immediate decision," the C3 concluded weakly.

"Look, General, this is not some lighthearted comic opera we're running here, no goddamned *HMS Pinafore*—always hated that nonsense," he added as an aside. "You know it's vital to Confederation security and stability that we keep this business with you-know-who quiet. If it ever gets out they're kicking ass, the panic will never end, and worse, everyone'll know the government's been holding a goddamned monster by the tail without warning anyone. We send in more Marines and that's just that many more people in on the secret. And what happens if they get wiped out too? No. Contain them—that's going to be my advice to the chiefs and to the President." Admiral Porter leaned back in his chair. "Now, General, on to something we can deal with: the CCS picnic next month!"

The army general gave up and pocketed his reader. "Well, we've got Burnsides to cater for us . . ."

"That worthless ass," General Aguilano muttered.

"Which one, sir?" the Marine Corps sergeant major, Bill Bambradge, asked. He was sitting in Aguilano's office, enjoying a morning cup of coffee.

"Porter. Sturgeon's request for reinforcements, Sergeant Major. The Combined Chiefs won't even consider Sturgeon's request until the regular session the following week. I know Porter will take this to the President, Bill. He'd never act on something like this on his own authority."

The sergeant major had not been read in on the Skinks, but he had a good idea what was going on with 34th FIST on Kingdom, and it was pretty much common knowledge at HQ Marine Corps that they'd had several contacts with sentient—and not very friendly—alien entities. "Well, the commandant could go see him directly. If he wasn't away in China just now."

"Yeah," Aguilano mused. "Funny thing, isn't it, Bill? We send men to the stars, but Earth is still a big goddamned place. Well, Sergeant Major, you know the old expression: It's better to beg forgiveness than to be blamed for doing nothing in a crisis."

"Yessir. I believe I invented that."

Aguilano touched a spot on his desktop and his computer morphed out of it. "Deployment status of all Marine FISTs within thirty days' travel distance of the Kingdom of Yahweh and His Saints and Their Apostles," he asked. A short list of units appeared on the screen. "Dispatch a deployment order to Commander, 8th Fleet, requesting 126th FIST on Gambini be released immediately on a combat order to CM 327. Send it under my authority as Acting Commandant, Confederation Marine Corps. Standard annexes except under Operations Annex, 126th FIST to be placed under the operational control of Commander, 34th FIST. Standard distribution on information copies."

The sergeant major laughed. "One twenty-sixth FIST will be on its way before the boys at the Combined Chiefs sort through their mail. But sir, you will be called on the carpet for this one, you know?"

"Yep, Bill, I probably will be. Probably have the cops down on me too. But you know what? Ted Sturgeon's FIST is in trouble, and goddamnit, I will not let him down. And you know something else? If they get these stars of mine, I'll go out with a big smile on my face because first thing I'm going to do is go over to the Combined Chiefs and kick old Joseph K. C. B. Porter right in the ass." He grinned. "Give me one of your cigars, Sergeant Major!"

CHAPTER
THIRTY-ONE

Staff Sergeant Wu led the dozen Marines of his recon squad through Haven's sewers. Their destination was the river behind the Skink locations, the river to which the Skinks would most likely withdraw when their attack on Haven was beaten off. The Marines had their faces covered by masks that tucked tightly inside their helmets and shirt tops. Even without having to smell the stench of the sewers or risk being overcome by them, the going was more unpleasant than the Swamp of Perdition had been. The Marines' ears were constantly assailed by the shushing of fresh additions to the sewers' water, glugs and pops of gas bubbles that rose to the surface and burst, the gurgles and clunks of things better left unrecognized swishing about or punting against their bodies, the walls, or other objects. The water in places barely sloshed over the tops of their boots, and in places it was chest deep to a short Marine. Their infras showed strange shapes that corresponded to nothing they knew in the world above. Their light gatherers gave shifting and shimmering images Edgar Allan Poe might have seen in drugged dreams. The unaided eye saw the eerie glow of bioluminesence.

The sewers didn't empty into the river, they fed into subterranean settling tanks. The river fed into the sewers, to add purer water to the tanks and help the settling process. The river's water flushed into the sewers a kilometer and a half from Haven's border via a waterfall high enough that even at flood stage the sewers' water couldn't back into the river. Alongside the waterfall a ladder of metal rungs had been stapled to the ferrocrete wall.

The Marines climbed the ladder, and it was clear that no maintenance crew had gone that way for a long time; the rungs were slick with lichenous growths. Wu, leading from the front, climbed slowly, scraping the rungs bare, careful to drop the scummy growth to the sides where it wouldn't slop onto the Marines who climbed below him. At the top of the ladder, Wu led the way into the coursing water from the river and let it wash away the things that stuck to their uniforms, let it wash away the stench of the sewers.

After an hour-long trek that felt more like a full day, the Marines emerged into daylight and deployed. Team one went a kilometer upstream, team two downstream an equal distance. Team three stayed with Wu. The thirty-meter-wide river cut its way through a forest so dense that tree branches met over it and turned it into a tunnel. The ground under the trees was thick with fallen leaves, decaying their way into the underlying dirt.

The recon squad leader found a place that would mask the infrared signatures made by him and the five Marines with him. He listened to the *crack-sizzle* of Marine artillery in the middle distance. More distant and muffled were the roars of Marine Raptors and Kingdomite Avenging Angels, low behind hills to protect them from the weapons of the Skinks. The weapons of the Skinks were inaudible, as were the reports from Marine blasters. There was no way to tell by listening how the battle was going. At least he didn't hear anything that might be that awful weapon the Skinks had. Wu set his men to placing detection devices; sound, motion, infrared, olfactory, seismic.

In good time teams one and two reported they were in place, and then that their detectors were out. Wu made his report to FIST. FIST gave a one word reply, "Continue." In this case, it didn't mean move on, it meant stay in place and monitor. They sat tight and monitored.

An hour later team one reported, "Approaching, fast." A moment later team two made the same report.

Wu's monitors showed indications of large numbers of figures to his front moving riverward from Haven. He gave a three word report to FIST: "Approaching, full, fast." The monitors showed rapid movement toward all three recon teams.

The recon Marines tried to melt into the ground, to become one with the mulch. The last thing a recon Marine wants is direct contact with the enemy. If the enemy discovers him, his mission is compromised; he is normally vastly outnumbered and outarmed; he has relatively little chance of survival if he's discovered. They didn't want to be seen.

Wu kept his eyes glued on the monitors, tried to make sense of what they told him. Hundreds of figures, mostly smaller than normal humans, though some were the size of exceptionally large men, were headed toward the river. Though their physical forms looked fully human in the dark of the forest, their infrared signatures indicated either much smaller masses or significantly lower body temperatures. The sound monitors picked up a language that sounded like low growls and soft barks.

Wu was so intent on his monitors that several nearby shouts and closer *crack-sizzles* caught him totally by surprise—they'd been spotted. A few meters away Lance Corporal Donat screamed in agony when a stream of acid hit him. Wu looked up in time to see a giant figure rushing straight at him, a sword held above its head two-handed. He pointed, fired, and rolled as the sword arced down at him, slicing deep into the ground where he had been. He was momentarily blinded by the brilliant flash when the giant Skink vaporized.

By the time he could see again, the Skinks were all in the river and out of sight underwater. The sensors he'd left in the water showed them moving rapidly downstream.

He called in his report. A few minutes later the Raptors were using the string-of-pearls guidance system to bombard the river downstream from the recon Marines, but there was no way of knowing what effect the bombardment had because the missiles' heat signatures picked up by the string-of-pearls through the trees that roofed the river were so brilliant they washed out any that might have been from flashing Skinks.

Wu called for reports from his teams. Five Marines were down; one of them would probably die if he didn't get immediate attention. Now that the mission was complete, the recon squad leader turned his attention to the sword that had so narrowly missed him. He yanked it out of the ground and held it for inspection. Its blade shimmered, and he marveled at it.

A sword. It was the middle of the twenty-fifth century, and a soldier in an opposing army had just tried to kill him with a *sword*. He realized he understood the Skinks even less than he'd thought.

Not long after the attacking Skinks withdrew, Brigadier Sturgeon and Ambassador Spears were again summoned.

"I have sent for more Marines," Sturgeon told the five religious leaders.

"How long will it take for them to get here?" Ayatollah Shammar asked. He was somewhat chastened after the Skink attack on Haven. He did not look at Kingdom's other leaders. Swami Nirmal Bastar gazed speculatively at Sturgeon; he no longer resembled a ferocious ancient god. Venerable Muong Bo looked serene. Cardinal Leemus O'Lanners's fingers twiddled as though he was worrying beads. Bishop Ralphy Bruce Preachintent fidgeted, but he kept his own counsel.

Sturgeon had already calculated the wait for reinforcements: two months for the drone to get to Earth, a week for General Aguilano to get the message and get orders issued, a total of three months for the orders and an amphibious ship to reach the base of another FIST and for that FIST to reach Kingdom; pad in a few weeks for delays anywhere along the line.

"About half a year, standard," he said.

"If you withdraw your Marines from the countryside, can you defend Haven from the demons for half a year?"

"We can try."

"Then do so."

"Immediately, Revered One."

As he and Spears left the chamber, Sturgeon couldn't help but remember a time not so long ago that he'd been less than assured when General Aguilano said he'd "try." Marines have a saying, "Don't try, don't do your best. Do it." Brigadier Sturgeon had just said he'd try.

"Say what?" Lance Corporal Joe Dean yelped.

"You heard me," Corporal Pasquin growled. "Saddle up, we're moving to a new position near Haven."

"Yeah, that's what I heard you say. What I didn't hear was, who's replacing us here?"

"The brigadier didn't think to mention that when he laid this on me over morning chow," Pasquin snarled. "How the hell am I supposed to know?"

"You're a corporal," Dean said defensively. "Corporals are supposed to be smart and know shit like that."

"Knock you upside the head," Pasquin snarled, but he didn't raise his hand. He was as bothered by the unexpected move as Dean was, and probably for the same reasons. They seldom caught the Skinks when they went after them, but the Skinks always broke off their attacks on the villages when the Marines showed up, so they were doing some good for the people anyway. And when they did meet the Skinks, they beat them. The problem with that, though, was when they fought, they always took casualties they couldn't afford. Guard duty near Haven would be easier, but there had been a major attack on the city. Would guard duty be more dangerous?

"Ready?" Pasquin hefted his pack onto his shoulder. They didn't have much with them. Packing had only taken a couple of minutes.

"Ready," Dean grunted, and picked up his own pack.

The soldiers of the 241st Defense Garrison looked hangdog as the Marines boarded the Dragon and left.

*   *   *

Third platoon took command of the 64th Defense Garrison, which was situated on a hill overlooking a crossroads five kilometers from Haven. If anything, Deacon Colonel Ramshorn, commander of the five hundred man unit, was unhappy at finding himself subordinate to an enlisted man.

"Deacon Colonel," Bass said as soon as Ramshorn made his displeasure known, "I don't give a damn if you don't like it. I wasn't impressed by the quality of the officers or the performance of the troops in the company-size Defense Garrisons my squads commanded. I don't expect to be impressed by you or this garrison. What I do expect is that you and your soldiers will obey the lawful orders I and my Marines issue."

"We neither want nor need you here!" Ramshorn blustered. "The demons haven't been active in this area. You should be someplace where you can be of use in defeating the demons."

"Your leadership thinks otherwise. So does mine. What you want or what I want doesn't mean anything. We have a job to do here, and we will do it. If you dislike it so much, you can go back to Haven. We can function quite well without you."

Ramshorn flinched. He wanted to say more, but the order placing the . . . some sort of senior sword in command of his battalion, was signed by Archbishop General Lambsblood himself. If he went back to Haven, he'd have to explain to the commander of the Army of the Lord why he'd deserted his assigned post. He knew he could not come up with a reason the archbishop general would find acceptable.

"You will keep me informed of everything you do before you do it." It was a feeble demand, but Ramshorn needed to do something to salvage the situation.

"Then you better stick close to me. When something needs to be done, I'm not going to take the time to find you before I do it."

Matters didn't get any better when Bass had his Marines begin training the Kingdomites. Along with the training, they patrolled aggressively. They also put out observation posts in a loose ring roughly two kilometers from the perimeter of the garrison's position.

"Gunny, you shouldn't be out here by yourself," Lance Corporal Claypoole said.

"I'm no more out here by myself than you are, Rock," Bass replied.

Claypoole was running a squad-size observation post some 2,200 meters north of the garrison perimeter, sited where it could watch a lengthy stretch of river that flowed out of a swamp on the horizon. Bass, accompanied by a lesser imam and five soldiers, was driving around in an APC to check the posts. Lance Corporal Dupont was with them. He kept watching his UPUD's displays.

"So how are things going?" Bass asked. He looked over the landscape instead of at Claypoole. The land leading to the river was farms; people and machinery were moving about.

"Quiet," Claypoole said. "Almost too quiet. You'd never believe this planet was under invasion from everything that's going on here, which is nothing."

Bass caught a worried note in his voice. "Except?"

"That over there. I wish we had someone in it." Claypoole pointed at a narrow stretch of forest that extended southeast from the swamp almost to the highway nearly a kilometer to his post's left.

Bass scratched his chin as he studied the woods. The wooded finger was a couple of hundred meters wide, though thinner or thicker in spots.

"Well, I don't have the people to put in there," he finally said, "but how about some sensors? I can plant a few on my way to the next post, leave the monitors with you now. How's that sound?"

Claypoole nodded. "It'll make me feel easier. You be careful in there, you hear me, Gunny?"

Bass grinned. "You ever know me to *not* be careful?"

Claypoole cocked his head and gave his commander a

quizzical look. "You don't really want an honest answer to that, do you, Gunny?"

Bass laughed and slapped Claypoole on the shoulder. "Don't worry about me, Rock. I'll be fine. You're doing a good job out here. Keep it up."

"Aye aye, Gunny."

Minutes later, just inside the wooded finger, a couple of hundred meters from the road, Bass said, "Hold it up here."

The APC's driver brought his vehicle to a clanking stop.

"Put out some security," Bass told the lesser imam. "I'll place the sensors. It should only take about five minutes. Then we'll head on to the next post."

"Yes, Acting Deacon Colonel," the lesser imam said. He told his five soldiers to dismount and go fifty meters into the trees and keep watch. He didn't bother to place them himself.

Bass carried half a dozen sensors; infrared, motion, seismic, sound. Dupont carried one more of each of those plus olfactory and visual spectrum. Bass busied himself planting them, some stuck in the ground, others hanging in trees where they were hidden by clumps of leaves. He was halfway through when Dupont interrupted him.

"Gunny, the UPUD's picking up motion deeper in the trees."

"It's probably the soldiers, they don't have good field discipline."

"I don't think so, Gunny. I have them. What I'm picking up is farther into the trees."

Bass grimaced. "I don't trust that damn thing." He reached into his pocket for his personal motion detector, a piece of equipment he knew from long use worked right. He was bringing it to where he could see its display when something hit his wrist with such force it felt like his entire arm was being torn off. Simultaneously, another blow tore off his helmet. The blows spun him around and knocked him violently to the ground. He landed on the side of his face. He lay there dazed. A couple of meters away he saw two bits of gore, one laying on the ground, the other hovering above it. They struck him as very curious in a distracted kind of way. He attempted to focus his eyes on them and realized they were the ends of ankles sticking out of a pair of chameleon boots. He was pretty sure they weren't his; he certainly didn't remember taking his boots off. Idly, he wondered if Dupont had blisters on his feet and had taken his boots off to ease the pain. But if Dupont had taken off his boots, why had he left his feet inside them? That didn't make any sense. Maybe if he closed his eyes and rested for a moment he'd be able to shake his head and clear it.

Claypoole watched the APC disappear into the trees, then returned his attention to his duties. He was turning on the sensor monitors Gunny Bass had left with him to see if any were working yet when he heard the distinctive ripping sound of the weapon the Skinks had used against the Marines in the swamp—it came from the woods where Bass had vanished.

Immediately, he got on the command radio. "Gunny," he shouted into it, proper radio procedure forgotten. "Gunny, come in. Are you all right? Dupont, what's happening?"

Bass didn't answer. Neither did Dupont nor anybody else with him.

Claypoole called base, and Staff Sergeant Hyakowa took the call.

"Hold your position," Hyakowa ordered. "Have all hands alert. Watch for movement in those woods. I'm sending someone out."

Claypoole didn't want to stay put. He wanted to go into the trees after Bass and bring him out. Instead he put his security squad on full alert. He watched the woods himself and kept trying to raise Bass on the radio. A few minutes later ten APCs sped on line toward the woods. The vehicles were spaced so widely that only the three in the middle entered the woods. The others ran along one side or the other of it.

*   *   *

"One and three, keep going until you reach the river," Sergeant Bladon, in command of the reaction company, ordered. "Come back if you don't make contact. Two, stop here. Kerr, get everybody in a defensive arc facing northwest, then join me."

It took less than a minute for Kerr to get his platoon into defensive positions in the woods. Bladon spent the minute staring in disbelief.

Two hundred meters from the highway the forest was chewed up. Chunks of metal, the remains of an APC, were flung about like fragments of a child's toy that had been frozen then shattered by something heavy. A couple of sensors lay on the ground, looking as if they'd been dropped before they could be placed. Blood and bits of bone and flesh were scattered everywhere. Nothing seemed to live save the small carrion eaters that were already congregating on the human remains.

"Where's the Gunny?" Kerr asked as he joined Bladon. He carefully scanned the ground.

"I dunno. We gotta find him," Bladon said numbly.

"There." Kerr trotted a few meters to where Dupont's boots waited, one standing, the other on its side. A helmet, visible from the blood smeared on it, lay near the boots. A few meters from it he found a broken, bloody identity bracelet. He read its inscription and closed his eyes to shut out the pain that washed over him. Slowly, he walked back to Bladon and handed him the bracelet.

"Moses, Jesus, and Mohammed," Bladon murmured when he looked at it. The bracelet had Charlie Bass's name and service number engraved on its outer surface.

Corporals Dornhofer and Chan reported they'd reached the river without contact and were returning.

"Roger. Dismount when you get here," Bladon told them dully. He had to give orders, otherwise he'd dwell on the loss of his platoon commander, a man with whom he'd been to hell and back more than once.

"Get your platoon on its feet and follow that," Bladon told Kerr. "Find out where it goes." "That" was the small tunnel the Skink weapon had bored through the trees and brush when it fired at Bass and his security squad.

"Aye aye. Second platoon, on your feet!" Heavy-hearted, Kerr left Bladon. He needed action and purpose as much as Bladon did.

"Where's Gunny Bass?" Corporal Doyle asked when Kerr joined the platoon.

Kerr merely shook his head.

"The Gunny's dead? The Gunny can't be dead!" Doyle's eyes grew wide and turned wet. His pupils closed to nearly pinpoint, his voice rose to a squeak.

"Marines die," Schultz said, thick-voiced. "Get used to it."

They found where the Skinks had lain in ambush, but found neither Skinks nor their weapons.

CHAPTER
THIRTY-TWO

Conorado called out Marta's name. No response. The apartment was empty. He set his bags in the hallway and walked into the bedroom. The sleeping accommodation was neatly made. At least Marta's clothes were still in the closet. He walked through the rest of the tiny dwelling. Everything neat as a pin. For the first time in his life he had put personal business above the business of the Corps, and look what it got him. "Goddamned women!" he said aloud. He picked up a small bag and left.

Captain Lewis Conorado had returned to Thorsfinni's World via a series of very boring hops, taking whatever ship was headed in that general direction. He finally made it to New Oslo on another of the Sewall Transportation Company's vast cargo ships—the voyage on that ship reminded him poignantly of the outbound trip—and then a suborbital flight to Mainside.

Now, as he boarded the shuttle bus to Camp Ellis, he got his second shock. The driver, a seaman third class, announced, "You got a *long* trip ahead of you, Captain! Thirty-fourth FIST's on deployment. You a replacement?"

Sure enough, Camp Ellis was a ghost town. Conorado stood in the swirling dust as the empty bus headed back to Mainside, and stared out over the grinder. He wondered how long the FIST had been on deployment and where they'd gone. He trudged over to FIST headquarters. A young lance corporal he didn't recognize was on duty in the foyer. He snapped to attention as Conorado entered.

"Where is everybody?"

"On deployment, sir. Left me behind, sir, because I lost my leg in a training accident." Surreptitiously the lance corporal reached down and switched off the trid he had been watching.

"At ease, Lance Corporal. I remember that accident. Colonel Ramadan was injured too. Is he still here?"

"Yessir. Up in his office, sir. We're both coming along just fine, sir, and hope to go out to the FIST any day now, sir."

Where'd they deploy to?"

"Never heard of it, sir. Place called Kingdom Something-or-other. Sir, are you a replacement?"

"No. I'm Conorado, commander of Company L. I'm just back from business I had on Earth. Now I'm going out to join the FIST. We'll all go together, maybe."

"Fine by me, sir. This place is really boring. And sir?" The lance corporal leaned forward over his desk and lowered his voice. "They've had some action! Some guys been lost. I don't know who or from which companies, but damn, I just can't sit around here any longer. Mike's my company, sir."

"We'll go back together, then. You continue your outstanding job holding down this desk, Lance Corporal, while I go up and report in to Colonel Ramadan."

"Lew!" Ramadan exclaimed as Conorado entered his office. "We knew you were on your way back but had no ETA." He came around his desk and shook hands with Conorado. "Lew, you've got a lot of catching up to do. Come on, let's sit down and I'll brief you first and then you brief me on what happened back on Earth."

Conorado listened silently as Ramadan told him about Marta's adventure. The more of the story he told, the whiter Conorado's complexion turned. When he was finished, Ramadan laid a hand on Conorado's shoulder and said, "Lew, that Marta, she's a Marine wife if ever there was one!"

Conorado cleared his throat. Marta a hostage, and she'd killed one of them? Goddamn, he thought, that's just what he'd have expected of her. Marta was a fighter. "I stopped by the quarters, sir, and she was gone. Looked like no one's been there in a while. I thought, well, I thought . . ."

"She's probably over at the hospital, Lew. They're treating her on an outpatient basis now. Hey, she's back together again! Looked pretty damned new to me, last time I saw her."

"Colonel, how can I thank you for—"

"Ah, rubbish! I had the time of my life, rescuing Marta! I suppose you're anxious to get over to see her, but first, how'd things go back there? With you?"

"Well, I'm back in one piece." He pulled a box out of the bag he'd brought with him. "I thought you might like these."

"Anniversarios! Lew, thanks, thanks a lot! But damn, man, this must've cost you a bundle. Let me pay you back."

"No, sir. Those are a gift from General Cazombi and the others who were on my side. I want you to have them. Of course, I'd like one right now."

They smoked the cigars as Conorado told Ramadan as much as he could about the *Cambria* and the trial.

"Lew, I know about the *Cambria*. We got an ultrasecret message on the incident that I passed to Ted. He has a need-to-know. The guys who pulled that stunt represent a dissident group on Kingdom that believes the depredations they're experiencing are a plot by the Confederation to bust up their cozy little theocracy. They thought blowing up the *Cambria* and everyone on board would focus attention on what they believed was a clandestine plot by the Confederation. Dumb bastards didn't count on having a Marine on board. Oh, I know what you did, Captain Conorado." He held out his hand and they shook.

"All that talk about jail and everything—"

"Doesn't apply to us. Lew, 34th FIST is in the shit out there. Here." He handed Conorado a flimsy. "It's the casualty list."

As Conorado went down the list his face turned white. He got to third platoon. "Ah, Jesus, Schultz wounded? Kerr wounded again? Thirteen men down out of the platoon? Colonel, this is worse than Diamunde! Who the hell are they up against?"

"Skinks."

"When do I leave?"

"Soon. As soon as we can lay on transport. Here, this just came in." He handed Conorado another flimsy. "Twenty-Sixth FIST been ordered to deploy to Kingdom. We'll go to Gambini and join up with them. I know the commander, Colonel Jack Sparen. Good man."

"Good outfit too. I notice they've been put under the operational control of 34th FIST."

"Draw your gear and then go home, Lew. Marta needs you. You know what she said when we dug her out of that snow bank? She looked up at me and she said, 'Lewis, I'm so glad you've come home.' Go on home. Meet me at Mainside passenger terminal at eight hours fifth day."

Ramadan stood and offered his hand to Conorado again. "Welcome back, Lew. And Lew, we'll have to stay on our toes out there. This is a bad one."

Marta was reading when Lewis walked back into their apartment. Her first reaction was to put the reader in front of her face so he couldn't see the plastic surgery that had replaced her nose, but then she threw it down and jumped to her feet.

"L-Lew, I'm so glad you've come home! I—I'm all messed up, Lew."

"Martie, you've been around Marines too long!" He took her in his arms and kissed the top of her head, then looked into her face. "Hey! You actually look better than when I left you! Maybe if I stayed away longer you'd have turned into a movie star!"

Marta began to laugh between her tears. "I got into a little scrape, Lew . . ."

Conorado laughed. "I heard. Me too. Little scrape. Met some interesting people too." He was about to blurt out the old Marine joke, "and killed them," but decided not to since he wasn't too sure how Marta was taking the fact that she'd recently killed someone herself. He paused, thinking how he would say what had to come next. "Martie, I—I didn't know if you'd be here when I got back, after—after what we said when I left—and I've got some things to tell you that you should know."

Marta punched him in the chest. "You dumb ass!" The tears streamed down her cheeks. "Of course I was going to be here when you got back! I'm a Marine wife, damnit!"

They talked for a long time. Conorado told Marta everything.

"This Jennifer, Lew, did you love her?"

"Yes. If you'd left me, I was going to ask her to marry me."

"She had guts."

"Yeah. Like you. Martie, I need you. That's all I know how to say."

"Well, when they were holding me hostage in that cabin in the mountains, you know what kept me going, Lew? I kept asking myself, 'What would Lew do in a situation like this?' I was not going to give in to them because I didn't want you to be ashamed of me. So when the time came—"

"Marta, we don't have much time. I have to join the FIST. We're leaving fifth day. Something real bad is happening out there."

"There've been rumors. What is it this time, Lew?"

"It's those things third platoon ran into on Society 437. They're back."

Marta went cold. She wasn't supposed to know about the Skinks, but once Brigadier Sturgeon had found out about the secret quarantine of the FIST and decided to tell his Marines the what and why, it wasn't long before the dependents found out as well. "You have got to stop them," she said slowly, decisively. "But fifth day's not here yet. Let's live a little. Let's go into Bronnys! Let's eat steak, drink beer, and smoke cigars with the 'Finnis, just like Marines do! Come on, Lew, my appendages are working again and, oh, hell, I haven't tied one on since the night you left!"

Big Barb's was roaring when the Conorados arrived. Several ships were in port and the crewmen were living it up raucously. Conorado had told Marta that they couldn't go to Bronnys without at least dropping in at Big Barb's. "That's where third platoon goes on liberty, and you haven't lived until you've met Big Barb herself." By the time they got to Big Barb's, the Conorados had drunk just enough beer that the place actually looked inviting.

A couple sat at a small table that had two vacant chairs. "May we?" Conorado asked.

The man stood. "Certainly, glad to have your company. My name is John Francis and this is my wife, Hilma." The men shook hands.

"Is it always like this in here?" Marta asked.

Hilma laughed. "It's worse on nights when the Marines are here."

"Capitan!" It was Big Barb herself! "Ve are not seeink you here too much! Ach, der FIST iss on deployment agin! Alvays dese deployments wid you Marines! Iss bad for my business. You are nod goink wid dem?"

"I leave on fifth day. Barb, this is my wife, Marta. Marta, I'd like you to meet the legendary Miss Freya Banak, for some reason known to everyone as 'Big Barb.' "

"I don' know dis 'legendary' stuff, ma'am, but der capitan, der Marines likes him lots 'n' dey spends der moneys here alvays when on liberty! I get you beer, iss on da house for da capitan and hiss lovely wife!" She bustled off through the crowd like an icebreaker in early spring.

Marta grinned. "So that's her? She seems to think highly of you, Lewis."

The beers came and they drank and ordered more and talked for a long time with John and Hilma. "How long have you been married?" Marta asked Hilma at last.

Hilma smiled at John and leaned up against him. "We just got married."

Suddenly it seemed to Marta that the place went quiet. The noise, the singing, the dancers swirling in the smoke, the overpowering aroma of stale beer in the sawdust on the floor, all receded into the background. It was just her and Lewis now. "So did we," she said. "So did we." And she kissed her husband on the cheek.

EPILOGUE

The flight from Gambini to Kingdom would have been a crushing bore for Captain Conorado except that Colonel Ramadan and Brigadier Sparen, the commander of 26th FIST, agreed that he could assist the men of 26th FIST with their prelanding briefings. Conorado was especially helpful to them because he could explain things about 34th FIST that they needed to know; in particular, details about third platoon's encounter with Skinks on Waygone and what they could expect once they encountered them on Kingdom.

Being part of 26th FIST's training program, physical workouts in the transport's gym, and long conversations with Colonel Ramadan, made the flight more bearable, but always in the front of Conorado's mind was the fate of the men in his company. The casualty list Ramadan had shown him before their departure horrified him. Sure, he had almost boasted about the 201 dead souls he carried around in his heart, memories of all the good men he'd known who'd died or been killed in the Corps. But facing up to more additions to that list was hard.

Am I getting too old for this? Conorado asked himself. *Am I losing my edge as an infantry commander?* He had it out with Ramadan on the eve of their landing on Kingdom. They finished the last of the Anniversarios that night too.

"Lew, you wouldn't be human if you didn't feel this way. I'm worried about the men too, and I'm a lot farther away from them than you are!"

"Sir, I know we lose men in combat, and I know that I have to take responsibility when that happens. I also know I can't let that prey on my mind when the mission's at stake. But this time . . ." Conorado shrugged and looked intently at the deck.

"You know what, Lew? Think of it this way: lots, and I mean *lots*, of good men who are alive now would be dead if it weren't for officers of your caliber. The only outright disaster ever to happen to your company occurred when one of your platoon commanders, Ensign—what was his name?—didn't work out."

"Baccacio."

"Yes, Baccacio. Lew, I have served with and under officers who were good men, but they couldn't hold the proverbial candle to you."

Brigadier Sturgeon welcomed Conorado back warmly but his command post was jumping with the demands of putting 26th FIST under his operational control. Sturgeon took Conorado aside briefly.

"Lew, I have some very bad news for you. I don't have all the details yet, but it looks like they got Charlie Bass."

Conorado's heart skipped a beat. "Are they sure, sir?" he said, not betraying his shock. He was back in combat again. No time for regrets, no time to show emotion.

Sturgeon nodded grimly. "Company L's CP is only a few kilometers from here. I'll have a hopper take you there directly. That Lieutenant Humphrey of yours? He's a fine officer, Lew, a natural company commander. And Staff Sergeant Hyakowa? He's almost a perfect replacement for Bass. Get him to go for his commission." Sturgeon paused. "Well, again," Sturgeon laid a hand on Conorado's shoulder, "I am very sorry about Bass, Lew. I can't tell you how sorry." He looked into Conorado's eyes. They were dry. "Got a staff meeting now, Lew. Van Winkle will be briefing company commanders at sixteen hours. Welcome back."

Lieutenant Humphrey and acting platoon commander Staff Sergeant Hyakowa were ecstatic welcoming their company commander back.

"Tell me what happened to Bass."

"It happened a few weeks ago, Skipper," Humphrey began. "Charlie was checking remote observation posts. Somehow, he walked into an ambush the Skinks had set. He and everybody with him got wiped out."

"There wasn't much left, sir," Hyakowa added. "We found his weapon, his bracelet and helmet, all bloody and badly damaged. DNA testing showed the blood was Charlie's. It's been a while, Skipper. We—We're putting it behind us now."

"They may have taken him prisoner," Conorado mused.

"Skipper, they don't take prisoners," Humphrey said.

Conorado nodded. "Wangs," he said to Staff Sergeant Hyakowa, "I know you've done a good job as acting platoon commander, but in this situation, third herd needs both a platoon commander and a platoon sergeant. Lieutenant Rokmonov, take over third platoon. Wang, you're back to platoon sergeant again. But let me tell you, Bass is not dead," he said firmly.

"How . . . ?" both asked at once.

"I know because," Conorado tapped his chest several times, "he's not here yet. He's not dead. He's *not*." Humphrey and Hyakowa looked aghast at their company commander. Seeing their expressions, he added, "I just know it, that's all. All right? Now," he drove a fist into the palm of his hand, "26th FIST's aboard and we are going to kick some Skink ass!"

Humphrey and Hyakowa exchanged glances as they left the CP. Had the Skipper lost it? they wondered.

Charlie Bass was dead.

Now they had to integrate the replacements who had come in with the Skipper.

STARFIST

by David Sherman and Dan Cragg

Book I
FIRST TO FIGHT

Stranded in the desert on a distant planet, stripped of their strategic systems and supporting arms, carrying only a day's water ration, and surrounded by a well-armed enemy, Marine Staff Sergeant Charlie Bass and his seven-man team face a grim future seventy-five light-years from home.

Book II
SCHOOL OF FIRE

Deployed to assist the oligarchs of Wanderjahr in putting down a rebellion that threatens the planet's political and economic stability, the Marines must fight two wars at the same time . . . one against the resourceful, well-led guerrillas and another with the entrenched police bureaucracy.

Published by Del Rey Books.
Available at bookstores everywhere.

STARFIST

by David Sherman and Dan Cragg

Book III
STEEL GAUNTLET

After a resource-rich planet is seized by the armed
forces of an industrialist, the Confederation Marines
face their most deperate battles yet against the mech-
anized forces of those bloody usurpers. Promised a
walkover by military planners, instead the Marines
must run a gauntlet of steel, with weapons three hundred years out of date. The Marines of the 34th FIST
must do the impossible—or die...

Book IV
BLOOD CONTACT

When a scientific team exploring an obscure planet
fails to make its regular communications check, the
Marines of Third Platoon are sent to investigate.
They prepare for a routine rescue operation, but
what they find on Society 437 is a horror beyond
description.

Published by Del Rey Books.
Available at bookstores everywhere.

**A few good men.
A couple of awesome adventures.**

**by David Sherman and Dan Cragg
Starfist: Book V
TECHNOKILL**

After the Confederation makes a shocking discovery
on an alien world, nefarious opportunists from the
highest echelons of power plot to steal the vast rich-
es for themselves. Now the Confederation president
is sending in Gunnery Sergeant Bass and the men of
Third Platoon to take on the heavily-armed forces of
corruption in a life-and-death battle.

**Starfist: Book VI
HANGFIRE**

The resort planet Havanagas is an empire of pleasure and debauchery without bounds—and a brutal
ring of crime bosses control it all. But three Marines
from Company L's Third Platoon are going in
undercover, with only their wits and training for
weapons, to break the kingpins' bloody strangle-
hold.

**Published by Del Rey Books
Available wherever books are sold**